About the author

George Taylor Files Professor of Modern Languages, emeritus, Bowdoin College, James Hodge offered a course in European Epic and Myth for circa twenty years and wrote a number of articles linking Tolkien's *The Hobbit* with Germanic mythology and Parry-Lord's analysis of "Homeric" style characteristics. From childhood, he has been fascinated by Germanic and Celtic myth.

FERGUS SPEAKS

*To Sukey
From me and your Mom and Dad, who gave me tours through the world of Shakespeare.

Jim Haf*

James Hodge

FERGUS SPEAKS

Vanguard Press

VANGUARD PAPERBACK

© Copyright 2020
James Hodge

The right of James Hodge to be identified as author of
this work has been asserted by him in accordance with the
Copyright, Designs and Patents Act 1988.

All Rights Reserved

No reproduction, copy or transmission of this publication
may be made without written permission.
No paragraph of this publication may be reproduced,
copied or transmitted save with the written permission of the publisher, or
in accordance with the provisions
of the Copyright Act 1956 (as amended).

Any person who commits any unauthorised act in relation to
this publication may be liable to criminal
prosecution and civil claims for damages.

A CIP catalogue record for this title is
available from the British Library.

ISBN 978 1 784656 76 8

*Vanguard Press is an imprint of
Pegasus Elliot MacKenzie Publishers Ltd.*
www.pegasuspublishers.com

First Published in 2020

**Vanguard Press
Sheraton House Castle Park
Cambridge England**

Printed & Bound in Great Britain

Chapter One
FERGUS

I am Fergus of the Mist and Taliesin of the Noble Brow. And other names you may know. I have been a king and a warrior, a prisoner and an exile and even a sorceress's apprentice. I have known the exultation of triumph and the gall of shame. You, who have stood on my unmarked grave and invoked me — perhaps all unknowing — have not called me as a warrior or a prisoner, a king or an exile, but as a bard, for a bard is the glory, the memory and the justice of his people, and you must wish to know the lore of those you call "Celts", who called themselves by many names, and warred upon each other as upon everyone else — who left their art, thought and bright spirit all across the lands you name "Europe", whose descendants now cling stubbornly to the western edges of the world they shaped. I cannot tell you everything I know. A bard who is worthy of the name has learned and retained the tales of his people through all his experiences and from all those who went before him. It would be more than your lifetime in the telling.

But I can tell you something that is worth the knowing, and something to be preserved and passed on, if you and your progeny are worthy of the message. It is not a tale like any other, for it will be in my way of telling, and it will hold truths that have been long forgotten. And I will take pity on you, for it is plain to me that you are meagre of stature and of a diminished time and place, so I will not sing my tales with all the mystic phrases and repetitions whose meaning is lost to you. More the pity, for a tale should not be told for its own sake, but for the nobility of purpose and glory of deeds it inspires by example, and as a way of keeping alive the heart and soul and most sacred beliefs of a people. But I can hope, can I not, that something of the greatness of the past will cling to the wretched minds of our offspring, and call up in them something of the grand and glorious spirit that does not walk the land anymore?

The tale begins in the land of the Cymry, sometimes called the Britons, but later called by their Sassenach enemies "Welsh", for that was the Sassenach word for "foreigner". They inhabited an island they called "the Isle of the Mighty", and their Gaelic cousins over the wave called "the Isle of the Giants". The names themselves have a story to tell, but that is for another time. Like many tales, it begins with birth and death. The birth was to the wife of a smith in a land called Gwynedd and the death was the death of its king, whose will and wit are the beginning of everything you are to hear. Indeed, there are those who believe that it was his nephew's spirit that entered into the body of the newborn. Do not be impatient, for this is no easy and thoughtless unravelling of a tale only for the sake of entertainment. A proper tale takes time, and this one must begin with a glimpse of the character of the king.

His name was Gwydion, and he was the last of the great sorcerer-kings of this northern land of the Cymry. Much of what he did was later attributed to a great war-chief named Artor. At the time of his most famous accomplishment, he was being fostered with his younger brother, Gilfaethwy, at the court of his uncle, Math, the greatest of all the wizard-kings of the north. Their parents had followed long-standing custom for nobly born children, who were sent to be fostered at the court of a friend, a relative, an ally, or someone desired as an ally. Children sent away like this had two sets of parents to whom they could appeal in times of need, and parents who participated in the custom had two sets of children and a trustworthy ally for their old age.

Gwydion was an assiduous apprentice of his uncle, who was a redoubtable warrior as well as a sorcerer. As one of the people of Dôn, ruler of the sky, Math derived his strength in battle and his shamanic knowledge from the forces of air and fire. His most fearsome counterpart — the giant, Pryderi — was the son of Pwyll, who had once been of assistance to the ruler of the Underworld, and had become its earthly ally and the beneficiary of its wealth and power. Pryderi, inheritor of Pwyll's title, "Pen Annwyn" or Head of the Underworld, ruled in the south, in Dyfed, the land of the sons of Llyr, lord of the seas. He was feared by all who had contested with him over honour or land. Some say that these two lands might never have met in battle if Gilfaethwy had not been too much of the flesh. Others say it was destined, as the conflict between the powers of the life-giving sun and those of the fertile land and teeming depths must always be.

Perhaps because of his great power, perhaps in order to contain it in a mortal body, Math was subject to a peculiar affliction. He suffered an excruciating pain in his legs, which disappeared the moment he rose from his throne, sword in hand, to do battle. At all other times, he found relief only by sitting on his throne and placing his feet in the lap of a virgin. Some who know the druidic secrets have claimed that this was because the raging passions of blood lust and sexual lust are one and the same. I cannot say. I know only that some of the body's signs are the same.

Math had had many such 'footstools' in his long reign. It was a court office open only to the completely unblemished young ladies of the land and greatly coveted by many maids and their families. Math's footstool at this time had been with him since her tender years and he regarded her with great affection. She had grown from a charming young girl to a winsomely captivating young woman, but showed no signs of wishing to leave her duty either because of boredom or out of love for any young man.

Gwydion and Gilfaethwy had been at their uncle's court for much of their young lives, had learned and had grown in stature and in powers of the mind and spirit, but Gwydion — despite the small difference in their years — had achieved a far greater maturity. And so it was that he began to worry when he noticed a change for the worse in his brother. Gilfaethwy alternated more and more often between distraction and irritability, he grew pale and even, finally, seemed to waste away physically. He turned aside his brother's concerned inquiries with a show of temper until, one day when they were quite alone, he hissed, "The wind!" Gwydion did not need to hear more. Math had a reputation of being able to hear on the wind anything said within a few miles of him.

"Tomorrow, you and I will go on a boar hunt", said Gwydion.

"No, I don't..."

"Tomorrow..." Gwydion repeated slowly and with emphasis, "you and I... will go... on a boar hunt!"

And so they did, the very next day. Despite the retinue of the hunt, Gwydion was able to find a moment when he and Gilfaethwy were alone.

"Now, brother, you will tell me of your sickness or I shall make you sore as well as sick."

"I have never loved before..."

"And now you do. But why this agony? Is she a maid?"

"Yes. A maid."

Gwydion breathed a sigh of relief. This was not the wife of a potentially outraged and dangerous husband.

"What then? Does she reject you? Ignore you? Love someone else?"

"She does not know... that I am alive."

"You are not naturally timid. This must be a very imposing young woman."

"It is Goewin."

"Math's footstool? But she has been here almost as long as we have. Why now?"

"I don't know. One day she was just Goewin. Then I began to notice little things about her. The way she speaks, the way she eats, the way she holds her head. Suddenly, she was someone mysterious, lovable, familiar, unattainable. I became a prisoner of her femininity. Lately, I can't eat or sleep. I can't stay away from where she is, but I must always leave immediately, because my body betrays me. I am full of raging fire and deep darkness. I want to sweep her away and make her mine... or I want to die."

"This must be serious. You haven't talked this much since you were ten years old."

"Did you go through all this to get me alone, so you could laugh at me?"

"Brother, laughter is sometimes a relief from desperation. You would have an easier time to woo the divine Rhiannon of the South than to make this maid take notice of you. And our uncle will be none too pleased."

"I know, I know. If it weren't for him and his fearsome power, I tell you, I would have simply carried her off by now. But I would not take three steps before he turned me into a toadstool. I cannot live with this lust! It is devouring me!"

"Lovesickness is a real malady. And its cure is drastic. You must live through the disease and survive your misery and even then it is not like other illnesses, because you can fall sick of it again any number of times.."

"Or partake of the cure. I cannot resist any longer! I will try, and take the consequences."

"I have not put up with you all these years to let you commit suicide now."

"It is not your choice."

"On the contrary. If this must be, then I will arrange that you have a chance to fulfil your desires. Punishment may come, but it will be delayed, and it will strike both of us together."

"How?"

"Contain yourself for a few days. I have been planning to propose a bold stroke to our uncle. It may be of use to us. When I am ready, you will hear. In the meantime, ride, hunt, mortify your body with too much activity. At night, stay alone. Drink yourself into a stupor, but stay away from the common table, because it is too easy to provoke a conflict, and we do not need a kill-or-be-killed situation."

"I can wait, if a solution is possible."

"I swear it, unless the sky falls. Do as I said. You will hear."

Gilfaethwy rode until his thighs ached, hunted until he was sick of the sight of blood, drank until he spent entire days squinting through the miasma of hangover. Then, finally, Gwydion was ready, and all Gilfaethwy had to do was hold himself in readiness. And now the tale begins in earnest.

Chapter Two
THE BATTLE OF THE SWINE

True to the meaning of his name, Math ap Mathonwy was a bear of a man. Even seated in his low throne at the end opposite the door of his extra-large house, his white beard flowing in ripples down his chest and forming a whiskered pool in his lap, his head was on the level of an ordinary man. His massive body suggested a bear-like overweight, capable of exploding into furious, destructive action. His features were composed, even serene, since he sat with his feet cradled in the lap of Goewin, the footstool who had been with him longest, who understood his every mood and imperceptibly adjusted her body to compensate for the passions and tensions which lay just below his fearsome surface. Gwynedd was at peace, and so was its king. But peace is not just serenity. To a warrior-king it is also, unavoidably, tedium.

When his nephew entered his presence, Math was serene, and just a bit bored. Gwydion, who was no fool, knew of the love of action which underlay his uncle's exterior. He also understood that a king always wishes something better for his people and his kingdom. This is an ambition which, in a good king, springs in part from a true desire to see his people happier and more prosperous and an equally strong drive to be first among equals — the wealthiest and most powerful of kings. Gwydion's plan had been some time in the making. First, he needed a perfect pretext to allow Gilfaethwy a chance to fulfil his desires. Second, as presumptive heir to the throne, he had feelings about the primacy of Gwynedd in Cymric lands. The only land, the only king with an equal claim to supremacy were Dyfed and its giant king, Pryderi. Even so, if he had not loved his brother as only an older brother can love a somewhat spoiled younger sibling for whom he has fought fights and told lies, he might not have considered the hazardous project he was about to propose. His plan had every advantage: help for Gilfaethwy, fame for himself, glory and prosperity for Gwynedd and satisfaction for Math. Or, if it miscarried, death and disgrace for both brothers.

"You requested a private audience, nephew. Do you have something unusual to report or to propose?"

"Both, Uncle. My agents in Dyfed — among my best — have reported something that deeply concerns me, something that will greatly increase the prosperity of our rivals in the South. They have a new source of food experienced by visitors to their land. It is unlike any other food we know, and yet it is not wholly unfamiliar."

"Visitors have come away from Pryderi's table singing the praises..."

"In the name of the great god of the sky, nephew, stop sputtering and tell me what you are talking about! Is this food a grain, a fruit, a root, what?"

"None of these, Uncle. It is a new meat."

"A new meat! Have they sailed to the Land-across-the-Sea to bring back some magical beast that is all meat and no bone! What foolishness is this?"

"No foolishness, Uncle. And yes, it is a new beast, but not from the Mystical Isles. It is from their treasure trove in Annwn, the entrance to the riches of the earth. They have a domestic animal that is like a cousin of the wild boar we hunt in the forest. Its meat is as sweet and far more tender. It lives in a small yard and does not run when the cook comes to slaughter it. And it has fat instead of gristle running through its flesh. Some call it 'pig' and some call it 'swine'. They do not easily let these beasts out of Dyfed, but I would like your permission to go south and try to trade for a few breeding pairs."

"How far do you suppose a company of warriors from Gwynedd would be allowed to penetrate into Dyfed?"

"Not warriors, Uncle, eleven companions, part of my retinue as a famous bard."

"Yes, you do spin a tale better than most. But if King Pryderi does not fall under your bardic spell and refuses to trade any of his... swigs?"

"Then perhaps I can persuade a young pair of pigs to follow me home on their own."

"And I shall have to post myself and a considerable army at the border to meet their angry response. Really, nephew, this is a most irresponsible plan," said Math, but in the depths of his eyes, Gwydion detected a glint of battle-joy.

"Uncle, I shall do everything in my power to conclude this business peacefully. But if I should falter, your superior warcraft and experience might well be needed."

"Yes." With a show of reluctance, Math shrugged his massive shoulders, "I suppose it is for the good of the land. Well..." Math removed his feet from Goewin's lap and stood slowly, extending his open right hand, into which a ready attendant placed the hilt of his sword. He essayed a few, tentative steps. "Well, it appears that the physical signs are positive. Choose your companions, and inform me when you are ready. I shall see that our army is battle-ready. I suppose your brother will be one of the twelve?"

"No," said Gwydion, hastily. "As you see, lately he has become moody. I could not trust him in the company. I shall choose eleven of the best and craftiest of your warriors and be ready to depart in two days' time. No one but our small group will know our purpose."

"See to it, then." Math returned his sword to the attendant and sat ponderously, placing his feet again in Goewin's lap. She smiled up at him. Realizing that he had been dismissed, Gwydion withdrew swiftly.

Gwydion's company of twelve travelled only by night and paced itself to arrive unchallenged on the evening of the twelfth day at Pryderi's stronghold. Gwydion was aware of the peril of the journey. Pryderi's powers, perhaps no greater than his own, were very different. Pryderi's strength was drawn from the earth and the sea, his own from air and the fire that lived in it. Every advantage must be sought; every occult nuance considered. A company of twelve, taking twelve days for its journey, was just one of many mystical precautions.

As he travelled, Gwydion thought of his brother. He had instructed Gilfaethwy to continue to show all the symptoms of mental and emotional dis-ease, so that Math would not call upon him to accompany the army to the border of Gwynedd. When, presumably, Gwydion had accomplished his double objectives of acquiring the pigs and infuriating his host, the army would be needed to repel the hosts of Dyfed at the border, and Gilfaethwy would be left at court with Goewin and the other women. It would be his only chance to press his case with Goewin when she was not preoccupied by her duties.

On the twelfth day at dusk, they arrived at the outer wall of Pryderi's stronghold. Like Math's, it was seated on an oblong hill, surrounded by three concentric walls — massive, earthen, grass-covered — which were pierced at one end of the oblong by a pounded earth road wide enough to accommodate a war-chariot, but sinuous enough to slow an alien advance. They were challenged in the usual manner by a warrior whose flowing moustache fairly bristled with suspicion: "What is your name and family? Whence do you come? What do you seek?" This man and his two companions had evidently had their fill of peace, since his hand grasped and released the hilt of his long sword and he glared eagerly into Gwydion's eyes, hoping to find a hint of hostility there. Assuming an unwonted humility, Gwydion announced himself as a bard, travelling with his companions to see the many lands of the world. He had heard of Dyfed's great power, he said, and had even learned some of their history, in order to have something pleasing to sing before their king. Somewhat mollified by the prospect of new tales and new versions of old tales, the sentinel led them up the ramp into the fortress.

The largest of the mound-like wood and thatch houses — presumably the king's — stood at the opposite end and next to it what appeared to be an oddly shaped tree. As they drew nearer, the 'tree' took on the shape of an incredibly large man, sitting on the ground. Of course, Gwydion thought, this is Pryderi, of whom it has been said that no house built is large enough to contain him. Perhaps this was not strictly true. Glancing at the entrance to the large house, Gwydion surmised that Pryderi could pass through the entrance on his hands and knees and curl himself up around the curvature of the wall to sleep. However that may have been, he was an impressive sight. The gold torque around his neck seemed to be the size of a child's play shield; the arms that hung from the short sleeves of his tunic were the size of young tree trunks and hard with muscle; the trews, gathered at the ankle, looked as though they could be converted into a sail for a sea-going coracle. The effect of enormous strength was palliated by his facial features. Looking into his deep blue eyes was like gazing into the depths of a deep, still pond. His expression was as mild and benign as a spring morning.

He listened with care to the quietly delivered report of his sentinel, dismissed him with thanks, and turned to the visitors.

"You are welcome," his voice boomed softly, like the distant sounds of the surf. "We are always glad to hear a new tale sung. Which of you will sing at meal this evening?"

"With your permission, I am the most practised," Gwydion said.

"So be it, then." He motioned to one of the men standing nearby and they were taken to a small house near the middle of the fortress area and furnished with water, so that they might wash and refresh themselves. There had hardly been time for this, when they were summoned to the king's house. He was already seated on the ground at the wall furthest from the door as they entered and Gwydion thought, fleetingly, that he would have liked to see how Pryderi had come through that door.

Mead flowed freely and there was meat in abundance, of a kind that reminded Gwydion of the taste of boar meat, but sweeter, tenderer and dripping with the most delicious fatty grease. The animal which filled much of the area inside the circle of men had the form of a boar, too, but it was smoother, rounder, pinker, less hairy, and the mouth under the boarish nose showed no tusks. From the select company allowed to share the king's meal, Pryderi awarded a choice, fat section of haunch to a superbly built, swaggering, very young warrior with flowing dark hair and luxuriant moustache that drooped his chest. This endowment of the hero's portion was contested half-heartedly by an older man, who seemed to feel it was good form to make his claim to be the best of all Dyfed's warriors. When he was roughly sent sprawling, however, he ruefully laughed with the rest of the company and did not reach for his eating knife to press matters further. Clearly, despite his youth, this Lot ap Llanuwyn was Pryderi's premier warrior, and would bear watching.

Then it was time for Gwydion to sing for his supper.

"Well, good bard, what do you have for us?" Pryderi asked with a smile, and Lot added in a hoarse murmur which Pryderi seemed not to hear: "It must be an excellent song that is worth a meal with Dyfed's king."

Gwydion replied modestly that he hoped to justify his presence, and began to sing. After a very short time, all — even the surly Lot — were spellbound by his art. He sang first of tales they all knew:

How Pwyll made a compact with the lord of Annwn and fought one magic battle for him, in exchange for which he gained an everlasting alliance with the land under the earth, and access to its riches, and he and his successors held the title of Pen Annwn — Chief of Annwn.

How Pwyll sat one night on the great mound, Gorsedd Arbeth, to test the rumour that sitting there would bring great pain or great adventure, depending on the worth of the man who sat there. And the divine Rhiannon came riding out of the world of Annwn to be his bride. How her old suitor had nearly tricked Pwyll into giving her up, and how she had devised the brutal game of Badger-in-the-Bag to turn his trick back upon him and Pwyll had earned his enmity from that time forward.

How the great Bendigeidfran once towed his entire army in its ships across the Celtic sea which lay between the Cymry and their foes, the Gaels, to rescue his sister from a cruel captivity and fought a great war which left only seven men alive on the side of the Cymry and only five pregnant women hidden in a cave to repopulate Eire.

How gentle and clever Manawydan foiled the revenge of Pwyll's ancient enemy from Annwn, saving by his wisdom Pryderi, Rhiannon and the entire land of Dyfed.

And then he began to sing songs that none present had ever heard:

Of a battle that had yet to occur between the armies of Annwn and the armies of the upper world, where warriors would contend with gigantic and magic shapes, like an oak tree with a thousand whirling, cutting branches.

Of an enemy just then taking shape to the East and beginning to appear offshore in raiding parties — the axe-wielding Sassenach and their war-loving cousins; and of heroes of the Cymry yet to appear in the final great battles against the foes that pressed them from all sides.

And of a new kind of belief that would inundate Cymry and Gael and Sassenach alike, overwhelming their ancient ways and defeating their ancient gods.

For a short time, the company sat in stunned and sated silence. Then Pryderi said: "Minstrel, you have sung for us as no one has sung in a long time. You are due a rich reward. Name your heart's desire and if it is within my power, I will grant it to you."

As soon as he had spoken, he felt his error. With just such an ill-considered, unconditional offer of the host's largesse had his father nearly lost Rhiannon to a competing suitor at his own wedding feast. Once made, the offer could not be withdrawn or narrowed. He must only hope that the bard would ask something reasonable... rich, but reasonable.

"My wish is simple and within your power, sire. I wish two breeding pairs of those animals whose delicious flesh we have feasted on tonight."

Pryderi's face showed none of his consternation. Driven by the knowledge of promises made, he attempted to explain. "Those animals have come to us from a very special source. We have promised to give none of them away beyond our borders, until they have become a thousand in number, and they are still short of that."

Gwydion appeared to reflect, then his expression brightened and he said, "I believe that there is a way to overcome this problem with no loss of honour on any side. Not far from here, I can acquire twelve stallions and twelve hounds that are worthy of a king. If you do not agree that they are as fine as you have seen, I will say no more and leave with thanks for your hospitality. But if they are the equal and better of any you have seen, we shall barter. Then it could not be said that you have given the animals away, for a trade is not a gift."

It would have been churlish to object or procrastinate, even though Pryderi suddenly had a dark premonition about this minstrel and his true purpose. "So be it, then."

Gwydion begged leave to withdraw immediately, promising to return in the morning. Once far enough along the road from the fortress to be beyond eye and ear, Gwydion led his company into the forest, stopping at a clearing, and ordered them to set up camp and wait for him. Then he plunged into the darkness of the wood. For hours, the company heard him mumbling to himself, naming herbs and trees, moving slowly in a circle around the clearing. Then there was silence. After an interlude, they heard his voice again, speaking words they did not recognize, accompanied by hissing, popping and rustling sounds and flashes of light that resembled the mysterious imp of the swamp — the light that dances over the marshes and can never be caught. Then again silence and darkness, followed by the neighing of horses and the throaty muttering of hounds.

When Gwydion re-appeared just before dawn, he was leading twelve magnificent, deep black stallions led on one long golden line and twelve black hounds with white chests, all on one silver lead. None dared speak, for they knew only that these were by no means real animals. Gwydion smiled inscrutably as he led them away. Twelve men, twelve stallions and twelve hounds marched back to Pryderi's fortress. Pryderi awaited them where they had first seen him.

He smiled a sad half-smile when he saw what they had brought.

"So, Bard, you have kept your word. In truth, I have seen no animals to match these. You shall have your four animals, and I hope that they will bring you and yours good fortune, as they have done for us." He turned to one of his men, "Fetch the swineherd and four of his young animals."

His mouth half open to object, the man looked into the king's face and obeyed. The swineherd was a boy fair of face, but grimy, and regretful at parting with his animals to strangers. He, too, gazed at the king's sad smile and brought the animals — young ones, squealing in sacks — to Gwydion, who smiled brilliantly and said, "It is known far and wide that the king of Dyfed is a man of spotless honour who holds to the word he has spoken. I thank you for your bounty. You will live in memory as a generous king."

"It has ever been my most notable virtue and failing," Pryderi replied. "Fare well through my land."

Thanking him again, they left the fortress, making their way slowly along the road until they were out of sight behind a curve. Immediately, Gwydion dispatched the fastest man of his company to carry the news to Math that they had their prize and were being pursued.

"Now, men, stride as if all the armies of Annwn were at your heels! That may yet be true, for the gifts I have left with the king will hold their form only a little while longer. When Pryderi sees that he has been deceived, he will be after us with both his soldiers and his great powers. The further we are from Gwynedd, the weaker my ability to counter them."

At a quick pace, they moved forward until dusk overtook them. Suddenly a light flared brilliantly and briefly in the sky behind them.

"He knows now! Forward with all your might!"

They strained to quicken their pace, but as they did, the ground seemed to give more easily beneath their feet and each step required greater effort than before. A mist rose from the earth as damp and all-encompassing as the vapour that rises in the morning from a pond. Their feet began to make squishing sounds, and sank further into the surface of what had moments before been a solid road. The mist became a dense fog and the ground they passed over became a bog in which they floundered blindly. Gwydion exerted himself mightily to dispel the fog and to weakly illuminate the way just in front of his little party. Behind them, they could now hear the sounds of a pursuing army. Desperately, they flung themselves through the bog, straining to see and hear ahead. Their every step pushed blindly into the fog, weighted down by muck, weary with exertion and fear. They ran slowly, fell slowly, rose slowly, cursed slowly. At last, one of them cried out, "I hear them ahead! It is Math and the men of Gwynedd!"

And so it was. As they broke out of the fog and onto hard ground, it was bright morning. The army of Gwynedd was forming directly before them, men running from their hard night's rest on the ground, Math already out front in his chariot. The man who had carried Gwydion's message stared at them in disbelief.

"How have you been so long in coming? I arrived five days since and we had word of a huge army making its way to the border two days ago. We have been waiting here ever since then."

It was true, then! Dyfed really was an extension of Annwyn, where time ran differently! So it had been that the divine Rhiannon, first to join the two worlds by marriage, had ridden out of the mound at Gorsedd Arbeth and her cantering horse could not be caught by the best mounts of Dyfed ridden at full gallop. Only when Pwyll called out to her did she come to pull her horse to a halt, and allow the two times to blend.

Gwydion had barely time to realize what this meant about the nature of the journey he had just taken as he slipped through the roughly organized ranks of warriors and sprang into his own, waiting chariot. He was ordering his charioteer to maneouver forward, when the chariot vanguard of the army of Dyfed burst out of the fog, followed closely by the main body of warriors on foot. Some wearing minimal armor, some naked but for shield and sword, some painted blue over the entire body surface, many heads adorned by a halo of whitish spikes created by pulling a solution of chalkstone and water through the hair. The men of Gwynedd, looking much the same, surged forward and the two hosts crashed together with a cacophony of battle shouts, clashes of metal on metal and metal on wood and already the screams of the mortally wounded mingling with the anticipatory screams of hungry eagles.

Javelin in hand, Gwydion braced himself against the back of his chariot. An exact opposite to the chariots of their Celtic cousins and most other peoples who used them in war, the Cymric chariot was tapered from a high back to an open front, protecting against low spears and missiles from the rear. As his driver crouched before him, steering a swathe through the enemy, Gwydion launched javelin after javelin at opposing warriors, dodging swiftly to avoid those aimed at him over the horses or the low sides, always seeking Pryderi, hoping to confront him and end the slaughter by defeating the king of Dyfed.

But it was not to be. Charge, retreat, counter-charge. Mud and blood mingled copiously. Energy and fervour drained, both sides returned ever more slowly to the battle after giving way. Day waned. The two sides, as by mutual agreement, drew back, separated, settled in to rest for the night. Without consulting his uncle, Gwydion sent a message to Pryderi, saying that too many lives had been forfeited. If Pryderi felt his honour had been stained, it was he, Gwydion, who was to blame. A fight to the death between them would decide the issue and spare many warriors on both sides. When Pryderi's acceptance came back to him, Gwydion presented Math with his already accomplished plan.

"It is better to lose one life than many," Math said wearily, and Gwydion realized with a chill that his uncle was eyeing him speculatively. "When this is concluded, if you are still alive, we will speak of your true motivation in this matter. If you have been worthy of my tutelage, you will be alive." So saying, he turned ponderously and walked away.

In the morning, the two armies faced each other across the formerly green field, now churned into a sea of brown clods and uprooted balls of grass. The dead and wounded had been fetched away, leaving some shields and weapons behind, with a few frustrated crows hopping from clod to clod, seeking a meal they had expected and could not find.

Gwydion stood in his chariot, watching for Pryderi, prepared to give his driver the order to begin as soon as the king of Dyfed appeared in front of his army. When he did appear, it was not as Gwydion had hoped. Because of Gwydion's message of the night before, Pryderi now knew with whom he had to deal. Gigantic, naked, surmounted by the customary white-spiked hair, carrying a great, oblong shield and an unbelievably long sword, Pryderi stepped majestically from the front ranks of Dyfed, raised both sword and shield above his head and uttered a booming cry of challenge. The strength and speed of the horses, the skill of the charioteer, the tactics of the warrior riding the lethal battle platform would play no part in their meeting. If Gwydion was to live through the battle, it would be his own strength, speed and skill and nothing else that would defeat the most formidable warrior in Dyfed.

With some quivering behind his knees, Gwydion jumped down from the chariot. Grasping his sword and the first shield that was thrust into his hand, he walked slowly forward, the sun of early morning glaring weakly on his face. When the two men met midway between the armies, the contrast was heartening for the men of Dyfed — their great king, naked and enraged, two heads taller than his foe, who, by contrast, scorned the limestone solution for his hair, the blue dye for his body, and retained his breeches although not his tunic. Uncharacteristically for a Cymric warrior, Pryderi did not bellow and charge. He seemed to be aware that this opponent and this battle were to be decisive in his life.

Only Gwydion's quickness saved him from the first, sudden swing of Pryderi's sword, which seemed to appear in front of him and overhead, as if flying directly out of the sun. Rather than raise his shield to be splintered by the first, tremendous blow of combat, he half turned, half skipped out of the path of the down-rushing blade and then stumbled backward, to the cheers of the men of Dyfed and the moans of the men of Gwynedd. Pryderi's blade buried itself in the muddy earth. As he bent his back to pull it up, Gwydion skipped again, to the king's unprotected sword side as he pulled on the buried weapon, and delivered a slashing blow which missed the sword-arm, but cut a horizontal gash across the giant's thigh.

Again, ominously, Pryderi did not roar, but moved forward one step at a time, stalking his opponent. His deep blue eyes were not filled with rage, but with adamantine purpose. Gwydion retreated as best he could, using his shield only when he could not use his speed and agility to avoid the king's strokes, any one of which could have been lethal. When he could not quite avoid the blow and had to use his shield, Pryderi's blade did not ring on the metal rim and slide off, but bit through to the wooden core. Eventually, Gwydion was left with a splintered wreckage of wood, dotted by a few of the round, protective metal bosses that had not been hewn off with the wood in which they were imbedded. The very weight of the blows which landed even indirectly had numbed and bruised his shield arm, and, although uncut, he moved now in a haze of pain, as if from a brutal beating. By his quickness, now and then, he was able to rush by the defences of sword and shield and draw blood. Pryderi's body from shoulder to knee was dripping in sweat, here and there coloured by blood from one of Gwydion's many quick strokes. But it was apparent to both sides that, should the contest go on in this way, Gwydion would be beaten into the ground.

As they circled each other ever more slowly, the sun rose gradually from its dawn position just behind the trees, to the high diagonal of mid-morning, then to its noon location directly overhead. Strangely, as the sun rose to its zenith, the comparative strength of the two combatants changed in Gwydion's favour, who seemed almost to draw strength from its heat, while Pryderi, who had sustained no serious injury, moved his feet ever more slowly, swung his great sword with less force. Finally, as if tiring of the game, the king flung his shield at Gwydion, who avoided it only by falling backward and then rolling to one side, supporting himself on the hand that held what was left of his shield. Pryderi took a two-handed grip on the hilt of his sword and half ran, half stumbled toward the not-quite-horizontal Gwydion, raising the sword for a stroke that would undoubtedly cleave him in two halves. Rising on the support of his one hand, Gwydion did not move back or sideways to evade the king's next blow, but propelled himself forward, under Pryderi's just descending sword arm, thrusting his sword before him, into Pryderi's mid-section and upward toward the heart.

The king of Dyfed rocked in place, as Gwydion withdrew his sword, then fell to his knees, still almost eye to eye with the man who had killed him. On a mouth that trickled blood from one corner, the sad halfsmile played briefly again and Pryderi said, "Well played, bard," and fell forward and died.

Through the army of Dyfed rippled a moan that could make a listener shudder at the desolation and loss it expressed. Pryderi's chariot was led forward and the dead king was seated in it, almost as if he intended to ride home in comfort. As the men of Dyfed withdrew, Gwydion limped unhappily to his own people. Somehow, triumph over Pryderi was not sweet, but depressing, and the success of his plan must now be followed by a dreaded conversation with Math.

Math, already standing in his chariot, instructed his driver to turn homeward, and moved off at a sedate trot. Gwydion allowed his driver to do the same without bidding. The journey back seemed endless. Arrived in the fortress, they found Goewin standing before the big house, hair wildly disordered, robe awry, the tracks of tears down her cheeks denied by the blaze of fury in her eyes.

Math dismounted slowly from his chariot and walked to her, asking, "What has happened here, lady?"

Goewin's blazing eyes stabbed across Math's left shoulder, skewering Gwydion where he stood, still in his chariot.

"Come inside, my lord. You have a family matter to dispose of."

As Math disappeared through the doorway, Gwydion's sweeping glance located Gilfaethwy back near the entrance to the compound. As quickly as he could without seeming to hurry, he stepped down from the chariot and walked toward his brother, who retreated before him until they had both traversed the path leading out of the fortress and were standing alone outside.

"Now, brother, without further ado, tell me what happened!"

Gilfaethwy shifted from foot to foot uncomfortably.

"I am to blame, but I could not... do otherwise. I... she was with the other maids most of the first day after the army left for the border. Until late in the day. When she was alone in the big house. I approached her. I told her of my feelings. She... she smiled and said that she was... was not ready yet to sacrifice her vocation for the love of a man."

Gilfaethwy fell silent, staring at the ground. Gwydion's agate-hard eyes bored into his scalp until he looked up and continued, "I put... my hands on her shoulders to plead with her, and she became furious. She was in a rage, but she was so beautiful! I could only think of all the months of waiting..."

Of course he had known this possibility, but concern for his brother had allowed him to suppress it. Now, faced with the deed, he felt a chill creep slowly down his spine and an answering rage rise in his throat.

"So you forced her. May the great Dôn curse you for a fool! Did you not know there is a difference between desire and rape? And by the red stripes down both sides of your face and a newly crooked nose, she seems to have defended herself vigorously."

Gwydion seized control of his turbulent emotions.

"So. At great cost, you have had your will. Is your fever broken?"

"Yes..."

"But there is no satisfaction, it seems. You would have done better to have borne the malady until it abated of itself."

"Yes."

"And this pretty story is what Goewin is telling Math at this very moment?"

"Yes."

"Then our only hope is to flee beyond our uncle's wrath, and immediately. We cannot go south. The men of Dyfed are of a mood to tear us to pieces. We must go north, through the heart of Gwynedd, and then east to Alban, where some of our kin still hold out against the Picts and Gaels and we can perhaps take service with some other lord. Come!"

"But we have no food, no drink, not even a horse."

"And shall we go back into the fortress and ask our uncle to help us? Think, brother! We must go now! Food, drink and shelter are never refused honest travelers."

So saying, Gwydion set off at a fast pace, half dragging his brother along until Gilfaethwy finally understood that this was indeed their only route, and pressed forward so fast that Gwydion had to restrain him, lest they tire themselves out in the first halfday. Constantly listening for the sound of pursuit, Gwydion forbade conversation after a while, for fear that Math's uncanny power could track them. "Not even loud thoughts!" he said.

By nightfall, they were weary enough to welcome the thought of hospitality even in the crude hut they came upon. But it was not to be. With pious regret, the old man who lived there alone informed them that Math had put a ban on their meat and drink. They would find no helping hand in all of Gwynedd, and possibly beyond, "For Math be feared in all the land of our folk."

It seemed incredible, even for Math, to have spread the word against them so far and so quickly. Yet, through the night and into the next day, they encountered the same answer — polite, regretful, firm or hostile. No one would break the ban. And so, with dread lying heavy and cold in their stomachs, they turned home again.

Math received them sitting, his feet in the lap of a young girl who looked as though she wanted nothing more than to escape the muscle-tightening tedium of her new office. Goewin stood at Math's right hand. He glowered silently at his nephews and they silently bore his gaze. Goewin stared impassively over their heads.

It seemed that they stood for hours in silence before Math spoke: "One of you has achieved a great victory and has brought a great blessing to our land. But these are the secondary results of a scurrilous plot which has robbed me of my most faithful servant, and would have despoiled Lady Goewin of her honour, had she not become my queen. It was a shameful thing you did, and I could choose to have you killed. I would not care to face my sister with that news. No more would I care to have it known that anyone, even the presumptive heir to the kingship of Gwynedd, will go unpunished for such a deed. This day begins the first of the three years of your chastisement."

Math raised his right hand holding his druid rod. He leaned forward to tap Gwydion on the head with it, and Gwydion tensed to flee, but he could not. Then Math did the same to Gilfaethwy. He spoke, but the words swam chaotic and senseless in their ears. An overwhelming weight seemed to press on them, forcing them forward and downward until their hands touched the ground. Looking up, Gwydion could see the look of sudden comprehension — and satisfaction mingled oddly with pity — on Goewin's face. He tried to stand, but when he pushed up with his hands, they scrabbled loudly and moved back and forth, like the hooves of a frightened deer. He felt his neck muscles grow and expand to great, smooth bands, supporting an ungainly weight which seemed to be connected to the top of his head. He heard a scrabbling sound next to him and, still on all fours, looked to his right at his brother. But what he saw was a frightened doe, fidgeting in place, terror in her eyes. As he understood what was happening, he felt the person who was Gwydion shrinking inside of his new body and retreating to a small place inside the head, where it could observe, comprehend, but no longer control the body in which it was housed.

Once again, Math pointed at them. "You will return to this place in one year's time."

Gwydion's body felt an overwhelming urge to flee from this place of human beings to the safety of the forest. Together, the stag and doe ran from the big house — the stag ducked his head instinctively, to keep his great rack of antlers from catching on the doorframe — then from the fortress and into the safe darkness of the forest.

"So," thought the observer who was Gwydion, "our punishment is to live as wild animals. We must escape the wolf and the bear and the human hunter as well. A nasty task, but not impossible."

He was right in this, for their strong bodies and acute senses were the proper tools for survival in the wild — to find food even under the snow, to sense danger before it burst upon them — to outrun it or outlast it. It was a hard life, but not an impossible one, and the observer within could bear the terror of the chase and the privation of little vegetation, because it understood that the body which housed it was admirably suited to its tasks.

The true horror came during the mating season. Two bodies responded to odours and movements that told an esoteric tale of their own. It was the time when male and female of the species are impelled by mysterious forces to join. But two brothers — one of them in the form of a male and one in the form of a female? Could Math truly have wished this? And, of course, he had. It was not just a penalty; it was a chastisement, accomplishing not just punishment but an education in the true and natural relationship between male and female, and a demonstration on their own bodies which did not cease with the perceived shame of the observers during the couplings, but continued through the time of gestation and the overpowering physical experience of birth.

At the end of a year, a demanding call resounded inside their heads, summoning them and their fawn irresistibly away from their haunts deep in the forest to the edge of the wood, to the open fields beyond and then, before the startled eyes of men and women, up the entry ramp, into the fortress, across the compound, through the door of the big house and directly to Math's throne.

Math tapped the head of the fawn with his rod and it stood on its hind legs, precariously balanced at first, then ever more firmly as its shape changed from fawn to handsome young boy.

"Hyddwn I name you, for as deer you began and man you have become. You are welcome to the family of Math. And as for you," turning to the trembling parents, "Go forth for yet another year, and the one of you which was a hind shall be a boar, and the one of you that was a stag shall be a sow." He tapped them with the rod. "Begone!"

Back, back into the forest, grunting and squealing in their eagerness to escape this place of people. For another year, they lived on the land, finding food where their senses directed them, fleeing danger when they could, facing it in rage and terror when they could not, killing or maiming would-be predators — animal or human — with the fury that made the boar a symbol of battle rage. And at mating season, again the coupling and the shrinking shame for the observer within, and a young one to protect, until the call resounded in their heads again.

Once more before Math's throne, they watched, panting, as he tapped their young one and named the handsome young boy, "Hychdwn, for as boar you began, and man you have become. You are welcome to the family of Math. And you who were a sow shall spend yet a year as a wolf, and you who were a boar shall be a she-wolf, and you shall re-appear here one year hence." He tapped them and they fled, howling, from the eyes of men and women.

"One more year," thought the observer who was Gwydion, "and then we can hope for redemption." He was a bit ashamed of his relief at being the female only once of three times. Indeed, he almost looked forward to serving his last year of durance in an alien body. At least he was a male, and the wolf did not spend its entire life with its nose in the snow or the mud, but honestly hunted its food.

Alas, he had not foreseen the driving, gnawing, burning hunger which drove his new body to pounce, slash, rend and tear — a blood lust quenched only by violent death and frenzied feeding, while the observer that was Gwydion was soon beyond surfeit to a gagging nausea without the luxury of a mouth to vomit up his feelings. The worst kill of all was a magnificent stag, which ran and fought with desperate strength, until it could fight no more. And when it died, the look of sad and peaceful resignation in its eyes was a duplication of the look in the eyes of the king of Dyfed when he breathed his last. Male and female relationships were not the only lessons here. The death of a noble being was strongly felt by the observer inside the driven body of the wolf and, for the first time, Gwydion truly regretted the passing of Pryderi. Yet another message was imbedded in this one: that Math himself had had to reconcile the hard necessity of Pryderi's death with its ignoble causes.

At last, at long, long last, the call sounded in their wolfish heads, calling the observers back to Math. They found him as each time before, seated with Goewin at his side, now flanked by two stalwart young men — Hychdwn and Hyddwn. Math raised his druid rod to tap the cub which stood trembling between its parents. "Bleiddwn I name you, for as wolf you began, and man you have become."

Again, a handsome boy stood between Gwydion and Gilfaethwy.

"You are welcome to the family of Math. Come, stand with your brothers. And now," looking at the waiting wolves, "if you two have sinned against me and mine, then you have also paid, and perhaps learned as well." He glanced at his queen, standing regally beside him. "We are none of us who we were. Return to the family of Math!" He tapped each of them with the rod. One moment, observers trapped in beasts' bodies. The next, men again. Free in their own bodies!

Gwydion thought briefly of his time as an animal mother, and of the eyes of the stag. "Uncle, we have learned all that you could have wished."

"And are you prepared to help me fill the void your actions have created?" He glanced kindly at the young girl holding his feet in her lap, whose face, like that of the girl Gwydion remembered from three years before, betrayed her awe of Math, her muscular discomfort and her unrelieved boredom.

"Uncle?"

"In the three years of your punishment, I have had many footstools, as was the case before I discovered the Lady Goewin. I would gladly find another such as she, but have found none. Have you any help to offer?"

Into Gwydion's mind stole the image of his younger sister, Aranrhod — cool, beautiful, aloof even as a child, and haughtily uninterested in "incompetent, arrogant, weakling, blustering boys."

"The only determined virgin I have known, Uncle, who was still of that mind when we began our recent servitude, is our sister, Aranrhod. She is no longer quite a child, but is that intermediate age between child and woman. Our parents abandoned their attempts to find a proper match for her rather earlier than is usually the case — she is not only determined, but... quite independent and stubborn. She has her own stronghold and her own people, settled on her by our parents, who still entertain the hope that she will, on her own, abandon her solitary life. She might be enticed by the honour and unusual character of this office."

"Will you undertake to be my emissary?"

"Gladly, Uncle. I shall depart today."

Chapter Three
NEVER A MOTHER, NEVER A WIFE

Even the talents of a bard cannot reveal that which is not known. The answers to some questions are forever shrouded in the mists of the past. None can tell you why it was that Math and his queen had no progeny of their own, or what became of Gilfaethwy after the adventure you have just heard. Of Gwydion and Math, there is more to tell which also bears upon the tales which are to follow.

Gwydion undertook the journey to his sister's stronghold — small but solidly built and well maintained. She received him with the supercilious manner he remembered.

"You must be here to beg a favour. I should not expect a visit for reasons of fraternal affection."

"Nor have you ever wanted affection from your brothers or any other man. And that is why I have come. To offer you a position for which you, as a determined, lifelong virgin are admirably suited, if you should wish it."

When Aranrhod heard Gwydion's offer, her eyes shone, as he had known they would, with the thought of prestige and reflected power not purchased at the cost of sweaty, distasteful grapplings in the bed of some "incompetent, arrogant, weakling, bullying" man. She agreed without false hesitation, and accompanied him to Math's fortress.

Math greeted her cordially. "You are aware, lady, of the special qualifications and duties of this office?"

"I am, lord."

Math stood heavily, walked forward three steps and placed his druid rod on the on the hard earth of the floor before her.

"If you please, lady. Just a small test. Step over the rod."

Aranrhod hesitated only a moment, then stepped quickly over the rod, turning as she did, to face Math. In the moment of time she took to take that one step, a small bundle fell from beneath her robe, bounced on the floor and stood up — a handsome, black-haired baby boy, who looked around, then ran with amazing swiftness on his baby feet out of the door, past nonplussed men and women, out of the fortress and away in the direction of the sea. Aranrhod, who had stiffened in shock, seemed not to notice that a second bundle had dropped as well, and rolled to Gwydion's feet. He crouched swiftly and thrust the bundle under his tunic.

Aranrhod, her face blanched of all colour, stood deeply still, as if she could make the event unhappen. Math turned to Gwydion, who was still guiltily supporting his illicit bundle under his tunic.

"Nephew, I thank you for your effort. It would appear that you have misjudged your sister."

"Uncle, I am speechless and embarrassed..."

"There is a little good in everything, nephew. Your unaccustomed humility is, in itself, an unusual occurrence. But paltry in comparison to what else has transpired here. The dark-haired boy, who has run off to join the wave of which he is part, is from the seed of his father, who must be one of the sons of Llyr. Because he is of the wave he shall be called Dylan. And if you uncover that babe you picked up, you will see that he is marked as one of the people of Dôn, a gift of the blood of your sister. Her coming together with a man of the South would have remained a secret, had she not risked the test. The power of the druid rod quickened the memory in her body and produced these two fine offspring."

Gwydion gingerly drew the small bundle forth and there, in truth, was a boy-child as blond and light as his brother was dark. Shaking with fury, Aranrhod pointed one slim finger at the babe and, before Math could speak again, said, "I have been demeaned by unworthy trickery. You say this child is mine. Very well, I put a destiny on him: He shall not receive a name but that one that he shall receive from my lips alone. Brother, you are not welcome in my home." With as much dignity as she could muster, she swept out of the door and away. She was a skilled sorceress in her own right, although not as learnëd as Gwydion, who had had the benefit of long study under Math. She knew that the destiny she had placed on the child was doubly strong, because she had phrased it in exactly seventeen words — a mystic number in wishes and imprecations, for, as is known to those who practiswe the mystic sciences, that is the number of words a person can say in one breath.

Without considering why and without a further word to his uncle,

Gwydion took the baby to his own house. He had to arrange for a wet-nurse, and make a small sleeping area for the baby. But it seemed somehow worthwhile.

It all flowed seamlessly together: picking the child up, taking him home, arranging for his care, watching him grow, overseeing his learning — becoming as much a father as an uncle. As days grew into years, they were an accustomed sight — uncle and nephew — hunting, practising with javelin, sword and shield. Sometimes, passers-by heard uncanny noises and saw odd-coloured puffs of smoke drifting up out of the smoke hole of the house. And now and then, strangely familiar but unidentifiable small animals ran out of the door uttering unnatural squeaks and squawks, hopped or sprang or crept around the compound, returned to the house and were never seen again. And every time this happened, the deep, lecturing tones of Gwydion's voice mingled with the merry chortles of his young charge.

One day, when the boy was just past that awkward age in which the bones grow so fast that the body must struggle to control its own limbs, Math sent for both of them. He looked thoughtfully at the young man with Gwydion and then said, "Nephew, it is not fitting that a boy should meet his time of manhood without a name that is his and his alone. A nameless man can do no lasting deed; his name cannot be sung in the songs of his people. Because of the destiny placed on him by his mother, he can receive a name from none other."

"I have considered this, Uncle, and I have a plan. It is time to put it into action."

"I hope," said Math with a hard-eyed look at Gwydion, "that it harbours no hidden catastrophes, like your last scheme."

Gwydion hoped so too, as he prepared for the journey to Aranrhod's stronghold. He gathered the tools of a shoemaker's trade, including some elegantly blue- and gold-dyed leather pieces. He dressed himself in patched breeches and a ragged tunic, darkened the colour of his skin, hair and moustache and even, I cannot tell you how, of his eyes. He dressed the boy similarly, as his apprentice, but did not otherwise alter his appearance, for Aranrhod had not seen him in all the years since his birth.

Aranrhod's stronghold was not only on the coast but at the head of a cliff, so they embarked on their journey in a coracle. The craft, made of skin stretched over a wooden frame, was rather round and ungainly, in the offshore swells easier to paddle than to sail, so they made slow and steady progress along the shore until they reached their destination and beached it at the foot of the cliff directly below the stronghold.

They knew that their presence would be noticed quickly; all strangers everywhere were of interest because they represented danger, trade or information. So Gwydion immediately set up a work-place and began to create beautiful shoes of unusual design. Before long, a boy came down the steep path along the face of the cliff and up to their coracle. He stood watching Gwydion for a while, then turned silently and climbed the path.

When he appeared again in a short time, he said, "My mistress wishes to have a pair of shoes made of your blue leather," and he held out a strip of ordinary leather representing the length and width of Aranrhod's foot.

Gwydion barely looked up from his work. "Return tomorrow at this time."

Gwydion carefully made an elegant pair of shoes, just a little too short and a little too narrow, and gave them to the boy the next day when he came down the path. Shortly after taking them up, he came down again.

"These shoes are too small. My mistress wishes you to make another pair," and he held the shoes out to Gwydion, who only said, "Come again tomorrow at this time."

Gwydion carefully made a pair of shoes just a bit too long and a bit too wide and gave them to the boy, who had dutifully trotted down the path the next day. The boy took the shoes up the path, and in very short order trotted back down again. "My mistress says that these shoes are too big, and she wishes to know if all of your custom have this difficulty in being properly served."

Suppressing a smile, Gwydion replied, "Even a very good craftsman can only do his best when he sees the foot itself. If your mistress could come down to us, to allow me to fit her, I could guarantee success."

The boy trotted obediently back up the path. A short time passed. Then a small retinue appeared at the top of the path — two warriors ahead, several young women attendants, then Aranrhod herself followed by two more warriors. She paused imperiously before Gwydion and extended her foot. He removed the sandal and cupped a piece of leather around it.

As he did this, her glance settled on the young apprentice, who sat idly nearby, pulling the thongs of his sling to test their strength. Just at that moment, a sea bird glided down to perch on the edge of the coracle. In one fluid motion, the young man picked up a pebble, fitted it into the pouch of his sling and threw unerringly, striking the bird and knocking it senseless but alive into the boat.

"The fair one has a long arm," said Aranrhod admiringly.

Gwydion smiled and spoke in his own voice, "A good name, Sister — Fair One With A Long Arm — Lleu Llau Gyffes. And now that he has a name from your own lips, will you not relent? He is a fine young man. One to be proud of."

Aranrhod faltered backward a step, then stood stiff and hostile, glaring down at Gwydion. "Was it not enough that you disgraced me before Math? Now you present me with this non-person and expect me to acknowledge him." Her eyes blazed and she pointed her slim finger at Lleu. "I put a new destiny on him. He shall receive no shield and he shall receive no weapon, unless they are from my hands. My people will have orders to be on the watch for you and your schemes."

One reason for Aranrhod's fury was as she had stated: that Gwydion had enticed her into a public embarrassment, and was now reminding her of her disgrace. Another, unspoken reason was the knowledge that she had irrevocably given this young, handsome embarrassment more than mere social viability. She had reserved to herself the right to name him or not, and now had been tricked into using that prerogative. Still worse was the fact that she had named him by chance, from something that had happened at the moment. All Celts know that this sort of casual name-giving, apparently by accident, is actually evidence of fateful intercession by powers beyond the human. At one stroke, she had made him a member of society and guaranteed that his life would be a significant one in the memories of their people. The rage that boiled within her as she stalked away from Lleu and Gwydion came from a helpless feeling of being manipulated by forces far greater than her clever, older brother. Perhaps it was only partly anger and equally a desire to test these forces that had caused her to put this second, seventeen-word condition on Lleu. Without weapon or shield, no man could be a member of the warrior class; he was excluded from all most noble endeavours

And it was no doubt these forces which blessed Gwydion's next venture against all the precautions Aranrhod and her people took. He was not so foolish as to begin immediately. He allowed three years to pass, while he considered various plans. At the end of the third year, he set out again with Lleu. His imposture this time approached sacrilege. He was disguised as a white-haired, white-moustached, green-eyed druid in a long robe and hood, leaning on a long staff. Lleu was his young travelling companion — perhaps his student — his light hair and recent moustache blackened, his lustrous skin dulled and darkened. He might have come from one of the southern lands to the east over the sea, where the sky and the ocean were both warm, and some of the Celts had settled long ago.

Gwydion timed their arrival at Aranrhod's stronghold as carefully as he had his arrival years before at Pryderi's fortress. When they were just within sight of the main, landward entrance, he spoke softly but urgently to Lleu.

"Now, Nephew, you know your mission. Do it well and your mother will suspect nothing. Make any mistake, and you are doomed to be the oldest apprentice in the land."

Lleu set off at a dead run, arriving at the entry ramp dishevelled, sweat-soaked and breathless, where he was challenged in the usual manner: name, lineage, business at this place,

"I am Culwch, son of Owein, in service to the druid, Rhonabwy," he gasped. "He has sent me with an urgent message to the Lady Aranrhod."

He was led up the ramp, to stand before Aranrhod, who was just then taking her customary evening walk along the inside perimeter of the wall. She did this partly for the pleasure of seeing her people and being seen and greeted by them, and partly for the feeling of safety and satisfaction she had from knowing that this fortification, though small, was well built and well manned. Told of the young man's mission, she looked him up and down, thinking he would be a handsome addition to her own people, if he could be lured away from the priest's service. She gestured elegantly with her right hand to indicate that he had permission to speak.

"The druid, Rhonabwy, sends me to you, lady, to warn of what we have seen in the north. He follows, but sent me ahead, so that you might have word sooner." While Aranrhod and her attendants waited impatiently, Lleu gasped for breath a few times, then continued, "A fleet of strange, wooden ships is sailing south along the coast, bearing the most barbarous warriors, who speak a harsh tongue and wear animal furs into battle and use axes to fight. They have taken and destroyed every fortified settlement north of here and, when they have satisfied their appetite for rape and plunder, they will be here next." Lleu paused again to breathe deeply, as one who has begun to return to normal after a long exertion. "My master begs you to prepare. He will reach here just before dawn, and will not be far ahead of them. I must return to help him on the way. By your leave."

Aranrhod, frozen in shock, gave a feeble wave of her hand, dismissing him, and Lleu ran out of the fortress like a deer pursued by wolves. He ran at full speed until out of sight, then lapsed into a fast walk. Not far up the road, he encountered Gwydion, who led him to a camp he had set up in the forest.

The illusion Gwydion intended to create would tax even his abilities. He needed the powers of his accomplished apprentice to be sure of achieving it. They set to work immediately. Gwydion arranged the implements and materials he had carried under his robe, while Lleu moved about in the forest, locating the herbs, fungi and flowering plants they would need. When everything was collected, they set to work in earnest. It required the complete concentration of all their spiritual powers and the rest of the night until just before dawn. Then they set out for Aranrhod's fortress. As it came into view, they quickened their pace, Gwydion stumping along vigorously, like a determined old man.

They arrived breathless and were conducted straightaway to Aranrhod, just as the first shouts came from the opposite side of the compound. A large fleet of wooden ships with square, striped sails was spread out along the coast, advancing inexorably. Aranrhod turned in panic as Gwydion and Lleu approached.

"Great Dôn help us, lord priest! Can we withstand this force?"

"The crucial time is the first long attack, lady. Like our people, they are most fearsome in their first assault. If we can hold them outside the walls, kill those few who get in, we have a chance. I will do my best with my poor powers. I will call on the Thunderer to help us. My apprentice is not yet skilled in the mystic arts, but he has trained as a warrior. He will be glad to join your defenders, if you can arm him." Gwydion stepped forward confidentially. "He admires you very much, lady. He would fight like a boar with arms he received from you personally."

Aranrhod spoke brusquely to a young warrior who ran off and returned almost immediately with a magnificently crafted sword and a stout ash shield with gleaming metal rim and bosses. She tied the sword girth on him herself, placed the sword in his hand and passed the loops of the shield over his other arm.

"Now," she said, smiling, "you are a warrior."

As she did this, the great fleet began to flicker strangely and then dissolved into a mist that was wafted away by a gentle sea breeze.

"So he is, sister. For it is by your own hand."

The colour drained from Aranrhod's face and then from her neck. She stared icily at Gwydion.

"My clever brother! Twice you have tricked me but a third time you will not!" Rigidly she pointed at Lleu. "I put a final destiny on him: he shall marry no woman that is born of woman, nurtured by woman or raised by woman."

With Aranrhod's triumphant smile burned into their minds, they were allowed to leave unharmed and unmolested, but the journey home was steeped in gloom. Until now, Lleu had relied on Gwydion, had known that his uncle was resourceful, tireless and very, very clever. But he could feel his uncle's mood and it was not anger or discouragement, but something close to despair. Gwydion could see the purpose behind the last destiny Aranrhod had put upon Lleu. No Celt could be considered fully a member of the warrior society without a name and weapons. Lleu now had these and was beyond doubt a member of the warrior society, possibly even fated to be a hero of renown. One thing remained that she could deny him: marriage, and children who would carry on his name and his blood. And she had phrased her seventeen-word destiny so carefully that a human wife was impossible. This time, it was not a question of deceiving Aranrhod into fulfilling her own terms. Even she could do nothing. There was only one hope.

And his name was Math. Gwydion's skill had grown until he was second to none but Math. But he was still the lesser sorcerer. And he wondered whether even their combined powers could meet this challenge. He wondered because, in everything he knew, there was not even a suggestion of a solution. He ground his teeth together and held his impatience until they reached home.

Math heard the tale of their journey, told without Gwydion's usual panache and humour, then he sent for his bards and his druids. He dismissed Gwydion and Lleu, who spent the rest of the day wrapped in silence and misery.

When they stood before him the next morning, Math was more drawn and haggard than Gwydion had ever seen him. He had still not found a more permanent footstool. The face of the girl-child who sat on the floor before him bore a placid expression, but her body spoke of pride, awe and joint-stiffening monotony. Given the choice, Gwydion thought, she would leap up and run out to seek her friends.

Math spoke slowly and wearily. "It will not be easy. It will require your best efforts as well as mine, but it is possible. I have done everything I could to enlist the help of the Horned One, who knows all the creatures and plants of the wild. He has revealed to me what we must do and it begins with collecting. You, nephew and great-nephew, will go first into the fields to gather the white flowers of the meadowsweet, for it is the colour of purity and cleanliness and has a greatly pleasing scent, and the plant is upright and proud in the open air and the sun. Then you will go the edge of the wood to gather the vivid yellow flowers of the broom, for it is a flower of strong and vivacious colour and the plant that bears it is versatile and serviceable. Finally, you will climb the lord of the forest — the oak — and retrieve its tiny flowers, for they are too modest to flaunt themselves, but the tree on which they grow is the most steadfast of all trees, sacred to our sacred mysteries, and its bark is a tool of our civilization, since it allows us to make usable leather of useless hides."

So Gwydion and Lleu went out with an oxcart to gather armfuls of creamy white meadowsweet, and to the edge of the forest, to gather the bright yellow blossoms of the broom. Finally, they went deep into the forest, where they used ropes to clamber up the tall oaks and collect their blooms, always careful to avoid disturbing the sacred mistletoe which grew on them, for only the druids dared harvest this holy vine.

When they returned, everyone was sent from Math's house, even his footstool. Lleu, too, was left outside. He had helped Gwydion create a great illusion that had lasted just as long as it was needed, but that was the limit of his ability. Gwydion himself had created twelve horses and twelve hounds, but their forms had stayed on them only until sunset. This enterprise required a permanent spell which would hold the form of its subject together forever.

The great illusion at Aranrhod's had required an entire night to prepare; the twelve horses and twelve hounds had required the same. Those who waited for Gwydion and Math passed the night outside expectantly. But the night passed, and the next day, and in all a fortnight, during which the only communication from inside was a brief appearance by Gwydion to demand that food and drink be brought to their door. On the morning after the fourteenth night, Gwydion appeared again and called for Math's footstool, who had been happily passing the time with her friends, to enter and take up her interrupted duties. After a short time, Gwydion came to the doorway again, and invited Lleu to enter.

Lleu's blood rose to his face, his head roared, his heart stumbled in its steady beat, he felt for a moment that he could not breathe. Then, almost involuntarily, he walked forward and through the door. As his eyes became accustomed to the darker interior, he saw before him a young woman incredibly beautiful in form and face. He felt an unbearable lightness in his stomach, as if he had just dropped unexpectedly from a high cliff.

"This," said Math weakly from his seat, "is Blodeuwedd. She comes from beauty and so is beautiful. Her name is unique, for it means 'Flower-Face', and no other has ever had so just a claim to that name."

Lleu stood, stunned.

She stepped forward and, smiling up into Lleu's face, took his hand and said, "I am yours, lord."

Math said, "You will have your own land and people, and will rule over them together. Remember, Nephew, she is a gift from beyond our world. Pay careful attention to her happiness, and to her faults."

The tale of Aranrhod and the remaining tale of Blodeuwedd may cause you to think, stranger, that I have no high opinion of women, but that is not so. I did not sing of the divine Rhiannon, whose wisdom saved herself and her husband-to-be from an underhanded trick, whose steadfastness bore even a long period of disgrace and abuse when all but Pwyll himself believed that she had killed her own child. And I have yet to sing of Mebd and Emher and Scáthach and Aoife. Like any other woman, or any other man, the Celtic woman is weak or strong, evil or good, steadfast or disloyal.

(Of course, everyone knows that Celtic women in general are stronger-minded and stronger-willed than any other.) Because the lives of Gwydion and Lleu are crucial to my story, I tell them as they are, including the involvement of Aranrhod and Blodeuwedd.

As you have guessed from this, the tale of Lleu and Blodeuwedd is not a happy one, but what happened to Lleu proved him, in the end, to be something more than simply a mortal warrior. Math and Gwydion had done their best, and their creation had the appearance of an incredibly beautiful, sweet-tempered and biddable woman. Lleu was blindly in love with her from the first moment, and could never get enough of the time spent in their marital bed. She, on the other hand, was acquiescent and charming, but never passionate. Lleu began to wonder, through his haze of infatuation, whether the magic of Gwydion and Math had been incapable of infusing feeling into their creation. The truth was far worse. Like the things of the wild, her inner nature awaited an elemental encounter that would truly awaken it.

Their life was idyllic — no wars, no disputes among the people to which Lleu was not equal as a judge, a prosperous land. As time went on, Lleu more often took his pleasure in hunting, honing his skills in riding and use of the javelin. Now and then, he stayed overnight in the forest with his hunting party. Now and then, too, he journeyed to Math's stronghold to visit his uncle and great-uncle. On one of these occasions, a chieftain from a neighbouring land hunted too far from home, and found himself in a place he did not recognize. He asked for shelter at the nearest fortress, which was Lleu's, and was given hospitality by Blodeuwedd herself.

As they sat across the eating circle from each other, Blodeuwedd's eyes met those of Gronw, the visitor, and it was as if the bee and the flower had met for the first time. Gronw was struck dumb by her beauty. She felt for the first time the heat of passion begin in her eyes and flow downward to engulf her entire body. From that moment on, neither of them looked back. They did not think, because they were incapable of thinking. When the meal was over, all others were allowed to go their own way, and Blodeuwedd spent a night with Gronw which ignited a flame that was capable of consuming all caution, concern for appearance or moral inhibitions. To be absolutely fair, I should say that Gronw lost his moral inhibitions; it is not certain that Blodeuwedd, creature of the wild that she was, was ever endowed with any.

Of course, Lleu's people should have told him, but surely in their minds was the undisguised devotion in his face when he looked at Blodeuwedd, and his naive, uncomplicated character. None of them had a long acquaintance of their master and mistress, nor the absolute loyalty that long association commands.

And so began a long, desperate, passionate, doomed affair between Gronw, the stranger to this land and Blodeuwedd, the stranger to humanity.

Their desire was like the flame and their calculations were cold as the breath of a winter's day. They knew that they could never overcome Lleu's love for Blodeuwedd. She could not simply run from him. His reach was the reach of Math and Gwydion, and that was formidable. But there was a way. A terrible way, and neither of them could face it at first. Finally, however, the only question was whether fear or desire would be the stronger... and desire prevailed. Lleu had to die, and he had to die in a way that left them untouched by the repercussions of his death.

It was said of Lleu that he could not be killed by any ordinary means, and that none but he and Math and Gwydion knew the secret of his mortality. It was for Blodeuwedd to discover the one and only way.

Uninformed and unsuspecting, unaware that the embraces he received from her were but the flickering light thrown by a great flame, Lleu continued to hope that a spark would one day ignite in Blodeuwedd. One night, as they lay side by side in their low bed, she turned away from him as if in distress, and he asked her why.

"I sometimes think of what would become of me if you should die," she said craftily.

"That should be of no concern to you. I was born with great protection, and can only be killed by an unusual combination of circumstances. When I die, it will be because it is my destiny to die at that time. I can only be killed by a javelin that has been created over an entire year — no more, no less — with a shaft of ash and a head of bronze. The craftsman may only work on feast days, while others are revelling or sacrificing, and the thing must be used on the first day of winter or the first day of summer. And there is even more. I must be killed in a very particular way. So you see, there is little to worry about. Until the day of my destiny arrives, I am invincible."

"I am relieved to hear it," Blodeuwedd said through gritted teeth. Her voice was so strangled that Lleu believed she was still in the grip of fear for him, and moved to comfort her. But she seemed, unaccountably, to have developed a headache.

For a year thereafter, Lleu hunted, embraced his wife and lived in hope of an answering emotion. Blodeuwedd used her headaches and other ailments carefully, only when she had to — when the thought of Gronw was too strong in her to bear the touch of her husband. And Gronw worked on the javelin only on sacred days, beginning with the raw materials, and pacing himself to finish in exactly four seasons, at the gateway to summer.

When the time was right, Gronw hid inside the compound during the day while Lleu was gone, and stayed in hiding for the night. As Lleu lay beside Blodeuwedd that night, she turned away from him as she had seasons before. When he asked her why, she said again that she was tormented by the thought of his death.

"What if someone hates you enough to prepare a javelin in the way you described? How could you protect yourself?"

"When someone knows enough to prepare such a weapon, that will be the day of my destiny," he said, "for they will also know what else they have to know. Many things must come together to accomplish my end."

"But... what are they?"

"Believe me, they are impossible until the day of my destiny. I must be neither wet nor dry, neither inside nor outside, neither clothed nor naked, neither eating nor fasting."

"Such a thing is not possible!" Blodeuwedd said with a force caused partly by her shock at the impossibility of creating such a situation. "You did not tell me that you were immortal! I will grow old and ugly, and you will remain as you are forever and become tired of me and put me away. The things you said cannot be done!"

"They can be done and I am not immortal. I am only destined."

Blodeuwedd looked miserable, as indeed she was beginning to feel, and cried, "I do not believe you! I do not believe you! I do not believe you!"

Lleu wanted nothing so much at that moment as to convince Blodeuwedd that he was speaking the truth. So he rolled to the edge of the low bed, walked to a water vase and plunged his hand into it. Pulling out his hand, he brushed the water through his hair. Out of an earthen pot hanging by a thin rope from the rafter, he took a leek and put it between his teeth. To cover his nakedness, he draped himself in a fisher's net that he had brought home a long time ago. Then he went to the doorway, keeping one foot down on the lower level of the floor and putting one foot up onto the ground level outside.

"You see," he murmured around the leek, which was not quite a food and yet not really not a food. "Now I am neither feasting nor fasting, neither wet nor dry, neither inside nor outside, neither clothed nor naked."

And as he turned to smile reassuringly at Blodeuwedd, Gronw launched the javelin, which took him full in the back. He fell quietly and softly, like a robe which has been held up and then released. But from the heap that lay just inside the doorway, a great eagle rose with a shrilling cry, cast a baleful glance first at Blodeuwedd, then at Gronw, and flapped noisily away into the sky and out of sight.

Blodeuwedd and Gronw did not waste much thought on the eagle that had flown away or on the obvious fact that Lleu's body was missing. They did not ignore these things because they were stupid, but because nothing further seemed to threaten them, and their desires consumed all thought. So they began a life together in Gronw's stronghold, leaving Lleu's people to their own devices.

It was some long time before any of them had the courage to face the necessary action. Finally, a concerned delegation appeared at Math's court to report the disappearance of Lleu and Blodeuwedd. Gwydion questioned them sharply, implying dire punishment for any who had contributed to Lleu's disappearance. Conscious of their disloyalty to Lleu, they reacted with terrified silence, until Math overrode his nephew.

"There will be punishment for only two things: doing direct harm to my great-nephew or his wife, and not telling us everything that might have to do with this disappearance."

This provoked a babble of information which gradually resolved into one or two voices, telling of the liaison between Blodeuwedd and Gronw. When Gwydion heard Gronw's name, his eyes blazed and he made as if to leave immediately, but Math forestalled him.

"There will be time for vengeance later, nephew, and it will be for Lleu to decide its form."

"But where is he, then, if not dead and buried or captive with the two of them?"

"Nephew, the lust for action in your guts is blinding you to what we know about him. He is greater in his own way than both of us together. He is not dead, but transformed. You must make a pilgrimage to his land and search for signs."

"Signs, Uncle?"

"The pigs you brought us from Dyfed are domesticated now all over the land. They are still, in their own way, creatures of Annwn. They will be drawn to the distress of a son of Dôn."

Gwydion knew his uncle well enough to perceive that he would receive no further clue. Even in such a serious matter, Math still found an opportunity to instruct his nephew by setting him tasks which he must unravel as he went. So Gwydion dressed himself again as an old druid and set out on a solitary journey through Lleu's small land.

It was neither easy nor short. Gwydion stopped at every large house and small hut. At last, footsore at the end of a long day, he discovered a pig farmer who was thrilled to find that his guest was the man who had brought the creatures to their land. He waxed eloquent in his praise of the food animal which had come from the South, then, growing confidential, he told Gwydion of something truly unusual.

"I have a sow that does not act like any pig I have ever had. When I let them loose to forage nearby, she runs off as fast as she can, over the hill and out of sight. None of us has ever been able to stay with her, to find where she goes. Even during the mast, when the acorns were thick on the ground, she did not stay to eat with the others, but ran off. And yet, she flourishes, as you see."

He pointed to a sow suckling her squirming young. She was as fat and healthy as any Gwydion had seen.

"Tomorrow, when I open the gate, she will rush out, leaving her young ones to squeal, and I will have to keep them apart from the others until she returns and gives them suck again for as long as they want."

"And tomorrow," said Gwydion, "I will be at the gate when you open it."

The day was dawning grey and cool, when the sow was released and set off at an ungainly but incredibly fast trot up the hill. Only because he was a superior tracker did Gwydion find where she had gone. When he caught up, he found the sow at the foot of a withered oak, with her snout pushed into a pile of what appeared to be rotted flesh. As he watched, another handful dropped onto the pile and drew his eyes upward. On a branch at the top of the oak perched a sickly, wasted eagle, peering down at him suspiciously.

Gwydion strode away to a nearby copse of trees and picked some toadstools. Then he returned to the withered oak, sat down cross-legged and began to hum a tune he had taught Lleu as a youngster. While he hummed, he tapped one of the toadstools with his druid rod. Suddenly, in place of the toadstool there was a small furry animal with the nose of a rat, the tail of a pig and the six hairy legs of a spider. It wobbled unsteadily around the oak until it came full circle, then stopped, gave a puff of smoke and became a toadstool again.

The eagle hopped down to a branch lower on the tree.

Gwydion kept humming, and created another whimsical animal, which ran around the oak and then returned to form. And the eagle hopped down further. Another animal and another hop, and the eagle was now just above Gwydion. He stood up and extended his arm and the eagle hopped down to perch on his wrist. Setting it down gently, Gwydion tapped it with his druid rod and there, in its place, sat a sickly and wasted Lleu.

Gwydion gathered him up — he weighed very little — and took him to the friendly pig keeper, who gladly sold him a cart and a bullock. Back at Math's stronghold, Lleu slowly recovered his health and his former strength, and told of what had brought him to such a state.

"But, Uncle," he said, fixing Gwydion with a quiet eye, "Gronw is mine. I cannot bring myself to do anything against Blodeuwedd. I leave her to you — to uncreate." Gwydion agreed, Math provided the men, and Gwydion and Lleu set out for Gronw's land.

They were seen and formally challenged by border sentries, who, having satisfied the formalities divided into two groups. One man raced to warn Gronw; the rest raced as fast as possible in another direction. Clearly, Gronw did not inspire great loyalty in his men.

While Gronw led his men out to meet the men of Math, Blodeuwedd, who knew the capabilities of Math, Gwydion and Lleu, gathered a few women about her and fled from the stronghold toward the mountains.

The confrontation between the two war parties was less a battle than a rout. Gronw raced back to his stronghold with a few men, but Lleu entered almost on their heels. As he came to a halt some yards from Gronw's house, Gronw paused in the doorway, one foot down in the house and one foot on the ground outside. As Lleu hefted his javelin, preparing for a throw, Gronw turned to his men and asked, "Is there no man of you who will take this blow for me?"

But they stood silent, their shields sliding off their inert arms. And this is why they came to be known in the Triads as One of the Three Disloyal War-Bands. Lleu said, "You must take the same blow that you dealt to me, and none can take it for you."

"I ask a favour of you, then. That I may hold a shield before me."

"Granted," said Lleu with undisguised contempt.

Gronw leaned inside the door of his house and pulled out the heaviest, stoutest shield Lleu had ever seen. He held it in front of himself at arm's length, to avoid being stabbed by the tip of the javelin if it penetrated. Lleu immediately launched the javelin in a throw so powerful that his throwing hand swept down to scrape the ground. The javelin pierced the shield with such speed that it did not cause an explosion of splinters, but drove an almost perfectly circular hole through the wood just above the large central boss. It sped between Gronw's outstretched arms, into his chest, out of his back and into the house with such force that it ended, quivering, in a supporting post. Gronw fell as silently as Lleu had done, and did not rise ever again.

Gwydion, meanwhile, was fulfilling the task Lleu had set him, by tracking Blodeuwedd and her companions into the mountains. He caught sight of them at the start of a treacherous, narrow path along the steep face of the first large mountain. Seeing him, Blodeuwedd urged them to hurry. They became bolder, less cautious, more worried about Gwydion than the mountain path. One by one, they made mis-steps, stumbled, put a foot wrong, and fell, until none was left alive but Blodeuwedd herself, pressed trembling and panting against the mountain. She eyed Gwydion fearfully as he came up to her.

"Your origins make you an immortal," he said, "so I cannot kill you. I must choose between oblivion and transformation. After the mischief you have caused, I cannot choose mere oblivion. You will become a creature of the air. As you should be in your human form, you will be scorned and feared by others of your kind, and you will live as a creature of the night, seeking your sustenance by preying upon other nocturnal beasts. You will still be called 'Blodeuwedd', but the flower form of your face will be a bitter irony to you."

And so it was that Gwydion created the owl.

This now, is as far as the story of Gwydion will go. He lived many years thereafter, succeeded to the kingship of Gwynedd when Math died, and — probably because of the foolhardiness of his early years and the knowledge and regret that came with age — ruled well and wisely. As he and Lleu travelled home, victorious but saddened at the thought that Lleu would leave no progeny behind him — even then, Gwydion's mind would not rest. He turned to Lleu and asked, "What was it like, to be an eagle?"

Chapter Four
GOWEN

Lleu never told his uncle or anyone else what it had been like to be an eagle, but it proved what Math had already known: that there was more to Lleu than anyone could imagine. Not just anyone struck by a javelin can transcend physical death by changing shape. Even Math needed his great knowledge and druid rod to accomplish transformations. Lleu's transformation had been without conscious intent, like blinking when water splashes toward the eyes.

Despite the favorable omens of his name and armour, it appeared that he would simply disappear from memory, and play no part in future songs. In fact, after a while, no one seemed to know his whereabouts or whether he was still alive and among mortals.

As it transpired, the answer was Yes and No. He was not dead, but never again was he seen among mortals. His brother, Dylan — he of the wave — was seen only the once, when he arrived out of the sea, years after disappearing into it. For those who believe in blind chance, his death was a clear example. Emerging onto the beach in Gwynedd, he encountered a kinsman who was — strangely — both a smith and a warrior, who gave him no time to explain himself or his unexpected appearance. Sensing from the corner of his eye the naked stranger's approach, he drew and swung his sword as he turned, and Dylan died as he had lived — a mystery.

What now has all this to do with Lleu? Well, it was this blacksmith who had a beautiful young wife, whose fate it seemed to be to remain childless. The couple had become resigned to the fact. They lived and enjoyed their lives as best they could and thought less and less about the lack in their lives. One day — the very day of Gwydion's death it was — the woman brought her husband a noonday meal, which they shared and washed down simply with the cold, refreshing water of a nearby spring. As she went to scoop out a drink for herself, an eagle flew overhead. A small something fell from the eagle's beak into the little drinking pot just before the woman drank from it. A small, worm-like thing, which swam or floated about in the water as she drank, and she drank it down. And it was only shortly after this that she began to have pangs of sickness in the morning.

She waited until she was sure before she told her husband, and when she did, they both rejoiced at this unexpected fortune... Ah, I suspect the question you are burning to ask: if the smith and his wife did not know about the small creature, how do I know? And why do I mention the eagle in a way that implies that it was Lleu in a form he had taken before? And what could all that have to do with the departure of Gwydion's soul from his body? If you are to understand this tale at all, you must accept that I am a true bard, and true bards know much that is not known to the throng. What everyone knows is the warp of the fabric and what we know is the weft. There is no cloth with only the one. It is not for me to know if you will believe everything I tell you, but I will not make it common to make it acceptable.

As I said, the couple rejoiced, and in time they rejoiced even more at the birth of a healthy boy-child, whom they named Gowen.

Now there was in Gwynedd at this time a warrior named Gwri, who lived apart and was said by many to have powers. A month after the child's birth, he arrived at the compound — tall, grey-eyed, neither friendly nor aloof. At his side was a large hound, walking stiff-legged with hostile watchfulness until its master was received with courteous welcome. Then the fire died from its eyes, but it did not leave its master's side. Gwri was offered hospitality, as was the custom. His reputation was such that he was offered shelter and refreshment in the king's own house. He smiled a slight smile of acknowledgment and walked directly to the house of the blacksmith, which was marked by the smelting oven beside it, ribbons and shards of metal radiating from its still glowing embers. None would dream of refusing hospitality to a traveller, and so Govannon invited him to stay the night, although we may suppose that he was not eager for strange company in a house with his wife and new child.

Entering, Gwri greeted Govannon and Branwen gravely and sat with them around the cooking fire, which was laid on a firestead of small circular stones in the middle of the living area. The hound walked straight to the baby, lying beside its mother on a soft skin and covered lightly against the air. Branwen started up apprehensively, but Gwri held out his hand, seeming to stop her by the movement. The dog lay down with its head on its paws, its nose but a short space from the child's face, and gazed with what appeared to be rapt attention into the lively young eyes.

It did not move or utter a sound after that.

Gwri proved to be an unusual guest, for he refused to be served by his host and hostess. Instead, he unpacked a small parcel, producing a small wineskin, a packet of herbs and a choice cut of meat that must have come from a freshly killed boar. Using the cooking fire, he prepared a meal for the three of them that equalled anything the king had ever seen on his table. Some of the herbs he kept aside, making a poultice of them with a bit of the wine and a few drops of blood from the meat. Govannon and his wife noted this with curiosity, but their courtesy restrained their questions, and they soon forgot it in the pleasure of the meal and the companionable atmosphere created by their guest's friendly inquiry into their lives. So they were caught unawares when he scooped up a handful of the poultice, leaned forward almost languidly across the remains of the meal to the baby, who lay on a blanket by his mother, threw aside the covers and lightly rubbed the aromatic mixture on the child's chest, stomach and bald head. He rubbed his hand with the residue of the poultice over the dog's muzzle, and it gazed softly at him as if it understood why. Re-covering the child gently, he spoke.

"I am here by a design greater than my own, because I have come to know of this child. You must take comfort and pride from the life that he is destined to lead, and no matter what happens, believe what I tell you now. The name you have chosen for him was not your choice alone, nor was it idle chance. Each name has its character, and the giving of it must fit the life of him who will bear it. I confirm by the gods the name of Gowen, and I tell you that this is only one of the names he will be known by. His life will be glorious and mysterious, even to those who know and love him. He will be a stranger and a hero in the lands where he lives, and his death will be both the affirmation and the glorious end of a way of life."

Rising almost before the couple realized what he was doing, he called the dog, which seemed to leave the baby reluctantly to rejoin its master. When they protested that he was welcome to stay the night with them — something they had expected from the start — he smiled and said that he had done what he had come to do, and there was more yet to be done. Thanking them, he departed, and left behind two people numb from the shock of his visit. What haunted them most was his phrase: "You must take comfort from.." for it seemed to bode separation from their only and deeply loved child. It would be many years before they understood, at least in a way.

Thereafter — once or twice in the course of each cycle of the moon — Gwri would return to look in on the boy and, when he was old enough to converse, Gwri took it upon himself to speak to him of the gods and traditions of the Celtic peoples. Gowen learned of Cernunnos, the horned god with his special understanding of animals; of Taranis, the Thunderer, whose great club and erect penis symbolized his power; of Epona, the horse-goddess whose rites legitimized each new king of the Cymry, of Teutates — god of war who received the sacrifice of captives as gratitude for victory. He learned that the king's power could not protect him against a time when the fortunes of his people faltered, and the druids declared that he must be sacrificed to persuade the gods and destiny to smile on their community once again. And he learned of the hag-beauty who appeared only rarely to mark a man destined to be an unusual king or an extraordinary hero.

"Why is she called that?" Gowen had asked.

"Only those who see her know the answer to that."

"Do you know the answer?" Gowen had asked slyly.

"No," Gwri had smiled enigmatically. "I do not, but I know someone who will."

As Gowen grew into an active young boy, it was clear that he would not resemble his father, who was a tall and powerfully built man. The boy was small, even delicate, and so it was thought that he favoured his mother. For all that he was small, he was filled with a boundless energy that soon came to the attention of his contemporaries. For it is a quality of boys that they will probe and test, to see who fits their image of what a "man" should be. Gowen — small, delicate-featured, with eyes and hair that could only be called beautiful — was a natural target for such testing.

His desire to be included in a small group of boys roughly his own age was responsible for both his early misery and his eventual transformation. They formed a clique that was a terror among their contemporaries: burly and handsome Llan ap Lot — the acknowledged leader, Cei — even then tall and thin and swift and dangerous, Bedwyr — born with only one arm but more fearsomely competent with his one arm than most others with their two, Culwch and Peredur — both quiet and intense and in their eyes the longing for something beyond the world, something that only they could see. Llan took particular joy in declaring that Gowen was not fit to tag along behind them, then punishing his attempts to follow along and emulate their feats of physical daring. For a long time, Gowen's desperate desire to be included trammelled his inner fury, and his acquiescence was taken to be timidity.

"Go home and help your mother at the cook-fire," Llan would hiss, and the others, but for Cei, laughed obediently. Cei was not quite sure what kept him from laughing. He always squirmed inside himself and looked away until it was over, then rejoined the group in their next endeavour, sometimes casting a look over his shoulder at the forlorn, small shape standing irresolute behind them as they frolicked ahead.

Finally, one day, it was enough — for both Llan and Gowen. As the boys set out to seek their adolescent idea of adventure, they spied a crow flying full speed, pursued by a much smaller bird which repeatedly dived to peck at the crow's head. The crow had been caught in the act of raiding the nest of a smaller bird, and was being driven away.

"See now," said one-armed Bedwyr, "how the little fellow overcomes his disadvantage and drives the bigger one before him."

"He is using his greater speed and manoeuvrability to overcome his bigger adversary," said Cei.

Llan murmured in agreement and Bedwyr continued: "His superiority gives him the victory and drives the larger enemy before him."

"No!" piped a small voice, and they all looked at Gowen, who said, "He does not know that he has an advantage, he only knows that he is right, and that gives him the strength to defeat any odds."

"So, rabbit, being right is enough to give victory," drawled Llan ominously.

"Yes," replied Gowen, tight-lipped, and Cei was startled to see what he thought was a glow in the boy's eyes.

"Then let us see the right of your hopping along in our footsteps every time we go out," roared Llan, and gave Gowen an open-handed blow to the face, to be followed, as was his wont in such disagreements, by a kick aimed at the ribs. The blow of his hand left a red mark over one whole side of

Gowen's face, and bent his upper body in the direction of the blow. He staggered one step to the side, but did not fall. Llan, meanwhile, had struck out so hard that his arm followed through and pulled his own body in the same direction. He pulled back and set his legs to deliver the finishing kick, but it was too late. Gowen's right hand punched into his midriff with such force that Llan emitted a loud "Woof!" and bent slightly forward, where his nose encountered Gowen's left elbow, travelling at incredible speed. He rocked backward on his haunches, then sat slowly and clumsily — almost as if on purpose. His laboured gasps drew in and bubbled out the blood running from his nose and lips.

From Gowen's point of view, it seemed as if the world had slowed down. While Cei looked on in bemused astonishment, Bedwyr, Culwch and Peredur stepped forward scowling, to defend their leader from this diminutive warrior. To Gowen's heightened sensibilities, they moved as if asleep. He struck first at Peredur, kicking his knee and aware of his sideways fall, even as he moved on to Culwch with a leap and a clawed hand at the face. Culwch fell back, protecting his eyes. Bedwyr, who understood the principle of surviving to fight another battle, simply turned and walked away. The expression on Cei's face transformed slowly from blank amazement, to comprehension, to exultation, and he stepped toward Gowen, carefully extending both hands upturned to indicate no weapon and no hostile intent. Gowen amazed him again, by solemnly placing his smaller hands palm to palm on Cei's own and smiling into his face with an expression Cei would in later years think of as "benevolent". Cei seized Gowen's wrists, swung the smaller boy in a wide circle and up onto his shoulders, then turned to his companions.

"Well," he said, "are you coming?"

And so Gowen became one of them.

Gowen's parents were aware at first of only one change. Their heretofore solitary son had acquired a small group of friends, each of whom seemed to acquire minor injuries of the kind acquired by typically Celtic boys in typically rough play. It was, after all, preparation for a life of war. That their son alone was always unblemished seemed to both of them a sad confirmation that he was not made of the stuff of warriors. Only later did they learn the truth, told to them in segments by the other parents.

In fact, from that day on, Gowen was the undisputed leader of the little band. His most avid admirer was the lanky, mystically driven Cei, and his most grudging follower the de-throned Llan. Cei believed that Gowen had been specially endowed by the gods, to fight the enemies of the Cymry, and said so to everyone who would listen. Wherever Gowen was, there was Cei; and whatever Gowen chose to do, Cei was his first and most faithful supporter. Llan believed that Gowen was a dark spirit from Annwn, but he did not dare say that to anyone, for even his former adherents — Peredur, Culwch and Bedwyr — were prepared to follow Gowen wherever he chose to go and to emulate every feat he undertook. When they could not duplicate his physical accomplishments, they simply smiled and shook their heads in wonderment. It was, as Cei often thought to himself, as if a reign of terror had been succeeded by a rule of example.

The truth is that the small, perpetually sad-looking Gowen — except when he was moved to hilarity, aroused to battle fury or plunged into thoughtfulness — was graced by a kindness of temperament, an ebullience of spirit and a sense of honour which gave the lie to his somewhat dolorous exterior. With the exception of Llan, Gowen's companions not only deferred to him, but liked him. Problems had only just begun to arise among some of his young band, because the girls of the community universally favoured him, when his promising career as a future Cymric war leader came to an abrupt end.

One misty morning, the compound woke to blood-curdling war-cries and the clash of weapons on shields, as the men of the night watch were driven inside the walls and into the central area by a party of raiders from Eire. For some time, unexpected Gaelic raids for treasure — animal, metal or human — had been an unpleasant feature of life along the coast in Cymric lands, so even waking abruptly, Gowen knew instantly what was happening. He bolted from the house on his father's heels and dashed headlong into the pandemonium, wielding his father's second sword. The first warrior he encountered — tall, broad, yellow-haired — beheld the spectacle of a three-and-a-half-foot boy swinging a four-foot sword. He threw back his head and laughed, and then howled as Gowen's sword bit into the calf of his left leg. He fell heavily, right on top of his diminutive attacker, and a mist of darkness settled over Gowen's mind.

When Gowen woke, it was as from a bad night's sleep during an illness, with an aching head, fuzzy mouth and aches and pains throughout his small body. He was face down in the bottom of a sea-going curragh — the Gaelic version of a coracle, immersed in the smell of stale sea water, sweat and blood. Without thinking, he rolled over to push himself up and go on fighting, when the same large blond sat on him hard and said, "Lie still, boy! 'Tis too late to fight and too late to get away."

Holding the bloodstained rag wrapped around his left calf, he turned and roared to his companions, "Did I not tell you that he was full of fire? This one will be a warrior, and no slave to do chores." And then to Gowen, "I know you're a fighter, young one, but a warrior knows when there is no more battle to fight. You will not see your home or your people again. We are a fierce folk, but a decent one. Take time to learn before you go attacking someone five times your size again." He eased his weight off the prostrate boy and crouched beside him watchfully.

It was to be said of Gowen many times in his later life that he had a young man's passion and an old man's wisdom. He had heard enough Gaelic from more peaceable traders and passers-through from the Gaelic land to the north to understand and reply. He rolled over onto his back, stared into the big man's face and said, "If it is too late to fight and too late to escape, maybe it is time to have something to drink."

As he drank from the skin passed to him by his friendly grinning captor, he looked slowly in all directions, and saw nothing but the sky and heard nothing but the gruff chuckling of the waves on the skin of the carcass of the curragh. They were well away from shore; only one of Llyr's deep-sea denizens could swim from here to the coast of his homeland.

"What is your name, boy?" asked the blond Gael.

"I am Gowen," he answered. "And who are you?"

"I am called Roigh, boy, and lucky you are that it is I am the one you are asking so boldly, for I have a bold lad of my own and I will not lay my hand across your face for it."

Gowen said not a word, but stared directly into the blue eyes of the big man, who laughed loudly, but spoke quietly, "I see in those strangely coloured eyes of yours what you're thinking — that my hand would come back to me with fewer fingers. Now keep still, speak when spoken to, and try to control that fire inside you. I would hate to see one of my comrades bloodied by so small a fellow. And I would hate to watch as they threw you into the sea."

Gowen understood better than he would have cared to admit. He clambered a bit higher in the curve of the craft, leaned back to close his eyes. Before he could will himself to relax, he heard the gossipy quacking of ducks and, looking up, saw a flight of them pass overhead. A moment later a melancholy cry announced the passage overhead of one lone seagull. As Gowen's heavy eyelids sagged over his vision, he had the thought that he had just seen something significant, but he could not understand why. And so he slept.

He woke to Roigh's large hand shaking his shoulder.

"Look up over the side, boy. It's the Green Land of the Gaels you're looking at. We have a long and careful way, still, to come home to Uledh. For if we make landfall in Munster or Leinster, we will have to fight across the half of the land, to our borders. And that is a great task, even for men of the Uledh."

The names had no meaning for Gowen, for how was he to know that Eire was divided into four lands with a mystic, invisible middle. He contented himself with inspecting the craft in which he was an unwilling passenger. It was not so different from the seagoing coracles used by his own people to sail from their island to the south and then to the east, across the arm of the sea, to maintain commerce and religious contact with their cousins, who lived on the coast of the great ancestral homeland. Nor, though he did not know it, from those skin-covered craft that sailed out to the west toward the Land of the Young and never returned, though some claimed to know that they had found another, unknown land, much like their own, far across the great, open sea.

It was a long and boring voyage for Gowen — sky, rolling sea and talk among his captors which meant little to him. But he listened when he could, because soon he would be living among these people, and everything he learned now could protect him later. When seasickness threatened, he closed his eyes, breathed slowly and occupied his mind with visions of what he would have done to the Gaels, if Roigh had not fallen on him.

Finally they arrived, wearily beached their boat and tramped determinedly through the darkness. And Gowen had his first view of Conchobar's court. It was a great *dún* — high circular stone walls and a torturous roadway to the massive wooden entry gate. They entered, and life changed forever.

Chapter Five
EMAIN MACHA

Inside, they faced a house of the kind he knew, but immense. Entering, they seemed almost to be at the opening of a huge forest clearing. Standing and sitting around the large area, men and women seemed to form almost random patterns. As Roigh's party made its way toward the opposite end of the long oval, Gowen spied three men. On a throne-like seat in the middle, a large, red-haired man with flashing blue eyes, teeth that gleamed white when he laughed and what seemed to be a cloak in a colour of blue Gowen had never seen before. The king he had heard his captors speak of — Conchobar. On the king's left stood a tall, strongly built warrior of middle years, reddish hair shaded with grey, green-grey eyes, and a stance which spoke of authority. On his right stood a stern, grey-bearded, black-eyed druid who stared unblinking at Gowen from the moment he entered the hall.

Conchobar glanced smilingly at Roigh's left leg. "Did you cut yourself on a hoe, friend Roigh, or did a Cymry dog bite you?"

As Gowen glared at the king, Roigh's laugh boomed out, but his next words were quiet and earnest. "It is, the one who swung the sword was holding it as high as he could," and he looked down at the boy. "If he did not cut the legs from under me, I would not have fallen on him, and me as big as a tree." He laughed again. "And he would have chopped down a few more of our men."

Now the king and the other man also looked intently at Gowen.

"And so," said the king, "you thought, 'Who has more need of a true hero than Conchobar and the men of Emain Macha, who are always having to fight one or more of their neighbours.' And right you are!" He paused thoughtfully. "But he must be fostered, and learn the ways of Uledh." Another pause and a glance aside at one of the men in the background. "Sualtim, you and your wife are childless no longer. This child will be your fosterling."

The druid spoke. "It is clear to me, Conchobar, that this child with the hair that seems to shift colour in the firelight and eyes that seem to hold every human colour will have no ordinary fate. He is destined to be here, and his education must be one that binds him to us through knowledge and love."

"Then who better to be his mentor than I, the model of all Uledh?" said Conchobar, with no false modesty.

"Unless it is the former king and one of the three greatest warriors of all Uledh!" spoke the warrior to Conchobar's left.

Conchobar glared and the tall warrior glared back. The druid spoke again, mildly but firmly.

"It is for this child to be reared by Sualtim and his wife, to be instructed in statecraft and strategy by the king himself, Conchobar, to be tutored — when he is ready — in the mysteries he will have need of by me, Cathbad the Druid, and in the ways of the warrior and the bard, by Fergus, the former king and great warrior."

Yes. You are asking with your eyes and I answer you: Yes, it was I who had been the true king of Uledh, who had been deprived of my birthright by a clever trick played by Conchobar's mother. At that time, I no longer bore ill will, but was content to be among the best of warriors in my land. It was only later, at Conchobar's low betrayal of friends and allies whose safety I had personally guaranteed, that I left Uledh forever. And ages after that, I was raised once before this from my grave by an ambitious minstrel apprentice who wished to know the whole story of the Tain, and I sang it to him, seven days long, wrapped in a druid mist, and he with his teeth chattering in terror even while he strained to remember everything I sang. But that is all for another time and another place.

It was agreed, and Gowen was sent with Sualtim and his wife, who lived in their own small house some miles away.

Gowen was wise enough to see that his foster parents were good people, and clever enough to understand that what the druid had said about him was a part of his life. They were good people — they just weren't his people. He tried hard to adapt, but it was difficult, and at night he sometimes thought of home and his mother and father and his friends, and a great lump rose up from his chest and lodged in his throat and his eyes hurt as if they were being squeezed like grapes to pop them out of the skin. But he would not cry. When the pain came over him, he hardened his spirit and thought of Cei, who felt he was a child of destiny, and of Cathbad, who had said the great thing about him. And he decided that if he could not have home and comfort, he would have glory and fame.

When he came to Fergus, he learned the use of weapons and the use of every part of his body in combat. For all that he was small, he mastered the throwing spear and longsword of a warrior, after a short while in training, and learned the use of the shield not only as a defensive but also as an offensive implement. Hands, feet, elbows, knees, hips and even head became weapons of attack, and his ability to leap straight up or sideways with amazing speed gave his mentor some hard moments, before he came to expect the unexpected and defend against it. Alone and unseen, they engaged in combat, one against the other, which might have killed a lesser man, even though I say it myself. They grew to know each other's strengths and weaknesses so well, that they came to an unspoken agreement not to exploit them, rather to hone their skills with mutual help. Perhaps because of this early time together, Fergus became the only warrior in Uledh, and only one of three in all of Eire, who could stand against the boy after he became fully a warrior. Of both of those, you will hear later.

The long hours they spent together also taught Gowen another aspect of war — the comradeship among warriors. A bond grew between the veteran warrior and his protégé that would, in later times, affect the course of a great war in which they faced each other as mortal foes.

The times Gowen spent with Conchobar were a joy to both of them. Sometimes the boy sat on the floor to one side of the king's chair and listened as he judged civil cases or conducted negotiations with chieftains from Uledh or elsewhere. Now and then, he would beg the king's pardon, approach diffidently and whisper in his ear. Always on such occasions, Conchobar would smile a slow smile, and return to the judgment or negotiation with a new perspective or proposal. Sometimes they would ride out together in Conchobar's great war chariot to this plain or that hill, and the king would describe to the boy the exact progress of a battle that had gone on there — who fought well, who fell and where, who won and why.

Conchobar also thought to entice the boy's military sense by teaching him his own favourite pastime, the game of fidchell. After only a few days of tutelage, the boy grasped the principles of it and began to overtake his teacher, so that the king soon ended his games by overturning a losing board and roaring with laughter at how easily he had been bested. No one before or since then was ever allowed to win from the king with such good grace — those few who were able and incautious enough to win easily often ended by holding their heads in their laps with the mouth still open to ask what they had done wrong.

Gowen's time with Cathbad was a time of legends and tales that held within them many secrets of the Celts. Never was a secret worth telling that did not also have an interesting tale wrapped around it. It was during his time alone with the druid that Gowen first heard the legends of Scáthach, who lived far away in Alba and of Lugh Lamfhada of the Tuatha de Danann and of Cúroi mac Dáiri, the wizard-warrior of Munster. Cathbad took special care to explain the origin of the sickness of the men of Uledh.

"In the dawn of our time in Uledh, a man lived alone, and did not feel the lack of a life companion," Cathbad said. "One day, in at his door stepped the most beautiful woman he had ever seen. She walked to the centre of the living space and knelt by the firestead, where he had laid out the makings of a simple meal. She gathered them together and mixed and cut and placed them in a small cauldron on the fire, and when she was done, she served him up a meal that was too good for the simple ingredients she had put into it. Then she whisked the dirt floor clean and inspected the herbs and meats hanging in baskets from the roof. And when she was done, she turned to the man, who was still dumbstruck, and said, 'I am for you, oh man, if you wish.'

"He did wish — how could he not? But then she said, 'I will be your life mate, and you will have cause to be glad of it, for I have come to you from a place you call the Sidhe only for that purpose. But I put a *geis* on you, that you will not speak of me to anyone, and if you do, then I must leave.'

"And the man promised, of course he did. And he lived in happiness with this faultless woman, who could do everything any woman could do and, if that was not enough, everything a man could do and more. Until one day, when she was great with child for the first time. He went to the king's horse races, where all the best and fastest were gathered to try their speed against one another.

"He was a simple man and a good man, but not a foolish man. This once was the only time he ever did anything mortally foolish, and it changed his life and the history of Uledh and maybe even the history of all of Eire.

"As he stood and watched the races, the thought of his wonderful wife — her beauty, her talents — rose up in him, and he could not keep her from the front of his mind. He ached with a need to tell someone at long last about his marvelous luck and happiness. He fought it until he could bear it no longer, and then he broke his vow to her and the *geis* that was upon him, and he did it in the way that there were most terrible consequences. As he watched the races, the man next to him exclaimed on the swiftness of the king's horse. The man laughed abruptly and said, 'My wife is so swift that she could outrun even the king's horse.'

"The king — a strong but brutal king — overheard the remark and called the man to come to him.

"We will see this woman of yours,' he said, 'and see whether can she really outrun my best horse. You will be bound and wait here while my men go to fetch her. If she does not come and race, your head will leave your body.'

"So the messengers went out to the man's house and found the woman and told her what the king had said.

"But I am close to delivering a child,' she said. 'If I must race, it will kill me.'

"The messengers were sorry, but the king had said what the king had said. It had to be.

"So they went with her back to the king, and she said to him what she had said to them. And he answered: 'Your man has made a boast, and you will contend to prove it true or false, or his head will bounce along the ground before your feet.'

"So she took her place with the best of the king's horses and raced with them the length of the course. Beat them she did, but when she came to the end of the course, her pangs overtook her and she fell down with a loud cry and gave birth right there to twins. The exertion of the race and strain of the birth were too much even for this unusual young woman. She died on the spot, but not before repaying the king's brutality.

"She placed a curse on him and his land with her dying breath: 'It will be with Uledh now and for all time as it was with me when you made me race, and the pangs that I have suffered here are no worse than those that will strike you at any time you have need of your manly powers. And this is my *geis* upon you: Whenever need is upon you, every Uledhman of warrior age will lie in his pangs thirteen days.' That was the curse, said in one breath and unbreakable."

Cathbad ended this tale by saying: "There are some who say that, at one time, each man took to his bed when his wife was in her delivery pangs, and suffered sympathetic pains with her. I cannot tell you if this is true, but I know, and every man in Uledh knows, that the pangs will come at any time when we are under attack, and an enemy will have free run of our land until we rise from our pain."

He looked searchingly at Gowen. The boy looked back steadily and said, "I see that you are telling me more than the origin of the pangs, for I am not of Uledh, and you and Conchobar and Fergus hope that I will one day fight for Uledh. And so it may happen that I alone will have to face some danger in the future, when all the rest of Uledh but for old men and boys lies in its pangs."

Cathbad smiled a slow, sad smile and inclined his head to indicate that Gowen had perceived the lesson in the tale. For his part, Gowen first felt a chill darkness rising in his gut — a foretaste of a time to come when he and only he would stand against a great force until the men of Uledh could rise from their beds of pain to join him. Hard upon the sensation of cold and dark, his insides were suffused by a glow which dissipated the sense of foreboding and replaced it with a fierce joy at the thought of himself facing a whole host of enemies and holding them off until the men of this land could defend themselves. Unbidden, the thought of Cei and of Cathbad's great word flashed across his mind. The sad smile of the druid was answered by a glow of joy on Gowen's face.

"I will do my part," he said, invoking an old Celtic oath, "unless the sky should fall."

Chapter Six
WHAT'S IN A NAME

It had been agreed that Gowen would not have to do with the Boy Troop until he was older. The Boy Troop were fifty of the boys of the best warrior families, just old enough to be in training with Fergus and with Cathbad to learn the ways of the warrior nation of Uledh. In their leisure time, they liked to split evenly into two groups and play the game of hurley. The game is not for the faint of heart. The hard, little ball is meant to be contested and the short, broad-bladed, hard sticks are to carry it balanced or to drive it along the grass or to scoop it into the air and send it with a mighty whack into the goal. But it is not unlikely that the ball or the sticks will on their way raise lumps and cuts on arms, legs, chests and heads — it is a rare game when someone is not carried from the field.

In hopes long since disappointed, Sualtim had once made a child's hurley ball and stick. One day not long after his arrival, Gowen told his new mother that he was going out to practise with them. With his ball and stick, he set out on the road to Emain Macha, hitting the ball high into the air, running to catch it as it came down, and sending it again into the air. When he arrived at the playing field, he stood aside and watched the game, which washed back and forth like a battle, each change in direction led by a single player's efforts, until he was checked — or levelled — by another.

Gowen wanted to join, but not one of the players bothered to look at the small fellow off to the side. So he began to amuse himself, hitting his ball straight up and catching it on his stick, first in front, then on the side, then behind his back. Then he began to hit the ball sideways, run after it and catch it on his stick before it hit the ground. Though none has told it before, this was the first sign of the many amazing feats that he was later to perform for his own and others' amusement. Still, though they could not but notice, the boys pretended to see nothing.

When the game ball rolled in his direction, followed by a thundering herd of boys, he dropped all pretence and took the ball on his own toy stick, driving through and around the boys and slanting it through the goal. A roar of fury rose from the Boy Troop, and they advanced on him as one, with their sticks raised. Gowen had not yet tested his young strength, except against Llan ap Lot and, humiliatingly, Roigh. He was also clever enough to realize that he had overstepped some boundary of proper behaviour, though he did not know what. Staying to fight might be unacceptable, as well as suicidal. So he took to his heels, heading in the direction of Conchobar's compound.

The king was outside the compound, in the shade of a rowan tree, playing at fidchell with Loeghaire mac Roigh — a young man, but already one of the three greatest heroes of Uledh, and the son of whom Roigh had spoken to Gowen in the curragh after his capture.

I will tell you another time of fidchell. Some now name it chess, but that is not so. It was a game of strategy that substituted for war, when no war was available.

Conchobar looked up from his game to see Gowen running ahead of the Boy Troop, straight to the king's game board.

"What is it you have done, boy?" asked Conchobar.

"I do not know, king. Tell me my fault."

"What have you tried to do, then?"

"To join the hurley game."

"Meagre as you are, that is a great undertaking. And did you ask permission?"

"No, king."

"Then that you must do."

Gowen faced the panting boys and humbly asked permission to join the game. Although he was smaller by half than most of them, and had just humiliated them by running through them to the goal, they felt the king's glare and granted permission. Off they shambled and Conchobar smiled at his own judiciousness.

Loeghaire, called the Triumphant because of his many victories in battle, said: "That youngster will either be a boil on the backside of Uledh, or a shield before its face."

They returned to the game and had been engrossed in it for a long time, when some few of the Boy Troop came racing by again, each one with a bruise, a bump or a bloody mark somewhere on him. They passed in a moment, and right behind them ran Gowen, red-faced and glowing with a battle fury. When the king held up his hand, Gowen skidded to a stop and stood politely waiting.

"Now then, I thought that you had nicely asked permission."

"That I did, king."

"Well then, what is all this?"

"Now it's for them to ask my permission," said Gowen and ran off, holding his stick high. Behind him, Conchobar laughed so hard and long that he scattered the game and pieces, even though he had been winning at the time.

From this time out, it was with the Boy Troop of Emain Macha as it had been with the boys of his village at home. There was not a one of them could play hurly, or run, or throw a spear, or follow the track of an animal, or speed a stone from a sling as Gowen could. And so, without ever a word being said, he became their natural leader. If Gowen said "Run," they would run. If he said, "Rest," they would rest. For all that they looked to him for leadership, he thought of himself as a comrade among comrades. It was only that he could not let a challenge pass or an opponent win. And for them it was an entertainment to think of new contests and challenges to test him and, when he prevailed, to congratulate themselves silently for having him in their midst.

One day, when Conchobar was going to a feast in his own honour given by a grateful subject — Chulainn the Smith — he stopped his chariot at the playing field, and called to Gowen to join him and his company at the feast. As Conchobar told it later, the boys were divided very unevenly in a game of hurly, with the smaller number on Gowen's side looking remarkably cleaner and less bruised than the great number on the other. And Gowen said that the boys had not yet had enough play of him and that he would come along later.

With that, Conchobar rode off. Now, Conchobar was a mighty warrior — even if not as mighty as I — and for all that he took my own throne from me, he was a better king than I would have been; for some are destined for fame and war, and some for kingship and war. His one greatest fault was pride of such magnitude that it exceeded his virtues, and caused him to think always of himself and the pleasure the moment gave him before all other things... except perhaps the needs of his kingdom. Indeed, it was this pride that doomed him, when his appointed time had come, and he was persuaded to turn aside from a journey by the women of Connaught, who claimed a great admiration for his manly figure. And so, when he arrived at Chulainn's stronghold, he was already anticipating the tasty boar and the great quantities of drink inside. When Chulainn asked if there were any more to his party, he answered "No" and did not think for one instant of Gowen. Hearing that, the smith turned out his great hound to guard the outside. He had raised the beast from a pup, and it was worth a small army as a sentinel, for it would tolerate no one but Chulainn himself or those who were with him.

Now as to Gowen, when the Boy Troop had had their fill of the game, he set off with his hurly stick and ball, hitting the ball into the air and running under it to hit it again. Passing the time this way, and thinking of nothing but the bounty of food and drink he would soon see, he arrived at the stronghold and glanced away from his ball and stick just in time to see the dog. It was huge. Its maw was wide open in a slavering roar and it seemed to Gowen that it stretched from the earth to the sky. His body turned cold with fear and then, almost as in reaction, hot with rage at the thought of dying before he had made a name for himself. Almost without thought, he tossed his wooden hurley ball a bit into the air and, with his stick, made a two-handed, full-shouldered swing, so hard that the follow-through twisted his upper body completely away from the hound. The ball flew straight into the mouth of the great beast, tearing out the roof of its mouth and a great part of its skull as it sped out the other side almost as fast as it had entered. The monstrous hound fell, silent and already dead, at Gowen's feet. As relief washed over him, his knees threatened to buckle, but he gritted his teeth and willed them steady.

Alarmed by the roar of the hound, the festive company burst out of the house, carrying their weapons and ready to repel any hostile party. Instead of a raiding enemy harried by the great hound, they found a small, sad-faced boy and a huge, dead guard dog.

"What then?" cried Chulainn. "What has happened here? How has my faithful guard come to his end? Tell us, boy, and we'll hunt the spalpeens down and bring their heads back on our belts!"

"It is I killed your dog, Master Smith," said Gowen, forcing his voice to remain steady, "and sorry I am for it. But he left me the choice of his life or mine."

Chulainn stared at the small figure stupefied. Conchobar's embarrassment at forgetting to mention Gowen was beginning already to fade before a mixture of feelings: awe at the boy's deed; fear of what he could do against him, the king; gloating triumph that such a young warrior should live in Uledh and not Connaught or Munster or Leinster. Cathbad regarded the scene with the air of one whose predictions have been ratified.

"Self-defence is something everyone understands," said Chulainn, "but it does not lessen my plight. For now I shall have to train one of the sons I bred to him, and until then, I will have many a sleepless night."

"I killed the guard and I will take his place while I train one to replace it," Gowen blurted, and then wondered at himself for pledging months of his life to mean and unwarrior-like duties.

"Bravely said, boy," replied Chulainn, "but it takes a knowledge of the craft to train a dog properly."

"I know dogs," Gowen said firmly.

"Have you had dogs of your own then, boy?" Conchobar inquired paternally.

"I know dogs!" Gowen repeated with a trace of anger in his youthful voice. He could not understand the problem. He had said that he knew dogs, hadn't he? What else did they wish to hear? He never said that he knew something unless he knew it.

Cathbad's resonant voice broke the apparent deadlock: "Chulainn, it will benefit you to accept the boy's offer. He will train the new dog like no one else can, yourself included. And you will have a better guard than any dog while you wait. Just give him a place by your fire and food from what you eat and he will fulfil his bargain."

"Well, then, boy," said Chulainn with some reluctance, "if Cathbad says you can do it, I will believe him. I will give you weapons of my own making and the wage of a warrior while you are here."

"Thank you, Master Smith. I am not ready to take up my weapons, but I will protect your belongings with my sling and the stones on the ground." Again an unsuspected impetus from beyond his own thoughts put words in his mouth: "And I will require no wage other than a training in your craft."

Chulainn did not let his surprise show on his face. Long since, the warriors and priests and others had forgotten that smithing was not merely a skilled labour, but a craft which required knowledge of mystic rituals to identify the best ore, determine the best day and time for heating and shaping and to recall the secret formulas for mixing metals.

Cathbad was too absorbed in the significance of what had happened to think of what Gowen had said. His gaze swept over Conchobar and the rest of the company, letting them know that he had something significant to say. He looked directly at the boy.

"You have killed Chulainn's dog, that was known by all to be the fiercest and best of guard dogs, and you will take its place while you train another. By this act, you will be known as Chulainn's Hound — CúChulainn."

This was simply too much! Now they wanted to take his name away from him! "My name is Gowen," he growled.

Cathbad stared intently into the boy's eyes: "The name you came to us with is a name of meaning where you were. The name I offer you now is created by an act of your own, and will be a name of meaning here."

The boy stared stubbornly back at the druid, but for the first time in his life could not hold a gaze. The priest seemed to peer through his eyes into the depths of his being, seeing things there that the boy himself could not see.

"CúChulainn," he said grudgingly, and Cathbad nodded with austere approval. Chulainn, Conchobar and the company were silent, sensing that something of major importance had occurred, but unable to comprehend its meaning.

"Your destiny is to be a great warrior and the shield of your people against those forces which will wish to drive them into the sea. Your first *geis* is that you must not refuse a proper offer of hospitality or sustenance made to you. Your second *geis* is that you must not taste the flesh of your namesake, the dog. Until you have fulfilled these geasa , you will not be killed."

The feast that night proceeded as planned. After that, Gowen remained with the smith and learned the secret rituals of his craft and trained the new dog by day, while he also guarded the property by night. He was strangely content during this time, feeling that, in a way, he was preparing for another stage in his life. He surprised himself by becoming fond of his routine. Training the young dog was no effort. He simply did what he wanted the dog to do, and the dog imitated him. It was as if it could read his thoughts through his actions, as if they communicated in some way beyond his own understanding. And from time to time, when he grew tired or faint from lack of sleep, a fiery eagle, or an iridescent figure with hair that seemed like flame burning up out of the top of his head, would appear and sit by him and wake him if anyone or anything approached. The few folk that witnessed one of these visitations knew that young CúChulainn's visitor was of the Sidhe, and that the fabulous people of the Fairy Mound — the Tuatha de Danaan — had taken him as a protectling. They appeared to share Cathbad's view of the youngster's significance.

Eventually, the time of his service as a guard for Chulainn passed, because he could leave behind him a dog as faithful and fierce as the one he had killed. And he never again questioned the giving of his name.

Chapter Seven
THE CHOSEN WEAPONS

He was still a boy, but he had already two names and two homelands.

And the second name was as true for him in the second land as the first had been in the first land. His life went on for a while as it had before the encounter with the dog. He spent much of it with the Boy Troop, but there were times when he could not be with them. They were older, and had to spend time with Cathbad, learning those things it was necessary to learn before taking up arms as men. At such times, Gowen amused himself by perfecting various feats of daring and skill with which he would then amaze his friends when they returned from their lessons.

It was not that he became bored with his own company, but his pride began to prick him; he began to ask himself what could possibly be revealed in these sessions that he was forbidden to hear simply by virtue of being too young. Pride and curiosity led him to find out one day. After his friends had been out of sight for some time, he used his tracking skills to follow their spoor, which, after a short distance, was joined by that of an adult whose stride he recognized as Cathbad's. Moving noiselessly, he crept up on a copse of ancient trees and there, in a man-created clearing of great age, sat his friends on a semi-circular, raised earthen bench. Low-growing foliage covered its sloping front and its extensive flattened surface, except where the feet or the buttocks of generations of boys had pressed, just as the feet and buttocks of these boys did now. Before them, in a spot worn similarly bare by himself and his predecessors, stood Cathbad and spoke softly in his resonant tones.

Gowen strained to hear, but even his unusually acute ears could not distinguish what the druid was saying. The boys sat absolutely still, listening with a mixture of respect, boredom and fear of failing to learn something crucial to their passage into manhood as warriors. Moving so slowly that an observer would have said he was immobile, Gowen crept closer and closer, stopping behind the huge trunk of an ancient oak tree, just in time to hear one of his friends say:

"What is the meaning of the day?"

"Yes," Cathbad smiled slightly, "I always tell you the special meaning of the day when we meet. Today..," he paused meaningfully. "Today is a special day for that young man who feels he is ready to take up arms."

Several of the boys' faces lighted from within at the thought.

"That special man will have unimaginable glory and undying fame..."

A few of the more self-confident boys leaned forward and tensed their leg muscles, as if they wished to stand up and offer themselves for this challenge.

"... he will have to face and overcome great dangers..."

All but two of the boys leaned back and relaxed.

"... and he will depart this life at an early age, leaving behind him grief and a name that will live forever."

The last two boys eased their tensed muscles as unobtrusively as possible, all the while — like the others — maintaining a facial expression which betrayed respectful attention, but no special interest.

As the light died from his friends' faces, Gowen crept away again, until he was safely distant from the clearing, then ran with the greatest speed he could muster, straight to Conchobar's house.

He burst through the door as the king was engaged in one of the tedious, but often rewarding, obligations of his office — adjudicating disputes and complaints between his subjects: who had taken whose cattle, whose were the rights to a particular pasturage or watering place, which man had alienated the affections of which other man's wife. A greybeard was just taking his grateful leave of the king, as was his disputant, a younger and much angrier warrior, whose case had obviously carried less weight with the king.

Conchobar smiled at the sight of the excited youngster, and beckoned him forward, past the row of waiting petitioners.

"Well then, my hot-headed little Cú, what is it that you are chasing into my house? You see," he smiled widely, and his teeth flashed white and strong, "of anyone else, I would ask, 'What is pursuing you?' But I am beginning to learn that our Cú is always the pursuer and never the pursued. What are you seeking that I may give you?"

"King, I am destined this day to take up arms and become a warrior of this land."

Shock silenced everyone, including Conchobar. This child, this mite, no matter how strong, wanted to take up arms before boys twice his size!

Conchobar, though accustomed to dealing with the outrageous as well as the ordinary, took a moment to recover his wits and even then spoke with unaccustomed clumsiness: "How can you know this, boy? How can it be that your time has come, all unexpected, before even your training? From where does this idea come? Who has said it?"

"Cathbad has said it," Gowen answered gravely, "and it is to you as king to help me carry it out."

"How has he said it? When?"

"The moment before I came here. It is the meaning of this day."

"I know Cathbad and his reading of days. He is rarely wrong. And yet... Let us put it to the test. I shall give you sword, shield and spear, and if you can handle them, you shall have a chariot, two horses and a gillie." He turned to Fergus and said: "Friend Fergus, bring the boy his arms." And he winked, so that Fergus knew he should bring the oldest, toughest and heaviest sword, shield and spear he could find in the armoury.

Which he did. The boy did not speak, only took hold of the sword and, walking outside followed by the king and everyone present, swung it over his head and brought it down with immense force on a rock that protruded from the earth. The sword shattered, and Gowen looked wordlessly at Conchobar.

"Who will bring this young man a better sword?" the king cried.

Several warriors stepped forward, proud to be part of a memorable event, and offered their own, favourite swords. Gowen thanked each one with grave courtesy, accepted each sword, and shattered it.

Conchobar laughed uproariously. "How can we furnish you a sword, if you break every one, boy?"

"There is one sword that will not break," said Fergus, not without some enjoyment. "The sword of the king of Uledh, which is called 'the Defender'."

Conchobar bit his lip so that his blood ran down through the red hairs of his beard. Under the boy's unwavering gaze, he slowly drew the ancient sword, which, it was said, could only be lifted by a king or by a warrior destined to be the shield of Uledh against a great peril. Of those alive in

Uledh, only Conchobar and Fergus had ever succeeded in lifting it. Gowen stepped forward slowly, grasped the hilt lying across the king's limp fingers, lifted it with both hands — slowly, not as he had lifted the others, but showing by the very slowness of the act that he had complete control of the great weapon. He raised it, still slowly, over his head, and brought it down in a smooth, fluid motion, cleaving the rock even below the level of the ground. The perfectly severed halves gave off wisps of smoke from the black scorch marks that traced the sword's passage.

Silence. Uneasiness. What does this mean? Then a loud cheer broke forth from the throat of Roigh, who had been standing in the crowd, watching the boy he had brought as a prize of war to his own land. Suddenly, Roigh knew that the mysterious prediction made by the druid was going to be fulfilled. And those around him understood why he cheered, and they cheered with him. A great roar rose from the crowd gathered there. A shout of wonder, jubilation and awe.

The king understood, but he asked Fergus with his eyes to hand Gowen the ancient, ponderous shield from the armoury. The boy slipped his arm through the leather grips, grasping the second and smaller one with his hand. He held the shield before him and, giving a wild battle cry, shook it as if in defiance of an a enemy. He shook it to pieces, to splinters, to particles. Nothing remained but the second leather grip, still in his hand. Pieces of the metal rim, hide covering and wooden core lay scattered on the ground.

Again, the king called for volunteers. And again, their shields met the fate of the first shield. Fergus did not need to speak. Conchobar silently offered the boy his own shield, and it alone withstood the boy's strength.

Conchobar laughed again, but with less heart than before. "Bring our young warrior a chariot and pair of horses."

Fergus raised his hand and a gillie guided a chariot drawn by two horses from across the compound to the front of Conchobar's house. Before the dust-swirl of its arrival had settled, Gowen jumped up into the chariot, pushed the gillie aside, seized the reins, gave a great shout and drove the chariot swiftly around and around and around the compound, throwing up clouds of dust, digging up great ruts and gasping in delight at the sensation of speed and danger. Finally, with a rending groan, the chariot fell apart, scattering wood splinters, leather scraps and wheel rims across the great yard. Suddenly relieved of their burden, the horses staggered a few steps and stood, foam-flecked and blowing heavily. Gowen himself let go of the reins and came to a skidding stop in the midst of the debris. As he walked back toward Conchobar, the king rolled his eyes upward, threw his hands widely into the air and laughed as long and as loud as he had laughed on the day when the young stranger chased the Boy Troop past his fidchell board.

"Bring my chariot!" he cried, and in a change as quick as the weather on an early spring day, his full good humour returned. His eyes twinkling, he handed Gowen his own spear, saying, "I will not let you disarm all of Uledh before you come to this spear, boy. Take it and use it against our enemies!"

Gowen sprang into the chariot beside the gillie, who set the horses in motion, and they trotted sedately out of the compound, down the long, winding entry road and into the open country. As Conchobar and the others watched, Gowen gave a sudden shout and the horses leapt forward. In a few moments, the chariot was obscured by its own dust cloud, and in a few more, it had disappeared over a hill.

After they had gone, the day seemed somehow tedious and long. Ordinary entertainments seemed to lack vitality. Even blood-challenges by one man to another over some real or imagined insult at the meal in Conchobar's great house were half-hearted. Scarcely any blood was drawn and no one was killed at all. It was as if the whole company realized that they were waiting for something, although none was sure what it was.

Then Conall, called Cernach, the Hundred-Fighter, came limping home with his dusty, disheartened gillie behind, leading a team of horses without a chariot. A shock ran through everyone when the lookout identified him, for Conall — Uledh's premier warrior — was supposed to be guarding the border at one of the most travelled fords.

"What enemy has brought you to this, oh, Conall?" cried one man, as Conall walked wearily across the compound toward Conchobar, who now stood frowning in front of his great house.

"Tell us where we must go to avenge this deed!" cried another.

Conall waved a weary hand and gave a dusty smile. "You shall hear it all when my gillie and I have soothed our parched throats. Lead the horses to drink, man, and then come back here as my witness."

By the time his gillie had returned, Conall was already draining his second horn of beer. The dust on his face was less and the smile was broader, but rueful.

"Resting beside my chariot I was, looking now and then in hopes of a stranger who would give me a good fight at the ford, but I saw none but friends pass by. It's a sad day when there is nothing for a warrior to do." He paused and shook his head.

"All of a sudden, from nowhere, like a spirit come up out of the Sidhe, a chariot flies into my sight, and it's not long before I see that it is the king's own chariot and matched team, and even his gillie. But beside the gillie is this little, sad-looking fellow whose head seems just to peep up over the front of the chariot. And it's our Little Hound, CúChulainn. And he calls out to me: 'What is it that you are doing here, friend Conall?'

"And I answer: 'It's guarding our ford I am doing, and you may be doing it someday too. And what is it you are doing in the king's own chariot?'

"And the gillie answers for him and says that he has taken arms that day, and that no sword or shield or chariot could bear the strength of him but only those of the king. And I am after thinking that the gillie is bragging for him and it's not to me to believe all of that. So then I ask: 'Where is it that you are going then, Cú?'

"And he answers me: 'I am going to seek some test of arms where I can redden my spear or sword with the blood of an enemy of Uledh.'

"And I see that he means what he says, and I say to him: 'If you are, then I am coming too, to see that you come back alive.' And I climb up into my chariot, and my gillie climbs up with me and gives rein to the horses, and we set out after the king's chariot, that has moved off again that fast that we had to race to catch it.

"And the boy turns back and says that it is to him to go alone, and I say that it is to me to make sure he returns, and he says 'Don't do it!' and I say right back 'I will.'

"And I never said another word. For into his sling he puts a small stone, swings it wide once and hurls it right at one of my wheels. The band of the wheel bursts and the spokes fly out and away, and I and the gillie with them. And the boy calls back that he's sorry, that he has to go alone, and away he rides. And that is how I come to be here without my chariot."

He looked at his gillie, who just nodded in agreement and buried his nose again in his drinking horn. And it was from this time out that Conall took a special interest in Gowen, and they became fast friends and companions in battle and drinking and all kinds of sport. And Conall vowed that the one who killed Gowen, he himself would revenge Gowen upon him in a way that no one would forget the event.

It was a good many drinking horns later when the lookout shouted out again that the king's chariot was approaching at great speed, and its occupants were a gillie and an odd-looking fellow who seemed to be aglow all over. And tied to the chariot and running and flying behind were several deer and a flock of swans.

Cathbad spoke quietly, but with intensity: "It is CúChulainn. He is in his heroic rage and we cannot let him enter the compound in that state, or he will kill us all and regret it later. His internal heat must be lowered or we are all doomed. Bring three great cauldrons of cold water to the top of the entry-way. We must put him into them one after another to cool him down."

"And how," spoke Roigh, who well remembered the young fellow of a few years before in the Isle of the Giants, "will we persuade him into those cauldrons if he does not care for a cold bath? I would not like to be the one to try to manhandle him into the first one."

Conchobar, who had listened carefully, knew of one weakness they could exploit — Gowen's modesty and sense of shame — which might override even his battle fury. "Naked women to him!" he cried, and every man and woman understood at once. Several men left to prepare the cauldrons. The women of the company rose as one and walked straight to the entry road and down a little way, so that they would stand directly in the chariot's path. With their backs to the compound, and thus still preserving their modesty before the world, they bared their breasts and stood, waiting. The men above stood at the ready to run down the path after Gowen had encountered the women.

In the time it took to wonder if this plan would work, the dust cloud of the chariot appeared at the bottom of the entry road and approached at breakneck speed. The women stood composedly in its path. The gillie tore back savagely on the reins when he saw them, and the horses stood almost perpendicular to stop their headlong rush. Through the dense cloud of dust, the men above could see Gowen turn his face away in embarrassment, while the gillie continued to stare in joyful stupefaction, until the nearest woman plucked the reins from his nerveless hands and delivered him such a blow to the face with them, that he made a backward somersault out of the chariot and lay stunned on the ground.

As the women covered themselves, the men sprang forward, seized the red-faced Gowen and threw him head foremost into the first of the three cauldrons. The water boiled and hissed and steamed away into the air, so they seized him again and lowered him, more gently this time, into the cold water of the second cauldron, which seethed and boiled, but did not evaporate. Finally, they dunked him in the last cauldron, where the water just reached lukewarm, and an abashed Gowen peered out over the top at them.

After he had clambered out with the help of some friendly hands, Gowen accepted a horn of beer, drained it at one swallow, apologized for any trouble he may have caused, said his goodnights to all and walked soddenly away, leaving a trail of drips and footprints behind.

"It will not do!" shouted Conchobar. "I mean to know of this adventure, and I mean to know now!" And he glared at the terrified gillie, whose face had the red stripe of the reins and eyes that were not yet able to focus properly.

Both men and women took up the shout that the gillie should tell all, and a few of the men carried him by the arms inside the king's house, where they set him down in the centre and supplied him with all that he could wish to eat or drink. After a few voracious bites and some chewing and swallowing, accompanied by a good deal of guzzling, his eyes seemed to focus again, and he began to tell his tale, looking around the circle of avid faces with the gratification of one unaccustomed to such attention. As he recounted his tale, he was careful not to look any one of the women directly in the eye.

An extraordinary tale it was.

They had ridden out to the ford at the border, he said, after leaving Conall behind, and over the ford and upstream until they encountered a marker stone. It was long and phallic, rounded at the top and with a spancel of challenge resting near the top. Gowen looked at the iron hoop with eager curiosity and asked who had placed the challenge, and against whom.

"And I told him, I did, that it was put there by three brothers who have been the bane and terror of the men of Uledh ever since their father was killed by an Uledhman and they had grown to warrior's age and stature. And that they boasted that a day that went by without the killing of some man of Uledh was a day wasted in their lives.

"And he smiled, he did, in that funny way of his and lifted the spancel off the stone and turned sideways to their dun that we could see above on the hill, and threw backwards-like, I mean with his right hand but from left to right across the front of his body, so the thing sailed like a swallow through the air and landed inside the walls. I've never seen the like..." And the gillie seemed lost in contemplation of this peculiar feat until the impatient shouts of the crowd and the outraged growl of Conchobar brought him back to the present time. He took a long, deep breath and continued.

"And I said to him that everyone in the world is allowed to be a fool a few times, but he had just made a mortal foolish mistake. And he to me, that the difference between a mortal fool and a hero is that a mortal fool doesn't know when he is going to die.

"As we spoke, out from the *dún* came the youngest brother in his chariot and armed to the teeth and I said that here was a man that could not be killed by the metal of any spear or sword. And Cú smiles as if he knew that already, and when the fellow is within spear-throw and ready to send his first throwing spear at us, he — Cú, I mean — lets his sling fall out to a ready position and fits a small stone in it and gives a throw like the one he threw at Conall's chariot, and the stone goes in at the eye and out at the back of the head, and the fellow drops off the back of his chariot and lies there, dead.

"And I hear a fearful shout that is half a cry of grief and half a cry of rage, and out comes the second brother, and I said to Cú that this was a man who always fought in water, because he always won in water and so stay out of the water, I said. And he smiles that smile and jumps right over the side of the chariot into the middle of the stream and waits.

"It was a man joyful with the killing rage that jumped from his chariot and ran down the slope of the bank and into the water to destroy the little fellow that stood there. And he rushes at Cú with his bare, empty hands, to seize him and drown him, and Cú seems to slide between his legs and ends up behind him. So he turns and makes another rush, but a little slower this time, so the little fellow shouldn't be able to slip by him, and Cú gives a jump, the like of which I've never seen, and sails heels-over-head above him and lands behind him again. Well you can see how it was going to come out. The big one is charging and grasping out in front of himself, and the little one is going over and under and around him, so that he finally stands still, right there in the middle of the water, and Cú leaps up in the air and one swipe of his sword and the big fellow's head sails all the way to the opposite bank.

"And I'm thinking to myself that we may live to see another day after all, when I look up and there he comes striding — the oldest brother. And I to Cú as loud as I can: 'This is the oldest brother, and the most dangerous altogether. They say he has a heart of ice, and if he gains a hold on you, he will grip you until you freeze in fear, and then he kills you.' And Cú laughs a happy laugh and up out of the water and straight at this big, dark, grim man, and I looking up over the side of the chariot and wondering if ever again I would see this hall or taste this good drink."

Whereupon he took a very long draught, closed his eyes and sighed contentedly. The momentary silence was broken by a guttural murmur from Conchobar, and the gillie took up the thread of his story.

"It's not long to tell now. The big man smiled a terrible smile as he stood waiting for the little fellow, who ran right up to him and leaped into his arms. The big man, he locked his arms behind Cú's back, as if to squeeze the life out of him, and Cú reaches out and rests his hands against the big man's chest, and there they stayed. It seemed forever. Cú's arms and legs, where they were bare, were all red, almost like they were hot, and his hair seemed to me to be three colours — brown at the bottom and red in the middle..."

"... and yellow at the top, like a flame rising upward," Cathbad said softly.

"That's it! That's it, indeed!" cried the gillie, and started to bury his nose in his drinking horn again, when he caught Conchobar's glowering gaze. "And so they stayed, until the big fellow's smile just started to fade away, and his eyes began to glaze over and his chest began to buck and heave and, all of a sudden, he fell down dead right there, and Cú on top of him. And so I said, 'Can we stop all this now and go home to our meal?'"

The laughter which greeted this last sentence was born of a knowledge of both Gowen and the gillie. Even Conchobar joined in with his booming laugh, and the gillie looked mightily relieved. Taking a quick swallow to fortify himself, he went on.

"So homeward we go, and as we're pelting along, I notice that Cú still seems to be hot all over, and I'm beginning to wonder, will he even know who I am, if he should take a disliking to something I say or do? So then we see a flock of swans, and he turns to me and says, 'How is it more heroic to take these birds, alive all at once or dead all at once?'

"And I say, 'Why alive would be much harder,' and I thinking all the while that he might spend a bit of that energy I'm in fear of in chasing after these birds until he is worn down.

"But out again comes his sling, and he fits in a small stone and lets it fly, and I cannot tell you how, even though I saw it, that one stone knocked the birds senseless, and over we drive and he picks them up one by one and ties them carefully to the back of the chariot and off we drive again, until he sees a small herd of deer and he turns to me again and says, 'What is the best way to take these deer?'

"And I am not a wise man, but no one has ever said that I fell on my head as a baby, so I know the right answer and say, 'Why alive, of course.'

"So it's out of the chariot he jumps and off on foot after those deer and runs them down one by one and brings each one back and ties it onto the back of the chariot. And that is how you saw us coming, a flock of geese and a herd of deer and a warrior still in his rage and a gillie who didn't know, should he be proud or scared out of his wits."

And this time the gillie's nose stayed a long time in the horn, while everyone laughed and shouted and exclaimed. And the telling of this story was in Uledh for a long time.

Like Lleu before him, Gowen had won the right to a name that was peculiarly his own and arms that would suit no one but him. Although only Cathbad knew why, Gowen carefully sought out and chose a gillie who had served Foragall and so was not of Uledh. As time passed, his abilities magnified his name in cattle raids into neighbouring Connaught and Leinster, and in repelling raids from the same. But he still did not have a wife, and that was a problem.

Was it his hair of the three colours, or his eyes of the shifting hues, or the sad-sweet look on his face, or the fantastic feats and tricks with which he entertained Conchobar's friends and subjects? I cannot tell you. I can only say that the men of Emain Macha became seriously perturbed because of his influence on their women. Mother, daughter or sister sat and watched Gowen performing the tricks he was challenged to do, and when they went home again, the wives were less admiring, the daughters were less obedient and the sisters were more contemptuous than ever. And these same husbands, fathers and brothers grew more and more discontent, until finally it came to speech among them and from a group of them to the king himself.

"What do you want of me then?" Conchobar asked in exasperation. "Shall I offend the premier warrior of the land because your women admire him? The man who has fought like a wolf in our battles... who has saved more than one of us from the spear or sword of an enemy? Shall I tell him that the skills we welcome in battle are not welcome when we are seated together at meat and drink?"

Roigh had the courage to speak for the rest: "It is not stifling we want for him. It's a wife."

"A wife?"

"If we find a woman worthy of him, he will marry, and the fantasies will fade from our women's minds. If we don't, there will be grief when some one of us has had too much of looking less beside him."

"So be it, then," Conchobar sighed. "Send the word out across the land. And only the fairest and wisest and most accomplished of young women should be suggested. If Cú is to marry, it must be a very special woman."

But it was with the search for a wife as it had been with the taking of weapons. Gowen watched patiently as the word went out and hopeful mothers, not only from Uledh, but Munster, Connaught and Leinster as well, herded their daughters before Conchobar, who introduced them with a great flourish. They were attractive, they were clever, they were charming, and Gowen said nothing, did nothing. They came, they waited, they left. Discouragement grew like a wave rising big, stark and blank out of the sea and towered over the spirits of everyone, even the admiring women. Was there nowhere a woman he would see fit to spend his life with?

Finally, one day, Roigh took matters into his own hands and approached Gowen himself: "Is it you are too good for any *caillin* in all of Eire and are you pining toward the girls of your old home, or did you have someone special in mind?"

Gowen smiled his sweet-sad smile and said: "Friend Roigh, ever since you had the good sense to fall on me, I could never deny you an answer. No, I don't think I am too good for anyone in all of Eire, but there is only one is right for me. And I see that all of you believe now is the time for me to marry, so I am going now to pay a visit on the woman of my choice, to see will she have me."

Stunned into silence, the company watched him walk to the door on the way to his chariot. As the heel of one foot — the last bit of him they could see — disappeared from the doorway, Roigh recovered enough to shout: "And who is it, then? Who?"

The answer came back faintly through the doorway: "Emher, daughter of Foragall.

And Roigh, who knew of both the young woman and her father, shook his head and could not decide, should he laugh or cry?

Chapter Eight
EMHER

If you rode out from Uledh, the land of warriors and cattle keepers, to the south and east, you crossed the border into Leinster, land of deer hunters and trackers, later land of the mighty Fionn and his *fianna*, the defenders of Eire against intruders from across the water in a future time. Across hills and streams and woods lay the rath of Foragall — warrior, sorcerer, implacable foe of Uledh. Some said that he was allied with the Fomhoire, that dark and frightening, monstrous and misshapen folk who had contested the arrival of every new people in Eire, indeed, annihilated some of them and exacted a crushing tribute from others. Until they had finally to give way before the high magic and battle prowess of the Tuatha de Danann, who themselves withdrew at the coming of the Gaels, and lived under the lakes and hills as the People of the Sidhe. And it was that the hero of their battle against the Fomhoire, the radiant hero, Lugh Lamfhada, among others, appeared from time to time among the Gaels. And he it was who sat with Gowen to guard the property of Chulainn. And his name it was that was the same as the name Lleu Llau Gyffes, for it was Lugh Long-Arm, the Bright One with the Long Reach.

And it was not just the Tuatha who let themselves be seen from time to time, for the Fomhoire were not of a sort to admit defeat and hide away in the fastness of their far islands. They, and their allies, were everywhere. And now and again they would strike out at those who had taken possession of their land, both above and below ground. Foragall's alliance with them was suspected, although not proven, but it was clear that he had great powers and mighty friends, for none in Leinster at that time offered any resistance to his wishes, until Gowen.

How it is that Gowen came to Foragall's rath, and how it was that he knew of the way, not even his gillie knew, for he followed the roads and paths and crossed the streams and hills as Gowen told him to do.

When they arrived, they came upon a small semicircle of young women, sitting in the grass outside the high walls, knitting, talking and laughing, watched over from a respectful distance by a few armed men. Facing and a little apart from the circle was a young woman with raven-black, lustrous hair and calm, grey-green eyes. Her beauty alone left no doubt that this was Emher.

As the chariot drew to a halt some distance from the circle and the armed men moved forward one step to challenge its occupants, Emher lifted her eyes to look at Gowen. She stood gracefully, dismissed her companions and waved off the small party of guards. The men were clearly disturbed; one of them protested. Although the smile never left her face, her eyes blazed as she spoke again. The man's eyes dropped just before he turned away to obey her command. She stood alone and waited as Gowen jumped from his chariot, leaving his gillie behind.

As Gowen walked toward her, he felt her eyes on him, and his throat constricted and his stomach felt light and queasy, as if he had just leapt from the highest branch of a tall tree.

"She is all that she was said to be," he thought. "But what if my feeling is wrong? Is she truly the one who is fated for me? Am I everything that I think myself to be? What will I do if she doesn't see me to be the one who is fated for her? Can I bear to be scorned? Is it too late...?"

At that instant, she smiled. Just a small smile, but he fancied that he saw recognition in it. And the warmth of it was like a glow throughout his body, melting away all his misgivings. He smiled too, and, instead of turning and walking away as he had thought of doing, he kept walking until he stood before her.

When they stood together, they were of a height, he no taller than she and looked directly into each other's eyes. Grey-green eyes looked deeply into eyes that seemed to change colour from moment to moment. Two young faces, and behind them, two timeless souls.

When they spoke, it was like a code. The gillie could hear what they said, but understood almost nothing of it.

Gowen said: "You are Emher, known in all five lands of Eire for your beauty and wit, and I know you for your wisdom."

She said: "I am. And you are the warrior born in the month of the dog, who has the name of the dog and the sickness of the dog."

"I am," he said and he glanced down the length of her from neck to ankles. "I have found the place in which I shall rest my weapon."

"No man shall come to this place until he has stayed in the white shadow from Lughnasad to Samhain and from Samhain to Imbolc and from Imbolc to Beltaine and from Beltaine to Lughnasad again."

"I have found the place where I shall rest my weapon."

"No man shall come to this place until he has taken what is not yet his from him whose it is."

"I have found the place where I shall rest my weapon."

"No man shall come to this place until he has defeated nine tens and spared nine out of all of them."

"I have found the place where I shall rest my weapon."

When they had spoken these curious things, she smiled a soft smile and put her hand in his and they stood for a while silently, smiling into each other's eyes. Then, abruptly, he said, "I shall be here," and she nodded her head in assent. He turned and walked back to his chariot and a very puzzled gillie. She turned and walked toward the walls of the *dún*.

The gillie was good at his work and had memorized landmarks along the way. He was prepared to retrace their route, but before they started again, he burned to know what this peculiar conversation had meant. As Gowen jumped into the chariot, the gillie opened his mouth to let the questions pour out. Before he could utter a sound, Gowen gave him directions, and they started out, but not in the direction he had expected, for they were headed eastward toward the coast.

"And now," said Gowen, as they flew through the countryside, "I will answer all those questions you wanted to ask."

The gillie blushed that his thoughts were so clearly written on his face.

"All I wish to know," he said, "is, what was the meaning of the strange speech you had with each other? I understand that you have the name of the dog, for you are CúChulainn from your youthful deed of killing the giant guard dog and taking his place. And if you were born in the month of the dog, it must be near the Lughnasad, at the time of the dog star, when the heat of the year is at its greatest. But what is the sickness of the dog?"

"You are right about my name and my birth date. I did not want the name, at first, but I accepted it, and I have come to realize that it tells something of me that is beyond ordinary understanding. There is a powerful man who is called Lleu LLau Gyffes in the land I came from and Lugh

Lamfhada in this land, and it is right that I was born on his day, because he is my protector. So I was born in the month of the dog and I have earned the name of the dog and one of my *geasa* has to do with the dog. The part you do not understand is what Emher knows without being told, because she is fated for me. When she said that I have the sickness of the dog, she meant the sickness that makes the dog go mad with battle fever, when he foams at the mouth, and will not cease attacking until he or his enemy is dead. And he does not always know friend from enemy. That is the way with me when the battle rage is upon me, and that is the thing that Emher knows without being told. And she knows that my madness will cause my death in the end, as the dog's does his.

"And what I said, that meant that I would have her to my wife, and what she answered each time was that anyone who wishes her to wife must perform certain tasks. The first of these is a sojourn in Alba, the White Land over the water, where Gaels have gone before, but the Cymry are also, and the wild Picts. And I must go to the country of Scáthach, the warrior queen, of whom no one knows to which race she belongs, there to take my apprenticeship. And I must abide there from Lughnasad to Samhain and from Samhain to Imbolc and from Imbolc to Beltaine and from Beltaine to Lughnasad again. That is, I must stay through each of our four great seasonal festive days, or one full year."

"Apprenticeship in war under a woman!?"

"Do you think Conall is a great warrior?" Gowen asked.

"Yes, of course."

"And is Fergus even greater?"

"Yes, and yourself is even greater than all of them."

Gowen hung his head, for he had not wanted to use himself as an example.

"What is it, then, that makes Fergus greater again than Conall?" he asked.

The gillie wrinkled his brow in thought. "It is that he has something in him from the Other Place," he said. "There is a power inside him that flies out to meet any challenge. I believe that Conall is the greatest of all the mortal warriors in Uledh and in Eire, but there are a few who go beyond the mortal. And," glancing sideways at Gowen, "with that power comes another kind of sight that lets them see the inner substance of a matter when others are blind to it."

"Who would you name outside of Uledh who has this kind of power?"

Again the gillie's brow furrowed in concentration, and he did not reply immediately.

"There are three," he said slowly. "Foragall in Leinster, who is in league with dark powers, Cúroi mac Dáiri in Munster, whose priests know the secrets of music and death, and..."

"And," Gowen prompted.'

The gillie sighed and said: "And Mebd of Connaught."

"Why do you name Mebd?"

"Because she is fearsome in battle and has powers within her that are greater than those of any warrior in her land. It is said that she knows the use and power of every weapon and can see the shape of any battle before it begins."

"And...?" Gowen prompted again.

"And she is a woman."

"And the woman I must apprentice under is the greatest of all women warriors. Indeed, it is lucky for the warriors of Eire that her home is in Alba, for many a mother's son would not be alive today if he had met her in battle."

"I have never heard her name. What does it mean?"

"She is Shadow, the one you see but cannot touch, the one you never hear until she is upon you, the one who can end the seeing of your eyes forever."

They raced across the landscape without speaking while the gillie absorbed what he had heard. Then he asked: "And what of the other tasks?"

"I will be able to carry them out after my year with Scáthach. Taking what is not yet mine from him whose it is — this means that I must take Emher away from Foragall, who does not want any daughter of his to marry anyone of Uledh."

"But you are not truly of Uledh..." the gillie blurted, and then swallowed his next words in chagrin at what might have been an insult.

Gowen smiled kindly. "You are right, but I fight for Uledh, and that is all he needs to know. So I must take her from him by force, and one of us will die in the doing of it."

"And what of the nine tens? Anyone who has seen you in battle will believe that you can kill many men, but how will you choose among them to decide who will live?"

"Ninety is the number of men Foragall will send against me. Nine of those men will be Emher's brothers, and I must find a way to spare them that will still win the day for me."

"How is that?! How can you kill the father and spare the brothers? Why would she wish it?"

"It is that she has the clear sight and knows that the time of alliances with the Fomhoire must come to an end, because in times to come they will not be the only threat, but others will come from across the sea, and great heroes will rise up in Leinster to defend the coasts of all Eire. Before that time, the Fomhoire must lose their hold on any folk in Eire, or they will destroy all five provinces from within, just when the enemy is coming from without. She and her brothers are of a new generation able to understand this. Her father is deeply committed to the Fomhoire and will take his death rather than yield the power that his alliance gives him. It is for the good of all that he will die."

Onward they flew, hills and trees and streams a blur in their peripheral vision, through the remainder of the day and the following night, until they came at dawn to the Leinster coast and a small fishing settlement. Gowen sprang from the chariot and turned back to the gillie.

"You will go back now. Follow the coast north until you know the landmarks. Cathbad, Fergus and Conchobar will want to know what has happened. Tell them everything, and, if Conall is not there at the telling, seek him out and tell him, too."

Before the gillie could ask any questions, Gowen turned and strode to the shore, where a number of curraghs lay beached, fishermen working near them to prepare for the day's work on the sea. The gillie watched him as he spoke briefly with one of the men, and then helped him launch his craft. At about knee depth, they entered the boat by sliding into it from their respective sides, the fisherman with an ease born of experience and Gowen with the lightness of a small fish leaping out of the water for the pure joy of doing it. The gillie continued to watch until the small boat disappeared beyond the breakers, then he wheeled the chariot and set out at a wild speed for Emain Macha.

It was many days after the gillie's arrival in Emain Macha that a gnarled, salt weathered Leinster fisherman appeared before Conchobar with a great, hide-wrapped bundle. It was the sword and shield that Gowen had won on his day of taking weapons.

"A funny little fella left these with me. He said to bring them to the great king in Emain Macha to keep them safe for him, and I'd be paid for his passage to Alba."

"So you shall," said Conchobar, "and richly. But did he take no weapons with him?"

"Oh, aye. I asked that too. And he smiles that funny smile and says, where he's goin', his body is his weapon. But he had a little dagger, he did, and his sling and some smooth stones."

Conchobar laughed out loud at the audacity of it, Cathbad looked solemn as if he had seen a vision and Fergus smiled to himself. Roigh now, clapped his two huge hands — one each — on the backs of his son, Loeghaire, and Conall Cernach and roared: "To the the Little One, wherever he is, a greeting and the favour of the gods!" and he drained his horn, followed by all the others. And the evening became a legendary night of drinking, storytelling and fighting.

Chapter Nine
THE WHITE SHADOW

North and east of Gwynedd, to the east across the water from Eire, lay the land called Alba. The oldest folk here were those called Picts, who painted and tattooed their bodies from top to toe with illustrations from their myths. Their weapons had not been the equal of the weapons of the Cymry and the Gael, and their discipline in battle certainly no greater, but their wild spirit compensated for much. They had been here when the first of the Cymry pushed up from the south and west, hoping and expecting to take possession of everything between themselves and the opposite coast. The Cymry had made some inroads, but finally had to settle for much less than the whole.

The Gaels who swarmed across the sea from Eire had left themselves no home to return to, so they fought more stubbornly and desperately to make a new home for themselves in the land of the Picts. The Picts never ultimately surrendered, for they did not have such a concept, and they did not retreat, because there was nowhere else to go. But in the end, the Scotian Gaels controlled the land. In their own country, the Picts lived as subjects, allies or rebels, depending upon their individual tendencies.

In this land of three warlike peoples, the most feared and respected name was Scáthach. No one knew from which of these three peoples her blood sprang, whether from one or more of them, or whether from some earlier folk that had long since disappeared from this land. It was not even clear to everyone that she truly existed. If she did, she lived in a remote valley, little travelled because of its reputation as a dangerous traversal. Whoever, or whatever, resided there was dangerous. Few who attempted the crossing of this territory were heard of again. The few who did return told tales of a fearsome woman warrior who exacted a heavy tribute from outsiders.

It was on the shore of Alba that Gowen landed, with thanks and the promise of rich payment to the fisherman who had ferried him over. Cathbad had told him the legends surrounding Scáthach, and now he was here, in her land. He remembered still the druid's final words on the subject.

"It is dark to me how you will arrive there, for I have never been, nor any man of the Uledh. But the powers that watch over you will provide."

Legends of how Gowen reached Scáthach's land are many. The most famous is the tale of how he encountered a lion and tamed it. Then, as the story goes, the inhabitants of this land were startled by the sight of a golden youth with his hands entwined in the great mane of a golden beast which seemed to know exactly where it was going.

Bards know many tales, but some are only for entertainment, and not to be taken seriously. The tale of the lion is appealing, but I know the whole of the life of Gowen-who-was-also-CúChulainn, and I know it to be a charming falsehood of the kind that springs up around any great name.

Ah, I know what you're thinking. The great bard, who tells us of marvel upon marvel, does not believe this marvel because it is not one of his own tales.

Little you know. It is not the marvellous that is unbelievable, but the illogical and the incongruous. It is true that many Celts found their way to that huge southern continent with its odd animals and exotic peoples, at least as far as some of the mighty northern kingdoms there, and lived the life of adventurers or fought as mercenaries. I could even tell you the story of a thousand young warriors fighting for one side in a great civil war over a vast empire. Trapped on an island in a great river, they knew that the coming battle would see many of them taken captive, so they chose to kill themselves instead. When the opposing army overran the island, they found a thousand bodies and a final defiant message carved on a stone. Although none could read the odd characters, they had little doubt about the nature of the message. But enough of side tales. No matter how many of our people went by land and sea to that far place, who has ever heard of one of those southern beasts living in the cold mountains and valleys of Alba? There is, after all, a difference between the marvellous and the silly.

The truth of it is that Gowen met an old, wild Pict almost as soon as he set foot on the soil of Alba. He recognized him as a Pict from Cathbad's extensive lectures on the peoples of Eire and of the Isle of the Giants, where Alba also lay. Around the old man's middle was a tanned hide and over his left shoulder a long, cloak-like length of tanned hide, tied at the waist by a leather thong. Slung on his back by a thick cord was a two-bladed axe. His feet were bare and coated with dust and he limped on the left one, which was clubbed. The tattoos which covered his skin were elongated and interrupted because his skin hung now over an old, enfeebled frame. In the mask of wrinkles that was his face, only his cool, grey eyes seemed not to be old, but rather, ageless. An ancient hound tottered along after him.

Gowen stared at the old Pict. The old Pict stared at Gowen, and finally said a word that sounded like: "Khuurkhii."

Gowen took this to be the old man's name and replied by saying, slowly and carefully: "CúChulainn."

The wrinkles of the old man's face rearranged themselves, moving from vertical sags to horizontal waves which approximated a smile. His teeth were short and brown and his tongue flicked in and out of his mouth as he murmured to himself. He motioned with his hand, to indicate that Gowen should follow him, and set off in a shambling limp along a narrow path that meandered upward toward a nearby mountain. Following the old man, Gowen was aware almost at once of movement in the periphery of his vision on both sides of the path. Climbing toward the base of the mountain, they came to a narrow pass between two heavily wooded rises. Quite suddenly, it seemed, Gowen and the old man were being followed, preceded and flanked by armed men — one in front, one to the right, one to the left, and two behind. From what Cathbad had taught him, Gowen identified the man in front as another, younger Pict, naked but so covered by blue tattoos that he seemed to be attired in a skintight garment. He was carrying an enormous spear. Gowen gave a quick glance behind and to the sides, recognizing behind him two Alban Gaels in their distinctive legless lower garments and, on both sides, warriors of Cymru.

On they climbed, without a word spoken or a pause taken, until dusk. Just before darkness descended, their five companions vanished as silently and swiftly as they had appeared, and the old man stopped to kindle a fire. After watching him laboriously start a spark for the fire, Gowen expected to see him pull some bit of meat or even a small animal out of some unnoticed storage pocket in his hide cloak. But he was disappointed. The old man looked intensely into his eyes, motioned for him to lie down and said, "Khuukhlen." Then he went to sleep, leaving Gowen to attempt the same thing.

At dawn, their five companions appeared as silently as they had vanished, and, without food or drink, the trek began again. The path spiralled up and along the face of the mountain now, tree cover became sparse, the air grew cooler and fresher. Gowen noticed that another mountain was growing closer, as if to intersect the one on which they climbed. The intersection of the two mountains was forestalled after a while by a deep, wide ravine. Still, not a word was spoken and so Gowen was also silent, seeing no advantage in attempting to begin a conversation with folk who had no mind to speak to him. Toward midday, the small company slowed and Gowen saw a peculiar arc, stretching upward from their side of the ravine and reaching to the other, somewhat higher side. It was a bridge of horizontal planks, supported underneath by meticulously arched supports running from one side of the arch to the other. It was then that Gowen remembered what Cathbad had said about entry to Scáthach's country:

"When you come to the land of Scáthach, you will know it from a ravine crossed by the highest curved bridge you ever did see, and no railing on either side. It is a property of this bridge that only the unusually gifted warrior can cross it. How that is, I do not know, but you must be on your guard. Mighty magic is at work there."

Looking back from his appraisal of the bridge, Gowen saw that the old man was alone again. Pointing toward the bridge with his wrinkled smile pulling at the planes of his face, the old Pict spoke for only the third time. He said: "Khuukhlen."

He said no more, but Gowen heard it in his mind, spoken faultlessly in the dialect of his childhood: "This is the bridge Cathbad described. It is impossible to keep footing long enough to climb up this side. But climb it you must, for this is the entry to the land of Scáthach."

So Gowen set about trying to climb the steep arch. First, he tried climbing slowly, bent over and holding onto the sides with his hands, moving one foot at a time. And he reached a third of the height of the arch before he could go no further, because the arch seemed unaccountably to grow steeper rather than shallower as he climbed. So he ran quickly, and the force of his speed carried his leap to two thirds of the height of the span, where he had to grasp the sides with both hands, hanging there, bent over and unable to move higher. And again he had to drop down, defeated.

Panting and discouraged, he heard the old man cackle at his efforts, and a flood of shame swept through him. He closed his eyes and thought of all the feats and skills he had mastered, and he remembered the Salmon Leap. By watching for hours at a time the great fish that fights and leaps its way upstream to found a new family, Gowen had taught his body to do the same. Concentrating the core of his being on the effort, he made a standing leap, turning head over heels in the air one time, and landed with his feet on the top of the span. From there he jumped lightly down to the other side and looked back triumphantly at the old man. But he was no longer there.

Gowen was in Scáthach's land, now. A small plain stretched before him, no dwelling in sight. Nothing but level meadow, bounded by hills and stands of trees narrowing slowly in the distance. Studying the ground, Gowen distinguished the spoor of people and horses, leading away from the bridge. Slowly and carefully, he followed the tracks, listening, scenting and feeling as well as seeing. Even as a boy with his friends at home, he had discovered that sharp eyes could be complemented by ears that heard the stirring of small creatures in the bush or the out-of-place cracking of a twig, by perceiving the scent of man or horse that had passed by recently, even by the touching upon his skin of damp or dry or cool or hot air that could tell him where he was in relation to a stream or a mountain or a hollow. Toward the end of his time among them, his friends — especially Cei and Bedwyr — delighted in testing him by covering his head and carrying him in circles and straight lines, to set him down somewhere as night fell. They would then quietly withdraw and find their way home. After waiting to give them time, the young Gowen uncovered his head and, using all his senses, decided where he was and took the most direct way home, often arriving before his comrades.

So it was now. As he moved swiftly across the plain, he sensed rather than saw or heard that human settlement lay before him. Still, it was a long and weary time before he had evidence of it. Distantly at first, then more loudly, he heard the clash of metal on metal and metal on wood, and the unworded noises of battle. Then, he was sure that the sounds were coming from just beyond a small copse. Slowly and carefully, he approached the low-standing trees, lowered himself to the ground and crept forward so that he could peer through the young trunks and underbrush.

Two young warriors were vigorously attacking a third, whose back was to him. Like some warriors of the Cymry, this third warrior was nude, except that a thin cloth hung by a cord from the waist. Arm, back, buttock and leg muscles played powerfully under the sweat-sheathed skin. The sight of a naked warrior was not strange to Gowen, but there was something hauntingly wrong with the image before him.

Suddenly, the powerful downward stroke of the opponent on the left was met with a wolf-swift upward thrust of the shield, loosening his grip and sending his sword skirling through the air. A swift step back and a turn to the side deprived the right-side opponent of his target. As he lunged and then stumbled forward, a smart whack from the flat of the sword on the back of his cured-hide jerkin sent him reeling to a fall. This second manoeuvre turned the warrior sideways to Gowen and revealed the secret of what had bothered him. It was a woman — magnificent in her battle fury, lithe, white-haired, full-breasted, but still young-skinned. It was undoubtedly Scáthach.

Blood rushed to Gowen's face. Women — even in battle — did not dress, or undress, like this! Women... But then, this was not any woman; it was Scáthach. And no rules applied.

As he slowed his breathing and forced a coolness through his blood, Scáthach dropped her sword and reached a hand to the prone warrior to help him to his feet.

"Back to your camp, young men. You will sleep without sup or drink and, if you wish to eat in the morning, tell me exactly what you did wrong here. Someday it will mean your life."

She smiled as the downcast young men turned and moved wearily away. Then she dropped the shield as well and sat down, propping her back against a small tree.

Gowen raised himself silently with both arms and legs until he was poised in a crouch on hands and feet. With one gigantic leap, he was beside Scáthach, holding the point of his dagger between her breasts, knowing instinctively that this — instead of a knife at the throat — was the only right thing to do.

"My request for your life," he said sotto voce.

Scáthach drew her breath in sharply, as if in fear. Her breasts trembled and Gowen thought in amazement, "Could she be afraid?"

But in the next moment, he heard her breath quicken into a sound and saw the smile playing at the edges of her mouth. She was laughing quietly to herself.

"So, Chullainn's Hound has finally come to me, as foretold. Welcome, Little One. Make your request, but make it correctly."

Like Gwydion and Aranrhod before him, Gowen understood what this meant: exactly what he wanted, phrased in exactly seventeen words.

"Teach me the secrets of battle I do not already know, as you have taught no other," he said without hesitation.

"Done!" she laughed, springing to her feet. "Your fame and mine are now inextricably linked. You will learn all that I have taught any other, and at the end, I will introduce you to the Gae Bolg — and to Aoife."

"Who is Aoife?" he asked.

"My greatest foe — a woman warrior who leads a company of women warriors and fancies that she is my equal in battle."

"Is she?"

"You will learn that in time, Little One. But one thing you must know — she values her prize team of horses and her chariot above all things in the world," she said.

"And what is the Gae Bolg?" he asked.

"That you will also know in time, Little One." She smiled and picked up her shield and sword. "Come to my house. Eat. And rest. We will talk in the morning."

She strode away in the direction taken by the two young warriors and Gowen followed. A short walk brought them to the camp of the trainees — young men from points far and near in Celtic territory, sent by hopeful rulers to learn the skills of battle from the greatest teacher in the world.

The camp was not remarkable for its comfort. A clearing with rough shelters made by the young men themselves from branches and plants, the ground itself to sleep on. Scáthach led Gowen through the camp to a longhouse like any other, except that it stood alone and unprotected by walls and sentries. A red-haired, blue-eyed girl already shapely as a woman served Gowen food and drink, looking deeply into his eyes over the edge of the drinking horn she handed him. Gowen pretended not to notice, but Scáthach laughed softly and the girl blushed from the open neck of her tunic to the roots of her reddish-blonde hair.

"Curl up in a corner, Hound of Chullainn," she said, "and pay no attention to the hero worship of my daughter. She has heard prophecies of your coming since she was able to understand. In the morning, we will begin in earnest."

Gowen ate and drank greedily and did not omit to smile benignly at the tongue-tied girl. Then he walked to the furthest corner, where he found a raised earthen bed covered with skins. As he laid his head down, his eyes closed and he slept. His dreams were a welter of Emher, the old Pict, Chullainn's deadly hound and a straight-limbed hunter who called himself "Gwri" and spoke to him in Cymry.

In the days and months that followed, Scáthach taught him much that he had already learned from Fergus, except that each time she demonstrated a strategy or move, he gained a deeper insight into it — a dozen new ways to make it effective. (I am proud, but I am not so vain that I do not admit when I am bettered.)

His privileged position — sleeping in Scáthach's own house with the powerful and desirable mother and the equally desirable daughter rather than on the ground with the rest of the trainees — caused some grumbling and scurrilous jokes among the other trainees, which he chose to ignore because Scáthach ignored them. And because it was a privilege which did not include the freedoms some of his contemporaries seemed to suspect. He realized that it was a mark of respect for a fate already written for him, and for Scáthach's role in it. It would have dishonoured their bond to press an advantage he neither deserved nor desired.

Personal restraint was not enough. Aran-Cet, a tall, blond, mustachioed Gaul from the former heartland of the Celts, could not be content with behind-the-hand remarks. He burned with jealousy and injured pride. His remarks became louder, more public and more challenging.

One day at general exercises, Aran-Cet pushed a number of others aside, demanding to face Gowen as opponent-partner.

"Let us see how Gullenn's House-Dog will faarrre against a Gaul," he snarled, in his thick accent.

Gowen said calmly, "Let us try our strength against each other, then, friend Aran-Cet."

"I am no frrriend of yours, Little One," the Gaul replied scornfully.

Gowen did not move, but he felt the heat begin in his groin and surge upward through his belly, his lungs, his throat and finally flame out in his face. Through a red haze, he saw Ferdiad of Connaught step up quickly to

Aran-Cet's side and heard him whisper urgently, "Do you wish to live to make mistakes later in life, or are you a complete fool?"

"Thank you, friend," said Gowen through clenched teeth. "It may be too late for a man so foolish that he does not realize only Scáthach has leave to call me by that name."

"Oh, aye, I should apologize for galling you what you are. Or perhaps you prrrefer the other names I have heard. How about 'Warped One'? I like that, too. It is said that in your anger you grow out of your bodily shape and become a verrry monster. Is that what goes on at night when you entertain the ladies?"

Quicker than thought, Ferdiad's left hand lifted Aran-Cet's sword arm high and his left elbow slashed down and into the Gaul's solar plexus. Aran-Cet fell forward, coughing in agony. Ferdiad planted a foot on the Gaul's neck, and as the retching warrior squirmed helplessly, he said: "You will pick yourself up and disappear. Do not let us see you for a while."

Aran-Cet rose groaning and trembling to stagger away. Gowen was still tight-lipped.

"I thank you for your support, friend, but it was not necessary. He would have had little comfort in combat with me."

"It was not for your sake I did it, O CúChulainn," said Ferdiad. "I did not wish to see my new sandals covered in blood, shite and entrails." And he smiled impishly.

Despite his anger, Gowen had to smile too. And then he began to laugh, and the whole company of trainees looked on amazed as he and Ferdiad laughed and then roared and then collapsed in laughter on the ground, while Aran-Cet skulked silently and fuming on the outskirts of the crowd. Scáthach stood watching with a smile which held just a hint of sadness at what the future held for these two new friends.

In the days and months that followed, Gowen of Uledh and Ferdiad of Connaught excelled all others in tracking, tactics and feats of arms. If one of them did not lead in some activity, then it was the other. Some even say that these were the only two warriors in the history of the world who mastered the shield-rim feat: leaping lightly onto the rim of an opponent's shield, whence they could execute the beheading stroke. I have never seen it done, but I have heard of it. If any in the world could do it, it would be these two.

Their comparable abilities and Ferdiad's first intercession between Gowen and Aran-Cet were the basis of a lifelong friendship. Ferdiad, too, was an only child, and so the two of them became surrogate brothers to each other. If they suspected what the end of their friendship would be, they did not dwell on it, or allow it to dilute the pleasure of their comradeship. Together, they could defeat the young elite of the Celtic world collected at Scáthach's, just as Gowen had been able to stand off half of the Boy Troop of Emain Macha. And they revelled in competing with each other, each one laughing delightedly when the other bested him.

Scáthach did not believe in fortifications to protect herself or her students, so both the camp and her house were open to attack from all sides, and the only protection was a sentry system which provided a barely sufficient warning of marauders. At the end of Gowen's fourth season in the camp, Scáthach's training reached a climax with a raid by her only rival in warcraft, also a woman: Aoife of the Swift Legs. Just after dawn one day, the trainees awoke to the mad, exultant yells of Aoife's warriors sweeping down on their camp.

Scáthach woke instantly and was the first to the field, rallying her students, confident that they would follow her eagerly, and so they did. All but Gowen, who was still deeply asleep. His comrades among the Uledh had learned early in his stay among them, that Gowen slept when and as long as he needed. Only one incautious, old warrior — who thought he was helping the young fellow out — had attempted to wake Gowen gently. The reaction was involuntary, swift and breathtaking, and the helpful warrior was grateful that it bypassed him, to split a nearby shield in half. Since then, no one had even thought about waking Gowen. Scáthach did not, but not precisely out of fear. It did not suit her purpose to endanger the student who would carry her name into the tales and traditions of the Gaels for all time to come. He was still not ready.

True to his nature, however, Gowen did awake and heard the noise of battle, which was an irresistible call to him. Seizing his weapons, he rushed through the door and into the fight, where he found Ferdiad fiercely pressing a redoubtable woman warrior.

"Who are they and why was I left to sleep?" he shouted.

"No one wanted a broken head for breakfast," gasped Ferdiad out of the side of his mouth, "and these are Aoife's warrior maids, who are far more fearsome than any of our comrades. Over there," he said, unwisely pointing with his sword and recovering just in time to parry a powerful blow from his adversary, "is Aoife herself."

Gowen saw a flashing movement in the centre of the shouting, flailing figures — a raven-haired, black-eyed whirlwind. She was pressing Aran-Cet fearfully. He parried and lunged as best he could, but at each exchange, another cut or slash appeared on arm, chest or leg, and he fell back panting with exertion and the beginning of fear before the mad and skilful strokes of the warrior-queen. Gowen forced his way through the hurly-burly of clashing warriors to Aran-Cet's side and spoke, almost joyfully, to his former antagonist.

"Friend Aran-Cet — do not say we are not friends, for I am about to save your life — move aside by a little and let me engage your charming companion."

Aran-Cet wasted no time or rejoinders, but moved aside gratefully as Gowen moved into place befoe Aoife.

"Show her what we gan do, Gú," he hissed fervently. "You are my frirrend now, if not before."

Gowen moved into place before the fearsome woman warrior and exchanged stroke for stroke, slash for slash and bump for bruising bump, as elbows, shoulders and hips came into play. Her eyes, over the rim of her shield, flashed with joy at an opponent who gave as good as he got. Shields held out, swords flashing suddenly from behind their shelter, each sought to draw first blood, to intimidate by speed or strength. And each stroke met a raised or lowered shield or a dancing step away from danger. They parried, lunged and slashed until the metal rims of their shields were torn through and their blades began to cut into the hardwood cores, and every muscle and bone in their bodies shrieked in pain.

Gasping for breath, neither able to gain an advantage, they fought on until Gowen remembered Scáthach's words when he had first arrived in her camp.

Looking somewhere over Aoife's shoulder, he cried suddenly: "Ah! Your horses! What a shame!"

She reacted only for a moment, to glance over her shoulder, but it was enough. As her head began to turn, Gowen sprang across her shield, knocking her prone and pinning her arms to the earth, his sword lying across her throat.

"Well, then, it is CúChulainn, is it not?" she breathed. "What do you wish from me?"

Without reflection, Gowen had the answer, and he never knew in his life thereafter whence that answer came.

"Peace for Scáthach henceforth and forever, my child in your womb, those conditions I put on it," he answered in exactly seventeen words.

"Done," she replied, exactly as Scáthach had before her.

With a gentleness that belied their just-ended battle, he disengaged and rose above her. Aoife rose on one elbow to shout — can a woman be said to roar? "Stop all arms! Back to our camp! I will join you soon."

Scáthach appeared as if from nowhere, smiling down at Aoife: "So now you, too, have fulfilled your destiny. Enmity between us be far!"

"Peace now and forever!" Aoife replied, and allowed Gowen to pull her by one hand to her feet. She was a bit younger than Scáthach, easily as attractive as Scáthach or her daughter and as scantily clothed as ever Gowen's teacher had been. She reached out to take his hand and the two of them walked to her chariot. The way to her *dún* was not far...

I know what it is you are expecting of me, but it is not to be. This was not the night of your imagining — a night of passion and romance, but if you had any understanding at all, you would know that it was a night of destined coupling which was written into the fates of both of them. And what came after was the same, for as Gowen rose up on the bed, pulling his body stickily away from hers, he gazed into her dazed, deep-black eyes and said, once more in seventeen words, and once more not knowing whence they came: "Send him to me battle ready, giving no one his name and giving way to no man."

In the same, distant way, she replied, "It will be done."

And after that, neither ever saw the other again.

It was Aoife's destiny to fade into the background of the legend from that time forward. It was Gowen's fate to recall his brief meeting with her many years hence, and to wonder at the cruel surprises destiny has planned for us, and the meaning of them, if they have any.

Back at the camp, he arrived to a hero's welcome and Aran-Cet — credit be to him — was the first to greet him and say, "My life and my sword when you need them, GúGhulenn." And Gowen smiled and embraced him as he would a dearest friend.

Next to step up to him was Ferdiad, who joked with him about whether the nine or ten warriors he had bested were equal to besting Aoife herself, and then unwarily remarked that he had not had such a reward from any one of them as Gowen had had from their leader, but his voice faltered as he saw the look in Gowen's eye, and he made a sweeping-away gesture with one hand, as if to say, "Let us pretend that I did not say that." And Gowen left it at that, but only because it was Ferdiad.

Finally, Scáthach appeared out of her house and said, "Well, Little One, it seems that you are farther along than I thought. If you can best Aoife, then I have only one more thing to show you."

"But," Gowen protested, "I did not truly defeat her. I tricked her."

"And that," smiled Scáthach, "was your penultimate lesson — one that you had to teach yourself, for what noble young warrior wishes to hear the truth of things: that trickery and deception are as much a part of warfare as the ability to throw a javelin or wield a sword. Who cannot make use of deception in warfare, will never understand or excel in it. Who refuses to use it, does not understand the nature of war or of the enemy."

She lowered her voice so that only Gowen could hear, "And with that recognition, comes the ability to accept my last gift to you, and an unfair advantage over all others."

So saying, she went into her house and, after enduring prolonged and rambunctious congratulations, so did Gowen. After Ferdiad, not one mouth had uttered a syllable in reference to his actions of the night before. Those who did not hold their tongues out of respect, held them out of fear.

It was the next day, just before dawn, when Scáthach came to Gowen as he slept. No fool, she stood five paces away and threw small stones at him until he woke, violently as usual, burying his hand like a knife in the earthen floor beside him.

"Come, Little One," she smiled, "it is time for your last lesson with me."

Silently, they stole out of her house and away from the camp to a stream nearby, but out of earshot of the camp. Already standing in the stream, weighted down at its feet by heavy stones, was the wicker figure of a man, the water of the stream splashing and whirling as it hurried by its two legs.

They strode into the stream, which flowed calf-high on Scáthach and nearly knee-high on Gowen. Reaching into a small bag hung at her waist, Scáthach withdrew a short object, sharply pointed at its front end, increasing to a roundness in its middle and sloping to end in a forked tail. It looked like an ungainly fish.

"This," she said with slow and grave earnestness, "is the Gae Bolg. It is destined that you should be the one to wield it, and that its secret will be lost after you. With it, you will fulfil your destiny in Eire, and through it you will lose what is dearest to you. It is power and pain. You cannot have one without the other, and no more can you refuse the gift of it, for it is your name only that is on it."

She offered it to Gowen, lying on her open palm. Without a word, he took it from her and thought: "It is forked like a throwing stick and we stand in running water. It cannnot be thrown like a spear — it is too clumsy. It is shaped like a salmon, but it cannot be that I should make myself vulnerable by stooping to throw it along under the water."

So he dropped it experimentally into the water which was running past his legs from the front, and it seemed to drift downward, with its pointed nose held forward and its forked tail upright, until he raised his right foot off the pebbly surface of the stream and caught the tail between his big toe and the next. He squeezed down with his toes to grasp it firmly, drew back the foot and gave a long smooth kick through the water. Then he watched.

The Gae Bolg streaked underwater like a pike after its prey, the surface waves obscuring it intermittently as they do all creatures of the wave. Reaching the wicker figure, it turned upward sharply, leaping from the water like a bass after a fly, and crashed from below into the crotch of the wicker figure. The figure seemed to dissolve from within, tiny straw-like projectiles, drops of blood and bits of bloody flesh flying in every direction from it. Then the whole figure collapsed into the stream, wicker floated downstream toward them and blood suffused the water around the figure before it dissipated in the current. The Gae Bolg itself lay misshapen on the stream-bed. Its swollen middle had burst open, thrusting tens of hooked points in every direction of the wind. It was no wonder the figure had disintegrated; and it was no mystery what the Gae Bolg would do to the insides of a warrior.

As Gowen reached into the water to retrieve it, his touch seemed to transform it again. The points retreated into the middle like bees into their hive, and it was once again the fish-shaped object he had sent on its way through the water. So that was how it worked.

He waded back downstream to Scáthach and held the Gae Bolg out on his outstretched palm. She plucked it from his hand, unslung the cord of her small pouch, dropped the Gae Bolg into it, pulled the pouch tight and draped it over his neck, to hang under his left arm.

"It is yours now, Little One... forever."

He blinked slowly in acquiescence and then looked down at the stream, where the last wisps of red swirled by their legs, and bits of wicker bobbed and skirled by on the surface.

"Something alive was in that figure," he said matter-of-factly.

"The Gae Bolg cannot find its way to wicker — only to flesh and blood," she said with equal impassivity.

"What..."

Scáthach's expression was a curious mixture of frown, smile and sadness.

"Do not ask what you do not wish to know," she said. "Rather think ahead. It is time to take leave of your comrades and return to your purpose. A young woman named Emher awaits you. I did not think four seasons would be enough, but I am proven wrong."

So saying, she jumped lightly onto the bank and strode away, her feet and ankles sending droplets of water before and behind her.

Gowen stood in the rushing water until his ankles groaned with pain at the cold. He felt it, but he could not move. He had truly almost forgotten why he was here, and now the image of Emher floated before his imagination — just as he had seen her at their last and only meeting. And now he was being declared ready to go back and win her! He needed to stand there a bit and think of all that entailed. What had she said? "No man shall come to this place until he has met nine tens and spared nine of all of them." Destiny it might be, but a powerful task, and for the first time since leaving Eire, he had doubts that he could do it.

It was almost dark when he returned to the camp, and a much more silent group than the one he had met on returning from Aoife's *dún*. Scáthach herself was not in evidence, but it was obvious that she had told them that he was leaving. Aran-Cet stepped out of a small group and confronted him gravely, "What I said about my sword I will fulfil. You have only to send to me. I will be home beforrre another year is gone."

Gowen was unwillingly touched and his eyes misted over, thinking of Cei and Bedwyr, who had also changed from enemies to comrades. He put both hands on Aran-Cet's broad shoulders. He had to reach up a bit to do it.

"I cannot tell when, but I feel that I will need to call on you, and when I do, the payment will be greater than the debt."

Aran-Cet smiled slowly, until his entire face was a huge grin. "Let it be so," he said, and turned away as Ferdiad appeared by his side.

"I, too, am here to say farewell," Ferdiad said, "but in my own way. Come."

The light pressure of his hand on Gowen's shoulder directed him out of the camp and into the surrounding bush, then further into a tall wood. Gowen noticed two short-handled, deep-bowled wooden spoons slung from a cord at his waist. They walked through the deep dusk of the forest, saying nothing, until they reached a small clearing, where a fat, round covered urn sat alone. Ferdiad slid the flat stone from the top of the urn, and the sweet, pungent smell of mead filled Gowen's nostrils.

"I have never felt the need to drink over much of the stuff," said Gowen.

"Well, it is the once you will have to do it," replied Ferdiad, "for this is the end of our time together and the swearing of our friendship for all time, whatever may come," said Ferdiad. "We are on the edge of our destinies, and they lie in opposite directions. You return now to the Uledh. I will remain a while and then return to to Connaught, to serve Queen Mebd and King Aillil. If we meet again, it may well be on the on the battlefield."

Gowen was silent for a moment, then he dipped his spoon into the urn.

"Whatever may come," he said, and drank, and Fediad did the same.

They drank slowly, gazing into each other's eyes, and what they saw there, no one knows. At first, they spoke reverently of all they had learned from Scáthach, and all they had accomplished together. After a time, they wondered what lay in store for them as warriors for their own lands and whether they would always measure up to their own expectations. Finally, as the urn neared the point of being empty, they were flushed with the anticipation of the heroic life and began playfully to uproot the smaller trees to use them as imaginary swords and spears against one another, staggering from one end of the clearing to the other, thrusting and bashing and laughing and falling down and leaping up again. Their sport grew more raucous and muddled, until they were charging together against the larger trees and frightening the creatures great and small within sound or sight of their celebration. And back at the camp, their comrades listened, and smiled.

It is said that they tore up so much of the woods and the ground itself that nothing would grow there again and the depression was so great that a small lake formed. But I myself have been there and know this not to be true. Where the older trees were torn up by their sport, newer ones grew and stand out from the forest around by their younger age and sometimes by being of a different species than the surrounding wood.

And if the wood was altered for better and worse by their antics, so were they, for they woke in the morning nauseous and aching in their heads, and yet not regretting that they had spent a night of leave-taking in time-honoured fashion. Ferdiad hobbled quietly and miserably back into camp, and Gowen set off for the mysterious bridge he had crossed four seasons ago to come to this land.

Chapter Ten
EMHER AGAIN

Gowen's mind as he made his way from Scáthach's land was engulfed in a whirl of sad and exuberant thoughts. Fond memories of Ferdiad and, indeed, of Aran-Cet and the sadness of parting from them, perhaps forever or perhaps to meet again as enemies, brought back similar thoughts of Cei and Bedwyr. Thoughts of Emher drove hot blood into his face and strength into his step; then thought of what he must do to win her formed a cold ball in his stomach and turned his legs to stone. Despite his matter-of-fact words to the gillie on leaving Foragall's *rath*, he felt something near panic when he thought of killing the father of his future bride. He even found himself thinking almost fondly of the Old Pict and asked himself, not for the first time, who he was, why he had helped a presumptuous stranger and above all, why his wrinkled and tattooed face had seemed familiar.

He returned the same way he had arrived, but this time, the bridge passively accepted him, and he saw nothing of the Old Pict and his four companions. Again he found passage with a willing fisher, who was glad to take him along on a long-planned trip to Eire to visit relations, and accepted with smiling skepticism Gowen's promise of great reward at the court of Conchobar. Again he witnessed the flight of the ducks and the gulls, and puzzled about its meaning. And again a skeptical fisherman made his way to Conchobar's court and found that the promise of reward was munificently fulfilled.

On the wall of Foragall's *rath* in Leinster, meanwhile, a lone figure stood, gazing across at the darkling horizon, waiting, expecting, certain in her mind that the one she awaited would arrive on the appointed day. She, too, anticipated both joy and sadness from the fulfilment of her destiny.

And so when he appeared as a tiny figure topping the horizon as the sun began its rise behind him, she gave a sigh of expectation fulfilled, but she did not smile. She went down from the wall and walked to the longhouse of her father, where she knew he would be now. She did not visit him gladly at this time of day, because she knew that he spent the night until dawn in conference with his allies, the Fomhoire.

The rumour among those who had not seen them was that they were either unnaturally handsome or surpassingly ugly — misshapen beyond imagination — and possessed of supernatural powers which had allowed them to oppress the whole of Eire and all of those who had arrived on its shores until the coming of the Tuatha De Danann, the people of the goddess, Dana, who defeated them utterly by courage and magic, and drove them back to their own, wild island in the sea. And as I told you before, it was these peerless magical warriors of the goddess, Dana, who were defeated by my own people, the Gaels, only because of our own great druid, Amergin, who out-magicked the whole of their magic men and gave the battle to the better warriors of the Gael. It was the bargain struck, that they would divide the land in half between them, and the sly Gael who was given the choice of which half said, "We'll have that half that is above the ground." And thus it was that the people of Dea became the people of the Fairy Mound, and lived under the lakes and hills. And the Fomhoire they had driven out still plotted to return and put both the Gael and the Tuatha under bondage.

Emher tapped lightly on the entrance to her father's wooden longhouse and he stepped to the doorway at once. When he saw who it was, he smiled and his smile spoke of both love and proprietorship. He truly believed that the future would lie again in the hands of the Fomhoire, and he planned that his children should benefit from his association with them. Emher was his only daughter and, as such, crucial to his plans. Her marriage to a Fomhoire prince would ensure his family's dominance in Eire for many generations to come. He made himself no reproaches on the subject of physical attraction, for he had already chosen the Fomhoire prince he wished for a son-in-law, and he was almost unnaturally handsome. And a wonderful fighter, who might put that upstart, CuChulainn, in his place. True, he was not swift of intelligence, but he would not be required to think too much.

Emher smiled too, and her smile also spoke of love, for she did love her father, but it spoke of sadness as well, for she and her brothers knew that the day of the Fomhoire was past, and even if it was not, they would give their lives to prevent its return. Sooner or later, they could find themselves ranged against their own father in a battle to decide the future of Eire. What Emher suspected and her brothers did not know was that the time was now, and the agent of the break with their family's historic alliance was even at that moment trudging across the plain toward Foragall's rath. Emher spoke quietly, "The one to whom you swore I would never be given has returned from Alba and will be here before midday."

She turned and walked slowly away, just able to hear that Foragall was speaking intently to his guests.

Gowen, road-weary but high-hearted from thoughts of Emher, trudged on toward the walls of the *rath*. He had with him only the Gae Bolg, and the dagger and sling he had taken away to Alba. There was no scarcity of stones on the ground of Eire, and so he had no worries about being weaponless. He had no need of practice, since he had supplied himself with food along the way by his strong throwing arm and his good eye.

He had given much thought to his bargain with Emher. The first part was fulfilled simply by his appearance here exactly four seasons from the day they had spoken. What remained was not just a battle for Emher's hand, but a careful tactical separation of enemies from prospective friends. How was it to be that he could destroy the father of the woman he loved and she could still love him? How could he lie beside her and not quail at the thoughts that must be running through her mind? How was it to happen that he could spare her nine brothers while disposing of the other eight men in each of the nine groups of nines? Was this not beyond even his newly acquired powers? And none of this, at all, at all, would take place in or near the water, so the Gae Bolg was useless to him. What he did now, he must do with only his sling, and as it turned out, it was the precursor and the rehearsal for a great thing he would do later in his life.

As he neared the *rath*, heads appeared at the wooden palisade that ran around the top of the great earthen wall, the wooden stakes of the entrance gate grated along the ground as it swung slowly open, and through the opening appeared the first of the group of nines Emher had prophesied, trotting forward, spears held forward at the perpendicular, no shields, swords swinging in leather scabbards from a cord at the waist. Otherwise, as was often the case with our people, they wore nothing, showing their contempt of both danger and the enemy.

The centre man of the nine was slightly in the lead and his grey-green-eyed, dark-haired head was so similar to Emher's that Gowen knew it must be her brother. He dropped a smooth stone into his sling and began to swing it slowly at an angle in an arc over his head, staring intently now at the leader who must be Emher's brother. On they came, and as they cleared the packed-down entry path, another identical group appeared behind them, coming on at a comfortable trot. Behind them then appeared another, and then another.

Gowen let his mind take control of his sling-hand. Just before the first group came into effective javelin range, when his eye told him it was exactly the right time, he let the stone fly. It flew straight and true, to the chest of Emher's brother, and struck a blow that was terrible enough to stop his breath in his body, cloud his vision and throw him twisting sideways to the ground. And there he lay, bruised and miserable, but breathing again and very much alive.

The four men on the right and the four men on the left of him heard him fall, and saw it from the sides of their eyes. They faltered, partly from fear of the long-distance marksmanship and partly from concern for their lordling, whom they loved more than his father, their master.

The second group of nine, seeing only that the first group had faltered, ran around them and met the same shot, unerringly placed with a delicate measurement of power to stretch their own lordling on the ground.

The third nine, now more clearly aware of what had happened, trotted a little less enthusiastically past the first two, and had the same experience.

With three lordly brothers now gasping on the ground, the following groups slowed to a halt by the first three, and soon there was a milling crowd of warriors, shouting and protesting at one another to decide how they must go on.

But they had no leisure to plan, for another stone flew through the milling throng and struck with pinpoint accuracy a fourth brother in the arm, breaking it above the elbow and sending him to his knees. Seconds later, a fifth — turning backward to address someone behind was hit so hard and embarrassingly in the buttock that his entire left side refused to support him and down he slumped in a cloud of imprecations and entreaties aimed at every god and demigod who came to mind.

"Enough! It is enough!" This from a grizzled veteran in the aimless mob.

"It is a clear message, it is, that we are hearing. We will get ourselves back to the *rath* now, for the sake of our young lords, or not a one of them will survive when that fearsome son of the Morrigan takes aim at them a second time. Sure, what is it to us that he wishes to marry the Lady Emher but a blessing? For he is better again than any of the cursed Fomhoire she may be forced to lie with. Better a son of Uledh who lives under the same gods than a misbegotten enemy of all of Eire."

And it took no more. They stooped to pick up their mortified lordlings and carry them back to the rath, while along the wall behnd the palisades, the watchers watched in their different ways. Emher trembled with laughter at the cleverness and audacity of Gowen's solution to the first of his tasks, but she wondered in a small, cold and isolated part of herself how he could accomplish the rest and leave a possibility of love betweeen them. Foragall also said nothing, because he, too, understood the message. It was to him and his allies to deny this little scourge of a warrior what he wanted, and preserve Emher for the grand alliance to come.

Beside him stood a Fomhoire warrior — not misshapen nor even ugly, but large, fully a head taller than Foragall or any of his men. His face was so massive that it seemed to take appreciable time to glance from one of his wide-set eyes to the other. He stared under lowered lids at the single greatest obstacle to his people's re-assertion of suzerainty over this land, and made a sound deep in his throat, for he knew it was to him now to crush this deadly pipsqueak.

But as his muscles tensed, he felt Foragall's hand on his arm.

"Let be!" said Foragall. "If I do not dispose of him myself, after all that he has done, I will lose all respect among my people and that will be the end of any alliance."

"And if you fail, you will lose your life," growled the Fomhoire, "and that will be the end of any alliance."

"If it is to be, then let it be now!" grated Foragall and walked unhurriedly along the wall to an earthen stair, then down into the *rath* where he called in a calm and imperious voice for his shield and sword.

Gowen had not moved since the retreat of the nine nines and his gut was cold and bunched within him. No matter how clever his solution to the first problem, there was no way to evade Emher's brutal prophecy of her father's death. Nor was he so witless that he misread her calm prediction as a sign that she would not mourn her father. She had had no more control over the compulsion to speak that foreknowledge than had he over his peculiar bargain with Aoife. And she was human. She could look upon her father's death as fated and necessary, but that was not the same as loving and living with him who caused it.

But as Foragall stalked slowly through the *rath* gate, there was no choice. Reluctantly, Gowen dropped a stone into his sling; reluctantly, he began the arc around his head. As Foragall neared majestically, the speed of the sling increased, causing a slight whir, then a whistle. Gowen calculated desperately just how much force was needed to make it appear to be a deadly cast, yet leave Foragall alive.

Suddenly a grip of iron lay upon the back of his neck. Swifter than thought, a hand slipped the ends of the sling from his own. Its arc increased in speed and diameter, and then the stone flew. It flew straight for Foragall's forehead, smashing through and carrying a fist-sized mass of brain and bone out at the back. For a moment, Gowen fancied that he could see straight through Foragall's head, to the astonished faces of the the men in the *rath*. Then he turned to stare up into cool grey eyes that somehow made him think of the Old Pict, and of someone else, he did not know who. The stranger was tall, but not gigantic, lithe and easy, dressed in jerkin and leggings of skin, hide upon his feet, the tips of bundled javelins peeking up over his back. His tall hound whined and sniffed familiarly at Gowen's hand.

"Why?" Gowen whispered. "Why?"

"Because you do not need this on your spirit," the hunter replied calmly.

"But..."

"No, you will not become a joke because I took your shot. They cannot see me."

"..."

"And no, you will not suffer in Emher's eyes, for I have allowed her to see me."

"Who are you at all?" Gowen whispered in fierce frustration.

"I am Cúroi mac Dáiri, Little One, and I knew you long before you knew anything."

"You're Munster — allied with Foragall and with Mebd of Connaught!"

"Not everything can be explained as you stand in full view of the world.

Go and greet your bride."

And Gowen walked toward the *rath*, numb, in a mist of his own thoughts. As he arrived alone at the gate, Foragall's men stepped back respectfully and even those of his sons he had injured smiled up at him. The loss of Foragall was clearly not so strong a feeling as their release from a terror which went beyond personal loyalty to lord or father.

Into the *rath* and up the steps to the top of the wall he walked, still only half aware of himself. And then he stood face to face with Emher, and, as his knees turned to water and his heart dropped into his stomach, she smiled into his eyes and said: "It is clever you are to 'spare' my brothers that way, although they won't thank you for it! But how is it that Cúroi mac Dairí has taken on the blood-guilt of my father's death? Does he owe you somehow?"

"I don't know," Gowen answered. "I only know that I recognized him, but do not know why. He has something to do with my time in Alba, and long before that, before I can remember."

"Well," she said, with a smile that turned his face to fire, "let us get on with our business together."

Chapter Eleven
THE CHAMPIONSHIP — TALE OF A PIG

When Gowen was spied from the high stone walls of Conchobar's *dún*, he was at the reins of Foragall's chariot with Emher beside him, and a guard of honour of Leinstermen sent by Emher's brothers — even those still smarting from their injuries.

The men of Uledh, who after all had occasioned Gowen's search for a wife, welcomed them with noisy approval, tempered only by a twinge of jealousy on their first sight of Emher. None was louder or more wholehearted in his approval than Roigh, who dragged his son and Conall to greet them. And none was quieter or more thoughtful than a gaunt and tough old Uledhman Gowen did not know well, for he was never in the first rank of battle, as Gowen was, but much more likely to spare his horses until the other side had been turned and was in flight. He was known, for good and sufficient reason, as Bricriu Poison-Tongue, and he delighted in nothing so much as in creating mischief.

As Conall, Roigh and Loeghaire surrounded Gowen and Emher in welcome, a booming voice cut through the chatter.

"And when, Hound of Chulainn, will I be granted the pleasure of greeting this lovely *caíllin*?"

There were two disquieting things about this apparently jovial demand. The first was the reminder to all and sundry, including Gowen, that the king was not to be kept waiting while others conversed. The second was the word he used to describe Emher, for she was no girl now, but a woman about to be married. To the king, though... to the king, she was a girl and his by right for the first night, through an ancient law called the Law of the First Forcing. That is, any girl about to be married in Uledh spent her first night in the bed of the king. What lay behind it even I cannot say. Perhaps it was a sacred ritual at one time. Perhaps it was a way of spreading the seed of the king throughout the land in such a way that it ennobled the blood of many families, but gave none a clear claim to the throne. Whenever it came, everyone knew of it and all — even Cathbad and his ownself, Fergus — felt a little clutch of apprehension at what might come. For this was no ordinary noble maid and surely no ordinary warrior. As if guided by a common thought, every man held his tongue, and his breath, and waited for the dangerous moment to pass.

But it was not to be, even if Conchobar had wanted to amend his statement, somehow, to soften its implication. For Bricriu knew that law as well as any other and he spoke in a strong and authoritative voice: "But a *caillín* she will be no longer, after the king has claimed his right."

Conchobar, who was a good king, nonetheless lived according to his appetites, and this would one day prove to be his death. So he did not pause, as another might have, to consider what the privilege of a first night with this delightful girl might cost him. He smiled broadly, looked her up and down slowly, as he would a prime mare, and shook his head slowly in anticipation.

Stunned, Emher and Gowen stared at one another. The fury which began to glow in Emher's face was fearful enough. Gowen, now, took a moment longer to believe what he had heard, and then the rage began to come upon him. His eyes flashed and seemed to pulse in and out of their sockets, his hair appeared to writhe upright on his head and his skin flushed so red that it seemed one could light a brand from it. Conchobar saw the signs, but he was helpless. He could not now be seen to back away from an ancient right. The silence in the great hall became absolute. It seemed almost possible that they could all hear Gowen's blood boiling in his body, ready to escape in a mighty explosion of vapour.

Into this dreadful silence cut the quiet, commanding voice of Cathbad, "The right of the king and the honour of CúChulainn and his lady may all be satisfied!"

Everyone gaped, first at Cathbad and then at Gowen, who had heard, and was making a supreme effort to step back from the full flowering of his battle rage. Trembling mightily, hardly in control of his own body, he glared at Cathbad in an attempt to understand.

"Emher shall spend the night in the king's bed," the druid said, drawing his voice out on the last words to show that this was not all, and raising his finger to Gowen to demand further attention. "And so shall I, and friend Fergus, and her own good bridegroom. And we shall pass the night in good conversation and games of fidchell, like civilized folk."

As he listened, Gowen's skin-colour lightened, his eyes calmed, and finally he understood. As much in relief as in appreciation of the ingenious solution, he threw his head back and laughed, and Emher joined him. Then Roigh, too, roared his amused approval, and soon the entire company of men and women roared and whinnied and shrieked and howled their appreciation. Even Conchobar, who, had he but realized, had seen the beginning of the end of one of his royal privileges. For never again would it be necessary to take the Right of First Forcing seriously, and never again would a maid, or her mother, or her bridegroom meekly assent, but would demand "CúChulainn's Right", and so eventually create the tradition of a night of festivity in the king's bedchamber, whenever one of his warriors married.

But that was yet to come. After the night of comradeship and discourse on Conchobar's massive bed, all went their own ways. Fergus to his own *dún*, Cathbad to his and Gowen and Emher to the *dún* the king had presented them. Conchobar himself flung himself backward, spread out his arms and slept through a day and a night. Even when it came to sleep, he did nothing in moderation. And it was like a visit to the Fairy Mound the next day in his house, with everyone tiptoeing about, hoping not to be the one to wake the royal glutton. But there now, enough of my small-minded chiding! Impetuosity and appetite were his failings, and they were also a part of a personality that was second to none in generosity or courage.

While he slept, Gowen and Emher became acquainted with each other's minds and bodies (You did not think, did you, that I would describe this night in detail? For shame! You can learn such things for yourself!) And Bricriu was out and about at his usual business when there was no battle to be fought — fomenting mischief. At that time in Uledh, there were four premier heroes — warriors who would surge to the front of battle and slice a path through the enemy for their comrades to follow. We will not count Fergus himself, who had been king and was never measured by the same standard as others, but was compared in his own way to Conchobar. Muirchedach was one of the four heroes, but he was not yet back from a long, adventurous expedition into Connaught with a few of his favourite companions. The other three, as the the Uledhmen saw them in order of power and priority were: CúChulainn, Conall the Hundred-Fighter and Roigh's son, Loeghaire the Triumphant. Conall, in fact, had some claim to being the greatest warrior in all of Eire, and that is a tale quickly told.

Part I: The tail of a pig

At a time before ever Gowen took arms, there was held a great boasting feast that included all of the four provinces: Uledh, Connaught, Munster and Leinster. As was the custom on such occasions, one warrior after the other stood and gave his boast, making his claim to the Champion's Portion — that part of the pig that he chose to take because it was the best portion, fuller of sweet fat or tender meat than any other. Each new boast was greater than the one before it, and forced the holder of the place to sit down. After a short while, however, a Connaughtman named Cet, who was second in reputation in Mebd's and Aillil's realm only to his own elder brother, stood against all comers. When each new rival stood to challenge him, he had an answer:

"Oh, is that your boast is it, young fellow? And are you not the youngster who stood by and watched me sweep his sister onto my horse and did nothing to stop me?'

or:

"Ach, Conn, old fellow, and what of the time, then, when I rode by your house driving your cattle and leaned down to give your wife a kiss before I drove them all home?"

And so it continued with men from the other three provinces, until Conall appeared, wild and sweating and filthy with the dust of travel, and said:

"Get away from the pig, O Cet!"

And Cet looked up in surprise.

"Is it you that has come late to the feast, O Conall?"

And Conall repeated, "Get away from the pig, Cet!"

And Cet replied, "I will that, but you would not dare to make that demand of my brother, if he were here."

"Ah, but he is," replied Conall, yanking a bloody head from his belt by its hair and hurling it at Cet so hard that he was carried backward and stretched out on the earthen floor.

And then Conall took hold of the pig by its tail, they say, and sucked all the fat and meat from its body in one breath. As one who knew Conall, I can tell you that I believe the first part, but not the second. He never ate that much in one sitting in his life.

Part II: Inviting the guests

Loeghaire, although he did not have such a tale to his credit, could boast of many a battle when he alone led the Uledhmen into the enemy. He and Conall and Muirchedach had all at times been the only spark and hope of their people in one battle or another. And when they all appeared together, it was almost always a bad day for the other side.

As you have seen in the tale of Gowen's taking weapons, Conall did not feel great rivalry for his new, young comrade-in-arms. He and Loeghaire and Muirchedach welcomed all the help they could get. But this latest instance now, in which their comrade, CúChulainn, was privileged like no other before him — did it not rankle just a bit? And what led up to it: the men of the land having to go to Conchobar to demand that he find Gowen a wife, so that they could reclaim the attention and respect of their womenfolk — did it not sting? So they were a bit more prepared than usual to be foolish. Besides, the essence of a Celtic warrior is not just to fight, but to compete. It's only natural, isn't it? Now, as to Gowen, well, he was still young.

As everyone knows, the nature of such as Bricriu is to do what they can to bring misery and frustration into the lives of others. Perhaps they feel some satisfaction from it, though I cannot tell you what that may be. Bricriu was only one of many, like Bald Conan of the great Fianna of Leinster, who did wonders both to aid and to harm his leader, Fionn, and like Efnisien of Dyfed, who caused the great and ruinous war between Eire and the Isle of the Mighty, which left almost none alive, and which he finally ended himself by bursting the Cauldron of Life that was reviving the Gaels as fast as they were killed, and bursting his own heart in the effort.

Now our troublemaker, Bricriu, had only recently built himself a great eating hall, and wished to give a feast to inaugurate it. He knew, of course, that the Uledhmen did not trust him. They expected some kind of mischief if they came. And right they were, of course. But Bricriu knew too much.

For instance, had he not been the only one to notice that this one fellow was once taken by the screaming panics? And even though he had done his part in every battle since then, it would not do for Bricriu to spread the tale. And did Bricriu not happen along just at the moment when an otherwise respectable wife had decided to treat herself to a bathe in the nearby stream, and happened to be standing waist-deep in the water and in the altogether when a young, handsome herdsman walked by? Not that anything was done, you see — especially since Bricriu made his presence known very soon — but it was unfortunate that the lady and the boy had gazed at each other a bit too long and perhaps a bit too longingly, and the guilty knowledge of that temporary aberration, pleasant though it was, made it impossible for the lady to refuse something reasonable like an invitation. So she worked to make sure that her man would accept. And so it went, with some accepting because they had little choice, and others because they saw their comrades accepting. All of them thought: What can he do, after all, but play a few pranks? He had played tricks before, but no one had been hurt. What they did not know was that Bricriu had planned only one trick for this occasion, but it would be the trick of all tricks.

For Bricriu, like all men, wished to be the best of what he was. What did it matter that once he had boasted he had the power to "set brother against brother, father against son, wife against husband and sister against sister, until no peaceful spot remains in the land"? His mischief-making until now had been petty. He hungered to do something truly, heroically mischievous. Something that would live in the tales of future generations. And for that he had to make use of true heroes.

CúChulainn was the key — the one who could spoil it all by holding back. Carefully choosing a time when Gowen was not in Conchobar's great house, but was walking the walls as he sometimes did, Bricriu clambered up the parallel steps and onto the horizontal surface of the wall, falling into step and speaking instantly, but with studied casualness.

"Glad I am that you and your good wife will be coming to my small festivity, O CúChulainn. I will search out and provide the very best of everything — the best of drink, the best of bards, the best of succulent roasting pigs."

"Um," said Gowen, who wanted to be polite, but did not care at this moment what was to be set in front of him.

"And I have myself the most magnificent of all roasting pigs, which I have saved for such an occasion as this."

"Um, mm hmm," said Gowen, trying to work up some enthusiasm, but still staring into the distance, seeing phantom warriors and phantom battles yet to be fought.

"And of course, I would wish the greatest of all warriors in Uledh to have the Champion's Portion."

"Ah, of course," Gowen said, now that his attention had been captured. "You mean Conall, who has already shown himself to be champion of all Eire."

"Well, yes, that is impressive. But that was a long time ago, and much has happened since then."

"Well, if not Conall, then Loeghaire, who is not named 'the Triumphant' for no reason." Gowen's accustomed modesty was being sorely tested, but he did not want to fall into the trap of competing with his friends and comrades-in-arms.

"Loeghaire has truly been triumphant — many times. But there is none at all in Uledh that compares to CúChulainn. And none with more right to claim the Champion's Portion!"

"Um," said Gowen again, trying to recapture his air of disinterest. But it wasn't entirely possible, after all. He knew that he had a claim to being the best in the land. On the other hand, these were his friends...

"I see," murmured Bricriu, perceiving that flattery would not make his point. "Well, I have heard some say that Conall or Loeghaire had the greater claim."

"Um, um," mumbled Gowen. But he wondered to himself, "Who exactly are these others, then? And why do they think that?"

"I have heard it said," continued Bricriu, lying audaciously, "that Loeghaire himself has wondered how far you would have come, if his own father had not sponsored you and watched over you."

"If he said that," Gowen snapped angrily, then caught himself, "then he may have thought he had cause. Roigh has been a good friend and protector from the time I was new here," he finished weakly.

"Of course, of course, and it is really of no importance that so many of the men believe that you have been unduly favored above all others, and that you would avoid a true challenge from Muirchedach or Conall or

Loeghaire."

"And if they believe that, they are..." Gowen began angrily, then, disgusted with himself, he continued, "What does it matter? Speculation is not reality."

"True, true, and I do not believe those who say that you would shrink from claiming the Champion's Right, if you had to face any one of the others to do it."

"I would take it if I chose!" said Gowen, and stalked away, sure in his own mind of his meaning, and soon forgot the conversation.

Not so Bricriu, who bit his lip as he watched Gowen descending the steps along the inside of the wall, and hoped that he would not come back to retract his last words. As the small figure receded, he breathed a sigh of relief, clambered into his chariot and ordered his gillie to drive to Roigh's *dún*. Loeghaire, who found it comfortable to remain in the seat of his family holdings, had his own longhouse there. Bricriu knew that Fedelm would be alone at this time, since Loeghaire and Roigh would be riding their borders, seeing to their cattle and fields. It was not without reason that Fedelm was considered one of the most beautiful women of the Uledh — clear blue eyes, blonde hair, a lithe figure and and a sweet smile that melted men's hearts in their chests. The admiration she inspired in men's eyes was matched by the envious glances women directed at her heroic husband.

Bricriu found Fedelm at home, gazing raptly into the polished metal surface of a small hand mirror, slowly closing first one eye and then the other. A close observer of his fellow human beings, Bricriu suspected that Fedelm was inspecting the corners of her eyes, hoping not to discover the beginning of those tiny wrinkles that herald the beginning of dignity but the end of beauty.

"A mirror is not capable of rendering beauty like yours," he said silkily.

Fedelm was not startled. She expected any man within speaking distance to be concentrating on her magnificent face and figure. She inhaled deeply, as if breathing in the compliment and tore her gaze from the mirror, just as she thought she might have detected the tiniest beginning of a line at the outside of one eye.

"And for myself, I still believe that golden hair and azure eyes are the most beautiful of all. I pay no attention to what others say," Bricriu continued.

"What others say about what?" Fedelm demanded sharply.

"Oh, only those with no true appreciation of beauty who are singing the praises of CúChulainn's new bride. I admit that she is lovely for a black-haired woman, but..."

"Well," Fedelm tossed her head and pointedly raised the mirror to her eyes again, "they may think what they will. Others know better." And she turned her head to smile so fetchingly at Bricriu that he almost forgot why he had come.

"True beauty knows its own worth," he murmured sycophantically. "Even so, it is hard to hear those same voices saying that CúChulainn is the foremost of all the warriors of Uledh, and that when he takes the Champion's Portion at my feast, it will be the triumph of the greatest beauty and greatest warrior united."

Fedelm looked up sharply from her mirror again.

"It is with prowess in war as it is with beauty. There will always be disagreements. And I would not say anything against those who are our friends and supports in troubled times. Emher and CúChulainn have ever been gracious to us."

"Oh, aye, I have noticed that the high and mighty have a goodly supply of grace for those they know to be inferior."

"That," said Fedelm, "is enough and to spare! Be off to ruin someone else's day! And do not count us among those who will attend your feast."

"Yes," Bricru replied mournfully. "It is as I thought. You are too generous-minded to believe that the Hound of Chulainn has already said that he will take the Champion's Portion if he chooses to, despite all that Conall or Loeghaire may do to the contrary, or even together.

"And, of course, if he does, and Emher arrives first among women at the feast, it will only lend support to those wagging tongues I mentioned. It saddens me indeed to see arrogance triumph unopposed.

"Well, forgive my overzealous devotion to you and your good husband. I am sure that you are right. Nothing is to be gained by a futile attempt to deny what is written in the stone of the ages. I bid you good day and leave you, as always with my deepest admiration."

And so, smirking to himself, Bricriu betook himself to his chariot and bade the gillie to drive to Conall's *dún*, where he had a similar conversation with Lendabair.

The result of these conversations must be clear. It was as you would expect. Even the best of wills can be overwhelmed by a feeling that the heroic service or the extraordinary beauty one offers are under-valued. And so, in turn, both Loeghaire and Conall announced their intention to claim the Champion's Portion.

One further visit by Bricriu to Emher completed the ensnaring of her husband. When she heard what the other champions and their wives had said (augmented and altered judiciously by Bricriu), she was determined that he should claim the Champion's Portion and, further, that she would be the first of the women to be seated.

To be doubly sure that none who had accepted would find reason to change their minds, Bricriu had commissioned his new feast hall to be, in one respect, unlike any other of its kind. For himself and his wife he had an enclosed balcony built onto the outside of the hall, with an opening into the interior, so that he could see and be seen, hear and be heard, but the assembled revellers would not be annoyed or threatened by his immediate presence, and he would not be within reach if they should happen to take offence at something he said or did. The very fact that he was willing to go to such lengths to entice the flower of Uledh to his halls should perhaps have caused some second thoughts, but it did not, and so preparations were made, and the day finally arrived.

Part III: The feast

It was the custom at that time for the men to go on ahead, to "warm up the hall" with a few toasts. By the time the women arrived, they were not surprised to find their men in various stages of good cheer, from jolly to prostrate, depending on how fast they drank and how great their capacity. The one thing they expected of them was a welcome in accord with the trouble they had taken to be as beautiful as they could be. On the day of the feast, therefore, the men set off in their chariots, shouting and laughing to one another, already anticipating a day of eating, drinking, jesting and boasting.

The women were more on their dignity. They met, by long-standing tradition, at Conchobar's *dún*, to make the walk together. It was not a long walk, the day was pleasant, and each of them was a magnificent sight by herself. Fedelm, Lendabair and Emher, coming as they did from the households of the greatest heroes, each set out with a small retinue of handsome, well-dressed young women.

Unlike the unruly departure of the men, the women's progress began sedately, with greeting of friends, subdued conversations, mild laughter. There was, of course, a tendency for all, including those most concerned, to inspect the comparative splendour of Emher, Lendabair and Fedelm. Except for Bricriu's malicious preparation, it would have been possible to say that they were all three splendid, and have done with it. As it was, the three women in question began now and then to glance — always smiling — at each other and compare the gleaming of hair, the flowing colour of the brat—the long, handsome, woollen cloak covered with clever stitched patterns and sparkling fibulae and other pins, the rich weightiness of brooch, the elegant twisting of the neck torque. And as they reached the crest of the first, modest hill, it seemed as if this inattention to their pace had made one of them — no one was quite sure who — step out a bit more vigorously than the others. The others, of course, did not wish to forfeit the chance of being the first into the hall and the first honoured, so they too increased their pace, just a bit. Conversation, which had flowed easily, now faltered a bit, as the rivals looked back and forth at each other and moved just a little faster, and then, just a little faster again. By the time they topped the second, small rise, conversation was staccato and disengaged, the pace had become a somewhat faster walk, here and there unruly hairs floated loose from the gleaming mass and gave the impression that all was not quite as well as it had been. As they started up the last, small rise, more than a few hairs had broken loose, some fibulae holding the brat or even the underlying linen of the tunic had twisted sideways — disfiguring the shape of both garments; worst of all, sweat spots began to appear at strategic points. There was now no conversation. Only panting. As they topped the last hill, the walk that had become a canter that had become a trot, now became a gallop, and the only noise other than feet striking the ground was a breathing and snorting that sounded for all the world like the laboured efforts of a hard-driven horse.

In the feast hall, the men had begun to drink, but were still on their good behaviour, because they expected the women any moment. Suddenly, one of the men raised his head from his drinking horn and, nose and lips still dripping, asked, "What is that then that is making such a noise?"

Others dragged their faces from their drinks and cocked their ears.

"It's an attack! We're set upon by some cunning enemy, come to catch us in our drink!"

But another, recognizing the truth of the situation, cried, "It's the women are coming! And if we don't open the door to them, they'll knock it down about our ears and kill us all!"

Gowen, Loeghaire and Conall each recognized that his wife would expect to be the first into the hall. Loeghaire and Conall leapt as one for the door and met before it, each straining to stand in the entry-way and restrain his rival from doing the same. As the Uledhmen looked on in fear, wonder and amusement, the two great heroes began to beat each other on head and shoulders with open hands and closed fists. And neither gave way. The men in the hall held their collective breath.

Gowen, seeing the futility of being a third in the battle for the door, walked to a spot on the wall between two of the great posts, placed his hands flat against the wall and gave one, mighty heave. A portion of the wall crashed outward. He stepped outside and was seen by Emher, who entered the hall first and with as much dignity as it is possible to have when entering a feast through a hole in the wall. Loeghaire and Conall, hearing the cheers of their comrades, looked around and saw that Gowen had bested them. Crestfallen but determined not to lose a second time, they stood aside from the door and led their ladies inside.

The cheer had not been for Gowen and Emher alone, but for a side effect of Gowen's assault on the wall. For the force of his blow had dislodged Bricriu and his wife from their outside perch and dropped them into the cook's refuse pit outside. As angry and offended as a chicken ducked in a tub of water, they climbed wetly and noisomely back up to their balcony seats. Bricriu saw that he must regain control of the situation and ordered a massive influx of drink and then the entry of the main course: a massive boar surrounded by spitted suckling pigs. Still dripping grease and offal, Bricriu rose to set his prank in play.

"It is happy I am to see all the greatest warriors of Uledh with us here today! I call on those who have a claim to the Champion's Portion of the great pig to come forward and state their claim."

No one stirred. It was as if all three of the contenders were embarrassed. Perhaps they were even wondering about taking part in all this. But Bricriu was not to be thwarted. He stared across the hall at Roigh and said:

"It is you, Roigh, who best knows the strengths of your own son. How do you say to the proposition that he should be declared the Champion of all Uledh?"

As one, Conall, Loeghaire and Gowen rose to their feet. No more than Loeghaire would Gowen or Conall allow Roigh to be made responsible for this choice. But each, seeing the other two standing, thought to himself:

"So it's that way is it? Well, we'll see about that."

And each of them took a determined step toward the pig. They were stopped in their tracks by the authoritative voice of Cathbad.

"If contest there must be, it will not be here, where every one of us can be drawn into it. Let a fair task be set or a fair judge be found away from this place."

Conchobar looked thoughtful and spoke for the first time.

"Though she is no friend to us, Mebd of Connaught fears no man and will have no favourites among us. Let us send a rich gift with our three champions and the request for a fair judgment among them."

The hall roared approval, and so it was decided. Each one carrying part of the treasure, the heroes set out on the road to Connaught.

Part IV: The trials

They had not gone far, when they encountered fierce winds, dark clouds and a driving rain. As they struggled forward, each one was picked out of his chariot by what seemed to be a huge hand and thrown against a rock or a tree, where they lay for a time unconscious. First Conall and then Loeghaire woke, looked around him, saw nothing of the other two or of their chariots and set off home on foot. They arrived at Conchobar's *dún* moments apart and from separate directions, as the late sun stood in the sky.

When they had told their tale, Conchobar asked, "And what of CúChulainn?" But they could not tell him.

As dusk settled and the men sat at drink grumbling over the disaster that Bricriu's feast had brought on them, a lookout entered, shouting, "There is the dust of chariots on the road and coming at a great speed."

They all rushed outside in time to see Gowen, driving one chariot and leading two others, swirl up the entry road and into the *dún*.

He told much the same story as Conall and Loeghaire, adding that he had wandered around and finally found tracks which led him to first one chariot, then another. Nothing had been broken, nothing taken. It was like some great joke played by the gods.

Bricriu, who had spent what seemed like a very long time listening to the threats muttered against him, repented — not the results of his prank but their possible consequences for him. Best to make an end of it.

"It is a judgment!" he cried, "And it shows that CúChulainn deserves the Champion's Portion."

A roar of approval from some of the men was met by a cry of derision from others.

"It is no fair judgment! It is a happenstance! Let them go on to Mebd!"

And so they set off again, and this time came safely within sight of the great walls of Mebd's huge *rath*. Mebd and her king, Aillil, were walking in quiet conversation along the wooden platform inside the wall, when the lookout peering over the wooden palisade called:

"Chariots approach, three, each with a gillie and a warrior!"

"Describe the warriors," called Mebd.

"In the first chariot is a large, red-haired man, with a red cloak about his shoulders and a long, red-handled sword."

"It's Loeghaire," muttered Aillil. "What does he seek here?"

"In the second is a great, yellow-haired man, with a blue cloak about his shoulders and a long, blue-handled sword."

"Conall, the Hundred-Killer," murmured Mebd.

"In the last chariot is a small, dark, sad-eyed man who wears no cape and drives while his gillie stands behind him."

"That's Loeghaire, Conall and CúChulainn," said Mebd. "Give them passage in and make them welcome. We will not start a war with these three if we can avoid it. Let us see what they want from us."

Three great heroes of Uledh stood before the mightiest woman ruler and warrior in all of Eire, who looked down at them from her raised seat. As always, when she was consciously serving in her capacity as queen or judge or warrior, Mebd's two ravens perched, one on each shoulder.

"How is it then that we can serve three great heroes?" she inquired.

When she had heard their story, no flicker of emotion showed in her features. She bade them be comfortable: eat, drink and sleep, and she would address them again in the morning. Then she and Aillil retired to their own bed, where most of their weighty decisions were made. Between Mebd and Aillil, there was mutual respect and sexual attraction, but also the tension which exists between two strong personalities. When they married, Aillil was already a king in his own right in a province of Leinster, but the love of Mebd and the power of Connaught were powerful attractions, and so he had come to Connaught as a king-consort, but he felt himself in no way Mebd's inferior. This usually meant that any decision they arrived at was well-argued and finely honed. When they could not agree, it could be disastrous, as we shall see later.

In this case, as Mebd summarized their discussion, their choice was clear.

"If we turn them away, we will have earned their hatred and the hatred of the Uledh to no purpose. If we oblige them, we will oblige Conchobar and all his people, and no war will happen until we wish it. And if the tests we give them are cleverly thought, we will do ourselves a service"

"But," Aillil replied, "if we judge among them, we will have two enemies we did not have before."

"As to that," said Mebd, "I have an idea that will gain us three friends instead of one, and cause friend Conchobar no end of trouble when they return." And she smiled a smile of malicious delight.

In the morning, she addressed the three heroes again. Again, her personal ravens sat on her shoulders. Some said that they symbolized the Morrigan, the Battle Crow — the ancient spirit of battle that sometimes appeared to individuals as a woman, sometimes over battlefields as a gigantic crow.

"You are well come to us," Mebd said. "As it happens, there are three equal and annoying problems on us. Three powerful families have refused us allegiance and have caused unrest in our kingdom." (When Mebd said "we" it was not always clear whether she spoke the royal "we" or meant to include Aillil.) "To prove you are best, we ask each of you to subdue one of these families, one warrior at a time or all together, however you choose. We will judge the results of each attempt and award a trophy to show our decision."

It was clear to the three heroes that Mebd was using them to solve a domestic problem. But they had asked for a judgment, and could in no way refuse the task. What they did not know, was that Mebd had carefully graded the tasks, giving the most powerful and difficult family to Gowen, the next most difficult to Conall and the third to Loeghaire. It was her estimate of their abilities — ironically the very judgment that Bricriu had tried to proclaim only a short time before.

No matter. Each of them went at his task with a passion and thoroughly terrified the family in question. Gowen was the first to return, then Conall and Loeghaire together. Mebd said that she wished to speak with each of them alone, and first called Loeghaire into her throne room. As Loeghaire stepped before her, his face betraying a mixture of pride and apprehension, Mebd spoke, holding a bronze drinking bowl out to him.

"This is your trophy, O Loeghaire, read the inscription."

On the base of the bowl was the ogham inscription. "Loeghaire, Champion of Uledh."

Glowing with triumph, Loeghaire dashed from the room, past his companions without saying a word, leapt into his chariot and ordered the gillie to drive for Conchobar's *dún*.

Next, Mebd called Conall, who left just as Loeghaire had left, and finally Gowen, who left also, but somewhat more thoughtfully.

The first to arrive at Conchobar's *dún* was Loeghaire, who proudly displayed his bronze bowl and was admired and congratulated by all. Into this general hubbub stepped Conall, who inquired what was happening and was told that Loeghaire had been declared Champion of Uledh.

"Not so!" he roared, brandishing a silver bowl that read, "Conall, Champion of Uledh."

Confusion, shouting, arguments. And then Gowen arrived.

Conchobar cast a suspicious eye at him and asked, "And what do you bring with you, O CúChulainn?"

Gowen answered by holding out a a golden bowl which read: "CúChulainn, Champion of Uledh."

It was a near thing indeed, whether there would be war right there in the king's own house, between the supporters of each hero. Each party claimed victory, despite the fact that the worth of the metals in each bowl told its own story. First Gowen, then Conall, then Loeghaire — that was the hidden judgment. But none would accede.

Again it was Cathbad who offered a solution.

"There is only one other in all of Eire who has a power and knowledge to match Mebd, and that is Cúroi mac Dáiri of Munster. Let them go to him and let us hope in the Dagda's name that he will give us a clear answer."

Now of the four provinces of Eire at that time, each was independent of the others and each was regarded by the druids as the ancient home of one of the peoples that had settled the land. In the land of the Uledh had settled the next-to-last invaders before the Gaels — the ancestors of the peoples of all four provinces. These next-to-last invaders were the Fir Bolg, who were connected in the druids' mysteries with the signs of power and battle. In Connaught had settled the last of the Tuatha de Danaan, before they spread out over all of the land to live in hills and lakes under the surface. This heritage marked Connaught as the land of magic and Mebd as a powerful sorceress and seer. In Leinster had settled the simple farmers and hunters who had come before the Tuatha, and so Leinster, later the land of the great Fionn mac Cumhaill, defender of Eire against outsiders and champion of the common folk, was the land of forest, stream and field, where the hunter was warrior and the warrior was hunter. And instead of one ruler, there were several, smaller kings, who cooperated in time of need.

To the fourth province in the south — Munster — had come the first settlers of Eire, who were outcasts from their own societies. As so often happens, those cast out of one society, when they go elsewhere, form a stable and powerful society of their own. For reasons not entirely clear, Munster was identified by the druids with music and death. Cúroi was the enigmatic ruler of this kingdom. A skilled and powerful warrior, he was said to have powers that rivalled those of Mebd.

Again Loeghaire, Conall and Gowen set out — this time on an even longer trek — and bearing the richest gifts Conchobar could contrive. When they arrived before the massive walls of Cúroi's *dún*, the outer guards stood quietly aside as if they had been expecting them, as did the guards at the gate at the top of the curving ramp and then those below inside the walls. As they dismounted from their chariots, Cúroi himself strolled toward them, dressed as Gowen had last seen him, in his leather and hide hunter's clothes, his tall, thin hound loping along behind.

"Three great warriors of the Uledh are welcome to my home and to my services..." And then, as the three opened their mouths to speak, he continued, aiming his grey gaze at Gowen. "We shall begin the judgment tomorrow, when you have had the chance to eat and drink and rest."

And he led the open-mouthed three into a round house where a great feast was prepared. To each of them was brought an exactly equal portion of beef and pork, and all that they could drink. As they relaxed, one of Cúroi's bards sang familiar and unfamiliar songs of adventure and heroism, until the three fell asleep almost at the same time.

When they woke, they were alone and all signs of the feast had been cleared. By common consent, they went out at the door and walked the *dún*, but caught no sight of Cúroi. They were fed in their own house again and then wandered some more, feeling more and more that they did not understand what was happening. In the evening, they were summoned to Cúroi's longhouse for a big meal, after which they and all of Cúroi's people fell silent.

"The reason you are here is to decide which of you deserves the title of champion among your people. My people tell me that a giant of a man wanders outside these walls at night, and none will face him. I myself have never wanted to test the truth of it. I will put you one after the other to a simple test. You will bide outside the walls for one night and we will see how you fare. On the third night, I will give my decision. Tonight it is to Loeghaire to go outside."

And so, not knowing what must await him, Loeghaire trudged through the gate whose great wooden door creaked closed behind him, down the ramp to the plain and seated himself with his back to a great oak tree and his spears and sword by his side. It was a dim night, feebly lit through the clouds by scraps of light from the moon and stars. At first, pure excitement kept him wide awake, but after a time, his eyelids grew heavy and he nearly dozed. Suddenly, a huge figure appeared out of the darkness, moving toward him. Loeghaire jumped to his feet, gripping his short, throwing spear and peering intently toward the oncoming giant. He was the stuff of tales told to children — huge, bearded, wild-haired, covered to his knees by one shaggy pelt, the rest of his legs and his feet bare.

"Ho, pipsqueak, throw your splinter before I mash you up to feed my horse," he roared, and took two faster steps toward Loeghaire, who threw with all his might at the giant's chest. The javelin struck the furry hide and fell to the ground.

Seeing this, Loeghaire reached past his long, stabbing spear and took hold of his heavy, slashing spear. Holding it in front of him with both hands, he ran straight at the huge figure. Loeghaire was no coward, and he would not give way to any threat, no matter how great. The heavy, broad head of his spear slanted upward toward the giant's chest, he ran with all his great strength, shouting out a battle cry as he anticipated the jolt of contact along his arms.

Just before that could happen, a hand that looked as big as a young boar reached down to grasp the shaft of the spear and lift upward with such speed that Loeghaire — still holding it — was carried high into the air, where the other immense hand grasped him around the middle, squeezed until it seemed that his ribs would crack, and then threw him and the spear over the wall, deep into the *dún*.

There he lay, groaning and breathing, until he heard the first sounds of awakening. Pride overcame misery, and he used the spear to haul himself erect, where he stood, swaying and cursing and waiting for the others to discover him.

When the first man came upon him, he shouted in amazement.

"Hail to Loeghaire! He has fought a great battle with the giant and then jumped over the wall to be here when we awake."

As I said, Loeghaire was no coward. He was also no fool, and he did not deny this miraculous explanation. Conall and Gowen, seeing the terrible condition he was in, went cold inside and wondered what had happened outside. Now when Loeghaire drank, he talked and laughed and told tales of himself and many other things. But that day, he began to drink in the morning; he drank steadily and stared into the brown liquid and uttered never a word. All those who gathered round waited in vain for his story; they hung on every sound as if it was the beginning of a tale, and they sagged in disappointment as the day wore on and Loeghaire finally slumped over and slept. Cúroi only sat and looked thoughtful and did not once ask. As dusk crept in at the door, he said only, "It is to Conall tonight."

You may guess that it went the same with Conall as with Loeghaire. Conall's throw was just a bit harder, his charge just a bit more powerful, but the result was the same. When he, too, was discovered leaning on his spear, Loeghaire was among the first observers. They gazed intently at one another, but said not a word. Conall did not take to drink, but pretended to, stared into his horn all day long and did not utter a word of explanation. As dusk fell, Cúroi said only, "It is to CúChulainn," and Gowen was escorted to the gate.

Of what happened next there are differing versions. I will tell you the most elaborate and let you decide what to believe. This tale tells us that Gowen had barely sat down by the same oak, when the local ogre and his three sons happened by, on their way to attack the neighbouring village and eat a few of it inhabitants. They were persuaded to change their minds. It was difficult not to, when their heads were separated from their bodies.

Next, the nearby lake revealed an unwelcome surprise. Out of its depths came a snake-like creature of great size, already opening its maw to swallow the small fellow who was once again resting under the oak tree after his tussle with the local ogre family. Without a thought, Gowen leapt straight into the monster's mouth, pulled its tongue out by the roots, reached down its gullet and ripped out its heart. The creature was so stupid that it took several moments for the information to reach its tiny brain, and when it did, the creature dropped dead in its tracks.

According to this version, Gowen had already had a hard night when the giant arrived. All versions agree on what happened next. When the giant appeared as expected and issued his challenge, Gowen reacted oddly. He sprang away from all his weapons and his shield and ran toward the giant, veering slightly to the left. As the giant bent and reached for him, Gowen closed his eyes, bent his legs and did the best salmon leap he had done since crossing the bridge to Scáthach's land. He leapt in the same direction he had begun to run, passing the giant to the left — the giant's right. The giant turned right, reaching again and just missing a grip on Gowen's leg as Gowen rolled head-over-heels and landed on his feet still running in the same direction. The giant turned and turned again. Gowen raced on, jumping, rolling, running, now and then using the salmon leap when the giant's hand came a bit too close. On and on he raced, always in the same direction. Round and round the giant turned, bending and reaching, turning, bending and reaching. Until, as Gowen began to wonder if his breath and legs would fail him, the giant stumbled, tottered, stopped still, holding both hands to his forehead and groaning at the vertigo he had created by his high-speed rotations. Then he sat heavily, sending a small tremour through the earth.

"Enough, O Cúchulainn. Enough! I yield. My eyes cannot see, my head aches and my guts long to puke up my dinner. Go with my blessing."

Gowen eyed him doubtfully, his muscles tensed for quick movement. But the giant rolled to his hands and knees, groaning, stood up slowly and moved painfully away in the direction from which he came.

"Well," Gowen thought, "this has gone well. I am not bruised and battered like Loeghaire and Conall. All I have to do is leap over the wall with my spear as they did, and I will be done."

He measured the distance with his eyes, then he ran strongly and heavily at the wall, at the last minute driving both feet into the ground with tremendous force and launched himself into the air.

Splat!

He hit the palisade set in the top of the wall below the top and fell to the ground.

"What is this now? Is it that Loeghaire and Conall both can jump better than I? I will not believe it!"

He backed away from the wall and tried again, but this time, he ran lightly as a butterfly, almost running across the tips of the blades of grass, and at the last possible moment, sailed loftily through the air with the spear held high and his other arm stretched toward the top of the wall.

Splat!

Again he fell at the base of the wall — dirty, tired, bruised and disgusted.

"If I do not succeed in this, I will lose. I do not care if one of us does not win, but I will not lose!"

As he said this, the Rage came over him as if he were in battle; red washed across his sight; his blood seethed. He stood in one quick motion and, without thinking about it, made the greatest salmon leap he had ever made, over the wall and deep into the dún, where he stood and waited to be discovered.

When the others came, they said all the same things they had said about Conall and Loeghaire. Conall and Loeghaire smiled a conspiratorial smile at each other and at Gowen, who smiled back, because he believed he had done only what they had done.

But when they all went in to Cúroi, it was not as they had expected.

Seated on a low, earthen bench, flanked by his reclining hound, his rejection of the trappings of power made him more rather than less impressive. As he sat and stared at them thoughtfully, the three Uledhmen shifted uneasily from foot to foot. As the silence became unbearably long, they breathed, sighed, stretched, scratched and waited. Finally, his cool, grey eyes focused on them and he spoke.

"You came here hoping — or perhaps not hoping — for a decision in your competition. Now, after three nights, you are each expecting to hear that there is no decision. That is because none of you can know what I know."

Again, a long, uninterrupted silence. Then Cúroi looked each one of them in the eyes and said, "Each of you knows what he himself did. Each of you acted with courage and honour. Each of you did what he was capable of doing. One of you was capable of more. The champion of the Uledh is CúChulainn!"

Three pairs of eyes stared in shock. Three jaws dropped in disbelief. Heat rose like a flame to Loeghaire's and Conall's faces, while cold seeped downward into Gowen's guts.

Part V: The championship

Three heroes had ridden to Munster with purpose and some apprehension. Three heroes rode home in complete confusion. For those waiting at home, they had no explanation for Curoi's judgment — only the bald fact that he had made it. Each faction muttered and complained. In the end, by unspoken agreement, the championship was forgotten. Life, other feasts and other battles, went on.

At one such feast — this one in Conchobar's Great House — the eating was done, the drinking was well underway and the storytelling had begun. Gowen, Conall and Loeghaire were not in attendance, but Muirchedach was, and It was to him to tell the tale of his latest raid into Leinster, and he was warming to his story, when a shadow fell across the gathering and everyone looked to the entrance. Towering over the seated and reclining men stood a fearsome figure. Taller by a head than any man there, he was dressed in the rough jerkin of a *bachlach* — a poor man of the soil — except that the garment's colour was an unnatural green. Under one arm, he held a heavy block of wood. From his other hand hung a great, double-bladed axe. Slowly, his shaggy head turned in a semicircle, scanning the room, and he said: "I have come to see, is it true what they say, that the Uledhmen are the bravest of all the warriors in Eire. I have a little game to play with you."

He dropped the heavy block with a mighty thump and leaned on his axe.

"Who has the courage to try my little game? Tonight, I will stretch my neck out on the block, and whoever chooses may take the axe and see, can he strike off my head. The only condition is that you will be here tomorrow to let me do the same to you."

At first, there was amazed silence, then uproarious, incredulous laughter, but the *bachlach* was unperturbed.

"Come, has none of you even the courage to take such a fair offer, or does the true Uledhman —" and he looked slowly around at the remnants of food and drink, "eat like a boar and run like a hare?"

This was too much for Muirchedach. Up he jumped and took the axe by its handle from the *bachlach's* unresisting hands.

"Lay down your head, big man! After you feel the whack I give you, you are welcome to get up and leave."

Muirchedach laughed and every man there laughed with him. The *bachlach* merely knelt without a word and placed his thick neck across the block. Unbelief hung heavy in the air. Even Muirchedach could not believe what he was seeing.

"O, what a foolish man you are indeed!" he cried. "But a pledge is a pledge, and you will suffer the payment of your own foolhardiness."

Muirchedach raised the great axe with some difficulty high above his head, then brought it down whistling with its own speed and struck entirely through the neck of the *bachlach*. The wild-haired head jumped loose and bounced across the floor to lie at Conchobar's feet. The axe dropped with a clang from Muirchedach's hands. There was no sound in the hall. No one knew a word to say or even a thought to think.

As they sat in stunned silence, the headless trunk seemed to slip sideways from the block, but, at the last moment, one large hand slapped down on the floor, the muscles of the large arm flexed, both big legs tensed, and the body slowly stood up. Before the eyes of the of the stupefied Uledhmen, the body picked up the block and tucked it under its left arm, picked up the axe and took hold of it with its left hand. Finally, it reached down again with its right hand to pick up the severed head by its hair, turned, and unhurriedly walked out of the hall.

Finally, into the silence came Conchobar's voice, "We will all be together here again tomorrow."

There was no doubt that this was a command, not a prediction, and yet behind the usual tone of authority, everyone detected a whisper of fear, even in the voice of the king.

The next night saw a very subdued gathering, with little eating or drinking. Dread hung on the company and none wished to speak of why, so that Loeghaire — newly returned from his travels — had just begun to wonder at the pall that hung over Conchobar's hall when the *bachlach* lumbered in again, dropping his block with a sound that seemed to shake the entire house, and said, "Where is Muirchedach?"

Silence. Muirchedach was nowhere to be seen.

"Is this the bravery of Uledh? Is he afraid to face me? Who will answer for him?"

Without hesitation, Loeghaire stood and said, "I will answer for him. There is no man braver than Muirchedach. What is your demand of him?"

"Only that he play my little game, and he has fled rather than play it." The *bachlach* smiled unpleasantly. "It is called the Beheading Game. You have only to strike off my head, and promise to be here tomorrow night, if I should return to do the same to you."

Why did no one speak up to warn Loeghaire that it was a game he could not win? I was not there, but I have been told that a strange dread lay upon the whole company, such that they felt they could not speak when the *bachlach* was present. So Loeghaire accepted the challenge and, like Muirchedach, struck the head from the body cleanly. As before, the headless body collected its block, its axe and its head and walked out of the hall. As before, Conchobar ordered them to be present the next night. As before, no one spoke and the company quietly slipped away until Conchobar was alone with Cathbad.

"What does it mean, O druid?" he asked plaintively.

"It is a magic and a power unknown to me," replied the druid, "but it is of our people and something great will come of this. Whether to good or ill, I cannot say."

And Conchobar had to be content with that, because Cathbad would say no more.

On the third night, just as Conall had returned from his foray into Connaught, the *bachlach* appeared again and, as you have guessed, taunted the Uledhmen and the absent Loeghaire until Conall could stand it no longer and accepted the challenge. And as before, the headless body collected its wooden block, its axe and its head and departed.

On the fourth night, Gowen had just returned from a trip with Emher to her holdings in Leinster, and when he approached the king's *dún*, he saw the last of the men entering. He followed them inside the walls and into Conchobar's Great House, where everyone sat in unaccustomed silence, eating and drinking. No one sang, no one shouted, no one jumped up to call the man on his right or left a liar and offer to cut off his head. It was a very odd night. Gowen kept his own counsel and waited. He knew that he would learn sooner or later what had caused this unusual civility.

Suddenly, it seemed as if even the subdued eating and drinking had ceased, and he looked toward the entrance, where he saw the *bachlach* for the first time.

"Well, this must be the cause of all the quiet," he thought. "What could such a rough fellow be seeking here? And more to the point, why hasnt't he been thrown out already?"

"Conall!" bawled the big man. "Loeghaire! Muirchedach! They are after leaving the country as fast as they can! Are these sneaking cowards the best you have to offer? Are all Uledhmen chicken-livered, rabbit-hearted and empty-headed? Is there not a real man among you?" He paused. "I have met all but one of those who are supposed to be your best. Where is this pipsqueak, CúChulainn? Does he dare to show himself?"

Gowen sat quietly and said nothing, for he could make no sense of this. And he was not about to fight without knowing why.

The *bachlach* took one long step to stand towering over Gowen.

"Is it that you are afraid to face me in my Beheading Game? You get first blow, after all. Are you a coward like the rest? No! Worse! They did not take so long to challenge me."

Still, Gowen said nothing, did nothing.

"What a useless crowd of clods you all are! Not a warrior among you. And your women are no better. If they are all as ugly as Emher..."

Without thought, his sight washed in red, Gowen was on his feet, swinging his sword. The *bachlach's* head flew from his body. One big hand reached out casually to catch it in mid-air. Hanging from the hand, it stared at Gowen and said, "It is to you to be here tomorrow night, when I will take my return blow."

Once again, the Uledhmen went their separate ways, now completely dispirited. If these four could not stand up to the challenge of the Beheading Game, then they could all look forward to facing the *bachlach* and running away, until there was no honour left in Uledh and every wild gang in Eire would think their cattle and women fair game.

Gowen left thoughtfully, speaking to no one, and spent the night and the next day quietly with Emher. It was clear that something gnawed at him, but he would not speak of it, and so she comforted him with her love and did not ask. Emher was not the shy and diffident type of woman, but she had an instinct for those rare times when Gowen not only would not but could not speak of his troubles. She knew this time, and he knew that she knew, that something fateful was about to happen. They had no task for the time at hand but to hold on to one another.

And so, the next evening arrived. The silent company assembled to endure their shame once more. But in their midst sat Gowen, and the whisper ran round the hall, "Cú is here. Does he not understand? Who will tell him?"

It was not necessary to tell him — he knew well that his life was forfeit that night. So he did not shrink like the others when the *bachlach* walked into the hall and dropped his block on the floor with a thunderous thump.

"Where is CúChulainn? Where is the miserable runt? Has he joined his comrades in a trip to Tir-nan-Og across the sea to escape his pledge?"

The *bachlach* glared around the hall, where none would meet his eyes, until a quiet voice replied, "CúChulainn is here and is ready to fulfil his bargain."

Gowen stood and walked slowly to the bloodstained block, knelt and laid his neck across the flat, rough surface.

"You call that a neck, do you, Little Fellow? How can I hit such a puny target? Can you stretch it out at all, or is this all there is to you?"

Gowen stretched his head as far across the block as possible, then turned his head slightly and said, "It will get no better. Strike now."

Not a breath was breathed as the *bachlach* raised his great axe high over his head and held it there. For eternities he seemed to stand that way, but Gowen would neither look up nor shift his position. I believe if it had gone on much longer, the entire adult male population of Uledh would have died from lack of breathing. But he did not. The great axe swept back behind his head and then began a lightning swift descent, fast and hard enough to split the block after severing Gowen's neck.

Every ear heard the *Whoosh*! of the blade, and every eye followed the edge as it swooped down toward the block... and then, impossibly, the great muscles of the *bachlach's* arms stopped it a hair's breadth from Gowen's neck.

A moment of silence and then, holding the blade above an unmoving Gowen, the *bachlach* slowly raised his eyes to look at the transfixed men before him and said, in ringing tones: "Rise, CúChulainn, Champion of Uledh!"

As Gowen rose slowly and dazedly to his feet, the *bachlach's* features seemed to waver and fade and, for just a moment, everyone there who knew them recognized the features of Cúroi mac Dáiri.

Then it was over. The *bachlach* picked up his block and vanished out the exit.

Of course, it was not quite over. The men talked to each other. The women talked to each other. The children overheard and talked among themselves. Gradually, they realized that Cúroi's second test had taught them something. Because they would not accept his judgment of the best and most skilled, he had revealed another facet of heroism: humility and a sense of fair play that prevailed even if it meant sacrificing life itself. Loeghaire and Conall themselves said as much to Gowen and Loeghaire added, "And my father says to tell you that, if I didn't figure it out soon he would be after explaining it to me with the broad side of his sword blade."

They all three laughed, and that really was the end of it for everyone but Gowen, who still pondered what Cúroi had to do with him, and why he seemed so familiar.

Chapter Twelve
THE GATHERING STORM

Although begun by mischief and perpetuated by silliness, the Championship was brought to a conclusion by wisdom and magic. So Bricriu had his wish in a way he could not have foreseen. His prank became not just the greatest of all pranks, but the greatest of all stories told in Uledh — a high point in history, after which much else that happened seemed ordinary.

Life returned to its accustomed path. The men of Uledh fought, feasted, loved and laughed. The women of Uledh loved them and put up with them. Only one shadow lay upon Gowen and Emher, who understood each other almost without speaking. They had no children: none to carry on the name or tell the stories, begin new families or give comfort in old age. After a while, they grew accustomed to their lot and did not think of it often. Only once in a while, watching other people's children at play, did they feel a heavy sadness in their breasts, and reach out to take each other by the hand. Their understanding was not perfect, but was extraordinary, as was proven by a few incidents which preceded the final conflict and the completion of Gowen's destiny in Uledh.

One of these was the episode of Niamh of the Sidhe — the woman from the Fairy Mounds of the Tuatha. In the tongue, the word for woman was *ban*, and so a woman of the the Fairy Mound was a *ban sidhe*, pronounced banshee (as in screaming like a banshee — now you know where that phrase came from). As I told you, the people of the Sidhe sometimes mixed with the Gaels, even sometimes, as in Cathbad's story of the naming of Emain Macha, marrying them. Niamh was blonde, blue-eyed and beautiful, and desperately, forlornly in love with Gowen before she ever sought him out. It happened then, and no doubt still happens in your time, that a man or woman could briefly see or even merely hear the description of someone who seemed to be the epitome of all virtues and fall into a deep, melancholic desire to possess that person. The compulsion was no less than that which moved Gilfaethwy to desire Goewin.

Niamh first approached Gowen when he was alone, having ridden out without his gillie to reconnoitre an area in which a few too many cross-border raids had taken place. He was resting on the ground against an ancient oak, when a vision of beauty seemed to appear out of a mist and walk toward him, arms outstretched. As he stared bemused, her garments slipped from her and she stood naked before him. Gowen's immediate reaction was to avert his gaze in embarrassment, just as he had after the taking of weapons, when Conchobar had sent the women of Uledh against him. Niamh was perplexed and angry. No man had ever reacted this way to her offering of herself. She simply walked back into the mist and disappeared from Gowen's view. He blinked, and wondered if he was having a waking dream. Then he went on about his business and forgot the incident.

Niamh, meanwhile, did what many a wilful young woman may do when she is thwarted. She went to her father. This father, who could refuse her nothing, was a man of note among the people of the Sidhe, and skilled in the mysterious sciences known only to the druids among the Gaels, but common among the folk of the Fairy Mound. So it came about that Gowen became deathly ill and could not eat, sleep or drink. He wasted away before the alarmed eyes of Emher and his friends. Cathbad, when summoned, could only say sadly, "There is a magic here which will reveal itself. Without knowing what it is, I can do nothing. Even knowing it, I may be able to do nothing, for it seems a powerful and personal spell."

And so, they waited and worried. Until the red-haired boy. In Eire, there were many signs that something may have come from the Sidhe. One, almost certain sign was the sudden appearance of a red-haired boy who belonged to none of the local families. Such was this boy, who walked boldly into Gowen's *dún* and asked to speak to Emher. When she stepped forward, he said: "I come from Niamh, who has heard of your trouble and knows the cure. If you wish CúChulainn to be cured, you must bring him to the ancient oak near the sidhe of Aengus, and leave him there for a day and a night."

He turned without another word and walked away.

The sidhe of Aengus was known to all as the reputed dwelling of one of the most powerful of the Tuatha, who had once been their king. He was also known to have a soft spot for the surface-dwelling usurpers of his people's land — the Gaels — and appeared on occasion to help them in some crisis or endeavour. The choice of location was reassuring, and so Emher supervised the loading of her severely wasted husband into his own chariot and rode with him and his gillie to the indicated spot.

When they had arrived, however, she did not wish to leave him alone there, but he said, "If it is a cure there is to be, and these are the conditions, I am prepared to face them. Anything is better than being helpless like this."

So she did leave him, but sent the gillie back with instructions to wait just a short distance away.

Later, she went to find him and ask, "Did you see or hear anything in the time you have spent here?"

"Yes, lady," he answered somewhat tensely. "I have heard soft sounds."

"Sounds of distress?"

"Nnno... not of distress."

"Of comfort and easement of pain then?"

"Not exactly that either."

"Well, what then, man?!" she snapped, out of patience.

"Erm, ah, sat... satisfaction, I think. Yes." His frozen face muscles cracked slightly to allow a small smile of relief at having found the most useful phrase.

"Satisfaction?" Emher asked impatiently. "What does that mean — 'satisfaction'?"

But the gillie became embarrassed and tongue-tied and could say no more. Emher finally tired of questioning him and rode on to seek out her husband. Gowen was leaning against the ancient tree. His cheeks showed the flush of good health, his eyes were bright and alive, but wary, and would not meet Emher's gaze openly.

"Well, husband," she said, "it seems as if this mysterious woman has cured you indeed. I am very grateful to her. Where is she? I would like to thank her."

"She has not stayed for thanks, but has gone to her home in the Sidhe," he said.

"Well, I am grateful nonetheless. And now let us get you home."

"She... she did say that I might have to... take the cure again, if this one does not hold."

"We will deal with that if it happens to be," said Emher, and continued to supervise preparations for taking Gowen home again.

Gowen was his old self for the space of seven days. He and Emher seemed as happy as ever in each other's company, although he was more distant at times than she was used to, but he would not speak of it. Then he began to sicken again.

"It is what she said," he told Emher. "I must go back again."

"If you must, you must. Though I do not like it much."

And so the whole trip was repeated. Apparently, Niamh would know without being told that Gowen was coming again and would come to meet him. Once again, Gowen was left at the oak tree. But this time, Emher had arranged her own transportation home and left the gillie just over the next hill with new instructions. He was to listen as before, but he was also to peek over the brow of the hill and report what he saw to Emher when she arrived. She wanted to know just what "satisfaction" meant.

The next conversation between Emher and the gillie was even more difficult.

"Well, man, did you do as I said?"

"Yes, lady..."

"Well?"

"Well, I... I heard... the same sounds as before..."

"Of course you did, dolt! Did you go to the brow of the hill, as I instructed you?"

"Yes..."

Emher drew in a long breath and exhaled slowly. The gillie seemed to be fascinated by the movement of her breasts under the fabric.

"Speak, man, or I will have your head hanging from my wall!"

The gillie gulped audibly, shifted from foot to foot, raked a hand through his hair, but still said nothing until Emher pulled a thin, nasty-looking knife from a sheath at her waist and laid the edge against his throat. She did not say a word, but her dark eyes bored into his. Slowly, his eyes fell from hers. He licked his lips and spoke.

"Sh... she appeared out of a mist, in the altogether, and Cú, he stood up as if he had no control of his own body and went to her, and..." His face screwed up beseechingly. "Lady..."

"It's all right, man. I know how it goes on from here. Go home. I will bring my husband."

She went on with her own driver and wagon and fetched Gowen, who again would not speak of his experience, but seemed somehow chastened and diminished within himself.

Seven more days passed. Gowen sickened again. Again, arrangements were made to deliver him to the oak near Sidhe Aengus. The gillie took him out alone, supported him to the ancient tree and leaned him against it. Then he drove off home. He had had no further instructions, and was more than happy to be left out of the rest.

What he did not know, was that Emher and a few of her most trusted women had left well before him and were even now within view of Gowen's resting place.

Soon, a mist seemed to drift in from a nearby hollow, and from the mist stepped Niamh, wearing an anticipatory smile and nothing else. As she walked toward him, Gowen stood as if in a trance, and walked toward her. She reached out to slip a hand under his tunic and he stood quiescently as she massaged his shoulder.

"My champion," she purred, "my own champion," and raked her fingernails across his flesh.

As she leaned her body close to his, she detected a movement from the corner of her eye and turned her head.

Just at that moment, a thin, nasty-looking knife slid close to her throat and a low, controlled voice said: "You will take your enchantments back to your hole in the ground where you came from, because, if you appear around my husband again, I and my companions," Emher indicated several grim-looking women with identical knives, "will carve you into pieces too small for your father to magic together again and feed them to the pigs. And when I tell Conchobar and Cathbad, they will lay siege to your father's sidhe and dig it out until they uncover him and all his people and hang their heads from the palisades of Conchobar's *dún*. Do we understand each other?"

Niamh said never a word, but turned and walked back into the mist, never to be seen again by anyone in Uledh.

After a few days had passed, both Gowen and Emher seemed to be happy to forget that the incident had occurred. Emher did not blame Gowen for something he could not control and he, for his part, seemed oddly proud of her for her solution to the problem. Only now and then, when Emher's temper threatened to reach epic proportions over someone or something, did Gowen deflate it by pretending to cower in fear and saying, "Oh, please do not use your thin, nasty-looking knife on the poor soul!" She could not prevent herself from breaking out in a great laugh. And when, just as rarely, Gowen seemed uncharacteristically proud of himself, Emher would glide up to him, slide her hand over his shoulder, rake his skin with her fingernails and purr, "My champion, my champion." He would blush, grin sheepishly and agree that she was right.

The incident of the Wild Boy was not so easily solved nor so agreeably remembered. It was during the hottest time of the summer, when the sun was at its brightest, just before the games in honor of Lugh Lamfhada — Lugh of the Long Reach, the bright god. At first, the boy was a dot on the horizon line of the sea. Then he became a tiny figure rising up from the round disk of a one-man curragh. As he neared the shore, he skillfully guided the hide-covered disk through the breakers and onto the beach, gliding to a stop on the sand. From a cross-legged position, he sprang lightly to his feet, casually twirling a small sling in his right hand. In his hand, it seemed a toy.

He was immediately confronted by one of the many men on coastal watch. It was a very short meeting. The sentry challenged according to custom by stating that this was the land of the Uledh, giving his own name and asking for the boy's name and what he wanted there. The boy would not give his name, but said that he intended to go to Conchobar's *dún*.

"I cannot let you pass without I know your name and intention," said the guard.

"And I cannot give you my name and I cannot let you prevent me on my way," said the boy, still twirling the small sling around and around with his right hand.

Faced with such effrontery, the guard abandoned caution and protocol and reached for his sword. Quicker than thought, the stone flew from the sling and laid him out lengthwise on the sand. When he came to his senses, the boy was still there, idly swinging his little sling.

"Off you must go now," he said to the bewildered guard. "And tell

Conchobar to expect me."

The guard rashly reached again for his sword, but found that he no longer had it, nor his spear. Painfully, he clambered to his feet and started out toward Conchobar's *dún*. On his way, he encountered Loeghaire driving his own war chariot, who asked, "What is it then that has put you in such a state, man? Why are you staggering about with no weapon at all?"

"It is a bit of a boy, it is, but so fast with his sling that he laid me out before I could draw my sword."

"What is the name of this wonder?" Loeghaire asked.

"It is what he would not give me, and then I reached for my sword."

"Off you go to Conchobar, then," said Loeghaire, "and tell him that Loeghaire is looking into the matter."

So the the coast guard went on his way to Conchobar's *dún*, where he told all that had happened. Shortly after, Loeghaire entered the long house, downcast and weaponless. A torrent of question flowed over him, and he held up one hand to still them.

"It is that the boy is still on his way, taking his own time about it, so I rode on ahead to bring the news."

Conchobar pulsed with suppressed excitement.

"Then tell us his name and his business here. And why have you left him your weapons?"

Loeghaire smiled bitterly.

"It is the wrong question, O king. Rather ask why he left me my chariot so I could be here before him. No doubt so that I could tell you that I had barely drawn my sword when he leaped up to a height even with me in the chariot and struck it from my hand. And quicker than I could think, he seized my spears and threw them on the ground. It is to a better man than I to reason with this wild boy."

Now Conall did not deceive himself. He believed himself to be just a hair's-breadth stronger and faster than Loeghaire, and that would not be enough here. But he was the only other present who had a chance of slowing this wild barbarian down and gaining some information from him. So he said nothing, but cast a look meaningful look at Loeghaire, who smiled wryly, and then he left to ride toward the beach. In a short time, he was back and had a similar tale to tell.

"If there is anyone in all of Uledh who can stand against this fellow, it must be Cú," he said, and Conchobar did not hesitate a moment before dispatching a messenger to Gowen.

Gowen and Emher, sitting quietly together, gasped at the the message.

"Perhaps it is at last someone I cannot defeat," Gowen said heavily, and leaned over to kiss Emher.

"I do not like it, husband. I do not like it as much as I did not like Niamh's plague," Emher said, using her usual, tart description of the Fairy Mound seduction. "There is more at work here than just a challenge. Stay away this once. You are not obliged to face magic when you do not know where it comes from or why it is here. This wild boy has not called you out by name. Let Cathbad have him."

"It is who we are, wife. We are the land of warriors before all else, not the land of druids. And when Loeghaire or Conall is shamed, so are we all shamed. I have to go."

Emher knew it was wrong, and a desperate, cold fear gripped her insides, deep down. But she could not put it into words, and tried to convey it in her look — something that had always worked when words did not. But Gowen's mind was closed.

"Tell Conchobar that Cú is on the way and that I will return with our honour or not return at all," he said to the messenger.

And with Emher's look of bitter anxiety hovering behind his eyes, he went out to his chariot and ordered his gillie to drive him toward the shore.

He found the boy only a little way from the beach, walking slowly and idly twirling his sling, as if he knew that another would come to meet him.

"Greetings, boy! I am CúChulainn of Conchobar's men. You are welcome here, if you will tell me who you are and why you are here. What is your land? What is your nation?"

The boy gazed mildly at him and replied, "It is my own land I am, and my own nation. I will come to Conchobar unless you stop me." He dropped the sling and picked up the sword he had struck from Loeghaire's hand and the shield he had torn from Conall's arm, smiling provocatively at Gowen.

"Will you not go aside from your way for a brief time, and we will talk. No one must die this day. What is your name?"

The boy smiled a bright smile that struck Gowen to the heart, and he nearly turned his chariot to leave. But it was the honour of his adopted land he was upholding.

"Stop, boy, or I will have to stop you!"

The boy playfully shook Loeghaire's sword and Conall's shield at Gowen and continued on his slow progress.

Feeling a worm of unease in his chest, Gowen slowed the chariot and stepped to the ground in front of the boy. Like the boy, he held his sword and shield. When the boy saw that Gowen stood in his way, he stopped and said, "You must step out of my way. The old generation is passing and I am on my way to announce the coming of the new."

Gowen said nothing, but held his ground. The boy smiled brightly again, distracting Gowen for a moment, then struck swiftly with his sword. Gowen's reflex action was barely in time to fend it off. And then they began in earnest.

The boy leapt to the very edge of Gowen's shield, balancing on his toes, in a move only Gowen had ever used in Uledh, and tried to strike down at Gowen's head, slicing a bit off the tips of his hair. Gowen shook him off and repaid him in kind, just to show him that he was a match for him. The boy smiled even more brilliantly and said, "You're spry for an old fellow."

Gowen half laughed and replied, "You're too young to give a good haircut, and I can still show you a few tricks of the trade."

But he found it to be no easy task. Each of his skills and tricks was a skill or trick known to the wild, young boy, and so they fought on, leaping, slashing, stabbing, hacking at each other's shields, parrying, pushing with the shield while striking with the sword. Gradually, each of them tired and they rested more and more often, but neither would give way. During one of these moments of rest, Gowen tried one more time to find a compromise.

"You know my name, boy, and you know the land you are in, since you know that you are on the way to Conchobar's *dún*. How is it wrong for you to tell me your name or your family or your country? Are you from here at all — from Connaught or Leinster or Munster? Are you sent by Cúroi to be another sort of test? Just tell me any little thing so that we don't have to go on trying to kill each other!"

The boy smiled and said, "I know enough. I am fighting the best that there is in all of Eire and I will not yield and I will not stop unless you give way before me and admit that I am the better man."

Gowen laughed bitterly.

"You are not a man at all yet and better you will never be. Give over or die!"

"So be it," said the boy, and attacked furiously, driving Gowen back down onto the beach toward the water and pressed him until they both stood knee deep in the foaming surf. He was tiring visibly, but so was Gowen, and the thought flashed through Gowen's mind that there could only be one of two ends to this battle. Giving way swiftly and creating a distance between himself and the boy, he reached into the pouch at his waist, pulled out the Gae Bolg and dropped it into the water. As the boy advanced to make up the distance between them, Gowen caught the projectile between the great toe and the next toe of his right foot and gave it a powerful shove forward. A wrinkle in the foam marked its path to the boy, where it shot upward between his legs and its many hooks exploded in his insides. Immediately, he sank to his knees, smiled weakly at Gowen and said, "That is a trick that Mother Aoife never knew."

"O Dagda and Lugh of the great power, O Brigid of the healing, take away this stroke!" Gowen cried out in anguish, catching the boy in his arms.

But it was not to be, and they both knew it. The boy smiled again, put out his hand to touch Gowen's face and said, "Don't grieve for me, Father. I have held to the *geis* that was put on me — to tell no man my name and give way to no man. And it took the best in all the land to lay me low. It is my destiny and I embrace it. I greet Conchobar and all the heroes of Uledh."

His eyes closed for a moment, then he looked sadly and deeply into Gowen's eyes: "Together we two could have conquered the world. Perhaps the gods will only let one such live at a time." Then he closed his eyes for the last time.

Gowen carried his son out of the water and across the beach and put him into the chariot. Then he drove slowly to Conchobar's *dún*, where Emher had gone to wait with the others.

Slowly he carried the boy's body to the centre of the *dún* and stood facing his friends and comrades.

"I bring you my son. I do not know his name because of a *geis* I placed on him before his birth. He could not give way to any of us, because of a *geis* I placed on him before his birth. He greets you through me and does not regret his own death because it was an honourable one and a destined one. I grieve for him and myself and for the land he could have served. I hate this destiny, but I accept it."

He laid the boy's body before them. Emher could not see through her tears, and many a strong warrior turned his head and blinked away an irritation in his eye. Bricriu Poison-Tongue, who had no children of his own and never had a good word to say about anyone unless it was meant to gain some advantage, walked slowly forward, sank to his knees and openly let the tears flow over his cheeks and onto the ground beside the boy.

Shock and sadness froze the entire company for what seemed an eternity. Then Roigh stepped to Gowen's side, threw a brawny arm around his shoulders and glared around the circle from under shaggy brows now beginning to grow grey.

"The greatest sacrifice any of us can make is our children," he growled in a curiously husky voice. "I pledge my treasure to the making of the grandest funeral feast ever seen in Uledh."

Gowen had managed to control his reactions until Roigh's speech, but now he buried his face in his hands, and Emher ran across the circle to embrace him. Sobs no longer stifled broke out among the women and a kind of groan went up from the throats of the men.

"It is fitting that we celebrate the life and death of a hero such as this on the Lughnasad that is soon to come." The calm, clear voice of Cathbad cut through the sounds of their sorrow like an icy breeze. "It is the day most suited to father and son in this tragedy."

He turned and left quietly, leading by example. One by one the others followed, leaving Gowen, Emher and Conchobar, who was unwontedly quiet and simply stood to one side as long as Gowen and Emher remained. When they had left, he went in search of Cathbad, to arrange the funeral ceremony for the day of the Games of Lugh of the Long Reach.

The competitions at the great mound (supposed to be the burial mound of Lugh Lamfhada's mother) would be remembered as the fiercest and best ever held in Uledh. Men, women and children felt uniquely more at one as a people than any could remember. Past victories were sung, but also past defeats and the tragic deaths of brave men in hopeless battles. Winners and losers in the games were more enthusiastic than ever in drowning their defeats or lubricating their victories in the drink supplied in generous amounts by Roigh. The only stipulation he placed on his generosity was that each drink must be raised and dedicated "to absent comrades", a practice which appealed so much to the warrior spirit that it continued ever after.

Gowen did not participate except by attending, and no one expected more of him. Emher had heard the story of Aoife shortly after Gowen's successful assault on Foragall's fortress but, like Gowen, had thought of his time in Scáthach's land as part of a distant past. Now, childless as they were, she had no feelings of jealousy or anger as she had had for Niamh. She felt only empty and cheated, for Gowen's son would have been hers too. So they sat together numbly, almost unable to acknowledge the friendship that reached out to them from all sides.

Even the worst pangs of loss will fade with time and life will seek its accustomed path. For Gowen and Emher, though, a no-turning-back marker had been passed and nothing would ever be the same, or as good, again.

Niamh had been a test of Emher's determination and her love for Gowen. The Wild Boy had been a test of Gowen's dedication to his adopted land and to the destiny he had so readily accepted from the lips of Cathbad years before at the Taking of Weapons. The Woman at the Stream and the Hag-Beauty were affirmations of his character and destiny and signals of the shape of the future.

The Woman at the Stream came first, of course. She had to be first, or he wouldn't have been ready for the other. He was riding the border on the eve of the high holiday of Samhain, that time of the year when the portals to the Sidhe open wide and much that is good, but far more that is fearful and dangerous can pass through into the world of mortals. Suddenly the gillie sawed at the reins and Gowen looked in the direction of his glance. Beside a small stream stood a young woman with raven hair and black eyes. She was signalling frantically for them to stop.

Gowen jumped out of the chariot and walked to her.

"Do you have some trouble? Can I help you?"

"I must speak to you alone," she said, and began walking along the stream, away from the chariot and the gillie. Gowen waved at the gillie to stay where he was and walked along beside her.

"How can I help you, lady?" he asked.

"You are CúChulainn. Warrior. Killer of men. Soon you will be facing your greatest test and you will have few friends. If you serve me, I will help you. I will give you victory forever in Eire."

Gowen stopped and turned toward her. She was, like most women, as tall as he was, so he looked directly into her eyes. Inside the deep black of each of them, he seemed to see an even darker shadow moving, like a great, dark bird against a darkling sky. A chill began in his stomach and spread up and down his body until he felt as if he were standing in the ocean in a winter tide. But he did not let this feeling enter his voice as he spoke.

"I know you," he said. "You have the power to make those promises, but everyone knows that you don't keep them. You are Morrigan, the Battle Crow, lover of blood and death. Who wins means nothing to you — only that there is blood."

"Yes," she said, and her voice sounded hoarser, her skin seemed suddenly coarser. "Death and blood are my meat and drink. I have lived in this land for longer than all the nations that are here now, and I have always been well served."

She paused and smiled slowly.

"You may believe my promises or not. But if you do not serve me willingly, I will come against you in many guises. And you will not prevail in your last and greatest test."

"I do not kill for power," Gowen said, "and I do not kill for love of killing. I will fight when I must for my people, but I will not fight for love of blood and death."

"Then I will come against you as a red and white, horned heifer."

"And I will break the bone of your foreleg."

"I will come against you as a grey wolf."

"And I will break the teeth of your mouth."

"I will come against you as a snake through the water."

"And I will put the eye out of your head."

He paused. "I will put these wounds on you and you will never recover from any one of them."

The woman knew, none better, that Gowen had made his *geis* in seventeen words exactly and that it was binding. She also knew that conditions to limit it could be made only at the time it was spoken. Gowen had said "never", so she could not set a term, but she did the next best thing.

"Unless I secure your blessings on myself, and then I will be healed of all my wounds," she said, quick as a thought, in seventeen words exactly. Then she turned from him and walked swiftly away. Gowen returned to his chariot and his gillie drove him home.

Emher was dismayed. Clearly the Cú she loved could not have accepted an offer which would have made him into a killer as heartless and automatic as those warriors once returned from death by the Cauldron of Life. As the tale told, they were the same in appearance, but existed only to kill and, after the battle for which they had been restored, no longer had the power to distinguish friend from foe.

No, he could not have accepted the Morrigan's offer of alliance. But no man could stand against her forever, and she was now a declared enemy. She might attack him at once, or let him alone for a time simply because he would be serving her by doing his duty to Uledh. No one in Eire, excepting perhaps Cúroi or Mebd was so likely to create the bloodshed she desired. In the end, she would claim him, but he might live for a while.

Gowen had similar thoughts.

"She will have to come against me in her three guises, but I feel it in my guts that my time has not come. Other powers are protecting me for now, for some great purpose. When they have done with me, she will have me."

And so it proved to be. On three successive days, as he rode the border near the stream where he had seen her for the first time, he saw her again. He knew it was futile to avoid the meetings, so he invited them, stepping out of his chariot and walking to the stream. The amazed gillie was the only witness, and the tale he told to those in Conchobar's house was considerably more vivid than the one Gowen was telling Emher at the same time.

"It was three days in a row it was, that he went out to meet the Battle Crow, when she came as she promised. And each one of those very days, he stepped out of the chariot, leaving behind his sword and shield and spears and carrying only his little boy's hurley ball and stick. It was to me as if he was saying, 'You can't touch me, Old One!' And he was as carefree as the birds in the trees as he went. He knew, he did, what was going to happen.

"It was the red heifer with the white hooves, the first time, it was, and she came snorting out of the woods and charged across the stream with her head down. I almost closed my eyes, she was so fearsome to look at, but I kept them open, I did."

"And a good thing for you, that you did, my man!" growled Conchobar, who did not enjoy Gowen's colourless descriptions of his adventures. The gillie, who was privileged to be CúChulainn's gillie, after all, was not a bit fazed by the king, and continued his narrative.

"Across the stream she charges, and he standing there, with the ball tucked into a pouch at his waist and holding the stick off to one side in his two hands, as if he was about to knock a ball into the goal from way out on the field. She's so close now, that I'm thinking he can feel her breath on his face, and then he turns a little to one side and pulls back the stick with both hands and — Whack! — gives her a fearful knock on the knee of her left foreleg and down she goes, and he stands there and watches as she pulls herself up on three legs and hobbles away.

"The second time, now, it was the grey wolf, it was, and I have never seen a bigger one of the beasts than the one that came snarling and ravening out of the wood the second day and, even with only three good legs, jumped straight for Cú's throat from the far side of the stream. It was such a far jump and so unexpected that I thought sure she had him this time. But he threw his little ball in the air as the wolf started her spring, and gave it a mighty whack with the stick, and it flew straight into the gods-frightening teeth of that wolf and broke out the front ones, top and bottom, and she landed yelping on our side of the stream, and bleeding from her muzzle, and ran away into the woods.

"The third day, he walked right into the stream and waited for the snake to come. But it didn't come, because it was already there and all unexpected stuck its head out of the water and the fangs of its mouth as long as a throwing spear, and the mouth bleeding in between them, and its head was already moving to strike, and Cú, he jumps into the air as lightly as a trout after a fly, and he sails over her head, he does, and as he passes, he jabs down with the handle of his little hurley stick and her left eye squooshes out in a hundred droplets and she drops back into the stream and swims away."

That was the story, as far as anyone knew — anyone except Gowen and Emher. Gowen knew that the Morrigan was forever, as long as people lived and fought in Eire. Standing against her had shaped his destiny, and he could do nothing to change that. I believe that he accepted that from the start and that he expected her next move and accepted it in the same spirit. It is not, after all, for mortals to quibble with immortal forces.

Some time after his successful struggles with the Morrigan, Gowen was riding the border alone on a particularly hot summer's day. As he stepped out of his chariot to rest in the shade of a lone tree, he noticed an old woman, sitting on a stool, milking a cow. She was seated with her right side toward him, but saw him out of the side of her eye.

"A hot day, mother," he said.

"A day in need of refreshment, O CúChulainn," she replied with a toothless smile. She levered the cow's teat toward him and squeezed a thin stream of milk directly into his mouth.

"My blessing on you, mother, for the refreshment," he said.

Instantly she stood with a triumphant shout and turned toward him, showing her two good eyes, and her perfect teeth in a broad smile.

"Cured by your own words, Little One," she crowed, as her old woman form melted from her and she stood forth young and handsome and wicked.

"So you are," he smiled serenely, climbed into his chariot and drove away. I could only wish to know what her face betrayed at that moment, but some things are not revealed, even to me.

Chance crouches at a fork in the road, leaping forth to wring meaning from apparently random occurrences. For most of us, this has little significance beyond our own selves and those close to us. For a few, chance becomes an instrument of destiny. So it was with Gowen and the Hag-Beauty.

When Gowen rejected the path of the Morrigan, his true path was decided. Of all those in Conchobar's entourage who were amazed, even shocked, at Gowen's actions, only one truly understood the significance of them. Gowen and Emher themselves understood only the surface reality of these events.

Nearly two cycles of the moon had passed since Gowen's final meeting with the Morrigan. On a misty, chilly day like many another in the cold season.

Cathbad paid a visit to Gowen and Emher's *dún*. He chose a time when Emher was occupied with domestic matters and left the two men to themselves in the great house.

Gowen sat quietly, waiting. His experiences with Cathbad had taught him that the druid was connected to things neither Gowen nor anyone else understood. The naming of "CúChulainn" and the taking of weapons were only two instances when the druid had set Gowen on a predestined path.

Now was obviously going to be another of those times.

Cathbad was carrying a yellowish calfskin, almost like a sleeping rug. He stood, holding the skin and making no move to discard his ornate cloak. Fixing Gowen with his sternest look, the druid asked: "Do you know what day tomorrow is?"

"I do not know the name of it," Gowen replied thoughtfully. "It is not like our four great festival days. Everyone knows the names of Imbolc, Beltaine, Lughnasad and Samhain. Only the druids know of the others."

He looked inquisitively at Cathbad.

"Tomorrow," said the druid, "is a Day of the Seeking Sun. It is one of two days on opposite sides of the year — the shortest night is in the warm season and the shortest day is tomorrow at the threshold of the cold season.

"Even the oldest of my colleagues do not know the origins of them. Some say that we have them from folk who were here long before our own people, and long before your people came to the Island of Giants. Some say that they are the secret, high holidays of the Tuatha de Danaan themselves. We believe they are two of four sacred days, like our own, but they mark the seasons differently. This Day of the Seeking Sun must have been the most important, because the greatest of the ancient structures marking the coming of the sun are dedicated to it. The old structures are compelling, even to those of us in the priesthood, that we think of this day as one of the five sacred days of the year. It may be similar to our Samhain — a dangerous and magical turning of the seasons.

"Today," he said, staring directly into Gowen's eyes, "you will take a journey that will last through the night, until the dawn of the Seeking Sun. It is the last of the trials you will undergo before the greatest battle you will ever fight. We will begin by riding out to your herds. Bring only your sling."

Suiting action to words, the old druid walked through the door and threw the calfskin into his wagon, hauling himself up after it. If ever there was a time when Gowen wished to ask another question, it was now. But he bit his lip, scuffed his feet into his sandals and hastily pinned his brat over his tunic.

Then he climbed into the wagon and Cathbad drove slowly out of the *dún*, down its curved entry path and away.

Neither man spoke, until they neared a small group of cattle — several cows and calves guarded by a tough, old bull. Cathbad pulled his wagon to a halt, bent down to pick up a large earthen bowl and stepped out of the wagon. Gowen followed. Murmuring softly and unintelligibly, the druid advanced on the old bull, which seemed spell-bound by the man's voice and eyes. It moved its massive head from side to side, as if hearing some rhythm Gowen could not hear. Foam flecked its muzzle and a droning sound leaked from its throat. Cathbad walked fearlessly within range of the wickedly curved horns, pulled a dagger from under his brat, and slowly, almost gently, drew the knife across the bull's throat. Blood gushed from the wound into the druid's bowl, but the bull continued to wag its head from side to side, as if nothing were happening. Then, suddenly, with a gasp like air escaping from a split bellows, the bull fell to the knees of its forelegs. It rolled onto its side, dead before it stopped moving.

Going again to his wagon, Cathbad fetched some tinder. Then he knelt to kindle a small fire. When it was well started, he held the edges of the bowl, circling it over the flame until the blood frothed and bubbled. Then he stood and held the bowl out to Gowen, who shrank away.

"No," the druid said sternly, "this is not a matter of choice. Drink the bull's blood. Now!"

Gowen was not squeamish, but the sight and smell of the blood brought bile to the threshold of his throat. He swallowed painfully and then put the bowl to his lips, tipping it very slowly toward his mouth. As the warm blood trickled into his mouth, his throat contracted for an instant, rejecting the drink and he feared he would vomit. But he forced his throat muscles to open and swallow. When he did, it was as if he were drinking the best mead, and the thought of Ferdiad at their leave-taking crossed his mind. He drained the bowl and almost smiled as he finished, seeing himself and Ferdiad as they had been that night. It did not seem at all strange to be licking the remains of blood from his lips. Suddenly, he felt warmed from within. He threw off his heavy cloak.

Cathbad had watched him intently. Apparently satisfied, he spoke slowly and emphatically.

"Now your journey begins," he said. "You will wear nothing and you will carry only this calfskin and your sling. You may use the calfskin to disguise your nakedness. You will eat and drink nothing until you reach the end of your journey. Do you understand?"

"Yes, but what is the end of my journey?"

"You will know that when it happens. If you are who I believe you to be, you will come to a place that is sacred to the Day of the Seeking Sun. When you are there, you will lie down on the calfskin and sleep.

"I will speak to Emher and tell her what I have asked you to do. When you return, you will speak of it only to me and Emher."

Gowen stepped out of his sandals allowed and Cathbad to unpin his tunic, letting it slide into a heap around his feet. Taking the calfskin from Cathbad, he slung it over his his left shoulder so that it hung down both before and behind, and held it steady with his left hand. He carried his sling in his other hand.

Then, as though he were outside his own body, Gowen saw himself set off. If he met anyone along the way, he did not notice it. It was as if the bull's blood had intoxicated and numbed him. He was aware of the steady movement of his feet, of the beating of his heart, of the rhythm of his breathing. His entire being was concentrated on the physical act of walking. Step, step, breathe, step step, breathe. He walked without feeling heat or exhaustion, or irritation from the stones in his path. He walked through the rest of the day, through the dusk, the darkening, through the rising of the moon and into the time of its fading. He walked until his senses responded to the first inkling of dawn and he spied what must be the end of his journey.

In the distance, the first rays of the sun delineated a white wall rising out of the grassy plain. As he drew closer, he saw that it was a great structure, as big in circumference as a fair-sized *dún* or *ráth*. Its base was contained by a circle of large, slightly oval stones, covered with carved figures — spirals, triskelions and other symbols of the eternal and the ineffable. Behind the massive stones rose a glistening white wall of large and small stones integrated into a faultless surface, made by that same, meticulous, drystone construction still used by the best builders in Eire. Above the wall rose a formidable, turf-covered dome, large enough for a small herd of cattle to graze on, if they had been able to reach it. He wondered idly why it had not gone to brush and bracken by now. The entrance, if that is what it was, was directly before him, nearly invisible behind the bulk of one of the great cylindrical stones, lying on its side, and covered, like the others with sacred symbols — especially interlaced spirals. He knew that this figure was recognized in Uledh and probably all of Eire as a symbol of death and the passage to the Otherworld.

To enter, he had to clamber up the face of the stone, using hands, feet, elbows, knees, thighs, with the calfskin draped over his back and his sling dangling from his neck. As he moved across the face of the stone and the carved tri-spiral figures, a wave of well-being gradually swept him from head to toe and settled into his bones. At the top, he sat and swivelled his feet around to touch ground and then stand on a smooth stone floor. After the climb and its odd sensations, he felt unusually serene, and prepared to explore further.

The entrance was high and narrow, covered by a massive, roof-like slab. To negotiate the tight passage between large standing stones, a man like Loeghaire or Conall would have had to turn sideways to work his shoulders through. Gowen was able to move slowly straight ahead. It was a long walk with massive, vertical, symbol-covered stones on each side and almost no light.

Then, suddenly, the narrow passage ended and he stepped out into a large, round, open space, topped by a sweeping, corbelled ceiling that appeared to be as watertight now as it had been in the ages shortly after it was built by some long-forgotten master craftsman and his helpers. In front and on each side, the space opened into spherical chambers. In the chamber on the left squatted a heavy, black cauldron. In the chamber on the right, stood a tall, phallic stone, bare of symbols. The chamber before him was empty.

In the moment he stepped from the passage, a shaft of sunlight shot through the gap above the entry roof and suffused the central chamber and its three adjoining chambers in yellow-white brilliance. The passage was constructed so that only on this day of the year and only for a moment would the sun penetrate to the end and light the interior.

It was clear that his journey had come to its end. The bull's blood had brought him here, the sun had followed him through the delicately narrow passage, and now the calfskin on his arm seemed to grow warm on his shoulder. Suddenly he was overwhelmingly tired. He laid the skin on the smooth stone and lay down on it Despite the lambent brilliance of the chamber, he fell asleep instantly and did not dream. Or perhaps he did.

Suddenly, he was awake, standing on the calfskin, holding his sword. The chambers were bathed still — again? — in a soft but penetrating glow. Facing him was an old crone. Rope-like strands of hair hung down on either side of her wrinkled, toothless face; her nose was so long that it almost bisected her mouth. Her wizened body was covered by sores. Her voice scratched and shrieked like that of an outraged rooster. Gowen was not sure what she had just said, but it could not be what he thought!

"What?" he murmured.

The voice skreeked again, "Will you give a poor old lady a little kiss, young man?"

She leaned her face into his and stared into his eyes. It would have been hard to imagine a less attractive woman. But it was his habit to honour all women, and to respect the old. And besides, he felt sorry for her. So he closed his eyes and leaned into a long, firm kiss on her beaky mouth.

At first, the only sensation was a warm tingling in his lips. That became an intense glow and spread up into his mind, where it exploded like an internal bolt of lightning, filling his eyes from the inside with sun-like radiance. His chest, then his stomach, then his groin seemed to catch fire. When the light in his head faded, he found that his empty sword hand was raised almost straight up. Gone was the old woman. In the chamber before him was the most beautiful woman he had ever seen. Flame-red hair and sea-green eyes surmounted a body as white as the sand of the beach. He could neither lower his sword arm nor speak. As he stared at her, she smiled radiantly.

"Who are you, then?" she seemed to say, but her lips did not move.

"I am CúChulainn," he thought.

"Are you, indeed. And who else are you then?"

"I am Gowen," thought Gowen, and wondered why.

"And which is the name from your homeland?"

"I... don't... know."

"Do you remember the fisherfolk who used to come ashore and trade when you were very young? Those folk who spoke your parents' tongue with a strange accent? How was it that they spoke your tongue?"

"My father said that they were our own folk from over the water."

"So they are, and so, in a different way, are the folk who have given you a home here, even though their language is not so familiar. Your people have lived all over the great land across the water, and all abroad the Isle of the Mighty. The time will come when they are pushed to the edge of the sea in those places, and they will live in Eire under the sword of strangers even fiercer than the Fomhoire."

"What has that to do with me?"

"You are the first to come to me by the path of the bull's blood, the sword and the yellow calfskin; and you are the only one who will not be a king of all of Eire. In times to come, the chosen will seek me out and I will come to them and judge their strength of mind. They will be tested by the magic of the blood —" she glanced to her right and Gowen followed her glance to the cauldron "and by the Screaming Stone —" she glance at the phallic stone, "to see, should they be king, and these will be the two great tests of kingship. You will not be a king, but, by your bargain with Cathbad, you will have a great name in all of Eire and you will symbolize the greatness of the warrior-blood of this island. You have already been tested by the Morrigan, and you are ready now for the trials that will decide your place in the tales of your people.

"Soon, you will fight an impossible battle, you will triumph and you will lose everything, but you will leave a legacy. When you are visited from the Sidhe, you will know that the end is near. Remember one thing above all: your strength is of the sun. As it waxes, so your strength grows, and as it fades, so your strength ebbs away until it is no more than that of an ordinary man.

"Go home to Emher and live your life, for soon it will end."

She did not leave, so much as dissolve away, leaving Gowen alone in the darkness, shivering from the oncoming chill of the night. He rolled himself in the calfskin and slept until morning, this time without waking or dreaming until the chill of the stone floor crept into his bones and woke him.

Chapter Thirteen
A MINOR DISAGREEMENT

It was all about cows. Well, to be exact, it was about a bull — one, particular bull. If you have not lived in a society that prizes cattle above all else, you will not find it easy to understand. In Eire, cattle were prized above sheep, goats, pigs and any other domestic animals. The number and quality of a man's cattle (or a woman's — women have very distinct property rights among the Gaels) is an index of that person's wealth. Rustling is commonplace and cross-border raids are especially frequent. The satisfaction of increasing your own herd is no greater than the satisfaction of diminishing an enemy's wealth.

You remember Mebd and Aillil — she the queen of Connaught and he a king of Leinster and her consort in Connaught. It was to them that I fled when I could not stomach Conchobar's treachery against three brothers to whom I had given my pledge of safe passage. Mebd had the reputation of always having at least one man other than Aillil, and that could not have been easy for a proud man such as he was. Without seeming immodest, I may say that my reputation as a man of great prowess was fully deserved. So it was no surprise to anyone that Mebd took me as a lover. It was said that I was the only man who had ever satisfied her. All I can tell you is that she was the only woman who ever completely exhausted me. It must have been very difficult for Aillil. He had his revenge in the end, but that is another story.

At any rate, I was at their court for the entire tale of the bull and all it led to. You remember, too, that many of their important discussions occurred in what is called "pillow talk." Disagreements during these discussions were commonplace, but none so fateful as the one I am about to speak of.

Aillil had brought with him from Leinster his own considerable wealth, but he and Medb had never really talked about it. On one particular night, however, their dialogue took a new turn. No doubt stung by Medb's insatiable appetite for other men, Aillil was in a waspish mood as they happened upon the subject of their marriage. Each of them assured the other that he/she was lucky to have such a strong, handsome and powerful spouse. Neither of them could gain an advantage in anything until they began to compare property: land, animals, personal fighting men, even to the earthen pots and carved wooden spoons in their kitchen. In a listing of belongings that lasted all night, they were equally matched down to the last wooden spoon, but for one thing. In Aillil's herd was a pure white bull unmatched for power and size, and therefore for potential as a stud. Not only did Mebd have no bull to equal this one, she had exactly one bull fewer than Aillil. Aillil had won the debate, but he valued his skin as well as his relationship with this powerful woman. So when she hit upon the idea of finding a bull equal to his, he fell in with her plans agreeably, pledging to share costs equally.

They discussed every bull they knew of in Eire. There was only one bull of equal pedigree and power, and that bull was in the herd of an Uledhman named Fingal, just over the border from Connaught. It was brindle brown and the prize of his small herd. But he was a practical man, so he received the delegation from Mebd courteously, showed them true Gaelic hospitality and listened to the queen's offer. The offer was extremely generous for any bull — even such a prize specimen. And Mebd's confidential messenger was empowered to add that, if that was not sufficient, Fingal might spend a night enjoying the favours of the queen herself. Now Medb was not only a powerful queen and a formidable warrior, she was also a famous beauty, so this was a powerful incentive. However, as I said, Fingal was a practical man, and he knew that he had no place in a queen's bed. He knew also that Mebd's offer would enrich him beyond his imagining. So he accepted; of course he did.

And that would have been the end of the story, if two of the Connaughtmen had not fallen into a drunken conversation on the very doorstep of the man whose hospitality had supplied them with the drink.

Once again, Chance crouched just out of sight — this time in a doorway. As Fingal was about to pass through the outside door of his house, bearing another generous measure of food and drink for the Connaughtmen, he paused to listen to the two fools who were about to change history.

"Sure and it's a good man is our host, and generous to a fault," said the first one blearily.

"And well he should be, for Medb is about to make him a rich man," burped the second.

"And lucky he is as well, for if he hadn't accepted the offer, we would have knocked him into a quivering blob on the floor of his own house and taken the beast and his wife and daughters into the bargain."

"Sure and he's not to know how lucky he has been."

"Ah, but he does," thought Fingal. A moment later, he stepped through the door and moved on past the two unwitting troublemakers to the small circle of men around a fire. He offered them the food and drink and bade them "Good night". Then he went back to his house, roused his people and armed them. He sent the youngest boy to Gowen with a message that he was about to have trouble with some Connaughtmen who had crossed the border.

By dawn, his house was barricaded. Mebd's chief representative, followed by men bearing the intended payment for the bull, called out for Fingal. From inside came the reply, "It's the quivering blob speaking from the floor and saying: 'Be off before the blob rises up and rolls over you.'"

To this completely unexpected reaction, Mebd's man said, "If there is an issue between us about the payment, you have only to say and we will adjust it."

"'Tis not a matter of payment any longer. You will take yourself and your men, and especially those two drunken spalpeens who were sitting on my doorstep last night, and clear off. I will not be made small of by two Connaughtmen."

No amount of cajolery could bring him from this decision, so the leader of the Connaughtmen gave the order to take the bull. Fingal opened the door of his house and stood, backed by his men and ready to fight. The Connaughtmen gripped their weapons. It was the blink of an eye from a battle between the two small bodies of men, when one of Fingal's people glanced over a hill to the east and cried out:

"It is Cú that comes and he is in his rage already."

Fingal laughed harshly and said:

"Let us put down our weapons and watch. The Little One will turn them into piles of blood and bone!"

At that, the Connaughtmen leapt to their chariots and pelted away in a cloud of dust and a hail of clods from their horses' hooves.

When Gowen arrived, the Connaughtmen had vanished, but he learned enough to know that Mebd had been thwarted. He did not need Cathbad to tell him that serious trouble was brewing.

As to Mebd, well, she was just as angry as you would expect her to be.

Chapter Fourteen
EIRE RISES AND ULEDH LIES DOWN

In fact, Mebd was so angry that her men did not dare to tell her the whole truth, so they said that an overwhelming party of Uledhmen had ambushed them and they had had to fight their way back across the border. They should have known better. It required persuasion — some clever, some cruel — but she finally knew the true story and made her judgment in her usual summary style.

"The two oafs who caused this farce will be in the first line of my armies when we begin our campaign against Uledh, and they will remain in the first rank until we win, or they die."

And thus it was that everyone else in Connaught learned of Mebd's decision to cross the border in strength and take the brown bull. Word went out across the land and the men of Connaught began to muster. Then, too, there was the example of Fergus, who had his own reasons for resenting Conchobar. Rulers and chiefs enough in Leinster and Munster had reason to resent Conchobar or Uledh, or just to like the idea of seeing them properly humbled. The secret of the Uledhmen's weakness — lost in the past — was unknown to most, and many had good reason to fear attacking Uledh on their own. As part of a great army, though, it was not so daunting, so Mebd found it possible to assemble a huge army from all three provinces.

One of those who did not respond to the invitation was Cúroi. Instead, he sent a messenger to Gowen to warn him of developments. The day after receiving the message, Gowen appeared before Fingal's house.

"It is time, man," he said, "to move your prize bull away from the border and to a safe place. Mebd is coming for him and half of Eire is coming with her."

That is how it started.

Two days later, the army crossed over the border from Connaught into Uledh and found nothing. Fergus was among them. Perhaps because he no longer felt he had to defend Uledh, he was not struck down by the pangs.

"Onward!" cried Mebd, brandishing her own, great sword. And when the first riders hesitated, she smiled at a secret she alone knew and said, "I guarantee that the fearsome Uledh will not be greeting us for at least thirteen days. They are otherwise occupied."

She moved her own entourage to the front and rode boldly further into Uledh. Seeing this, the great mass of chariots and foot soldiers moved behind her.

Mebd's entourage, now, that was something else again. She rode in her own chariot with her own gillie, but she was surrounded on all sides by picked warriors in their chariots: two ahead, two behind, two on each side. Medb herself, with her raven on her shoulder, was the magical middle and the magical ninth in this formation.

At about the same time that Mebd led her army across the border, Conchobar was seated in his high seat at Emain Macha. Suddenly he cried out, bent forward and tumbled to the ground. Cathbad took one step as if to help his king, then clutched at his abdomen and sank slowly to his knees. As he curled up into a position that somewhat relieved his pain, he murmured, "CúChulainn, it is to you now."

At Roigh's *dún*, Roigh and Loeghaire were already writhing on the ground and the women were dragging them and the other men to the protection of the great house, where they would spend the next thirteen days.

When the pangs struck Conall, he was in his chariot, entering his *dún*. Like the others, he had heard the story of the pangs, but he had always thought it to be a fantasy. Now he experienced the overwhelming bite of pain in his guts and could not hold himself upright. As he sank to the floor of the chariot and women ran from every direction to help him, he cried out, begging the gods for help and cursing them in the next breath. He never ceased during the next thirteen days, except those moments when he felt strong enough to roar in anger and challenge Lugh himself to battle if he did not find a way to lift the curse.

And all the while, Mebd's massive army moved slowly and inexorably in the direction of Emain Macha, finding no resistance — in fact, no people at all, until they approached the ford of a medium-sized stream. The first man carefully picked his way across the stones below the swift waters, finding the best way for those behind him. He stopped suddenly, then dropped backward, as if he had been struck on the forehead by a giant hand. When they pulled him back to the bank, they found that he had indeed been struck in the forehead, but by a rounded stone. He was quite dead. Fergus stepped up to the stream and pointed across it to a pillar-like stone on the other side. Crowning the tall stone was a spancel — a wreath of twined branches.

"That," I said, "is a message from CúChulainn."

"That cannot be!" roared Mebd. "The Uledhmen are in their pangs and cannot move from their cots of pain for thirteen days!"

Fergus was amused that Mebd, for once, did not know everything.

"Cú is not of Uledh, Mebd; he is not even of Eire."

Mebd was silent for moments. No one dared speak into the quiet. Finally she shook her head as if to shake off a bothersome fly. Wearily she asked, "What is the message of the stone?"

"It is that we must retreat from the stream and make camp, then send one man to meet him tomorrow. If the man returns, we move on. If he does not, we must stay another day. And we will be challenged in this way at every ford between here and Emain Macha."

"Ha!" cried the angry queen. "And how will he enforce that prohibition?"

"Just as he stopped this man before us."

"No one is that fast and that accurate. You!" She pointed out a Connaughtman. "Get over that stream!"

The man said never a word, but walked swiftly into the stream, not bothering to find the best path. Halfway across, he fell backward, and we had to pull him out. Like the man before him, he was dead of one blow to his forehead."

Mebd's face was purple with rage.

"You! And you! And you! And you and you and you and you!" She shouted, pointing to seven men, and they did not ask what she meant, but rushed together toward the stream. One of them dropped on our side, two in the middle and another on the far side. The other three made for the cover of the woods as fast as their feet would carry them.

Mebd opened her mouth wide to shout another order, but it never came. As if by magic, the head of the raven on her left shoulder exploded in a shower of feathers and blood.

Fergus spoke again, "That was his way of telling us that he can kill anyone at any time."

Mebd was silent now for what seemed like a very long time. Then she threw up her hands and said disgustedly to Fergus, "It will be as you said." And to the others, "Back to the meadow we passed through. We will make camp. Captains will report the names of their best fighters to Fergus, and he to me."

The night passed in a review of the best the army had to offer. One day had already passed, so Mebd knew that she had only twelve more days to proceed comparatively unmolested. If only she could find someone to rid herself of CúChulainn! Finally, she and Aillil had reached a decision.

The first chosen to go against Gowen at the stream was Niall — the best warrior of the seven kingdoms of Leinster. They met in the morning, advancing from the banks into the ford. Gowen threw his short spear immediately and Niall caught it quickly on his shield, replying with his own. Then they went to their swords, and Gowen found that Niall was a strong fighter. He was still not reconciled to killing Mebd's people just because they were following her orders, so he did not press for a kill, but tried to wound and incapacitate. It was a costly strategy. Niall would not yield, and some of his strokes were telling, cutting Gowen's arms and legs. Blood flowed freely from both men. Still, Gowen only felt stronger as time passed and the noon sun approached. At noon, he was so fresh and strong that he pressed Niall almost casually, taking no care to husband his strength, using it lavishly and still trying to wear Niall down and make him yield. But as noon passed, Gowen tired again, rapidly, so that he began to fear for the outcome of the battle. He could not afford to lose this early. He had to hold on, defeat Niall and above all avoid capture or defeat.

Now he had to watch for every opening, not spurning chances for a deadly stroke. In a move he remembered from his first sight of Scáthach, he caught Niall's shield with his own and pushed upward against the faltering muscles in Niall's shield arm. As the shield rose, Gowen struck beneath it and the sword sank deeply into Niall's side. He withdrew it slowly, caught Niall as he sagged forward and brought him to the opposite bank of the stream. He threw his head back and gave a great shout, then he dragged himself away to find his gillie.

When Fergus heard the shout, he said, "It is CúChulainn shouting to tell us that we must come and fetch our man. We have lost for today."

"That is not acceptable!" Mebd shouted, and Aillil added a snarl of his own.

As the body of Niall was prepared for transport to Leinster, the king and queen spent much time alone in their travelling house of skins. They did not appear again that afternoon or evening, but now and then sent out for this man or that. It was only afterwards that the whole army knew what was happening. The men who went in to speak to them came out again, feeling that they had been put to the test: How many men had they defeated, how many battles fought, in which weapons were they skilled. Mebd and Aillil were calculating their resources, in case Gowen should last longer than one or two days.

Their next move was not a surprise. Fergus was summoned to them. Aillil was happy to tell the lover of his wife that he was now to repay the hospitality he had enjoyed in Connaught. He was to meet CúChulainn at the ford and drive him from it. Mebd's mouth formed the first sounds of the word, *kill* but she looked into Fergus's eyes and swallowed the word. Fergus knew where his duty lay and what his obligations as a refugee were. He left silently, but those outside who saw him described a face wreathed in storm clouds.

On the next day, Fergus did indeed go fully armed to the ford, where he found Gowen, still bleeding through the cloths his gillie had wrapped around his wounds. Gowen looked up in disbelief at his friend and mentor.

"Is it you indeed, friend Fergus? Is it so soon that we must try to kill one another?"

Fergus looked at him calmly.

"Take up your sword, Oh CúChulainn, and allow me to drive you away from this ford. You will have a day with no new wounds upon you and I will fulfil my debt of honour to the land that took me in."

Gowen appeared to think for a moment, then his face was brightened by a grin as he remembered how he and Ferdiad had massacred the trees and bushes in Scáthach's land.

"That I will, friend Fergus," he laughed. "And I will show you how to make war on the trees and rocky outcroppings, such that your comrades will believe that the Tuatha and the Fir Bolg are fighting the battle of Magh Tuireadh all over again."

And so it was that those watching were moved to cheers when Fergus advanced on Gowen with flashing sword and wide, sweeping strokes barely parried by the smaller man. Quickly, it seemed, CúChulainn retreated into the woods, until they could no longer see either of the combatants, but they could still hear the clashing of metal on metal and follow the disturbance in the trees, as if a mad giant were passing through the woods.

The moment they disappeared from view, Mebd ordered the advance and her entire army crossed the ford and headed once more for Emain Macha. At the end of the day, a weary, dusty Fergus slumped back into camp. No one dared to ask in what condition he had left Gowen, but it was clear to all that he would have said something if he had badly injured or killed his old friend and apprentice.

Fergus had made most of the noise and had tired himself so thoroughly in merciless attacks on trees and stones that he returned to Mebd's army a hero. Gowen, on the other hand, had had a refreshing rest and an odd but welcome visit with an old friend. Mebd had ten days left.

The next day and the next and the next passed slowly for Mebd but quickly for Gowen. He had learned from his fight with Niall. He no longer thought of exhausting Mebd's men and sparing them. He struck at the first opportunity, and he struck a fatal blow. The rest of his day was healing and recuperation. Mebd spent the remainder of her day alternating between helpless fury and a frantic search for another champion. On the evening before the sixth day, Gowen received a furtive visit at his campsite, where he was tending to his wounds while supper bubbled in a small cauldron. A shadow fell across the light from the fire, and Gowen stood in one fluid movement, his sling hanging already loaded from his hand.

"Is it a midnight chat you're seeking? Come out into the light."

"CúChulainn?" A short, broad man stood forth in the flickering light. "It's Lugaid I am. My brother and I are taken away from the keeping of our animals and made to be a part of the great army against Uledh. My brother — you know him — he is so strong that he thinks he can do anything, and they've offered him such things... such things... and he's agreed... to come against you. Tomorrow."

Lugaid was someone Gowen remembered from his long-ago trip across the border to ask for Mebd's mediation in the matter of the Championship of

Uledh, and from a few forays since. He and his brother were not fighters, but swineherds who willingly shared their bit of food and drink with a passer-by, even if he was from Uledh. Simple, friendly folk who had been sucked into the undertow of war.

"Go back to camp, Lugaid. Your brother will come back to you, but he will be no good to you for a while after."

"Thank you, Cú, thank you! I knew you..."

"Say nothing of this to anyone, or I will regret my decision. Get yourself back to camp. Now!"

And so, on the sixth day, out to the ford plodded Lugaid's brother, with no shield or sword, but a huge club he used for protection against marauders, human and animal. He was easily twice his brother's size, but slow and clumsy for all that. Gowen sighed. It would be so much easier just to cut him. But he felt something different for these two. Pity. Pity and a kind of brotherhood.

"I am sorry, Cú," rumbled the big man. "I have come to beat you into the ground. I have to do it, Queen Mebd says so. They will give me things, but I don't want them. I have to do it because it is my duty as a good subject of the queen. It is, it is..." His voice trailed away and he stood like a small boy expecting to be punished. The he raised his club over his head and took a step forward.

Gowen took a long, forward step for momentum, then launched himself feet first at the big man's ankles. He flew between them, reaching out when he had almost completely passed the massive legs, grasped each one in one of his hands and yanked them toward each other. With a muffled boom and a cloud of dust, the big man fell forward. Before he could rise to his knees, Gowen leapt onto his back, flattening him again. And then he danced a wild dance on the big man's shoulders and up and down his arms and down one side of his buttocks and one leg and back up the other. He danced and pranced and stomped until the big man just lay there and groaned, because every muscle on the rear half of his body pulsated with pain.

Gowen leapt off the the moaning mound of misery, threw his head back and gave a great shout to let Mebd's army know they should come and fetch their man. Then he melted into the landscape and waited to make sure that the big man was found. It was not long before he heard the scuffling of several feet and then four men appeared on the other side of the stream and crossed the ford. Lugaid was one of them, and he called out, "Larine, is it yourself? Are you with us then?"

A rumbling moan was the answer. And as if it had been a song of joy, Lugaid jumped into the air in his happiness and cried: "Come on, fellows! It's a living disaster he is, but living, living! Let's drag the poor, stupid soul back to my fireside and I'll feed him broth and tell him he's an eejit and luckier than any two fellows I know! Come on now, all together!"

And it took all four of them to drag him upright and prop him up from fore and aft and right and left and stagger off across the stream and slowly out of sight. As the sound of the moans and footsteps receded, a loud whisper floated back down the incline and over the stream: "Thank you!"

Now there were seven days until Uledh should rise from its pangs and fall like a ravening wolf on the armies of all of Eire. On the next three days, the best of the best from the armies of Connaught, Leinster and Munster were sent against Gowen. None of them returned alive, but the battles he had to fight were fearsome and took a terrible toll on him. Even his gillie's best skills could not keep pace with the his terrible wounds. At last, with only four days left, Ferdiad appeared at the ford.

Gowen did not want to believe it.

"Is it really you, then, my best of comrades? How have they brought you to this?"

Ferdiad stared sadly at Gowen and said, "They offered me riches and the hand of Finnabair and the friendly bed of Mebd herself and I still said 'No!' But after a long night of argument, Mebd pretended to hear some news from one of her men and turned to me and said that you had been heard boasting aloud that no one could stand against you since you had survived Fergus, not even your one-time friend and second best to you in everything, Ferdiad. And in that moment, I lost my reason to my pride and said I would go against you, and that is the word I have given, so now I have to try, are you good enough to survive even me."

"It is a sad thing, one of us to kill the other. It's a sad thing for me, to kill my best comrade," said Gowen.

"I told you when we were with Scáthach — I said we would be going back to our own lands and if we ever faced each other again, it could be as enemies. I do not love this task. I do not love this vainglorious and silly war. But it is a war like any war, because its business is to kill, and now it will kill you or me."

Gowen bowed his head in profound sadness. Then he looked up with a melancholy smile and said, "It is the way it is. Come to my fire and eat with me and then we will try our weapons."

And so they breakfasted together, and told of their lives since Scáthach and reminisced about their time there, and speculated about the fate of old comrades.

"Aran-Cet will be a fat, Gaulish chieftain with fifteen children and a strong arm feared by friend and foe alike."

"And the only thing more feared than a blow of his arm will be that he could sit on an enemy and squash him as flat as a cowpatty."

They talked and laughed and even choked a bit on their nostalgia, until tears came to their eyes. And their two gillies stood by and marvelled at the behaviour of these two men who were soon to try to kill one another.

But then it was time. They moved to the ford and began by throwing their short spears, each one in turn and the other turning each one away with his shield as if they were children's darts. They fought with their long spears, battering each other's shields and, with the butt of the spear, each other as well. Bruises were given and taken, but no cuts at all, and finally the spears were blunted and broken and the shields punctured here and there. And so, finally, they had to go to their swords.

Ferdiad was Gowen's equal in every weapon, including the sword. They had both learned the many feats of skill that Scáthach could teach, and now the swords clashed and rang and struck fire as no one had witnessed since Fergus went out to meet Gowen. But these blows were in earnest, each of them suffering grievous cuts, and Gowen the far worse because he had begun injured. As they took to the swords, the sun had just passed its apex and Gowen threatened for a short while to overwhelm his friend by the ferocious energy of his attack. As the sun declined, however, his strength did too, and Ferdiad — unaffected by the strength of the sun — pressed him ever more dangerously. Panting, glaring through a bloody haze at his friend and nemesis, Gowen retreated step by step down the bank and into the stream. Wearily and with a heavy heart, he reached into the pouch at his waist and drew out the Gae Bolg. He dropped it into the stream, catching it in the fork between his toes, drew his foot back a half-step and then swiftly forward, launching the fateful weapon for the second time in his life.

Ferdiad knew the instant it struck him what had happened. He smiled sadly and sweetly at Gowen and said, "I see that Scáthach made sure that you would fulfil your destiny. I do not complain. I have fulfilled mine."

Gowen stepped forward and caught him as he collapsed, sitting down in the middle of the stream with his legs crossed under him and Ferdiad's head in his lap. Ferdiad smiled up at him, but did not say another word, and died almost instantly. The Gae Bolg fell innocently back into the water, where Gowen retrieved it and put it into his pouch. Ferdiad's gillie came forward sadly and retrieved his master to return him in his chariot to Mebd's army.

After this battle, Gowen was one of the living dead. Both his body and his mind were battered by his wounds and the fate of his friend. He lay down that night unsure that he could rise again the next day and survive another contest at arms.

Mebd, too, was wakeful. The delays had gone on far too long and the danger point was near when Uledh would rise from its pangs. There were no champions left who could compare to Fergus and Ferdiad. Furthermore, there were none who would go willingly to their deaths for the promise of riches and the hand of the most desirable young woman in Connaught if not all of Eire. Even the magic beauty of her daughter, Finnabair, and the offer of Mebd's own friendly bed would gain no more eager warriors. Cost what it might, she decided to move her army across the ford and over Gowen's dead body the next day.

Chapter Fifteen
AN ENDING AND A BEGINNING

It was to be a surprise, of course. Mebd's advance troops would sweep across the ford and overwhelm a sorely wounded Gowen, still rising groggily from his uneasy night's sleep. And indeed it was a surprise for Gowen, who was just sitting up when he saw the first men splash into the ford from the other side. He was still in the act of rising — one knee still down and one hand reaching for his sling while the other plunged into his pouch in search of a stone — when the second surprise appeared, rumbling and bumping down the hill behind him. It was a caravan of the oldest and most decrepit chariots, the boniest horses, the gauntest, toothless old gillies and warriors of Uledh. And in some of the chariots, a woman of one of the warrior houses.

They had travelled through the night to arrive, bringing nothing with them but the clothes they stood up in and the weapons they intended to use. As time wore on at home, the incapacitated men had become more and more frustrated and this feeling had transmitted itself to the rest of the community. Finally, the older men decided that it would be a lesser shame to die in an uneven battle than to sit quietly while their only defender attempted to hold off an army. When the women heard what was planned, some of them had insisted on coming along too, despite the fears and pleadings of their husbands and brothers, and the older men did not turn away this extra help. In the first of the chariots, driven by a bearded and ragged gillie and occupied by a fierce old man who looked much like an older Conall, stood Emher herself, armed with short throwing darts and vicious-looking little knives. It was, in other words, a cooperation of all the men past the age of sexual potency, and therefore past the effect of the curse, with a number of the women who chafed at home, knowing their men could not yet help with the defence of their land.

The men in the ford stared unbelievingly at this incredible, almost comic juggernaut bearing down on them, all wobbling wheels, flapping beards and flying tresses, and most of them were cut down where they stood, still staring. As the next wave of men pushed forward, Medb recognized the new threat and hesitated not a moment to send a wave of her chariots against them. Gowen knew where he could be most effective. He retreated up the incline, away from the ford and monitored the one-sided battle, keeping an especially careful eye on Emher's chariot.

The Gaels of Eire, like all their Celtic cousins, were known for the furious abandon with which they entered battle. The "Celtic rage" was known and feared among many peoples. The old men, though, were past their age of passion and fury, so they entered this final battle with an ice-cold determination to make every movement count and sell their lives as dearly as possible. In the swirl and eddy of clashing chariots, and the flurry of flying and slashing weapons, the coolly calculating old men held their own, even making deadly use of stones from piles they had loaded into their chariots, since they no longer kept so large a stockpile of swords and spears in battle-ready condition.

When a chariot was flanked dangerously by more than one opponent, Gowen sped a deadly stone to the forehead or temple of the gillie or warrior, sending one of the enemy vehicles racing confusedly off at a tangent to the battle. The apparently uneven battle between Gowen, the old men and some women on one side and the advance wave of the armies of all Ireland on the other lasted much longer than could be expected. There were, indeed, men in Mebd's army who refused, even as they were being cut down, to reply in kind against women and old men.

Finally, however, the pure weight of youth and numbers prevailed and one by one the old men began to fall. When the remaining chariots all had women in them as well, Fergus approached Mebd.

"If it is a victory today that you want, you will have it soon. If you are thinking of having a long life after this war, it is time to call back your troops, before the women are killed as well. The men of Uledh will praise their grandfathers and fathers and uncles for their glorious deaths and will come to fight us and drive us out when they rise from their pangs. But if they rise to find even one of their women dead by our hand, they will not be content to drive us out of their land. They will not rest until they have hunted down everyone who is responsible for this war. And no one's rank or power will be proof against that vengeance."

Mebd mumbled something about men who have no stomach for success, but then she turned to her closest aides and gave the word to call back the troops for the day.

As the sad remnant of the Uledh contingent gathered its dead and straggled homeward, Emher jumped from Amergin's chariot and ran to Gowen. When she threw her arms around him, he stifled the inevitable groan and shudder of pain, but she sensed it anyway, and stepped back to look at him. Without another word she pushed him gently but firmly to the ground and began to clean and bind the wounds that had opened again. Amergin approached, no doubt to offer his help, but she said:

"I will have Cú's gillie take me home when I have finished, and he can return here before morning. Go back and tell everyone the women and the old men of Uledh have given a good account of themselves."

So she stayed and comforted Gowen in more ways than one, deep into the night. And this visit was more than mere sleep to him, so that he woke from his short sleep the next morning feeling more vigorous and optimistic than he had for days.

Alas, Mebd had not given up, but only waited for the next day to repeat her tactic of overwhelming him with numbers. Again, he rose to see a phalanx of foot soldiers approaching the ford and chariots rolling along at some distance behind.

But again, there was a surprise both for him and for Mebd. Shouting and cheering as they crested the hill in their miniature chariots behind their gallant ponies, there came the Boy Troop of Emain Macha — all the future warriors of Uledh who were not yet pubescent. That is, they were heartbreakingly young. And yet they were spurred on by the same feelings that had driven their grandfathers and mothers to this place. Had their mothers or grandfathers known of their intent, they would not have been allowed to leave home without a struggle; but, knowing this, they had prepared quietly in the early, dark hours of the day, left silently and then ridden hard to arrive by dawn.

Down the hill they charged now, shouting in excitement and exultation, poising their child-spears to launch at the full-grown enemy. Their training, even at this age, had been rigorous, and their spears found a surprising number of targets, throwing the foot soldiers into a tumbled, shouting confusion, and blocking off the surge of chariots from behind.

They were swift, and they were small, and so they were hard to catch and strike, and many of Mebd's men found themselves perhaps even more reluctant to strike down children than women and old men. This disinclination grew as it became obvious that the boys could strike accurately with sword or spear, but only rarely and by some odd chance was the wound mortal. Most often, the stricken warrior was inconvenienced or even incapacitated, and this seemed to most of them a small price to pay, not to become a child-killer. As before, Gowen chose his targets carefully to protect the boys as well as he could.

Mebd glowered and fumed at this second obstacle to her plans on the penultimate day of the opportunity given her by the miseries of the men of Uledh. Sparing children was not an excuse for shirking the duty of a soldier, but she had to choose carefully among her own men of Connaught, to find those who were willing to do unquestioningly what their monarch told them. It took time to find and assemble the right men for the job, and so it was already late in the day when a large group of chariots rumbled menacingly down the hill toward the ford and the still exuberant and triumphant children.

It was not easy, even for determined men, but not all of the boys' enthusiasm nor all of Gowen's deadly stones could prevent the inevitable outcome. One by one, rammed, overturned, crushed under wheels, the small chariots were halted. Their young occupants, those who were able to jump to the safety of the ground, whirled their small swords in fierce patterns, cutting at men when they could and horses when they could not. But no boyish panache, no idealistic dream has the force to undo reality. Gallantly, willingly, unvanquished, one by one, the boys of the Boy Troop of Emain Macha died, to the last young life. And as that last young life ended, so ended the day, and Gowen stood alone in impotent grief and rage.

The night passed in agony: unhealed wounds of mind and body gave no peace, and Gowen knew that there was no further desperate miracle in Uledh. At least, he hoped with all his heart that there were no others there who would sacrifice themselves tomorrow to delay his defeat and death by one more day.

And he would die tomorrow. There could be no doubt now. Even if the men of Uledh rose from their pangs with the dawn, it would take much of the day to prepare and the rest to travel to the aid of their one defender.

They would first of all have to eat, just to make sure that they did not faint from hunger in the midst of battle. Then the gillies would have to inspect the horses and equipment. Finally, they would set off and probably arrive in time to intercept Mebd's army as it drove forward from the ford.

But Gowen would die. A flurry of stones and a trail of dead men leading over the ford, then, when they were upon him, one last, wild battle rage and a circle of dead bodies, his own in the middle.

He walked to the pillar stone on which he had set his spancel of challenge, and leaned his back against it. He thought of how he might use the reins of his chariot to bind himself to the stone at the end, to make sure he finished upright, still facing his enemies.

It finally occurred to him to ask himself what he was dying for, in a land that was not even the land of his birth. And he could only dimly perceive that he was just one figure — albeit an important one — in a great, godly game of fidchell. He was not dying for his love of Emher nor even for his love of his friends, but because of some great conflict of powers beyond his ken, represented on the one side by Mebd the warrior-shaman queen — symbolic of an ancient matriarchal tradition, and on the other, by Uledh — the new, usurping, patriarchal society, even now being punished for its once-upon-a-time ruthless application of patriarchal rules to a not-quite-helpless woman of the Sidhe.

Well, dead was dead! And in a few hours, he would not be thinking of matriarchy and patriarchy. He would be killing as long as he could breathe, and then his enemies would finally exult and the light would die behind his eyes.

He regretted all the days and nights he would not spend with Emher, and all the carousals he would not have with his comrades. Most irksome, he regretted never knowing the answer to some questions, like: why indeed was this war taking place — and, unbidden it crept into his mind: who was Curói, and why did he care what happened to Gowen? Why, above all, was he here instead of home (what an odd ring that had: "home"!) with his mother and father — who might well be dead by now, and his friends, Cei and Bedwyr and Peredur. By what fateful or divine stratagem had he been brought to this wild and beautiful place to die?

As he leaned against the upright stone and thought all of this, he gradually became aware of another presence. His eyes focused; he saw, in front of him and slightly to one side, an almost exact replica of himself. This Gowen-figure seemed bathed in a low lustre, almost seemed to pulse with energy, and Gowen had somehow the sense of great antiquity. He looked questioningly at his new companion.

"I am Lugh of the Sidhe," said the figure softly. "In the land you came from, I was called Llew Llaw Gyffes and here I am known as Lugh Lamfhada. It is all the same. I am Lugh of the Long Reach. I can reach out as you can with your sling, and touch with death at great distances. I served the Tuatha well in their battle against the Fomhoire, and I am your father in a way that you cannot understand.

"I and my kind have always been and always will be. And some of us, like Aengus, meddle in the lives of your kind, now and then. I am here to help you on the last day before your companions rise from their pain."

He extended his right hand with an ancient drinking horn — pale-yellow horn wrought in gold at the tip and the mouth with an intricate design of delicate, intertwined figures.

"Drink, for your survival."

Gowen had heard the story of Llew Llaw Gyffes. He had heard it from... someone at home among the Cymry. Llew had been a legend among Gowen's people.

That long-forgotten tale, Lugh's demeanour and his physical resemblance to Gowen banished any doubts Gowen might have had. He meant to help; that was clear. And no help could be better than help from the Sidhe. Gowen reached for the horn and drank deeply, his nose tingling from unfamiliar herbs and spices. Almost at once, he had a feeling of well-being and relaxation. Lugh was speaking again.

"I will be in your place today when the armies come. No one will know that it is not you. Your friends will arrive only in time to find your body, and they will wreak a terrible revenge for your death."

Gowen stared. It was all he could do. Lugh's words were enigmatic, if not nonsensical, and yet he believed. He opened his mouth to protest. The word that wanted to form on his lips was "Emher". But he could not utter a sound, and Lugh went on speaking.

"Your time is not yet. It will not be too long now, before you can join me in the Land of the Young, but you still have things you must do. And you must do them at home — in your old home. You will drift away home, while I take your place here, doing what you would do."

Again, words that sought life in sound forced Gowen's lips to part, but Lugh continued serenely.

"When you come home, you will find much that is new and much that is disturbing, and you will not be able to change any of it. It is your destiny to be the last witness to the end of a time, and to make the manner of your leaving a statement for all of us."

"I AM NOT GOING ANYWHERE!" thought Gowen, and opened his mouth yet again. But no sound emerged. Haze settled across the pupils of his eyes and he saw as if through a waterfall. "I AM..."

Sight became darkness, sound became silence, thought ceased.

Gowen awoke. The curragh rocked seductively, but he forced his eyes to stay open. He was already a-sea, out of sight of the shore. He could not even guess where shore had been. It was to be as Lugh had said. He was going "home".

He unfastened the pouch with the Gae Bolg and hefted it thoughtfully in his hand. It was of the place he was leaving and was of him in that place. Almost reverently, he allowed it to slip from his hand into the waiting sea.

As he sailed, he found the answer to at least one question. Again he witnessed the solitary flight of a gull and the ordered formation of ducks and this time he understood.

"Our enemies," he thought, "the enemies of all our people in Eire and on the Isle of Giants and in the great land beyond, they are like the ducks. Alone, they are not formidable, but they flock together. We — we fly like the gulls, each man for himself, each tribe for itself, and we fight each other as much as we fight outsiders like the Sassenach. And in the end, the others have a place to be, and we are blown away by the wind. Somewhere, we must make a stand."

Thinking that, he slept.

The last day of battle was just as Gowen had known it would be. The-man-who-was-not-Gowen was awake, vigorous and ready when the first wave of men dashed down the slight incline and poured into the stream at its narrowest point. His sling whirled with incredible rapidity and its missiles sped to their targets like the numberlesss flight of bats in the evening.

Falling like deer in a hunt, Mebd's men nonetheless kept on, across the ford and up the other side, reaching Not-Gowen and besieging him on all sides with swords and spears. His sword flashed brilliantly, swiftly, fatally, and they drew back from the deadly circle of his reach to attack him with spears at a distance. But he would not leave them in peace. He charged through them, flailing madly with his sword and leaving behind him a trail of severed limbs and heads. As the sun rose to its zenith, he was suffused in a golden glow and his strength and speed were irresistible. He charged through them, ran to a distance, cut them down with his sling until they reached him again, then charged through them again.

As the heat of noon receded, his speed lessened, his strokes were less powerful, his sling less deadly. Gradually, he pressed them less and they pressed him more, climbing over the bodies of their comrades to reach him. Maddened by their own helplessness, they scrambled forward together, forcing him back now, in the direction he chose to retreat, until he reached the pillar stone. His left arm shot outward and backward and from his left hand floated a strong, supple, leather chariot rein, around the pillar stone behind him and snaked twice around the stone and himself and into his waiting right hand. Quick as thought, he fashioned a knot to hold it across his chest and just above his waist, and stood now, half on his own and half supported by the cord, as Mebd's men closed in on him. He parried and thrust as he was able, but the blood now ran freely from many wounds and soon his arms were hardly moving at all.

Cét — the very man faced down by Conall years before — stepped forward with his sword already swinging. The blade cut cleanly through the neck of the man tied to the pillar stone and clanged dully on the stone itself, as the head fell to the ground.

A ragged cry of triumph rose from the circle of men and died in their throats as they turned their gaze to the top of the hill before them, already tinged by the darkling fingers of evening. For over that hill, like some precocious night-time apparition, the chariots of the men of Uledh soared into view. Down, down, down the hill they flew and when they reached the vanguard of Mebd's army, they fell upon them like wolves upon a boar piglet in the forest. The first man to fall was Cét, whom Conall found instantly, sword still dripping the blood of the man tied to the pillar stone, his other hand holding the severed head by the hair, turning now to defend himself against the new enemy

"Never again, O Cét!" Conall roared, and his sword flashed — once right, once left — severing first Cét's sword hand and then his other hand, and leaving him staring stupefied at his bleeding stumps. Unseen on the ground, the severed head smiled.

The mere sight of that terrible vengeance completed the disheartening of the armies of all Eire. Half of them turned and fled and the other half offered token resistance before following after them. Down one hill, up the other, and into the broad meadow beyond stretched a roadway of bodies. It was the last, great victory of Uledh and would be remembered not only around the fires in Emain Macha but around the fires in all the capitals of Eire.

And should you ever journey to Eire, to that once-upon-a-time Viking village called Dublin, there is, I have heard, a great house called a "post office", and inside it for all to see is a great statue of CúChulainn (we know who it really is) lashed to the pillar stone, Mebd's raven perched on his shoulder, his head just leaning over toward death. And it is there because this tale from a time of giant deeds may still inspire the people of later days to struggle on against great odds.

What happened with the bulls? It is an odd ending to a great event, for the men of Uledh captured Aillil's bull and put him into a field with the Brown of Culaigh, and they charged each other. The signs were all there that this was the beginning of the waning of Uledh. Their last great victory was crowned by the mad rush of the Brown who ripped the bowels from the White and tossed them from his horns into the watching crowd, where the blood spattered Conchobar himself. And the charge of the Brown as he raced toward his enemy took him one unexpected step to the side, so that he trampled none other than Bricriu, who had not even time to shout in alarm. Many among the Uledhmen thought that this was but his due for the troubles he had created, but others saw that it was the accidental, and fateful, passing of yet another one of the great figures of their day.

And what of Emher? She grieved her life-long and never took another man into her bed. But she administered Gowen's holdings in Uledh and, from there, her own in Leinster. Every so often, there came to her one or two of the children of her brothers and she accepted them in fosterage. Later, there came children from other houses in Leinster and Uledh. It was custom to foster children with man and wife, but Emher was an exceptional woman among already exceptional women — the women of the Gaels — so her protection and aid were sought out by those who knew of her. She lived as full a life as possible for one who will never love again. And man after man who helped her to control her estates desired her and pined away for lack of comfort from her. There was only one CúChulainn.

Chapter Sixteen
OLD FRIENDS

Roll and grate. Roll and grate. The curragh rolled in the wavelets that lapped the stony beach, and grated on the stony bottom. Gradually, feeling and sound woke Gowen and he raised himself on one elbow and peered over the rim of the small skin boat. A pang of memory brought a vivid picture to his mind of how he had peered just so over the side of the large curragh on the day after his kidnapping by Roigh. His life had come full circle, and still he did not understand its purpose. Lugh, Curói, Scathách, Aoife, Cathbad, Mebd, Emher, perhaps Cei again. What did it all mean? What was it for?

Slowly and without enthusiasm, he rolled out of the the curragh and onto the ground of his homeland for the first time in his adult life. His possessions were few: his tunic, his hide trousers, his sandals, his sling and the pouch for stones, the simplest bronze torc around his neck. He emptied the pouch onto the beach and filled it with native stones. Whatever he did from now on, it would be as Cymry. Cautiously, unsure of whom or what he would encounter, he dropped a stone into the sling.

As he turned to walk away from the water, two figures appeared in his path and stood facing him — clearly challenging his right to be there. They would be the coastguards. In a moment, they would ask his name and family and his reason for coming here. Their backs were to the sun and their faces were shadowed, but there was something hauntingly familiar about them. One of them was tall and thin and seemed to be in motion even as he stood still. The other was half-turned away, even though his face was turned toward Gowen, and the side of the body toward him seemed incomplete. He moved suddenly, just as Gowen understood the significance of this incompletion. The side toward him was empty. The man was one-armed, and his movement now — lightning quick — was with the half-hidden left arm, revealing in the moment of launching a broad-headed spear. The thin man moved one hand as if to say "Wait!" but it was already too late.

Gowen's sling whirred half a thought after he saw the spearhead. His stone shattered the shaft of the spear when it had travelled little more than half the distance between them. The spear jerked, jumped and fell to the earth like a bird shot in flight.

"Child of Dôn!" hissed the tall man, and took an involuntary step toward Gowen.

The one-armed man threw back his head and laughed.

"Don't you see! You, who always said he would come back! Don't you see? Who else could have done that?"

Gowen's inner eye cleared as if it had been washed clean of a misty covering.

"Cei?" he said in a whisper, "and Bedwyr?"

One-armed Bedwyr continued to laugh as Cei rushed at Gowen, seized him around the waist and threw him into the air, where Gowen, as he remembered doing when they were all young, turned in mid-flight and landed lightly on his feet. Cei's face collapsed in joyful amazement and he sat down heavily.

"How... where?" Cei threw his hands out and laughed.

How and where indeed! Gowen smiled ironically.

"Have you time before you go to evening meal? It is a long story."

Bedwyr — always before prepared to follow Cei, even second to him in accepting Gowen when they were young — took the lead. He held his hand out to Cei, who took it and allowed himself to be pulled upright.

"Our post is just up from the beach," said Bedwyr. "There is fire, food and drink. We will all go there. You will tell us your tale and we will tell you ours."

And so they went — three old friends — but not laughing now. Each thinking of what had happened in the years since they had seen each other. Gowen, suddenly overwhelmed by thoughts of Emher, Conall and Roigh, nearly choked on the lump which rose into his throat and felt just like the lump he had had to swallow when he was but a child in Sualtim's house and thought of his parents and friends on the Isle of the Mighty. Then and there, he decided that he would return and take up his life again, no matter what explanations he had to offer. Those he loved would accept them.

For now, however, he re-acquainted himself with the best friends of his youth. He told his story first, glossing over his less believable exploits, but telling of Scáthach, Emher, Mebd and Curói and closing by telling the story of Lugh. When he had finished, the silence of his companions spoke to him and asked: Lugh and Curói, and Llew and... who?

Cei said thoughtfully, "The names are difficult for my tongue, but this Lugh —"and he painfully produced the comparatively simple sound 'Loo', "who says he is also Llew —" and he said it with confidence, giving the usual guttural rasp before the L: 'kh-loo', "it is a great thing to think of. We already know that we can speak easily to those of our people who live on the great land to the east over the water, and many of our ways are the same. But the Gaels of Alban and Eire — that they are from the same roots — yes, that is a great thing. And the thought comes to me, that you may have forgotten your steady visitor when you were among us. He was just as you describe your Curói — tall, silent, a hunter always accompanied by his dog. He first told your parents that you were fated for something. His name..."

"Was Gwri!" Gowen exclaimed.

"And is that not as close to Curói as Lugh is to Llew?"

For a while after this, there was silence, as all three struggled to understand what they had been saying. Finally, Gowen spoke again.

"What of you, and our home, and my parents, and our other friends?"

Bedwyr stared past his feet into the fire and said nothing.

Cei spoke huskily, "Your father was killed in a raid some years ago. Your mother died only recently."

Through the deep sadness which filled his mind, Gowen heard that Cei was still speaking.

"... brother."

"What are you saying, Cei?"

"After you left, it was as if the gods had decided to compensate for the loss of an only son. They had another child, and he is one of us."

"Gareth," spoke Bedwyr angrily.

"You do not like him, Bedwyr?"

"It is not that," Cei spoke for his companion. "It is the re-naming he hates."

"Re-naming? How so? To what and to what purpose?"

"Well may you ask. It is something Artor has allowed because of his love for Llan and Gwynhyafar."

Gowen's head whirled: who was Artor, who was Gwynhyafar and above all, was Llan the Llan that Gowen remembered?

Cei saw the bewilderment on Gowen's face and said, "It is a long story. Settle you down and we will tell it.

"After you were gone from us, our people were pressed not just from the sea any longer, but also from the east. The Sassenach have come westward and would subjugate us or push us into the sea if they could. We had to defend ourselves on the coast and in the mountains at the same time. We could no longer be as separate and divided as we had been before."

"So it is happening here already," Gowen thought. "The coming together to make a stand."

Cei continued, "We needed more than a council of small chiefs. Even Gwynedd was not enough alone. We needed a war leader who would unite the Cymry. And Artor came to us.

"No one is quite sure of his family, but there was a prophecy that a man of the blood of dragons would appear to lead us, that his name would be Artor and that he would have a magic sword. Artor appeared in Gwynedd shortly after the prophecy, said he was the son of someone called Pendragon, and challenged the strongest of us to battle to prove himself.

"Well, of course, the one who thought most of himself was Llan and he answered the challenge. At the first stroke, Artor's sword hacked a huge piece out of Llan's shield. At the second, it shattered Llan's sword. It could have been only that Llan's sword had a fault and was waiting to be tested. But it was all so much like the prophecy. We acclaimed him war-leader. Not much fighting was necessary to convince Dyfed, Powys and the other lands to throw their lot in with us. They were all as pressed by the Sassenach as we were.

"He has been a good war-leader. He has an instinct for tactics in battle and for overall strategy that none of us has. We have fortified the coast with small guard posts and garrisons. There are always at least two coastguards, so that one can ride for help at the first sign of a raid. In your case, we didn't think that a single coracle with a dead body was much of a threat."

Gowen smiled and Bedwyr grinned back at him as Cei continued.

"After that, Llan worked hard to ingratiate himself, picked a lot of fights with men who were not too sure of Artor. He became a favourite of his and life has been like it was before you surprised him and took away his leadership."

"Not quite," said Bedwyr. "Artor has enough sense to see who is a real leader and not just a blustering bully. Llan is his personal friend but Cei is his second in command."

"And Bedwyr is just as fast and ferocious as you remember him, so we always put him in the battle front, to terrify the enemy." Cei smiled as Bedwyr unexpectedly bowed his head in embarrassment. "Still, Llan can stand that, as long as he is Number One Friend and no one crosses him. He won't be happy to see you."

"I don't look forward to seeing him either," Gowen said. "But who is Gwynhyafar?"

"Gwynhyafar is Artor's queen-to-be. Llan brought her back from the great land across the water. He went to see the great world and he didn't stop with the Cymry there. He went on to some very grand places — where the houses and fortresses, according to him — are bigger, stronger, more comfortable. He returned with his head full of how everyone but the Cymry understand civilization. Talks about things called 'courtoisie' and 'chevallerie.' As if we have spent our lives squatting in the woods and bashing rabbits on the head for dinner!"

"It's almost better than what happened to Peredur." It was Bedwyr growling again

"Yes, Pedredur wasn't interested in 'civilization', so he went further. No one is quite sure how far, because he speaks in riddles like a druid."

"Peredur went with Llan and none of the rest of you went?"

"Peredur has never been the smartest among us," muttered Bedwyr. "Llan wanted a travelling companion and a stooge. He just didn't count on Peredur going off on his own."

"Live and let live," said Cei.

"Tell that to him and the great Lancelot."

Gowen stared from one to the other. "Who is Lancelot?"

Bedwyr smirked and Cei frowned.

"Lancelot," Cei said in a pedantic, bored tone, "is the grand new name for Llan ap Lot. Even worse, it's 'Lancelot of the Lake'. Nobody seems to know what lake he means, but it all sounds very grand. He... Well, you'll see."

"At any rate, he has re-named everyone, including the woman he brought back as a perfect bride for Artor. Artor was always a tough and crafty war-leader — led us to many a close victory when we should have been defeated. But he has given his approval to all this nonsense. Seems to agree that it is time for the Cymry to stop being barbarians. And he is completely bewitched by this woman Llan brought back.

"She is a Cymry of very good family who went abroad long before Llan, to learn foreign ways. She has returned not as Gwynhyafar but as 'Guinevere.' It is supposed to be 'modern' and 'up-to-date'." Cei's upper lip curled involuntarily. "And there is something a little funny about the way she and Llan act around each other. Everyone sees it, except Artor..."

"Arthur!" growled Bedwyr, viciously drawing out the odd sounds. "Aarththooo-ur!"

Cei flinched and smiled. "... Except Arthur and Peredur, that is, Percival..."

"Please, tell me," Gowen implored, "that this foppish name is not for my old friend Peredur — he who always seemed to be looking beyond our world in search of something greater. How could he stand to have his name taken from him?"

"You will have to ask him yourself," Bedwyr snarled. "Just don't make the mistake of saying what you think before you hear him rant and rave."

"Peace, Bedwyr," Cei reproved gently.

"And," Bedwyr overrode him angrily, "I would like you to meet your old friend Kay." He slashed his hand in the of direction Cei and then, thumping himself on his chest with his fist. "And his closest companion, Bedivere."

"Gods above and below!" Gowen choked on his laughter and bent forward to cough the misdirected liquid from his windpipe. When he straightened, he saw that Bedwyr was smiling sardonically, but with no real joy, and Cei's face was like a thundercloud.

"Laugh while you can," he said. "Soon enough it will not seem humorous."

"When may I meet this Arthur?" Gowen gasped, trying not to laugh again.

"Artor, when you speak around me," Bedwyr ground out, "or may you spend eternity in Manawydan's fortress of bones in Caer Sidi!"

"We and a few others do not conform to the new name-giving. To us, your brother is still Gwalchmei, as your parents named him. We are few, but we are valuable to Artor and the matter is trivial to everyone but Llan and Gwynhyafar, so no one complains of us," Cei explained. "But the time for us to be relieved of guard duty is soon, and then you will see it all for yourself."

All three fell silent for a while, mulling over what they had heard from each other. Gowen thought again of Emher and wondered whether he could just escape the fate Lugh had predicted for him and go back to her and his home in Eire. He thought of Curói and his odd, benign meddling in Gowen's life. He thought for the first time in years of Gwri and the similarities between the two men who had appeared on the fringes of his life at crucial times. Thinking of the two of them, he suddenly realized what had bothered him about his trip to Scáthach — "Khuurrkhi," the wizened old Pict had called himself. Unlike Gwri and Curói in every other way, he was also a hunter. He had the same, deep grey eyes and his constant companion was his dog. He was the same! Like his people, he was ancient, for they were ancient in this island. Curó/Gwri/Khuurrkhi was the only figure Gowen had encountered in all three of the peoples of these islands who had been here before the Sassenach — Pict, Gael, Cymry. He was the proof of what the bright-haired woman had told him in the cave. All these peoples were related somehow. Their bloodlines and their fates were intertwined.

And if that was so, he also understood the similar meaning of two other names: Gwynhyafar and Finnabair — Fair One, White One, Pale Spirit. Mebd's Finnabair was a living expression of woman's powerful sexual attraction for all men. It would be interesting to see whether Gwynhyafar also fulfilled this description. And to meet this Artor, who was a brilliant war-leader but such a poor judge of character that he could have Llan as a friend.

Chapter Seventeen
HOME IS THE STRANGER

When it was finally time to leave, Gowen received another shock. Bedwyr and Cei untethered two horses. Each one bore a blanket on its back and, on top of that, a kind of leather seat. They vaulted sideways into these seats and Bedwyr looked laughingly down at Gowen, extending his hand. Gowen took the hand and allowed himself to be half hauled, half thrown into the seat behind Bedwyr.

Cei smiled sourly, "This is what warriors do in the great world, instead of riding in chariots. Even our enemies, the Sassenach, ride like this or go on foot. Personally, I think that one good chariot charge would scatter them to the four winds."

"But then," Bedwyr interjected, "we would not be 'chevaliers' who know all about 'chevallerie'. We'd just be poor, benighted Cymry barbarians."

"He means, 'cheval' is the foreign, fancy word for horse, and the other word comes from it. So a man who rides around with a horse between his legs is somehow better than a fellow who stands upright in his own chariot, as our fathers did," Cei explained.

"Well, to be fair about it," he continued, "Artor has seen one advantage in this thing. A man on a horse can go over rough trails and no trails at all, over places that would defeat chariot wheels."

Gowen, who was already beginning to feel sore on the insides of his legs and just a little bit motion-sick, didn't know whether he wanted to laugh or shout in anger.

The ride would not have been long in a chariot, but on horseback, it seemed eternal. Finally, however, they came in sight of the biggest and grandest fortress he had ever seen — bigger than Conchobar's *dún*, as big, even, as Mebd's gigantic *rath*. It occupied the entire top of a long hill, and had not just one wall with a ditch-and-mound defence before it, but three, immense walls with intervening defences and a broad, snaking road to a massive, two-doored gate surmounted by a watchtower. Arriving inside, he saw that the houses were on the same scale as the fortress and that the walkways were not just beaten-down pathways made by passing feet, but stones or wooden boards laid out to show where one should walk to get from one place in the compound to the other.

Cei snorted when he saw Gowen puzzling over these innovations, and Bedwyr said sarcastically, "Even the wild Sassenach know about these walkways, and that proves that they are necessary to civilization."

"Say rather, that some of the folk Llan was so impressed with on his journeys had been conquered and ruled by the Sassenach and by others. He has brought the soft and beguiling ways of the great world to us, as a great favour to the Cymry!" said Cei.

"Oh gods!" Gowen exclaimed. "Just lead on, so that I may see all that there is to see as quickly as possible."

Cei led the way to the largest of the houses, with a doorway so great that the tallest man could pass through without bending and two strong men could pass each other in it. Inside, the space was filled on both long sides with low, wide tables, covered by vast amounts of food and drink in a variety of containers. Both men and women sat on low stools and benches eating and drinking. A long aisle led straight to the opposite end of the great space, where Gowen spied a large, wooden seat with an ornate carved back, raised above the hard-earth floor on its own platform. In the seat was a man as big as Roigh or Conchobar, with yellow hair and beard, just beginning to show traces of grey. On either side of him stood tall, burly warriors like a protective phalanx.

"Kay! Bedivere! Come forth! What have you brought from your watch on the coast? Who is this young fellow?"

Cei began, "He is an old friend —" but a booming voice overrode him.

"He is not young, Arthur, he is just little. And he is a friend only to some." Llan — massive arms crossed in front of his chest — scowled down at Gowen from his place beside the throne of the war-leader.

Gowen tensed, ready for any action on Llan's part, and waited for Cei or Bedwyr to speak.

Bedwyr looked defiantly at Llan and said, "This is the friend and companion of our youth who was taken from us in a Gaelic raid — Gowen. He has returned to us from across the sea. He has lived a marvelous..."

But he never finished. A roar of joy and recognition erupted from one of the other men beside Artor's seat."

"It is GúGullenn! It is my old gomrade from the training gamp. It is no Gauwain, it is a GúGullen!"

And Aran-Cet lumbered down off the platform to seize Gowen in a bear hug that would have snapped the spine of a lesser man. Then, ridiculously still holding Gowen like a child's toy, he turned to face Artor and Llan: "Little he may be, but take my advice and don't say it to him twice. He is fearsome when he is angry." As Llan's face turned deep red with the memory of his childhood encounter with Gowen, Aran-Cet dropped Gowen with a thump.

"I thought never to see you again — never to be able to pay my debt."

Gowen smiled, feeling a mixture of happiness at seeing Aran-Cet again, and sadness as it reminded him forcibly of their comrade, Ferdiad.

Llan would not be excluded from the conversation. He turned to Artor with a smirk and said, "The big Gaul has named him well — he shall be 'Gawain' in our company."

As Gowen opened his mouth to protest, his mind's eye conjured up Cathbad on the day of the death of Chulainn's dog. Naming by chance both that time and this. And this time, it came about by an odd agreement between a friend and an enemy. How could it be entirely bad, if Aran-Cet was partly responsible for it?

And so he said nothing, as Llan smiled triumphantly and Artor smiled benignly. The war-leader looked at him with interest.

"I have heard many a tale of you from your friends. For such a short time among them, you made a great impression."

"In childhood," Gowen smiled, and glanced casually at Llan's slightly misshapen nose. "Some impressions last longer than others."

Llan's face turned, if possible, an even deeper red. Behind Gowen, Bedwyr snorted with suppressed laughter and Cei suddenly became interested in how well his sword scabbard was fastened to the girtle around his waist. Aran-Cet looked from Gowen to Llan and back again with dawning comprehension.

"War-leader Arrthorr," he said, "my friend has gome a verry long way. He is tired and hungry and thirsty. Allow me to take him to a table for now."

Artor smiled again and nodded in agreement. "We will speak again,

Gawain of the Cymry."

As they walked toward a space at one of the long tables, Gowen turned to Cei and Bedwyr and said, "This is Aran-Cet, one of my most valued comrades at the camp of Scáthach I told you about. We shared a great battle before I left."

"Some of us shared more than others," the big Gaul said with a rueful smile. "I was not a bit insulted when friend GúGullen took away the fearrrsome woman who was about to garve me up like a boar for the feast! And that was after our other frriend had saved my life from GúGullen himself because I thought myself greater than I was. Our frriend...?" he looked questioningly at Gowen.

"Is dead... in battle not long ago," Gowen replied very softly.

Aran-Cet bowed his head in sadness and said no more. Cei and Bedwyr, who could guess what battle had killed Ferdiad, and how, were also silent.

As they found some empty spots and sat down at table, Llan's musing stare followed the four of them. Cei and Bedwyr had been predictably partisan in their welcoming attitude toward the little horror. But the big Gaul he himself had brought back as an emissary from their cousins on the Continent... that was unexpected and unpleasant!

Aran-Cet was just explaining this to his companions.

"I am not your frriend, Llan's first choice as emissary. He had a favourite gompanion who taught him all about manners and how to dress grandly."

His companions stared at his simple tunic and trousers.

"Yes," he laughed. "I am not a fancy drresser, and GúGullen knows that I am not a smart, smooth speaker." He laughed again as he saw Gowen struggling to control a smile.

"This gompanion also showed your Llan how to behave arround the ladies. And he paid special attention..." he stopped suddenly and his voice died away.

Cei interrupted. "Yes, anyone can see who that was."

Aran-Cet, continuing, did not attempt to hide his embarrassment.

"So your Llan wanted to brring this fellow back as an emissary to your Arrthorr, but my war-leader would not have it. I am just an ordinary fellow — I plant grops and keep livestock, I have two fine daughters and a strrrong son — but when I have to be, I am a warrior, not one of these fellows who sit around trrrying to decide if this wine is better than that one or whether this herb smells better than that one when it is grushed up and laid into the glothes chest.

"My leader chose me because he wanted to send someone who gares about how things are and whether an alliance with your Arrthorr is worthwhile. These fellows who call themselves Frranks — they look and sound a little like your Sassenach — are pressing in on us from the north and west. They are fearrrsome warriors, but no better than we are. But they are goming in such numbers — I don't know how long my own land will be my own.

"But now I have been here and I gan see: you have your own troubles, and we must each survive without help from the otherrr."

Gowen and his two old friends, who had heard him talk of the family of the Celt, sat in gloomy silence, thinking of Aran-Cet's bleak analysis and wondering what would become of their cousins across the water. Then Gowen felt a large hand rest on his left shoulder and an unfamiliar voice said, "Is this the prize that was thrown up on our shore, Cei? It seems small and harmless enough."

As Gowen tensed yet again, he saw Cei look up and smile and Bedwyr grin. As he turned to look up at a blond, blue-eyed warrior as tall as his companions, Cei said, "Gowen, meet your 'little' brother, Gwalchmei."

"Or Gareth, if you listen to Llan and his followers," smiled Gwalchmei. "It is good to see that you are not just a legend, brother."

Gowen stood and felt himself folded into an affectionate bear hug.

"What other wonders will I encounter before the day is out?" he mumbled from inside his brother's arms.

"Good that you should ask," muttered Bedwyr, and Gowen freed himself from Gwalchmei's embrace in time to face a woman who was making her way along the aisle toward Artor's throne. She was only slightly tall for a woman, slim-hipped and lithe and she walked with an abandon that spoke to every man who saw her. Passing Gowen and seeing that he was new, she smiled provocatively and trailed the fingers of one hand across his chest where his tunic hung open. The raw sexual power she exuded struck Gowen like a physical blow and he felt himself begin to harden. Frantically calling up thought of Emher and of the women of

Conchobar's people who had halted his battle rage by baring their breasts to him, he was able to damp the fire of unexpected lust, and he watched the emotional devastation she caused as she made her way forward. Men's jaws fell open, women's eyes danced with fire. His own companions, already inured to the effect, stared with hard, cold eyes as she passed.

As she reached Artor, the strategic wizard of the Cymry smiled like a child who has been given a new toy, and stood up to greet her. Gowen, who had been warned, could see that the glance of amused affection Gwynhyafar bestowed upon Artor was pallid in comparison to the heat of the glance that passed between her and Llan.

"It is too much for one day," Gowen said, loudly enough for his companions to hear. The roar of laughter he provoked spoke as much of the release of tension as of appreciation of the wry remark, and it caused the entourage around Artor to glance inquiringly in their direction. Bedwyr, never at a loss, swept his one arm across his body in a mocking bow and Gwynhyafar wrinkled her pretty nose in disgust.

"Come," said Cei, standing swiftly, "let us go to our berths in the warriors' house. We will find Gowen a mat for the night and then we can talk more if we wish."

He paused uncertainly as Aran-Cet also rose.

"Of course, you have your place with the leader's circle, friend Gaul..."

"The frrriends of GúGullen and the sleeping place of GúGullen are good enough forrr me. I will send word to Arrthorr," said Aran-Cet with such matter-of-fact determination that no one argued.

Bedwyr threw his long arm around the Gaul and said, "It is good to know that you are not a lapdog and some of your people are more like us than the 'manners' that have come our way from the great Continent."

Aran-Cet's broad face was covered by his all-encompassing smile and he said to Gowen, "It is like the gamp. Thrrrough you, I meet the most interresting people. I was beginning to be bored. Life," he said with great satisfaction, "is going to be morre interresting now."

Picture the main players now, as the scene closes. It was a collection of heroic eccentrics not likely to be equalled ever again in that land: the noble and naive war-leader, the steamily passionate woman who was to be his bride, the trusted friend who found some satisfaction in both the lady's embrace and the knowledge that he was besting his own leader; and down on the main floor the simple, bear-like Gaul, Cei of the perpetual movement and future-seeking eyes, one-armed Bedwyr whose every move was so fast that no one could say that he had made it, tall and handsome Gwalchmei and his older, smaller brother whose battle rage had once terrified his own king. Rarely has a poet of the Cymry had such rich material.

Do not be surprised. Were you paying attention at the very beginning of my tale? When I introduced myself? "I am Fergus of the Mist and Taliesin of the Noble Brow. And other names you may know. I have been a king and a warrior, a prisoner and an exile and even a sorceress's apprentice."

Well, a sorceress's apprentice of sorts. Actually, I was chosen by a powerful witch to stir a cauldron while she took care of a call of nature. The liquid was almost on the boil and contained a formula that was intended to compensate her monstrously ugly son by endowing him with wisdom, poetic inspiration and a little bit of magic craft. Unfortunately for her son, she turned over the the care of the brew to me at just the wrong moment. I had barely begun to stir, when it boiled, bubbled and sent a drop of the spicy concoction directly into my mouth.

Nothing could be done. The first drop is the same as the whole cauldron. I had whatever powers the liquid could bestow. The disappointed mother pursued me, with vengeance in mind. My little bit of magic allowed me to change forms, but she was more than equal to that. I was a cricket, she was a bird; I was a rabbit, she was a fox. Finally, I became a small kernel among many kernels. Undeterred, she became a hen and ate up every one of the kernels. Unfortunately for her, the kernel that I was became a child inside of her, and when I was born, she could not bring herself to kill me, so she set me adrift on a bit of bark on the river. I fetched up in a weir where a fisher found me and exclaimed in surprise when he saw my nobly shaped brow, thus giving me my name — Taliesin.

Among the gifts of the cauldron was the talent of poetry, which I used to immortalize the human greatness of that folk and those times. In vain. The many tales I set to verse about Artor and others were transformed by the same influences so keenly resented by Cei and Bedwyr. The characters — those two included — and their actions were transformed over time into something more luminous, and more grandiose. The heroes and heroines were remarkable for the superficiality of their faults and virtues, for the glittering triviality of their motives to action. Evil existed independently and without reason, and warred upon Good, whose petty benevolence prevailed in all challenges until the end, when their very evanescence betrayed them and their power vanished for as little reason as it had risen. And the truth of the times now lies buried underneath the tales of pretty and inconsequential adventures pursued by lovely, shallow figures. But that is progress. Let us return to our tale as it is.

Chapter Eighteen
QUESTS

In the warriors' house, before sleeping, Gowen told his story one more time for Aran-Cet and could not avoid this time the death of Ferdiad. The big Gaul had tears in his eyes as he laid his hand on Gowen's shoulder. He smiled through the tears as he said in a voice rough with emotion. "You see, you werrre both right about me. I am a fat Gaul with many children. And I gan still fight equally with anyone but you."

As Aran-Cet spoke of his home, family and friends, his broad face glowed with pleasure and longing. But he also spoke of the division among his people — those who wanted to fight on for their independent lifestyle and those who just did not want to fight any more.

"They say this thing, *garpe diem*. It means to enjoy yourself while you gan, begause you will not live foreverrr. It means that fighting for yourself is a waste of time." He shook his head in disgust and the others nodded and made noises of agreement.

"There are those here who feel that too," said Cei. "And I begin to fear that our leader is listening to them." He turned to Gowen. "Maybe you remember what it was like when we were children? Cymry fought each other all the time. But not one Cymry, in Gwynedd or any other land, decided that his nation could not win. No one said that it would be better for all of us if we just stopped fighting and accepted terms for peace. Just so we could go on living in our own land! Now there are those who not only say that. They've even started calling Cymry by the Sassenach name for us — welsh."

"And," continued Gwalchmei, "even when I was a child, there were none among us who believed that this world is unfit to live in and all we can do is seek a life after death."

"But there is life after death or at least life instead of death," Gowen said. "In Eire they talk about Tir-nan-Og — Land of the Young, because you never grow old if you get there."

"Yes," said Cei, "there is that for us too, by a different name. But your brother is talking now about our friend Peredur, who journeyed on after leaving Llan and his company. He says he met a magical person who told him that there is only one god, not many, and promised that Peredur would have an important role in making this worship the only one practised by Cymry and Gael and Gaul and even all the nations of the Sassenach. It will be the end of druids, and that's not all."

"And then there will be no more war or fighting," sneered Bedwyr, "because this new worship demands that its people be peacable. It hasn't done much for Peredur. Anyone who speaks against his 'Christ' finds himself on the ground with a sword point at his throat and either converts on the spot or dies. Looks like hypocrisy to me!"

"He met a man who wore a funny hat with a colorful feather in it, who said he was the Fisher-King, but he never caught any fish," said Gwalchmei. "He took him up to his big fortress where there was a great feast, and a great drinking mug called the 'Grail' that people worshipped, and young men were running in and out holding spears with blood dripping off the blades, and women wailing and the Fisher-King sat in a great chair — grander than Artor's — and seemed to be in great pain from some unmentionable injury that would not heal. Peredur's mother had always taught him not be rude, so he didn't ask what ailed the man, and that was against their hospitality, so they threw him out and made the fortress disappear. Before he came back, he wandered all over, looking for this man and this fortress."

"Where is Peredur now?" Gowen asked.

"Out knocking people off their horses and threatening their lives, no doubt," said Bedwyr. "He is at all times as one in a battle rage — what the Sassenach call a berserker. Even his friends approach him with care."

"You may just get to see him before he leaves again on what he calls his 'final pilgrimage' to find the fortress or die in trying," said Cei. "And he will be as useless to us in our battles against the Sassenach as will those who want to appease and surrender."

"I am almost afraid to ask about my other old friend," Gowen mused. "How is Culwch?"

"Ah, Culhwch is a different story altogether," said Cei. "While Peredur was off finding and losing magic fortresses and magic drinking vessels, Culwch was on a quest for his bride."

"Unhappily, I was still too young to go, but Cei and Bedwyr made the trip with him," Gwalchmei interrupted wistfully. "They had to travel far to the north and north-east and had a grand adventure."

Gowen looked a question at Cei, who said, "It all began on the day Culwch became of marriageable age. His aunt laid a destiny on him that he would never marry unless it was a maid called Olwen. He asked why she had done that to him and why he had to go so far away to find himself a wife, and she said, 'The seventeen words of the destiny I have laid upon you have been in my mouth since the time you were born, and I have no control of them but to rid myself of them by saying them at the right time. I cannot tell you how I know, but I know that this maid is the only one suited for you, and you would not be happy with anyone else.'

"So he decided he must go and he asked which of his friends would share the quest with him. Bedwyr and I volunteered at once. Llan was too self-centreed to go on a quest to benefit someone else, and Peredur was ruled by his widowed mother, who refused to let him go."

Gwalchmei broke in: "When he finally got up his courage much later and rode off to catch up with Llan, she didn't find out until he was gone, and she dropped dead on the spot. So now he has guilt about that and guilt about not asking the right question at the Fisher-King's banquet and he takes it out on everyone he meets by trying to recruit them for this otherworld army everyone will join after dying, so they can live peacably doing nothing for the rest of time."

Controlling an urge to smile, Cei continued. "Before we set off, we went to a druid for advice. He cast the sticks and studied the entrails of a fowl, and told us that we would never even find Olwen's father's fortress unless we first asked the oldest of creatures where it was. Olwen's father was a man who had trained to be a druid, but could not stand the discipline. In the end, he hated everyone in his home, so he ran away north, where there are other Cymry. He married and had a daughter, but his wife died in childbirth and he cut himself and his daughter off from everyone. Only the creatures of the forest and water knew him because he hunted them.

"So we consulted together and found that we did not even know what the oldest of creatures was. We paid the druid a good price to come with us and we set out to the north-east.

"On the first day of our trip, Culwch spread lime on a tree branch near our campfire and we waited to see what would catch itself. Soon enough, a magpie landed on the branch and the sticky surface trapped it there. The druid made a magic spell and the bird was able to talk. So Culwch asked it how to get to the fortress of Ysbaddaden. The bird said, 'I am not the one who knows. Ask a creature who is older and wiser. Ask the stag,' so we let the magpie go.

"The next day, we travelled until midday, then we dug a large trap covered with branches and spread nuts and grain over the middle of it. By afternoon, we heard a crash and a high, keening sound and ran to the trap. Sure enough, there in the trap was an old stag with wondrously large antlers. But when he knew what we wanted, he said, 'I am not the one who knows. Ask a creature who is older and wiser. Ask the owl,' so we let the stag go."

Gowen was sure he knew how this search for the oldest and wisest creature would end, but he did not interrupt the flow of the story to say so.

"So we travelled for most of the next day and when we made camp, we caught a mouse and tied it by its tail to a low tree branch near our fire and waited for nightfall. When finally, in the deepest dark of the night, an owl flew down to the branch to inspect the mouse, the druid cast his spell and the owl spoke to us. But it said, 'I am not the one who knows. Ask a creature who is older and wiser. Ask the eagle,' so we let the owl go.

"That was difficult. We climbed a nearby mountain. It took days, but we reached a spot where the eagle kept her nest. We just waited for her to return from hunting, and as soon as she soared into view, the druid cast his spell, so she knew what we wanted and that we were no threat to her young ones. She did not hesitate a moment. She said, 'I am not the one who knows. Ask a creature who is older and wiser. Ask the salmon,' so we left the eagle and made our way down the mountain and camped for the night near an eddy pool of a large, rushing brook. In the morning, we set a weir at the edge of the pool and waited. Before long, as if having planned it, a huge old salmon swam into the weir and waited patiently for the druid to cast his spell. He knew the way to Ysbaddaden's stronghold, and told us clearly and simply how to get there.

"It was a difficult path at the end, up a narrow path on a steep incline. It kept getting narrower and narrower, until there was little more than room for the path. Then we came to a well-built stone wall stretching from one side to the other, and a small wooden door in the middle, with a small portal near the top.

"We pounded on the door with our spear shafts and shouted, but no one came. We thought about scaling the wall or trying to batter down the door. Finally, we decided to camp right there and try again in the morning."

"Tell the truth!" growled Bedwyr. He threw Gowen an ironic glance. "We had no idea what to do, and we were exhausted, so we just had something to eat and went to sleep."

"Yes, well," said Cei, "that's true. We lay down to sleep, but sometime after dark fell, the little portal opened and a blue eye peered out and a woman's voice asked, 'Who are you and what do you want here?'

"And we answered that we were searching for Olwen, because one of us was destined to wed her. And the voice asked, what was the name of the one, and Culwch spoke up and said, 'It is Culwch of Gwynedd,' and the portal snapped shut and the little door swung open slowly.

"We entered very slowly, spear points first, because of everything we had heard about Ysbaddaden. But there was only one person there — it was a young woman who had to be Olwen herself, for she was so beautiful that I would have wed her myself if she had not been destined for our comrade — eyes as blue as the sky, hair like golden grain at harvest..." Cei's voice became wistful and nostalgic and Bedwyr grinned at the others and said, "Either one of us or the druid would have cheerfully cut Culwch's throat and run away with her then and there."

Cei smiled. "It wasn't quite that bad, but we could see that our friend had been given a happy destiny. She took Culwch by the hand and led us to the house that perched at the end of the precipice we had climbed. Behind it, from what I could see in the darkness, the cliff fell sheer.

"She led us into the house, which was lit only by a central fire. In the flickering of the fire, we could see a very large man, standing. He crossed his arms and said, 'So this is how you repay years of care from me. You bring the man who is to be my death.'

"The girl looked at him and said, 'It is the destiny you chose for both of us when you turned away from other men and came here. We have both known that this day would come.'

"He didn't even seem to have heard her. He looked straight at Culwch as if he knew which one of us it was, and said, 'If you are the one, you are fated to have my daughter and by that act, to be the death of me. I will not make it easy for you, for I am not done with this life. There is a wild boar in the forest below us who has gored me and chased me every time I have hunted him. I tell you that you will not have my daughter until you bring me that boar, trussed up and alive, to this house.'

"The girl stood calmly and did not protest, so it seemed to be all part of some destiny that had been worked out long ago. Culwch turned to go, and in that instant, the old man threw the heavy mug he had been holding in his hand straight at Culwch's head. I stepped in front of it and caught it. The old man just stared at me as I threw it back at him and bounced it off his forehead. He fingered the lump that was beginning to rise and said, 'What a terrible son-in-law! Already he gives me a headache!'

"Culwch went out with the girl, who motioned for us to stay. When she came back, she served us with meat and drink and we sat and talked with her and — believe it or not — the old man, telling stories and hearing stories of his adventures in this place, and it was as if we were welcome guests.

"As morning dawned, the girl went out of the house and we could hear her open the small door in the wall. We had heard no one knock, but when she returned, it was with Culwch, who was tired and filthy, but carrying a very angry boar — bound and slung across his back. The old man reached behind him to grasp a spear and flung it straight at Culwch. It would have gone straight through his head and into the body of the boar, I think. But friend Bedwyr was too fast. His hand shot out to grasp the shaft of the weapon. He flipped it around in his hand and sent it back to Ysbaddaden with incredible strength and speed, and it pierced the old man's chest. He stared down at the bit of shaft that still protruded from the front of his body and said, 'A terrible son-in-law. He makes me die of heart-ache." And he died right there.

"The girl told us what we must do next. We released the boar, which now had the spirit of the old man, and it ran back down the mountain and into the forest as fast as it could go. 'My father tried to kill my suitor and the boar at the same time. If he had succeeded, he would have gone on living in his own body. It was a destiny he created when we came here, and he knew what it meant. He did not want to live after I left here. He will seek out some of this old enemies and harass them until they finally kill him.'

"And so we came home. Culwch is always with us in battle, but he lives apart with his family."

Gowen laughed and said, "It is like evenings in Conchobar's great house, when one story followed on another, and each teller tried to outdo the previous one. This would have been the champion tale of one of those nights."

The story of Culwch and Olwen filled his mind as he felt the similarity with the destiny which had led him to Emher. Longing and sorrow flowed into his body. In the circle of his old friends, he felt an equal measure of physical exhaustion and an exhaustion of spirit — a sadness for the life he had not lived here, and a greater sadness for the life he had left behind him in Uledh. Without willing it, he allowed his eyes to close.

When he woke, it was bright day and his companions were gone, but for Aran-Cet, who smiled as Gowen sat up and said, "I have told them how dangerous it is to wake you up. They are in Arrthurr's hall, waiting for us."

Atypically for the Aran-Cet Gowen remembered, they walked in a companionable silence to Artor's great hall and Gowen found himself wondering what manner of woman it was who had had such profound impact on the bluff Gaul that his face glowed with joy when he spoke of her, and more, that he had learned the wisdom and utility of silence.

As they entered the hall and walked toward Artor's throne, Gowen subliminally sensed something. It was a few more steps before he realized what it was. It was unlike any time he had walked the length of Conchobar's hall, when — even after he married Emher — girls and women followed him with mischievous and flirtatious glances. Here and now, he was just another man among many men. Clearly, Cymric women were not a different breed of creature from the women of Eire. The change was in him. Life with Emher, and especially the certainty of death and final separation from her after she had left the battlefield that last night, had forged a new inner man. The instinctive, febrile glow of sexual attraction that he had never consciously controlled had guttered and died.

"Just as well," he thought, "just as well! I have had my happiness and now I will have my destiny. And at the end, maybe I can get back to my happiness again."

They reached Artor's end of the long hall just behind Cei, Bedwyr and Gwalchmei. Llan stared down at them. With a sneer in his voice so clear that Gowen wondered why Artor did not notice it, Llan turned to

Gwynhyafar and said, "Lady, this little fellow is the newcomer you have heard of. Gawain, this loveliest of all ladies is the bride-to-be of our leader and king, the Lady Guinevere."

A half-smile twitched on Gwynhyafar's soft red lips as her glistening blue eyes bored into Gowen's own with an unmistakable message of lust and pleasure.

"A new hero is welcome here," she said with soft intensity and waited expectantly for his reaction. But he had witnessed both her power and her corruption on the previous day. Unsmiling, he allowed his eyes to drift down her face, to her slender neck, to the softness of her breasts under the light cloth of her robe, to the darker green of the kirtle around her slender waist, to the folds that hung over her long, slender legs, to the shapely ankles that peeked out from the hem, and finally the dainty feet in sandals so elegant that they recalled to Gowen's mind an old tale from his childhood of how the great Manawydan had once supported himself in exile by making the most elegant footwear ever seen.

Raising his eyes to meet hers again, he said in a tone so neutral that he might have been reporting the disposition of an enemy army or the size of a harvest from a field: "The lady is lovely."

Llan clenched his teeth so that his jaw bulged. Gwynhyafar's neck turned a dark red which rose slowly to cover her whole face, dyeing even the roots of her blonde hair a faint rose. Artor smiled uncertainly and said, "Thank you. I am a lucky man."

Turning to Cei he asked, "Have you invited your old friend to join us in our campaign to keep the Cymry free?"

"No need, war-leader," Gowen answered. "This is my home as ever was. I offer my arm and my sword in its defence."

Gwynhyafar was recovering from her first reaction, and still unwilling to believe in the power of any man to resist her attraction.

"And your heart?" she murmured.

Gowen stared past her at Llan.

"My heart is like many others — given to her who knows she has it. And no others matter."

Artor's gaze shifted in mild bewilderment from Gowen to Llan to Gwynhyafar. Llan's jaw muscles bulged even more. Gwynhyafar's blush deepened further.

Cei smiled at the king. "Our friend has led a rich and complicated life far from here, but he is still the hero he was. Bedwyr and I welcome him and friend Gaul —" Aran-Cet beamed "into our little company. When the Sassenach send their patrols, we will be ready."

For the first time In the conversation, Artor's face cleared and he smiled the genuine smile that had solidified his control over the men and women of the Cymry.

"We have heard of great movements near our border — a great gathering of the Sassenach. Their scouting parties will come very soon, and our best border guards will be waiting for them. I need not tell you the most important thing about engaging them?"

Bedwyr said flatly: "Allow none to escape, leave none alive."

"Yes." Incongruously the warm smile was back in answer to this stark comment. "It is best to make them fear us as much as we fear them. The mystery of their missing patrols will be more powerful than any tales the survivors might tell."

As the five friends silently pondered this ruthless remark from a man who so obviously preferred love and friendship to war and death, the sound of a commotion penetrated from outside. Shouts of anger, thumps and thuds, clangs and clashes of metal on wood. Artor stood and moved commandingly through the hall, causing all others to move out of his way. Slipping into the train behind him came Bedwyr, Cei, Aran-Cet, Gwalchmei, Gowen, then Llan and finally Gwynhyafar. The others in the hall crowded in behind them and oozed out of the large central door, just as Artor stepped into the centre of a circle of men and demanded:

"What is the cause here and who are the combatants?"

Turning toward him was a tall, raw-boned warrior with a wild glint in his eyes and a sword held by the hilt with both hands, as if to begin a killing, overhead stroke. Opposite him and also turning toward Artor was a warrior, or perhaps a hunter, dressed entirely in green. He was at least a head taller than his opponent, his face hidden by waves of hair cascading from under a green, cloth cap. Held vertically in front of him was a thick, wooden staff.

Gowen gasped as recognition struck. The wild-eyed warrior was much like an adult version of his old friend, Peredur. There was also something hauntingly familiar about the green figure, but he could not identify it.

As they all stood, gazing at this spectacle, Bedwyr said softly into

Gowen's ear,k "No matter the size, this fellow is in for a drubbing. When friend Peredur gets that look in his eyes, he is nearly as fearsome as you in your rage."

Just then, Peredur/Percival growled, "This interloper will not say what he seeks among us, and I am by the way of teaching him some Christian values."

Suiting action to his words, he raised the great sword above his head with as little effort as if he were throwing a twig over his shoulder. His powerful downstroke began, but the stranger did not step back. He stepped forward, into the path of the stroke. His staff twirled to the horizontal and moved with the speed of a peregrine falcon to intersect Peredur's hands where they gripped the massive hilt. The sword flew up and over Peredur's head. His hands flew outward and then down, hanging sore at his sides. Grinding his teeth together so that the sound could be heard by those standing around, Peredur half-turned to retrieve his sword, but Artor said, "You have done well, Percival. Let us hear the man."

As Peredur subsided, muttering to himself, the stranger said, "I am in search of a champion. This good warrior did not care to listen. He is clearly in the grip of some powerful passion which rules his every act. I have no wish to harm or humiliate him."

Cei and Bedwyr, who had recently told Gowen of Peredur's obsession, exchanged a glance of stupefaction — that the stranger could not only read their friend so clearly and quickly, but that he could so easily disarm him.

Artor spoke again, "Tell us your errand, friend, and if you are not on the business of the Sassenach, we will hear you."

The green man answered softly, "I am in search of a champion who can storm the fortress of innocence, who can conquer with love and make a virtue of his pleasure."

Artor spoke softly into the bewildered silence. "You speak in riddles, warrior. Explain."

"Which among you," said the stranger, "has done wrong but is yet pure, has loved and never wavered, has lost everything but never hope?"

Bedwyr spoke, "It is still not enough, man! Leave the language of the druids, and speak your meaning plainly."

It appeared through the waterfall of hair that the stranger smiled and one, grey eye sparkled out at Bedwyr. "Bedwyr, known to all — you ask much.

"Know then: my home is but one day's ride from here." He pointed directly north. "I am not the commander of a great army, so I live in a hill fortress, where my people also come in time of trouble. I live to hunt, but they are tillers of the soil and keepers of goats, sheep and pigs. Good and simple people..."

"Will you come to it, man!" Bedwyr again.

"Ah," smiled the green hunter, "who was it who ever said that we are a people of poets? But yes," he hastened on, seeing the fire in Bedwyr's eyes, "the point is this. A curse has been laid upon me and my home, and it can only be cleansed by an outsider — a man of unusual virtues. And so I have come to the greatest gathering of good men to ask your help."

"How may the right man help you?" Artor asked.

"He will journey to my home, bide one night in it, experience whatever adventure may befall him, and leave on the morrow. If he does this successfully, he will lay the curse and my people and I will be free and prepared to reward him richly." He paused to stare at Artor and the group around him. "Is there any who will brave the trip, measure himself against the magic that afflicts my home and receive reward and gratitude?"

Gowen noticed that Gwynhyafar's hand came to rest lightly on the back of Llan's shoulder. Llan stepped forward, swelling his chest like a bullfrog's neck at the beginning of his mating song and said: "I will try it."

Gwynhyafar smiled as Llan half-turned his head to give her a glance that would have melted a spear point or baked a clay jar.

The hunter nodded and said, "I thank you, friend. I must not be there when the curse is raised, so I will travel on, but a guide will come for you at dawn, just at the edge of the forest outside, and bring you safely to my home." He looked at Artor and said: "War-leader, I thank you for your courtesy. I will do all I can to help you in the battle against the Sassenach. Perhaps we can prevent them from overrunning what is left of our country."

And then he was gone so quickly and unobtrusively that it was almost as if he had not been there.

Chapter Nineteen
IT'S NOT EASY, BEING GREEN

At the first blush of dawn, Llan waited at the spot where the Green Hunter had indicated. He was not alone. Artor and Gwynhyafar, Gowen and his friends, as well as a number of other curious men and women, waited with him. They did not wait long. Out of the path in the woods came a girl-child riding a pony. Blonde, blue-eyed, wearing plain jerkin and leggings of softest green leather, smiling slightly and completely unafraid, she rode directly to Llan and, from her pony's back, looked him straight in the eye.

Unaccountably, she pointed her pretty nose at Gowen for just a second and grinned at him. He smiled back at the spark of mischief in her eyes. Then she turned a serious gaze upon Llan and said: "I am to bring you to my master's house. We must start now."

And she turned her pony smartly about and trotted off toward the entry to the path.

"Ho, there...!" Llan spluttered, then fell silent and swung himself up on his horse to follow. He turned his head and shoulders back to wave at all assembled, then disappeared into the woods behind the child.

There was little more for those left behind than to gaze after the two vanishing figures, then quietly disband. Artor wore a small frown of disquiet; Gwynhyafar scowled as she strode long-legged up the entry ramp.

Gwalchmei, staring in the direction Llan and the girl had disappeared, asked slowly, "Has anyone ever heard of this fellow before? What do we know of him?"

Cei looked thoughtful, Bedwyr shook his head sharply in the negative, Gowen was trying unsuccessfully to transform the odd emotions caused by the Green Hunter's appearance into coherent thoughts. Into this silence flowed the rough bass voice of Aran-Cet: "In my homeland and among many peoples arround us, there are tales of a Grreen Man who appears, and does a grreat thing — good or bad — and disappears again. I gannot tell you what he is, but I do know that he is not only ourrrs, the Gauls', but the

Frranks know him, and the Alemanns and others."

Cei's gaze bored into Aran-Cet's eyes: "What is the purpose of his appearances? Is there no common thread in the skeins?"

Aran-Cet cleared his throat, "I have neverr seen him, but some think that he appearrs to test someone, or some grroup of someones."

"Test them for what?" asked Bedwyr. "If he is testing for conceit, our Llan is a sure winner."

As everyone smiled at the typical Bedwyr barb, Aran-Cet replied slowly and thougthfully, "They believe that he tests for gourrage — for the gourrage to face some test that will gome. And what is seen as a good that he does is when the one he tests is egual to the test and when it is seen as evil, he is not. I believe that too, but I think from the stories I have heard that it is not just gourrage, but honourr as well."

No one had an answer to that, or, for that matter, anything at all further to say. The matter rested where it was until four days later, when Llan reappeared.

In the middle of the day, when the sun hung high and hot overhead, an odd figure appeared on the path where Llan and the girl-child had left. He held a cape or coverlet of intricate design wrapped around him, one shoulder free like an exotic Roman senator. His hair was dishevelled, his bare feet were grimy, he cursed with the names of all the gods and demons he knew as he limped out of the woods, up the entry ramp and past the astonished guard at the great gate. Belatedly, the guard raised the cry and everyone within earshot spilled out of the great house and from every other direction to witness the homecoming.

Artor asked softly and affectionately, "Lancelot, what has befallen you? Have you run afoul of thieves or brigands? Is the child all right?"

"The child!" snarled Llan, and hobbled with startling discourtesy past his war-leader and friend and disappeared into his own small house — the private residence was a privilege afforded only a few, but Llan's gratitude was not in evidence at this moment.

Artor cleared his throat in embarrassment, Gwynhyafar wrung her hands in distress, but did not dare to openly follow her lover. Even Artor might find it odd. An uneasy, shuffling silence ensued, then, one by one and two by two, they all drifted away.

Gowen remained standing with Aran-Cet and and Cei. As they

exchanged aimless speculations, the girl-child rode startingly past the gate guard and straight up to the small group. Looking directly at Gowen, she said, "It is for you to redeem the honour of your friends and comrades. Be outside at sunrise tomorrow, prepared to travel." Before he could say a word — or even think what he wanted to say — she turned her pony smartly as before and trotted through the gate and out of sight. Bedwyr and Gwalchmei, when they heard, agreed with Cei and Aran-Cet that Gowen had been visited by a destiny. He had to respond.

And so, through the afternoon and deep into the evening, Gowen prepared, grimly holding his seat on top of Gwalchmei's horse. At first, his brother held the reins and led the good-natured animal in a large circle. Then he gave the reins into Gowen's hands and coached his older brother as he cantered around the same circle. Finally, in the grey predawn of the next day, Gowen stood surrounded by Cei, Bedwyr, Gwalchmei and Aran-Cet. Nibbling something green on the ground, Gwalchmei's horse was placidly unaware of his soon-to-be-rider's unease. Despite the practice session of the preceding day, Gowen's technique was lacking, to say the least, and his thighs and buttocks still ached. He wasn't sure, but he was afraid that there might even be the beginning of blisters.

As the slivers of the rising sun filtered through the trees, the girl-child trotted out of the forest path and stopped immediately before Gowen.

"It is time," she said, and smiled a smile at Gowen that the men found impossible to classify — was it impudent, joyful, childishly gleeful, or even affectionate? No matter, with some help from his brother, Gowen clambered laboriously onto the horse, the girl turned her pony smartly about, and they rode together onto the path and out of sight.

The ride did not begin pleasantly. The child's pony trotted effortlessly ahead and Gowen held the reins loosely, allowing his horse to keep pace. As much as possible, bracing himself upward with his hands, he kept his affected parts from contact with the horse. But "as much as possible" was most unsatisfactory, and his attempts to minimize the pain were obvious to the girl.

After a while, the child allowed her pony to slow and Gowen's horse to catch up. Staring up at him in contemptuous amazement, she said, "Have you ever before ridden a horse?"

"Oh, yes," he replied with a groan, "all of yesterday!"

The child laughed and he laughed with her.

Then, serious again, she looked up at him and asked, "Did you not fear to come with me, after your great hero returned in such a state? He is so much bigger and stronger."

"You invited me for your mysterious master, so there must be a reason."

Sharply but not aggressively, almost to herself, she said, "And he so handsome and you..."

Gowen smiled despite the pain in his buttocks and thighs.

"... small and dark and sad-looking," he said, staring down kindly at the child as if she were a niece confused by some aspect of life and looking for guidance.

The girl nodded slightly.

"My name is Lynedd," she said, "and I am of age."

"What age is that?" Gowen asked in astonishment.

"Why, the age of consent, of course. I can be chosen to be the intended of a worthy warrior."

And she stared up at him frankly. Her large blue eyes seemed so capable of swallowing him up that he momentarily forgot she was a girl-child.

He shook himself mentally, and smiled down at her.

"Were I not already committed, it would be an honour to contend," he said with as much gravity as he could muster, "and until your true suitor shows himself, I will gladly be your champion."

Again, she nodded to herself, and this time she smiled a small smile.

"There are some dangers along this path, so you must be alert."

"Dangers?" Gowen echoed. "How then did you survive them?"

"They know me," she replied cryptically.

"They know her?" thought Gowen. "Who knows her...?"

At just that moment, they rode around a gentle curve, beyond which an old woman sat on a fallen log by the side of the path, staring disconsolately into the woods.

"Good day, grandmother," said Lynedd. "What is your sorrow?"

The old woman sighed but said nothing. She held a slender willow switch in her right hand. Its tip trembled and flicked up and down as she moved her hand ever so slightly up and down, like a herder lightly encouraging his animals onward.

Lynedd asked again, "What is your trouble, grandmother?" and the old woman's eyes cleared. She focused on Gowen and said:

"He took my creeturs."

"Who did, grandmother?" asked Gowen.

"A big fellow with a big club. He just came out of the bush and took them away and said never a word."

"Where did he go?" Lynedd asked and glanced out of the side of her eye at Gowen. He knew he was being manipulated, but he only smiled and waited for the old woman's answer.

She pointed the trembling switch across the path, where broken small branches marked the fast and violent passage of a large body.

It was almost with relief that Gowen slid carefully down his horse's side to feel the wonderfully solid earth beneath his feet.

"I will see to it, grandmother," he said softly, and stepped toward the opening made by the big man.

Lynedd rode her pony across his path, stopping him and looking down sideways from her seat.

"Your big warrior made the same... kind of mistake," she said, and Gowen noticed the small pause to repair her initial statement. It was clear that Llan had confronted precisely the same situation and had reacted in precisely the same way, by following the trail of broken twigs and branches alone to find the big man who had taken the old woman's "creeturs" — sheep or pigs or cattle.

Giving the girl a quick smile, he bent down to retrieve a few extra, small stones for his pouch.

Straightening, he said, "Thank you for the warning." Then, after a pause, "I would be happy of the company, if you don't feel you should stay here with grandmother... Especially since you are acquainted with the dangers of this place and may keep me from some misjudgment."

The child suddenly sat up straight, as if he had tweaked her nose or said something unacceptable. Then her small frown turned into a ironic smile and she said, "I will come," and slid from her pony to land lightly on her feet.

"Mind your feet," he said with a grin and a glance at her delicate feet, protected only by sandals.

"Lead," she snapped, "and we shall see whose feet are sore at the end of this venture!"

They were but a short distance into the woods, when they heard the stuttering, guttural conversation of sheep close ahead of them. Gowen did not slow, but slipped a small stone into his sling. The path of trodden bushes and broken twigs ended suddenly in a clearing where they saw first a huge, ramshackle lean-to, and sitting in it a giant of a man, gnawing on what appeared to be a leg of mutton. A pile of bones lay in front of him, and a fire blazed merrily in a circle of stones. To one side, the old woman's sheep milled about, possibly one less than they had been.

A shaggy head raised to reveal a shaggy beard, and two large brown eyes stared with a minimum of understanding at the two newcomers. He stood slowly, grasping with his right hand the slender end of a massive cudgel.

"What?" he said, and Gowen assumed he meant, "What do you want?"

"We have come to take grandmother's sheep to her," he said gently, and smiled up at the big man. The giant seemed so like other big, harmless men he had known, like Lugaid's brother, that he hesitated to attack him.

The big man decided the issue by raising the cudgel and stepping toward them. Curiously, the girl did not flinch or run, but regarded the scene with detached interest. Gowen whirled his sling and loosed a stone at the big man's hand. The stone struck with a vicious crack. The big man gave a short cry, dropped the cudgel and cradled his wounded hand in the other. Then, with a sound that might have been a snort, or a sob, he made his undamaged hand into a fist and raised it level with his head, as if to pound Gowen into the ground. Gowen slipped a second stone into the palm of his hand and, instead of using his sling, threw it hard and fast at the small toe of the big man's foot. This action was followed by a howl and a crash as the big man sat down hard.

Gowen walked slowly forward, holding his hands out in front of him, as if to say, "Don't do anything," and the big man stared at him like a chastened child.

"It will be al lright," Gowen said. "We will take the animals and leave. You stay here. It will be all right."

The big man's lower lip slipped out from beneath his upper and he looked even more like a bewildered small boy. He stared up at Gowen as if to memorize his features, but made no move to stop him and the girl as they drove the sheep before them back to the path.

When they rejoined the path, the old woman stood up with a small cry of happiness.

"My creeturs, my creeturs," she crooned, and bent to touch them as they flocked around her legs. "Thank you," she said to Gowen, and as he was on the point of answering, Lynedd cut across his first words:

"It is well, grandmother. Take them and go with our blessings."

The old woman seemed to want to say something to Gowen, but she swallowed whatever words had been in her mouth, turned slowly down the path in the direction Gowen and Lynedd had come from, and urged her flock along ahead of her.

Lynedd did not appear to notice anything unusual in the old woman's behaviour. She pulled herself lightly onto the back of her pony and stared over her shoulder at Gowen.

"We have still a long way to go."

Sighing with resignation, he pulled himself laboriously onto his horse and looked down at the child.

"On to our next adventure," he said with a sour smile, and she ducked her head to hide whatever reaction he might have seen on her face.

As they rode, she began to question him about his life, and continued unrelentingly for some time. She was appalled and fascinated that he had been kidnapped and taken to the land of the "wild Gaels", where he had lived his life until recently. She insisted on hearing about his adventures — she even seemed to have heard something about them, so that she could refer to the "championship contest," or the "coming-of-age battles", and he fleetingly wondered which of his two old friends could have been so loose-lipped. On second thought, he dismissed that idea. Something else was at work here. And for some reason, he found that he could not — or did not want to — refuse to answer the child's questions.

He answered as briefly as possible, allowing the glory, where possible, to reflect on others than himself. He praised Roigh, and Loeghaire and Conall so often that the girl finally gave an impatient snort and said that she had asked about *him*, not about every Gaelic barbarian he had befriended. But when he came to speak of Emher, she listened attentively, and about his sojourn with Scáthach, and how he had come to meet Aran-Cet (although his Gaulish friend was better in the re-telling than he had been in the original encounter), and how he had come to know his beloved comrade, Ferdiad.

Even now he could not bring himself to speak of Cathbad and the beautiful woman in the cave. But, with ineffable sadness, he told of his last meeting with Ferdiad and, after that, his last meeting with Emher when she tended him on the battlefield. Tears were standing in Lynedd's eyes, when he remembered to mention belatedly the name of the mighty sorcerer/ warrior/ *bachlach* who had helped him at the walls of Emher's father's fortification and had awarded him eventually the championship of Uledh, and he wondered aloud what considerations had made grey-eyed Cúroi an interested party in the fate of someone born to the Cymry, fostered and accepted as a warrior by the Gaels of Uledh, and now returned to his birth-land at a time of great crisis.

As he spoke, her eyes grew huge and the tears, suddenly released from them, trickled down her cheeks like tiny streams, and dripped and dried away. In a deepening silence, she simply stared up at him, paying no attention to the path and allowing her pony to find its own way. Gradually, then, her eyes returned to their normal size and customary blazing blueness, but she did not speak again. And so they rode, each deep in thought, for what seemed to be a long time.

Gowen was not completely silent. Small, suppressed groans and sighs escaped from his compressed lips. Lynedd, however, stared straight ahead and did not take the opportunity to laugh or ridicule or even sympathize. It was as if she had discovered something in the tales she had heard that changed everything for her. It had happened, Gowen was sure, when he mentioned Cúroi, and he thought back to his not-long-ago conversation with Bedwyr and Cei, when they had spoken of Cúroi and Gwri.

Then, into their pensive silence intruded a loud, shuddering, and very long sigh. It was clearly from a male voice somewhere ahead of them. They heard it repeatedly and increasingly clearly. As they came finally to a widening of the path, where travellers had often turned aside to rest and had trodden a level area extending some distance into the forest and several horse-lengths along the perimeter of the path, they saw a doleful figure. A man of medium age, dressed as one of the warriors in Artor's army, was sitting on a fallen tree, toying with a branch he had apparently whittled into a walking stick. He sighed again lustily as they approached him.

"What is your trouble, friend?" Gowen asked, noting with amusement that Lynedd had her mouth open to ask the same question.

Another loud sigh was the only answer. Lynedd slid from her pony, walked to the doleful fellow and took one of his hands in both of hers. He looked up then, first at Lynedd and then at Gowen. When he saw Gowen, he cowered, peering up at him sideways from an averted face, as if to say, "Please don't hit me!"

Gowen repeated his question as gently as possible and did not stir from where he sat on his horse.

"I have nothing more, nothing more. Your comrades have taken my horse and my weapons, and left me not even my pride. They have gone that way," he said, pointing into the forest behind him.

"Can you lead me to them, friend? And I will see, can I get your things back," Gowen said, and noticed even as he spoke that the anticipation of real, warrior-like action had caused his speech patterns to return to those he had learned in Uledh.

"One man, one small man?" he cried in horror. "There is no chance. They are strong and ruthless..."

"This is a mighty champion," said Lynedd softly. "If anyone can retrieve your horse and weapons, it is this man."

"He is so little," answered the man doubtfully, as if Gowen were not a part of the conversation.

Tiring of this whining, Gowen slid from his horse, handed the reins to Lynedd and said brusquely to the man, "Lead me to them and we will see."

As if he had been ordered, the man stood and stepped silently into the forest. Gowen turned to Lynedd and said:

"It will be of most benefit if you stay here with the horses until we return. If we should become lost along the way, how much further is your master's home and how many more paths must we travel?"

Lynedd did not protest as he had expected.

"It is now but a short time, all on this path and few turnings."

Gowen nodded and followed the sad man into the forest, noting as he turned away from her that Lynedd's face had an expression partly of amusement and partly of sadness.

At first, there were clear markers — broken branch ends, small plants flattened by passing feet. After a while, the Dolorous Warrior (as Gowen thought of him) appeared to be following a trail that Gowen could no longer perceive.

"Either," he thought, "this is a truly remarkable tracker, or he is inventing the direction as he goes."

But he said nothing to his companion, and finally the other man came to a sudden halt, stood quite still for a short time, leaning on his walking stick, then beckoned Gowen forward with his free hand.

Gowen stepped to his side and peered into the leaves and branches before him, but he saw nothing. His companion pointed forward, insistently waggling his finger at something beyond the leafy cover before them. Gowen stepped forward, peering even more intently. He saw nothing but leaves and branches and shadows. Then suddenly, a brilliant flash of light followed by darkness.

He was lying on the ground, and the back of his head hurt. In fact, he had a very bad headache. And a very big lump on the back of his head. When he touched it, his hand came away pink with the little bit of blood there. He sat up slowly, gingerly, and his head hammered.

He was in the forest but not where he had been. There was no sign of the trail he and the sad man had broken. There was only the forest. He still had his clothes, sandals and pouch, but his sling and sword were gone.

Standing up slowly, he waited until his head stopped pounding, then looked around. He found a young oak tree, small enough so that he could reach the offshoots of one of the lower branches and break off one slender stick. He looked at the break. It was even, with small sharp points jutting from the break. He pressed his fingers carefully along the stick and broke it again, slowly. This time, one long, sharp point extended from under the bark on one side. Sitting down again, he poked the sharp point into his jerkin, just above the lower seam and began to rip and unravel the threads holding the seam. He had to remove the jerkin to finish separating the seam. Using the pointed stick again, he opened the seam, making a small pocket. Then he opened a rip in the opposite side of the circle, using both the stick and his teeth, and tore the strip apart. Finally, he held two ends of the seam in his hand, and below them dangled the loop of the rest of the seam, with the small wide space at the very bottom. Reaching into his pouch, he chose a small stone and slipped it into the pocket he had made in the seam. Whirling the makeshift sling over his head and to one side, he released the stone. It flew straight and true to another branch of the oak, striking with a sharp crack and carrying the end of the branch away. Gowen smiled. He was never completely at a loss when he had his sling.

Now his early games with Cei and the others came into his thoughts. He closed his eyes, finding somewhere in his mind a sense of where he was and where he needed to go. It was just as it had been when he was a child. He was like a soaring bird of prey — a falcon or an eagle — and he could look down on the whole area of the forest and its paths. He began to move through the forest at a trot, almost silently, keeping his face turned in the direction he knew he must go. Twisting and dodging past trees and large bushes, jumping supine trunks and small ravines, frightening small animals into pell mell flight, he accelerated to a run, then kept on without halt until he intersected the path.

When he crossed the path again, he knew he should be ahead of Lynedd, so he leaned against a tree and waited. In a short while, he heard the sound of hooves and of two people talking. The man was talking excitedly and laughing, but the girl was answering in monosyllables. Gowen's eyes seemed to be covered by a red haze. The heat on the surface of his skin became nearly unbearable. Almost without thinking, he slipped a stone from his pouch into his new sling and began to whirl it, casually at first, then increasing in speed when he heard the voices very near. In spite of his rage, it was a wounding speed, not a killing speed. As Lynedd and the Dolorous Warrior rounded the curve in the path, they saw him simultaneously. The man's jaw dropped in stupefaction while Lynedd's eyes sparkled with joy. Neither of these reactions was of much duration, for Gowen loosed his stone at the forehead of the man, knocking him backward off the horse to land in a sprawl behind it. He did not move. Lynedd gave a small cry and stared at Gowen.

"How could you..." she began.

But Gowen snarled, "How could I not! Treachery and assault must be repaid in kind."

"But if he is dead?"

"I do not think he is. But if he is, then he chose his own death when he struck me down. I thought to help him and he betrayed and attacked me. I believe this is another one of the little "dangers" you warned me of and Llan experienced before me. If they are meant to keep me from arriving at my destination, then they will fail. I do not make promises or undertake tasks lightly. Wait while I throw this wretched spalpeen onto the horse, then we can go on. I am sick to death of torturing the insides of my legs, so I will trot while you take the reins of my horse and lead it."

He paused and glared at her.

"And do not think to gallop away. I have more stones in my pouch."

"You are, you are... an uncouth Gaelic barbarian."

"And don't you forget it!"

With that, he hefted the limp but already groaning man over his horse, took back his sword, scabbard and sling, handed the reins to Lynedd and began to trot alongside her pony.

In a short while, they came to a great clearing. Stretching out before them and to the right were fields of grain and vegetables, meadows with pasturing animals. Men, women and children were at work tilling, weeding, herding. To the left was the steep curving path which led to a hill fortification. Without asking, Gowen simply started up the path, followed by Lynedd and the still groaning warrior lying across his horse.

At the top of the path, a heavy wooden door stood open in a timbered doorway capable of accommodating one chariot — or nowadays perhaps two horsemen side by side. A youth of no more than twelve or thirteen, dressed entirely in subtly tanned green leather, stood at the entrance.

"Welcome, Gawain, friend of Lancelot!" he said with apparent sincerity.

"Gowen," drawled Gowen in a dangerously low tone, "who is no friend of Llan, accepts your welcome, and would appreciate somewhere to sit after a long journey, and something to eat and something to drink."

The boy's eyes widened at this calculated rudeness. He turned on his heel, beckoning Gowen to follow him to a large, round, drystone construction with a massive thatched roof. It was located toward one end of the compound and was the second largest building, after the massive longhouse which took up the entire middle of the area and was apparently the common dwelling in times of siege or other danger.

Entering the house, Gowen paused on the threshold, to allow his eyes to adjust to the darkness, which was relieved only by a few fat and low tallow candles in bronze sconces on the walls and by the leaping fire in the fire circle directly under the smoke hole in the centre of the roof. To one side of the fire stood a low table, built up leglessly on a mound of clay and topped by a massive stone slab. Stools which appeared to be sections of a large tree trunk stood around it. On the opposite side and stretching along half of the rounded wall was a large bed/sitting area covered by furs.

The boy who had led him into the house said, "There will be food and drink soon. Please sit at the table."

He had barely settled on one of the stools when Lynedd entered, followed by four women bearing tantalizing platters of squirrel, partridge and hare and a large jug of what appeared to be fresh beer. The women placed their burdens on the table and silently filed out the door. Lynedd, apparently recovered from her earlier distress, sat down opposite Gowen and served from the platters onto two plates, passing one to him, and pouring from the foaming jug into two large pottery cups with handles designed in the form of a young boar climbing the side of the container and seeming to to peer over the edge at the drink inside.

While they ate, Lynedd talked of this place: the good people, the rich farmland, the master who protected them all. But she said very little that could not apply to any other place. For a child, she was surprisingly adept at making a conversation about nothing appear to be a conversation about something. As Gowen ate and drank, the day finally took its toll, and he became heavy-headed. He barely kept from nodding off while Lynedd spoke. Finally, she noticed. Standing up and pointing to the large sleeping and sitting area on the wall behind her, she said:

"This is our master's bed. He begs you to make yourself comfortable. He looks forward to seeing you on the morrow."

"But what of this curse?" Gowen sputtered, attempting to rise and finding his head so heavy that he had to lean forward and push up from the table.

"Of that, in the morning," said Lynedd, on her way out the door.

"But..."

Gowen was sure that this was not what he had been led to expect, but he could not think clearly. There was no question. It was time to lie down. So he moved heavily to the fur-covered bed, crawled over it until he had reached the wall, and settled down to sleep with his back at the wall and his sword in his hand.

It was dark. Only the low flames in the fire's circle lighted the area. Someone was standing at the edge of the bed, facing him and leaning forward slightly. As his eyes focused, he almost gasped. A beautiful woman stared down at him. At first glance, he had believed he was seeing Emher, but as he focused, he could see that the resemblance to Emher was no greater than the facial resemblance to Lynedd. A sister of the latter — a distant relative of the former? He willed his eyes to see more clearly and was shocked to discover that she wore a robe of the most diaphonous material he had ever seen. It was almost as if she wore nothing at all.

Gowen watched fascinated as she leaned forward a bit further and her breasts swayed with the movement. A longing he had not felt since his last sight of Emher washed over him and, in embarrassment, he felt himself respond.

"My husband," said the beautiful apparition, "cannot be here tonight, but he wishes you to have everything you might desire as an expression of his gratitude to you for undertaking this perilous task. I am here to see that your night is pleasant."

She smiled and slid one stunningly white knee across the furs. Then another, until she was on hands and knees, smiling at him. He was paralyzed by a conflict of thoughts and feelings.

"This is just his way of saying 'Thank you.' It would be churlish to refuse," he thought.

She reached out to stroke his leg above the knee, and he nearly groaned aloud with desire. Then she sat back on her haunches with her hands resting lightly on her thighs and smiled a friendly and inviting smile.

Somewhere inside of the swirling, rambunctious lust which gripped him, Gowen was able to imagine himself in the place of the absent husband, and it was a sobering picture. He swallowed noisily and rolled over onto his other side, presenting his back to the woman. He closed his eyes, pretending to fall asleep again and hoped desperately that his throbbing lust would soon subside. He had lain that way for some time, hardly daring to breathe, when he felt a light touch on the nape of his neck. Almost instantly, his body relaxed and he sank into a deep slumber.

Then it was bright morning and he woke to the sounds of lowered voices, dishes being set down on the stone table-top, feet moving softly by him. Rolling over to face the room, he saw that the table had been set for two and that Lynedd alone remained. She was seated at the table and she smiled at him with more warmth than he had seen in her until now.

"Perhaps I am forgiven for my temper of yesterday," he thought. "But I would do the same again."

Lynedd served a thick porridge into two bowls and poured clots of cream over it.

"Come and eat, champion," she said, still smiling. "You have passed the night and the trials."

"But you said we would speak of that this morning," Gowen objected, sitting and sliding to the edge of the sleeping area. He dropped his legs to the earthen floor and stood to take the few steps to his side of the table, where he he sat down and picked up the wooden spoon near his bowl. As he began slowly to eat, he stared at the girl challengingly.

She grinned impishly at him. "If only Guinevere —" her use of the name had a slightly sarcastic ring to it, "could know that all the rules and etiquette she brought back from Gaul are nothing compared to true 'chivalry.' Her Lancelot —" again that tone of voice, "was beaten by the giant, left behind by the sad warrior, and still he was brought here for the ultimate test. If he had passed it, he would have returned a hero, even though he failed the first two."

"Speak sense, child! I met the giant and the dolorous trickster, but you sent me off to sleep without ever explaining the horrors that would visit me in the night. And in fact, none did. I slept deeply and well. How have I withstood the ultimate test when I have apparently slept through it?"

She smiled at him again, but differently this time: warmly, almost — if she had not been a child, he could have sworn — seductively. His senses whirled and he feared for a moment he would lose his balance and fall off the stool. She had to be a close relative of the beautiful apparition of the night before.

"Explain..." he began haltingly, but then he stopped, unsure whether he wanted to hear the explanation.

She stood and leaned over the table at him, just as the beautiful woman of the night before had leaned over the bed. With no trace of a smile, but in a gentle tone, she said, "Once before, among the wild Gaels, you were tested for courage, humility and loyalty to your name. Now, among the Cymry, you are tested for steadfastness, compassion and decency. That last thing is what some in the new Gaul call "courtoisie", and is looked upon by them as a measure of worthiness. But what they have to learn, you already know. And where they may use their rules as excuses to do what they want, you will not do what does not feel right to you. You passed the test when you turned your face to the wall and your back to the temptation to take something that was freely offered, but was not yours to take. Why you have been tested is not for me to say."

She paused and looked embarrassed.

"I did not believe that such a 'small, sad man' could be the champion to pass these trials, but I was wrong. It has been a pleasure to know you, Gawain."

"I'm not," he began, but she interrupted him with a quick gesture.

"You are who you are," she said, "and now you must return to Artor and his men. Your horse is rested and ready and two bags are hanging over his neck. The small round one is provisions for the trip, if you should become hungry or thirsty. The long, heavy one is to be left unopened until you arrive back with your friends." She smiled, this time sadly, and walked around the table to take him by the hand and lead him out of the house.

His horse was ready, and standing with the reins in his hand was the dolorous warrior. He smiled at Gowen as he handed him the reins.

"I hope you will forgive me the knock on the head as I forgive you the crack you made in my forehead. If my brains had leaked out, I should be no smarter than my poor friend here."

Gowen gazed up in surprise as the giant stepped into view from behind the horse. Before he realized what was happening, Gowen felt himself lifted gently by the huge hands and set lightly on the back of the horse. The big man smiled shyly at him.

Lynedd said, "We all wish you well and a good journey, even the lady of last night," and she smiled again in a way that made Gowen grip the mane of his horse with both hands to withstand a moment of giddiness. Then the sad man lightly slapped the rump of Gowen's horse and it cantered out the gate, down the winding path and into the forest path. When he looked back fleetingly before turning out of sight of the fortification, he saw the big man, the small man and Lynedd all standing in the gateway and staring solemnly after him.

His return journey was peaceful and relaxing. Even his martyred buttocks and thighs seemed more comfortable than they had on the journey of the day before, and he almost began to enjoy the new form of travel. He drank in the restful sights and sounds of the forest and thought back to his childhood in these woods. He stopped briefly at the Dolorous Warrior's resting place to drink some of the good wine and eat some of the chewy cheese and the small round, crisp-crusted loaf of bread.

Finally returned, he was received with friendly surprise by the gate guard, who called out his arrival. As he dismounted — the action was actually smooth enough to deserve the name — Artor led a crowd out of the door of his great house. Llan, clean and rested after an experience that Gowen had only partly shared, hung back and said nothing. Gwynhyafar stood by Artor's side and Gowen's friends and brother just behind them as the war-leader said, "Well, Gawain, it seems you have already justified the boasts of your friends, since you have returned on your horse and with a rich reward... I suppose that is a gift to you from the Green Warrior?" and he pointed to the long object, wrapped in green and gold cloth.

Gowen held it in front of him and said, "I was told to open it only when I had arrived here again," and he began slowly to unroll the cloth. Bedwyr stepped out quickly to hold the loose end and move backward as the object rolled slowly on Gowen's upturned hands. At last, Bedwyr gently pulled the last of the cloth away and there, glittering in the late afternoon sun, lay a long, wickedly sharp sword. Gowen raised his hands above his head so that all could see and there was a collective gasp as the crowd saw the whole weapon. The blade was superb, but the hilt was a masterpiece. The handguard, which was curved away from the hilt to catch the blade of an opponent's sword, was in the form of the splayed back legs of a great hound. The slightly arching body of the hound was the handle. At the top end of the hilt, the front paws reached out with curving nails, while the hound's head reared back on the opposite side. The hilt was of a greenish material, but — except on the head and paws — overlaid with a hard, smooth, yellowish, translucent coating, which Aran-Cet later identified as amber, a favoured material of craftsmen from the north. Found in a naturally hard state, it could be boiled in oil and brushed onto a hard surface, forming a somewhat yielding, protective surface.

At that moment, however, the details of construction were only part of the general impression. Peredur, who had had his share of magical encounters, stepped forward from the group and peered earnestly into Gowen's eyes. With more than a hint of the old comradeship, he said softly into the dead silence, "This is a sacred sign. You have a challenge. Do you know what it is?"

Gowen smiled at his old friend and shook his head in the negative. For a moment, they simply stood like that, staring into each other's eyes. Then Gowen reached up to put his hands on his friend's shoulders.

"I do not know my challenge, but you know yours. And I know you. In your eyes, I see my old, far-sighted friend. No matter what others say, you will pursue your goal — into the Otherworld if you must. I believe you will succeed. You are no longer of this place, but you will always be in my thoughts."

Peredur nodded in understanding, smiled broadly at Gowen and abruptly turned to leave, striding long-legged to where he had left his horse. He mounted wordlessly, raised his hand in farewell and rode to the gate. He was never seen among Artor's men again.

None who saw him leave could have known that. Nor could they know that a time would come when the religion he sought would roll back over them all — Cymry, Sassenach, enemies and allies together — like a great flood, sweeping away old faiths, banishing and vilifying old gods and old ways.

In Peredur's place, a quivering silence remained, and the implied question, which Aran-Cet finally, impatiently, put into words.

"What does it mean, this wonderrrful gift?"

The answer came softly but clearly from just inside the gate: "It is a weapon with the sign of the hound to be carried by him who was born under the Dog Star." Walking toward them was the hunter, a tall, grey-eyed figure familiar to Gowen. He was still in green, but his hair fell away from his face to reveal grey eyes, and in his wake trotted a long, lean hound. "It is the proof of trials withstood," he said. "It is a sign of the end of this time and of a new beginning."

"Cúroi," Gowen whispered.

The Green Hunter smiled and said softly, only to Gowen: "Or Gwri or

Khuurkhi. But to you I am most vivid as Cúroi mac Dáiri of Munster. And now that you have proven again that you are who you are —" Lynedd's voice saying these very words sprang unbidden to Gowen's mind, "your trials are over, but your challenges, and final victories and defeats begin."

Raising his voice again, he faced Artor.

"This time will be your time, war-leader, until your final battle. In times to come, many tales will be told of you and those who surround you — some of them true. When you leave this place, you will journey across the water to the place our people tell about and you will learn the meaning of everything you do not know. You will meet our small friend here, and he will be your guide. Until that time, I will help as I am able to hold back the Sassenach and save this remaining land for our people."

He turned and strode away toward the gate. Gwalchmei, Bedwyr, Cei and Aran-Cet surrounded Gowen, smiling, talking all at the same time, pounding him on the back until he felt like Lugaid's brother. Artor stared at the group quizzically, as if he were newly arrived in his own land and trying to understand its peculiar customs. Then, with a melancholy smile, he turned back to his house and the others dispersed, some with Artor, some in other directions.

After that, Artor had a habit of consulting Gowen when important decisions were to be made. Llan, still the best friend of Artor, to say nothing of Gwynhyafar, glowered at each new demonstration of Artor's deference toward his old nemesis. Hate radiated palpably from him when the two were in the same place together and it was obvious to all that he was only awaiting the proper opportunity to strike at Gowen.

Cei advised him of this pedantically, Gwalchmei affectionately, Bedwyr sharply and Aran-Cet gruffly. But Gowen only replied, "Let come what will come. Nothing can be taken from me that has not already been taken from me, not even my life." And saying this, he thought of his parents and of Emher and of the bright figure of Lugh.

Chapter Twenty
EARTH AND SKY

When the second challenge to Artor and his people came, it was not so benign as that offered by Gwri. Without fanfare except the announcing shout of the gate guard, a visitor appeared just after evening meal, entered the great house flanked by two of Artor's warriors and made his way to Artor's seat. He was so tall that he saw almost eye to eye with the shortest of the bodyguards on the platform. His body was heavily muscled and yet lithe and flexible. Gowen felt an eerie similarity with the intrusion of the *bachlach* into Conchobar's hall. But this was not Cúroi. And he was sure that this was not a test aimed specifically at him.

Artor stared with interest at this newcomer. Every inch a king, although he disdained any title but war-leader, he asked mildly: "What is your business with us, Stranger?"

"I am Tygrnwn of Dyfed," the tall warrior said in a deep bass voice. "I am here to dispute the leadership of the Cymry in the great war that will be against the Sassenach."

His voice grew louder, declamatory.

"Legend tells us that a man of Gwynedd met the king of Dyfed a long time ago and killed him in single combat. I claim the same right of single combat. Will Artor meet me to decide the issue between us?"

The astonished silence was not long, for Cei rose quickly and asked, "Your name in the old tongue means 'Great King' — are you such?"

"I am here in the cause of the king," the tall man replied stiffly. "And in my own cause as his war-leader. Artor is not called king among you."

"It is not good enough," snapped Cei. "You will not come here as an emissary and challenge our leader. If your king wishes to measure himself against our war-leader, we will all be happy to watch as Artor carves him into stewing pieces. But our leader is not to be tested by an underling — not even one who calls himself 'war-leader'."

"I claim the right with the war-leader who is not even of your people.

None knows his origin. How can you follow him when you do not know who he is?"

"You will take one of us or take yourself off, warrior! None here fears you," said Cei. The facial expressions on many a warrior in the great room gave the lie to this statement. Llan, who had been humiliated so recently, was inscrutable. Cei, Bedwyr and Gwalchmei stared pugnaciously at the intruder. Artor smiled at Cei's display of loyalty, but said nothing, watching his warriors as a teacher might observe his students in their first test. He reminded Gowen of Scáthach at the battle with Aoife.

"Who among you is worthy of my time?" asked the stranger. "Have you any one who is the equal of your war-leader?" And he gazed with scorn around the great room.

Bedwyr rose at once to stand beside Cei, and Gwalchmei a heart-beat after him, but the issue was decided by Aran-Cet.

He rose ponderously and said, "I have seen it beforrre, in Scáthach's gamp. And you have all seen it again in the ventuurre of the grreen warrior. There is only one who should answerr this challenge. He is one of you, he is my old gomrrade and he is a man of the Gaels.

"It is Gau-wain, my friend, GúGullen. He is fated forr some grreat thing here. He knows it. All of us know it."

Gwynhyafar's tongue flicked swiftly in and out; she cast a cursory glance at Llan. He stared steadily ahead and did not acknowledge her look.

"Which of you is this wonder?" asked the tall man.

Gowen sighed. Sometimes one's friends could be a trial! He was sure in his guts that this was not the "grreat thing" Aran-Cet expected. It had nothing to do with him. But he stood. And the tall man laughed.

"Have you no adult warriors? Must you send a child against me?"

Before Gowen could think how to respond, Gwalchmei walked up to the tall warrior and stood chest to chest with him, looking up only slightly to meet his eyes.

"If you can survive my little brother, then you can come back and claim a full-sized warrior for your challenge. None of us expects to see you return."

The stranger stared at Gwalchmei, then turned his head to look at Gowen again. Finally, he shook his head angrily.

"Let him set out early on the morrow, southward on the trail that begins outside your walls. I will meet him before midday. And when I have finished with him, I will return for your next champion."

Turning on his heel, eyes straight ahead, he walked stiffly through the entry and left a bemused audience behind — not least Gowen, who wondered whether he should thank Aran-Cet for his naïve confidence or join the stranger in laughing out loud.

In the end, no one laughed. Gowen spent the evening in quiet discourse with his friends and brother. They talked of the tales they had heard of how the Cymry had come to this land, of how they had once ruled it far and wide excepting the northernmost land of the Picts, of the coming of the Sassenach — now already shrouded in legend which told of ferocious invaders who arrived by the thousands in strange plank boats and appeared out of the mists of the beaches wielding strange weapons and shouting strange war cries. They talked of the old rivalry between Gwynedd and Dyfed and why it should now re-appear. Then, finally, without directly addressing what would happen on the next day, they slept. Gowen had not thought it possible after such a strange day, but he fell asleep instantly.

Just before dawn, after the briefest of meals, Gowen dragged his protesting body onto Gwalchmei's horse and rode out of the compound. Gwalchmei, Cei, Bedwyr, Aran-Cet, Artor himself said words of encouragement and watched him ride away. Unexpectedly, Gwynhyafar was also there, studying him from a distance, as if trying to classify some unfamiliar creature. As he began his journey in the damp and dusk of morning, his horse's steps creating puffs of vapour, he found that he was not as sore as he had feared, and decided he might at least survive the ride.

It was not yet mid-morning when he encountered a man and woman of middle age, taking their rest from working in their small field. They sat under a tree, at the base of a small hill, just where a lively spring bubbled into life and began a small, meandering stream. He stopped to greet them and they invited him to have a cool drink and a rest in the shade of their tree.

He inquired about their family — three older boys, presently on the hunt to put some meat on the table. He told them openly of his errand here and they both looked grave. The tall warrior was indeed the war-leader for Dyfed and was their local master as well.

"Some say he has powers," said the woman, and blinked at the ground by her feet.

"He be strong and cruel," said the man. "Most folk stay out of his sight. Take care, sir, take care."

Gowen thanked them and continued thoughtfully on his way. Later, just before midday, he found himself entering a broad meadow, overgrown by knee-high wild flowers. At first, he was lost in the peaceful contemplation of colour. Then he looked up and lost all interest in the flowers. Facing him across the sea of blooms was Tygrnwn on a horse both taller and heavier than Gowen's. Under his right arm and supported on his extended and upturned right hand, he held what appeared to be a long, thrusting spear. Without a word or a wave, he kneed his horse's sides to urge it forward. In a few steps, the equine behemoth was thundering at full speed toward Gowen, the thrusting spear pointing directly at his chest.

For precious moments, Gowen was paralyzed by this odd behaviour. Finally, before the point of the spear came close to passing over his horse's head and directly into his chest, he leaned forward to put his hands on his horse's back, and brought his feet up and over, flexing his arms. It was the second half of a salmon leap, rising from the strength of his arms rather than his legs. Barely clearing the blade of the spear, he soared, face-up and feet-first into the body of Tygrnwn, driving him backward off his horse. They landed hard, Tygrnwn on his back and Gowen sitting on the big man's stomach.

With a roar of rage, Tygrnwn sat up, using his strong arms to lift Gowen and send him spinning through the air. As he hit the ground rolling sidewards, Gowen sensed the world turning red and felt the heat touching his skin everywhere. Tygrnwn stood, pulled his heavy sword and, bellowing like the Brown Bull of Culaigh, rushed at his small opponent.

Gowen was beside himself with rage. The unfairness of the attack, his opponent's unjustified anger at being unhorsed — it was all too much!

As he rose to one knee, he grasped deeply to scoop some earth from the ground beneath him. He half rolled, half jumped to one side, throwing his handful of earth with devastating accuracy into Tygrnwn's eyes. The big man howled as his sword swept down with deadly effect on the wild flowers. Gowen — untouched and pulsating with fury — used the hilt of his sword to strike Tygrnwn's sword from his hand and then, unsatisfied with such a small revenge, swung the sword hilt-first in a wide arc, ending with tremendous force on the big man's chest. Tygrnwn sat heavily, gasping for breath and stared through tears of pain at Gowen.

Still unable to cool his anger, Gowen used his sword to slaughter dozens of wild flowers, sweeping it widely on all sides. Finally, he buried it nearly to the hilt in the earth. Then he directed his still burning glance at Tygrnwn, who was staring at him with naked fear on his features.

"Are we finished here?" Gowen grated.

The big man's reaction was startling. Tears of pain were succeeded by an expression of abject misery. The man was impossible! Gowen ground his teeth in frustration.

"Man, you will take hold of yourself instantly, or I will send you home swordless and horseless!"

Tygrnwn was astounded.

"Will you not do that in any case?" he asked.

"We will have a small talk. Then I will decide."

Gowen's view of the world had cooled from red to pink and the internal heat had begun to abate. He looked speculatively at the big man who seemed quite abashed, and still confused at how this confrontation had ended.

"First," Gowen asked, "why did you challenge Artor's leadership as you did?"

"I thought the king would be grateful to me for upholding the name of Dyfed."

"I would not call this 'upholding'," Gowen said sharply, and then felt a small twinge of something like regret when he saw the utter devastation in Tygrnwn's facial expression.

"How long have you been war-leader?"

"Not long. I only defeated the old war-leader a short time ago."

"And how did that come about?" Gowen said, forcing himself to be patient.

"I challenged him."

Gown sighed, "WHY did you challenge him?"

"Some other lords who are my friends said he was too old, and someone had to replace him before the big war with the Sassenach. I was clearly the strongest."

"And did these friends also suggest that you should challenge Artor?"

Tygrnwn looked surprised.

"Yes," he said, gazing up at Gowen with something like wonder.

"And how long have you been lord over these lands here?" Gowen asked, already suspecting that he knew the answer.

The big man looked very sad.

"Only a short time — since my elder brother, the heir after my father — was killed in a personal battle."

"Is it fair to say," Gowen mused, "that your family is renowned for its temper and readiness to fight?"

"My father always said that we were a proud family," said the big man with just a touch of his old hauteur.

"Have you any brothers or sisters?"

"No."

"A wife?"

"No." The big man looked more and more puzzled.

Not without some pain at the thought of Emher and her grief at the loss of Aoife's son, Gowen said softly, "Do you not see that if you go on like this — challenging everyone, treating your own people like slaves instead of people you are sworn to protect — that you will have a very short life with no one to mourn you and no heirs to carry on after you?"

Tygrnwn's face reflected a massive effort to comprehend what Gowen was saying. Then his eyes narrowed and his lips thinned.

"You are saying that my friends are not my friends. That I was wrong to fight with the old war-leader and to challenge Artor. That I have been used."

"Let us test that idea. Where is the old war-leader now?"

"He is still with the king, as an adviser."

"And if some crisis like a battle with the Sassenach — or with Artor — arises, do you think the king would turn to you for advice, or to the old war-leader?"

The big man stared at his feet, upturned before him in the ruined wild flowers and said, "Yes, I see."

"And finally," Gowen continued, "what made you come riding at me with that big spear? I have never seen anything like that."

"My friends — some of them — said it was a way of single combat. They have been..."

"... over the water to visit our cousins in the great land there. May the birds of Rhiannon peck the unseeing eyes out of your head! May the mare of Epona ride over your body until it is as weak as your mind! May..." Gowen stopped his tirade when he saw the look on Tygrnwn's face.

"Man," he said more temperately, "will you not take some advice and some help as your penance for losing this battle?"

The big man nodded, almost eagerly.

"Then it is this. I will return to Artor and tell him that we have met and you have declared your loyalty to the war-leader of all the Cymry. I will also ask him to send one of his own, trusted people to you here. You will make him welcome and listen to what he has to say, especially how to deal justly with your own people. And if your friends do not agree with what he tells you to do, you will do to them what you tried to do to me."

Tygrnwn nodded his assent, but still looked miserable.

"What is it then? What more?" asked Gowen.

"I will be a joke in my own land and my former friends will no doubt be the first to laugh at me."

"Leave that to me too. Lead me to your compound."

Holding any further questions or comments behind clenched teeth, Tygrnwn stood, sheathed his big sword under Gowen's watchful eye, mounted his big horse and led the way to a fort of about the size of Gwri's. Unlike Gwri's, it was situated on a small island, several horses' lengths from the shore of a small lake, and could be reached by a stone and earth causeway leading to a large entry. The large wooden doors swung open before they had to slow their horses, and they rode through into the compound, where people busy at various tasks stopped and collected around them. Without dismounting, Gowen looked around him and said, "I am a representative of Artor, war-leader of all Cymry. Your lord and I come from a battle where he bested me. As a result, I have pledged him my help as a new lord in this land. Soon a steward will arrive to help him in his duties as your lord. Give them both your help and trust and they will give your theirs."

A somewhat uncertain cheer rose from those gathered around the two riders. Tygrnwn appeared stunned.

"Thank you for your generosity," he said tentatively.

"It is nothing,' Gowen said loudly enough to be heard by all. "It is the least I can do for a mighty warrior who is sworn to help Artor in his battle against the Sassenach."

Fearing that any further conversation would only confuse or worsen the situation, he waved vaguely, turned his horse and rode out and away from the compound.

His return was awaited with some misgiving. After passing through the entry, dismounting and entering Artor's great house, a hum arose in his wake. When he stood before Artor — as well as Llan, Gwynhyafar and two of the ever-present bodyguards — the war-leader looked at him with genuine concern.

"How have you fared, Gawain? And what was the issue of your meeting with our unpleasant intruder?"

Artor's tone was brittle but firm. It was clear that he was prepared to finish the dispute personally, if necesssary.

"Tygrnwn has met with me," Gowen said, "and has pledged his loyalty to you as war-leader of the Cymry. He is new in his role as lord of his family's lands and asks that you send him a temporary steward who will help and advise him as he learns to manage his new responsibilities. I have promised in your name that you will send him someone reliable and strong."

Artor was non-plussed for the span of one breath, then he smiled at Gowen and said, "Well, done, Gawain. You have our thanks."

Gwynhyafar gave him another appraising glance, Llan stared stonily ahead and Gowen's friends came forward to fetch him back to their circle for food, drink and, of course, an accurate and complete recitation of what had actually happened.

After he had told his tale, Cei looked thoughtful and said, "Your instinctive reaction to his charge with the big spear — that is not something I could have done."

The others nodded their heads in agreement.

"But it was not merely your fighting ability that was needed. Any one of us might have met this fellow. And if I had bested him in my own way, I would not have been so generous. And we would have a hidden enemy instead of a friend." Again the others nodded. And Cei concluded, "It is as I said when we were young. You are destined to do something of importance here, among our own people. And you have already begun."

When he had finished and the others had clearly agreed with him, the look Cei directed at Gowen reflected a pride almost of ownership. Not for the first time, Gowen felt humbled and not a little confused at why he had been chosen. But he said nothing more and the evening waned in further talk and drinking.

It was to be said later that Artor had no more implacable nor loyal captain in the great war against the Sassenach than Tygrnwn. As to the others: Aran-Cet would soon be recalled to his own land. He was needed in the increasingly desperate efforts to stem the almost tidal advance of the Franks and their allies. Gwalchmei, careless of his own safety, disappeared beneath the axes and swords of surrounding Sassenach in one of the first major battles. Bedwyr survived much longer, but finally rode in the front line once too often. Cei was scarred all over his body, but still alive and active by the time of the truce which — although neither side knew it at the time — set the line which finally divided Sassenach from Cymry.

Of all of Artor's warriors, however, the most ferocious and foolhardy — the one who may have made the ultimate difference between victory and defeat — the one whose ravening fury paralyzed the Sassenach and overwhelmed even their berserkers, was Llan. How that came to be, you will learn soon.

Chapter Twenty-one
MY FAIR LADY

Reports, rumours, inferences drifted in from the eastern mountains with travellers through the territory controlled by the Sassenach. Great movements were taking place. Clearly Artor was right to expect a major effort soon. For the moment, his men rotated on patrol, concentrating on trails and roads that ran directly from the better-known passes. Cei's company now comprised Bedwyr, Gwalchmei, Aran-Cet and Gowen. It was not a big patrol, but they had agreed without speaking of it, that they were stronger alone than accommodating, and possibly having to protect, people they did not know.

The first encounter had the nature of an unexpected turning in the wood. They had stopped to eat and drink at midday, dismounted, and were talking quietly, munching, swallowing, when suddenly Bedwyr stiffened, held up his hand for silence, rose fluidly in one motion from sitting to standing. It was clear that he had heard something, something that he suspected was the enemy. The rest of them rose as one, unsheathing their swords, and stood side by side, almost perfectly in line, just off the path. Then they all heard it: a measured tramping sound, like a number of men jogging slowly, more or less in step with one another.

Suddenly, Bedwyr stepped forward and turned right to face up the path, bringing his one arm around with the turn and throwing his spear, completing the throw at the moment he planted his feet, and continuing in one, unbroken motion, down, then up and behind his back for the second spear carried there. There was a muffled thump, a strangled exclamation. Then roars and howls of rage, rattling of weapons, pounding of feet, and the rest of Cei's small company leapt onto the path to face the onrush of ten infuriated Sassenach warriors, already leaving behind one comrade, face-up on the path, Bedwyr's spear rising straight from his throat.

Even as Gowen stepped into the fray, he was taking note of this enemy he had never seen before. They were big — both tall and broad, and they were hairy. From under rounded helmets, blond hair cascaded, framing blazing blue eyes. Furry animal skins swung from massive shoulders and strained across broad hips. Round shields waggled back and forth as they ran and upraised hands held either longswords or battle axes — a weapon Gowen had never seen before. A momentary chill ran through him as he faced the onrushing phalanx, and a wonder at what kind of warrior would choose to use such a cruel and clumsy weapon. Perhaps the very sight of the weapon was enough to undo some opponents. The thought was instantaneous, and then two of the huge men had reached him, one slightly ahead of the other.

Instinctively, he sprang into his salmon jump, somersaulting at the apex, so that his head was down and his feet were up, as he momentarily faced backward. At that moment, he faced the back of the second warrior's head. Quick as the thought of it, his sword hand flicked out, his sword plunged into the back of the man's neck and out again. Then he was continuing his roll to land on his feet facing away from the two Sassenachs. In a glance, he took in the others. Bedwyr had already finished his second and third warriors with several lightning stabs of his heavy spear, the last of them teetering, already dead before falling. Bedwyr was turning to go to Cei whose fierce energy was holding off two burly Sassenachs; Aran-Cet and Gwalchmei were back to back against three axe-wielding warriors, the fourth already still on the ground. Gowen's inner eye still held this picture as he was turning to face his own two enemies. But the one he had struck in flight lay prone, blood gushing from the back of his neck. His companion had skidded to a halt, turned and was now half-charging, half-stalking Gowen. As Gowen completed his turn, he had barely time to raise his shield hand against the fearsome swing of the axe, which crashed into the shield just below centre, slicing through the leather cover, smashing the ashwood core into splinters and tearing the metal edging open at the bottom. As he drew the axe hand back to prepare another blow, Gowen jumped straight up, in one of the moves taught by Scáthach, and swept his sword horizontally across the big man's shoulders, severing his head even before its face could express surprise at the counter stroke.

By the time he had turned and caught sight of the others, their opponents too lay dead on the ground, but Cei was gripping a gash in his left forearm; Gwalchmei was seated, leaning against a tree, wrapping a rag torn from his tunic around his knee; Aran-Cet leaned over him solicitously, paying no attention to the blood that was streaming from his own scalp.

"Well," Bedwyr grinned, "that was stimulating."

Cei grimaced, waving his uninjured arm at the scattering of bodies.

"Will someone instruct me how we are going to dispose of these bodies so the the next patrol can't just pick them up and take them back? If they find them this way, they can just assume that they encountered superior numbers and died. That is not the terror Artor wants. And we are in no condition to meet the next patrol right now, so we cannot tarry here to bury them or hide them."

"Leave the bodies," Gowen said, thinking of Conall and the story of his challenge to Cet of Connaught. "Take only the heads. One thing the Sassenach fear about us — one thing that all others fear about us — is our headhunting. They don't comprehend that it has to do with the seat of the soul and the power of the human spirit. They see it as a fearsome thing. If they find the headless bodies of their eleven comrades, it will send a shock all the way to Lugdunum. And," he added softly, "the heads will be easy to carry."

All right! Widen your eyes, wrinkle your nose, twist your mouth, make horrified noises. Why are you surprised? Perhaps the tale engrossed you so much that you have not paid attention before now. Perhaps you just didn't think about it. Believe me, I am used to it. Gowen was right, of course. No one not of us understood. All of them hated, or feared. There was one — a great war-leader against our people in Aran-Cet's homeland, Gaul — who told of the barbarian human sacrifices done there by our cousins across the water. He and his people were horrified. Of course, at the same time, they were killing our cousins by the hundred, by the thousand, just because they wanted to rule over the land where they lived. They captured Vercingetorix, the greatest war-leader of the Gauls, who had united them for first time. They paraded him through one of their great communities in chains, then threw him into a dark place under one of their fortifications. After he had spent twenty-four seasons there in his own filth, they dragged him out for one last time and had him strangled to death. Such civilized, sensitive people!

In Gaul, there was a famous cave where the skulls of the best of their thinkers and warriors, and also of the best and bravest of their enemies, were kept in niches in the walls. Aran-Cet's people went there to find strength and wisdom by touching one or more of them. Some even went to be cured of long-standing illnesses. And do you know what happens there now, now that all those old barbarian skulls have been removed? That religion of Peredur thinks of it the same way! Folk who have troubles or illnesses will go there and slide a hand into one of the niches and hope for something good to happen. And they don't know about the past, so they cannot even ask themselves whether the power that lives in the niches in this cave comes from what they believe or from something that was there before them.

At any rate, they did as Gowen suggested and the heads were eventually given a fitting place to rest, with many others. The next Sassenach were so unnerved and infuriated by the sight of eleven headless comrades that they attacked a nearby fortified farmstead with berserker strength, taking the fortification and slaughtering both people and animals. Then, in accordance with their own custom of honoring the war-god, Tiu, they cut up not only people and animals but tools, weapons and other artifacts and consigned them all to a nearby swamp. To each his own barbarism.

Not all patrols were as fortunate as Cei's. Some returned with wounded, some with dead, all with tales of fierce encounters. Cei's patrol itself rotated back to its duties several more times before the kidnapping of Gwynhyafar.

It was completely unexpected. Once, as Gowen and his comrades arrived back from a difficult several days, other patrols had been gone for a day or more, Llan and his hand-picked followers among them. As Cei's small group straggled through the entry gate, men, women and children were milling about in the centre of the compound, directly before Artor's house. Artor himself stood in the entry, his ordinarily untroubled face creased with worry. Looking up at Cei pushing through the crowd on his horse, Artor's expression betrayed relief. Words tumbled from his lips with unaccustomed speed.

"Thanks be to the gods! Llan is unreachable, on patrol. I must go after her and I need someone here who can keep discipline and morale..." His distress was even more apparent in his use of Llan's Cymry name.

"War-leader!" Cei said more sharply than was his custom when addressing Artor, "After whom? Why?"

Artor drew a deep breath, making a visible effort to control himself.

"Guinevere." He paused, drew a deep breath, exhaled, than began to speak more deliberately. "Llewellyn of Powys. He is a war-leader who... had feelings for Guinevere when she was still a child, before her parents took her with them across the water. He has never accepted... me. He must have been watching for his chance. And saw it with the rotation of patrols, men coming and going, sentries attuned to watching the gate and who came there. Guinevere..." he drew a ragged breath, "she chafed at being inside the fortification. Took her ladies with her on walks outside. Never far. It seemed harmless. Always within sight of the main gate. Just hours ago... He appeared out of the forest with a party of warriors. It was all over so fast that the sentries at the gate barely had time to raise the alarm. They... they scooped her up and rode away. I... I must go after them. Take some men..."

"No!"

The single word was so loud and emphatic that Artor and Cei, as well as all others with earshot, jumped in surprise and stared at Gowen.

"He will not have come with only the few men you saw. He would be foolish if he did not have a larger party waiting close by, in case of immediate pursuit. He would probably welcome a chance to test himself against the war-leader and the small group of men you have here. He would leave with an even bigger prize. Your people would be demoralized."

"But," Artor protested, "I cannot abandon her. Who knows what he intends? What would she think?"

"What will she think if you and this small group of warriors is taken and everything you have worked for is lost?"

Artor's mouth twitched, but he did not speak.

Bedwyr asked waspishly, "What do you suggest, O Wise One? Shall we send a negotiator after them?"

Gowen could not help smiling, even now, at Bewyr's caustic wit.

"Yes, in a way. One small person, dressed more like a child than a warrior. Someone who can find his way through the woods to intersect their party and surprise them when the time is right." He turned toward a boy who was big for his age, as tall if not quite as broad as Gowen. "What is your name?"

"Ywain, sir," said the boy politely.

"Well, Ywain, how would you like to loan me some clothes and sandals so they can go on an adventure that I will tell you all about personally when I return?"

Still polite, the boy's answer was unexpected.

"Begging your pardon, sir, I go where my tunic goes. And you may not remember how to be a boy any longer, so you will need an expert." He smiled somewhat impertinently.

"Boy... Ywain," Gowen said as kindly as he could, "if you ever hope to wear a warrior's sandals, you must first live to earn them."

"If I do not go with you now, I will never know myself worthy," the boy replied with such force and simplicity that Gowen was forced to remember himself before Conchobar, claiming the destiny of the day and demanding to be armed.

Still, Gowen had opened his mouth to continue the argument, when one of the few warriors at home on rest between patrols stepped to the front of the crowd.

"The boy is our adopted son. Loved as if he were our own, but all the same not of our blood, and constantly proving that his origin is something special. If you do not take him with you, I will have to bind him and tie him to a post to keep him from following you. And," he cast an ironic and affectionate glance at the boy, "I could not guarantee that he would not chew his way through the bonds and follow you later."

Gowen sighed in resignation and allowed himself to be led to a corner of the great community longhouse, where he and the boy selected tunic, leggings and sandals and the boy stooped to retrieve his well-worn, deerskin sling. Outside again, Gowen gave his sword into Cei's keeping and selected several lengths of heavy twine, which he wound around his waist. He and Ywain left the compound followed by a small group of interested adults and children — the boys shouting words of foolishness and encouragement to their comrade. Gowen and Ywain had their pick of smaller and older horses not deemed suitable for war or agriculture, and so available for the training of children. As they mounted and prepared to leave, the boy's mother — slim, brown-haired, hazel-eyed — came forward and laid her hand on the boy's leg. Gowen braced himself inwardly to hear of her fear and grief at taking leave of her son. Her words startled him.

"Behave yourself, obey this warrior as you would your father. And do not leave him if he is in difficulty."

The boy nodded soberly and she turned to Gowen.

"I know of you and I know you will not leave him behind," she said simply.

Gowen nodded, swallowing a lump in his throat, and they rode slowly across the clearing and directly into the woods. His last view of Artor was standing near the bottom of the ramp, staring blankly after them.

The boy must have heard some of Cei's and Bedwyr's tales of childhood, for he followed Gowen's lead, as he led his horse on an apparently meandering path through the forest. Before long, he, too, dismounted and led his horse.

"How soon?" he asked finally.

Gowen smiled. The boy reminded him of himself.

"Soon, now."

And, indeed, it was a short time later when they intersected a path leading south.

"We will wait here, out of sight. When they come, wait for my word to use your sling. We will knock as many as possible from their horses before they react. Then we will appear and pretend we are youngsters who have made a stupid mistake, thought they were Sassenach."

Again, the boy said nothing, merely nodded.

It seemed forever, but was really only the time it would take to sharpen a spear, before a large troop of men appeared, riding hard, but not as if they were being pursued.

"Is that the large party you meant?" asked Iwain.

Again, Gowen had to smile. The boy was calm and attentive, as if he were playing a difficult game of fidchell. ("I must remember that the game here is gwyddbwyll," he thought.)

"Yes," he said answering Ywain's question. "Llewellyn is sure now from his rear scouts that there has been no pursuit, so he is sending the main body home, in case Artor has made a leap in strategy and plans a move against him there. He will be riding more leisurely with his hostage, feeling absolutely secure."

And, indeed, in a short time, they heard the sound of horses cantering unhurriedly along the path. Moments later, the party appeared: a warrior leading, another following, one on each side and, in the middle, a tall, grim warrior — doubtless Llewellyn — and next to him, head bowed dejectedly, hands bound in front of her, Gwynhyafar.

The boy had let his sling hang loose from his hand, swaying slightly from the weight of the stone it held, but he made no move to throw, looking sideways at Gowen's eyes. As the last horseman drew even with them, Gowen nodded, pointing with his left hand at the rider in the rear and on their side of the path. He and Ywain struck simultaneously, the boy's stone striking the man in the rear and spilling him from his horse as Gowen's struck the man on the opposite side. Again, within moments, the man on the near side tumbled just as Gowen's stone flew so close to to Gwynhyafar's ear that she felt its passage, and then the man in front tilted sideways and slid to the ground. Llewellyn's left arm snaked out, grasping Gwynhyafar at the waist and pulling her with him to the ground, where he stood, now grasping her hair with his left hand while his right held his sword at her neck.

"Artor," he roared. "Step out now or see your intended spill her blood on the ground before her!"

Ywain looked stricken. Gowen dropped his own sling, pointed wordlessly at Ywain's, then stepped from the underbrush onto the path.

"There is no Artor here, sir. No boar-god or any god at all. Only me, sir."

Llewellyn stared, torn between confusion and fury. Gwynhyafar glanced at the face of the boyish figure in front of her and swallowed a gasp of astonishment.

"Who are you, fool?" Llewellyn grated. "What are you babbling about? Where are your weapons?"

Gowen smiled a little foolishly and spread his arms wide, as if to say, "I don't understand." As Llewellyn followed him with narrowed eyes, he moved slowly to his left, clearing a path for Ywain.

"Sir, I thought you were a warrior. But no warrior would threaten a woman with his sword. You are all dressed up like a mighty warrior. But you are acting like a farmer who doesn't know what to do. Are you a farmer, sir?"

Llewellyn snorted with rage and swung his sword away from Gwynhyafar's neck to point it at Gowen's chest. Feeling the prick of its tip, Gowen forced himself to freeze in place. As the blood began to trickle lightly down his chest, Ywain loosed his stone — a perfect shot to Llewellyn's mouth, breaking out his front teeth, snapping his head back. Gowen leaned forward swiftly to pluck the falling sword and finished Llewellyn's fragile consciousness with a sharp blow of the hilt to his forehead on its way to the ground.

Gwynhyafar sank slowly to her knees, trembling visibly, now that she could finally loosen the iron grip she had kept on her emotions. Something like a sob escaped her, but she suppressed any further demonstrations of feeling, stood slowly and held out her hand to Gowen. He took it with some misgiving as a tremulous smile flitted across her mouth. However, with no evidence of her seductive charisma, she looked deep into Gowen's eyes and said, simply: "Thank you."

Then she looked questioningly at Ywain, who had stepped into the open.

Gowen nodded toward the boy.

"Artor," he said, "was on the point of riding after you with the few men he had. We had to restrain him first. Then we had to show him that there was a better way. The boy is called 'Ywain'. He volunteered."

Gowen ran out of words and waved one hand vaguely. (Why did life among these people make him do that?) Ywain smiled at Gwynhyafar and she smiled back at him. Her smile shone in the boy's face like a sunrise. Gowen could see that he was instantly enslaved.

"We must be on our way," he said, trying to sound casual. "I will bind Llewellyn. We can bring him along as guarantee against attack, and Artor can decide his fate."

The unconscious men were dragged to a tree by Gowen and the boy. They were seated around the tree like guardians of the trunk and tied intricately but loosely to the tree and to each other. When they woke, it would take time to work themselves free, possibly not before the advance party became suspicious and returned to find their leader. Llewellyn himself was bound hand and foot, thrown belly-down over his horse and secured by a length of thick twine that ran underneath the horse from his wrists to his ankles.

By now, it was late in the day and the sunlight trickled weakly through the trees from a point near the horizon. Gowen gave no thought to stopping for the night, but urged Gwynhyafar onto the horse she had been riding, took two others for himself and Ywain, and ordered the boy to lead the remaining animals from his own horse. Gwynhyafar followed Ywain, while Gowen brought up the rear as guarantee against any pursuit. They rode as fast as possible, given the extra horses and Gwynhyafar's still shaken condition. It was just possible that they could be in familiar territory before darkness fell.

It was deep dusk, and they were very near Artor's fortified settlement — Gowen estimated that the next turning would reveal the walls of the stronghold — when Ywain, who was in the lead, gasped and pulled back hard on his reins. Before them was the figure of a woman, hovering just above the path. Her outline shimmered in the gloom; deep-blue eyes set in a face of surpassing beauty; an almost girlishly slim figure. As Gowen pulled abreast of Gwynhyafar, she breathed in raggedly.

"Rhiannon, Great Queen, protect us from the spirits of Annwn!" she murmured.

The beautiful face smiled — a sad and almost kindly smile.

"Child, it is not seemly to be in fear of your own mother."

Gowen and Ywain gasped, but Gwynhyafar stared searchingly at the ghostly image. Then, soundlessly and without warning, tears began to stream down her cheeks and splash onto the fabric of her garment where her breasts swelled gently outward.

"Mother!" she said softly.

"Not worthy of the name," said the ghostly, sweet voice. "I set you no good example, I loved too much, and too many. I thought myself above the small rules of life. You could not have been ignorant of it, even as a child. I feel my failure still, among the sacred dead. It leaves me no rest. And now I must know that you are pledged to a man who holds the future of our people in his hands..." She paused. Not one of the three stirred or breathed.

"... and that you hold his peace of mind in your hands but you are pledged falsely to someone else.

"I know," she continued gently. "I know the passion, the lust, the need that will not be stilled. I know the blindness of acting without thought or control. I know the dull madness that rules inside your skin. And I know the surge of power when you look at a man and he melts like cheese on a hot stone. Your father and I were well matched — he was no better than I. But this man who will be your husband is no ordinary man. His spirit must be free for a great work. You must be better than I was."

Gwynhyafar reached out blindly to her side, grasping Gowen's hand and crushing his fingers in a desperate grip. He held the grip and returned the pressure firmly but not with his whole strength. Ywain had lowered his eyes and was now laboriously backing his horse and the string he was leading away from the pair of them and the apparition.

Gwynhyafar seemed incapable of words. Tears continued to stream from her wide-open eyes, soaking the fabric of her robe. Her breathing had slowed to the rhythm of a sleeper. Her face had lost all trace of fear and was, Gowen thought, rapt — bespelled by the figure before her.

The Ghostly Lady, as Gowen thought of her thereafter, turned her luminous gaze upon him and said with ineffable sadness.

"It is to you, Gawain —"though she could have said, CúChulainn, as, eerily, she seemed to pronounce the Gaelic syllables at the same time, "to make the final sacrifice that will close the circle of your life and validate the sacrifice you have already made."

At this gnomic statement, Gwynhyafar stared intently at Gowen. His face reddened, but he did not speak, only nodded, and it seemed to him that something heavy and cold had taken up residence in his breast, never to leave again.

The two of them sat side by side, moving gently in time to the quiet prancing of their horses' hooves. Gwynhyafar turned her face forward again. The luminous lady raised one hand as if in benediction, and as they stared, became translucent, then transparent, then dissolved into small clouds, wisps of mist, nothing. Gwynhyafar's fingers loosened, slipped from Gowen's grasp. They still sat and stared into the space that had been the vision.

"It is dark." Ywain's voice startled them. Gwynhyafar started, then hung her head. Gowen reached reflexively for his sword and stopped when his hand found no hilt where it should be.

"You are right, Ywain," he said. "It is dark and we must ride the final, short distance."

He threw a quick glance at Gwynhyafar and, catching her glance, gave her an encouraging smile. They prodded their mounts into motion and in almost no time were riding up the ramp to the entry gate. The guard had hardly uttered the first syllable of his welcome when Artor appeared in the doorway of his house and other figures appeared in the flickering light of the great central fire.

"Guin! Guinevere!" He choked as he walked toward them and stopped, holding his arms out. Gwynhyafar slid from her horse and walked into his embrace. After a long, intense moment, Artor opened his eyes and looked over Gwynhyafar's shoulder at Gowen.

"Gawain! I have never been shown greater service, never been more indebted, never felt the reward of loyalty..."

His voice trailed away and Gowen waved his hand vaguely. Something in the air in this place seemed to make him do that.

"It was something I could do," he smiled deprecatingly, "and no one else was small enough. Except my excellent partner here. Without him, we would not be so happily returned."

Ywain, who had begun the adventure with such presence — even impertinence — blushed and smiled and looked suddenly as young as he was.

Artor gently held Gwynhyafar at arms' length and opened his mouth to speak, but what came out was an unexpected snort of happiness. Even he looked startled for a moment, then he threw his head back and roared with laughter. Ywain, infected by the same spirit laughed a high, young boy's delighted laugh. Then the others standing around them — men, women and children — broke into a chorus of snorts, giggles, guffaws and gurgles.

Gowen really didn't see anything comical in the situation, but he could not withstand the general merriment, and laughed too. Finally, when only a few gasps could still be heard and everyone felt that their stomach muscles had never ached quite so much, Gwynhyafar spoke to Artor.

"I must take a moment privately with my two champions, to thank them properly."

The war-leader smiled and stepped back, allowing Gwynhyafar to lead Gowen and Ywain some distance from the crowd.

She faced Ywain first, bending her twisted gold torc to slip it from her neck and reaching out to slide it on his. The boy's face flamed with pride and adolescent worship as she said, "No other could have done what you did for me. Thank you."

She smiled into his eyes and waited pointedly as he realized that he had been both rewarded and dismissed. Torn between joy and reluctance, he turned and walked toward his beaming parents.

Then she turned to Gowen and, again with no trace of coquetry or seductiveness, she spoke very softly.

"For one who has been so badly treated to act so generously to help me when I most needed it — that is humbling. To meet myself in the spectre of my mother — that is life-altering. I think I know you better now than I did when you arrived, so I will not embarrass you with lengthy words of gratitude.

Gowen bowed his head. He still awaited the "but" that would change the tone of what she was saying. But her tone was that of a petitioner asking a favour.

"Rather, I beg your help in keeping my determination to be worthy of our war-leader. If you see me faltering, do not fail to speak. If I feel myself weaken, I may ask for help."

She smiled at the skepticism which clouded his eyes.

"I do not blame you for what you are thinking, but give me a chance; help me find honour!"

"I will, lady," he was surprised to hear himself say. "I will help as I can."

"You have loved someone deeply. You love her still. How did I not see that before?" Her eyes fell, and Gowen knew that she was thinking of their first meeting and her own 'surge of power' when she had trailed her fingernails across his chest.

"Lady, we are all blind in our own way. It seems I must change my ideas about you, too. We will find the way to honour together."

Gwynhyafar blinked new tears from her eyes, reached out, and put both hands on his shoulders.

"Thank you... Cu... Cúkullen."

And with that awkward attempt to pronounce his Gaelic name, she won him completely, not as a lover, but as a loyal friend and supporter.

Chapter Twenty-two
HAIL AND FAREWELL

Life in Artor's compound, which had been richly complex already, was made even more complicated by Gwynhyafar's new view of herself. It took some time for Llan to understand. She had tried to explain when he first returned from patrol. And several times thereafter. But he was completely unable or unwilling to absorb what she was telling him. It was as if she were speaking a foreign language. So he simply kept on as before. He expressed his desires by smouldering glances in Gwynhyafar's direction. When she did not react, he sidled closer, so that his hand or arm could touch her casually.

The crisis came one day when, as usual, the signals that had always served had no effect. He waited for the moment when he could catch her alone, just outside Artor's house.

"Guin!" he croaked. "What is wrong? What has happened to our love?"

Gwynhyafar's look was a mixture of sympathy with his confused suffering and guilt for what she now perceived as their betrayal of Artor.

"Llan," he recoiled at the use of his Cymry name, "I have tried to explain how I feel. What we felt was not love, it was something else... a madness. And it was a great betrayal! I cannot do that any longer."

"YOU cannot!? How can ONE of us stop? You don't know what you're saying!" His eyes were glazed; his voice trembled with emotion. He gripped her shoulder roughly and she winced, but her glance did not falter.

"Llan, everything is different now. You have to understand..." The pain of his grip, increasing in intensity robbed her of words.

Then, as suddenly as it had begun, the pressure eased and was gone.

Llan stared down in fury and stupefaction as Gowen's hand forced his away from Gwynhyafar's shoulder.

"Is it you, rabbit? Are you standing in my way again? We are not children now. Do not mistake my abilities."

"Llan," Gowen began, then, in a conciliatory tone, "Lancelot, I do not wish to thwart you or make you more my enemy than you already are. This is Gw... Guinevere's decision — a very hard one and taken all on her own. Please respect it."

Use of his and Gwynhyafar's romanticized names did not appease Llan, but seemed to inflame him further, if that was possible. He wrenched his wrist free from Gowen's slackened grasp and stared impotently at his old nemesis and his ex-lover. His chest heaved with the twin passions of desire and fury.

He did see something new in Gwynhyafar's eyes, but it was not what she had hoped he would see.

"I will wait Guin," he said with quiet intensity, "and you will come to your senses. I will wait as long as I must and you will need a man," he glared poisonously at Gowen, "a full-sized man. Even after you are married, you will need a man to give you true satisfaction."

He paused, almost thoughtfully.

"I love Arthur as a friend and a leader, but he will never be enough for you. And," he stared into her eyes, "no one else will ever be enough for me."

Then he turned a gaze full of bitter hatred on Gowen.

"As for you Gau-wain," he drawled the name in bitter parody of Aran-Cet, "the time of your death approaches. Be ready for it!"

He turned with what dignity he could muster and stalked away. Gwynhyafar's cheeks glistened with tears as she watched his stiff-backed retreat. But it was not love, but pity that shone from her eyes.

Gowen, for the first time in his life, had conflicting feelings about Llan. It had always been a simple thing, to return Llan's hatred in almost equal measure, aware of what the former leader of his boyhood friends would do to him if he could. On returning to the land of his childhood and seeing Llan for the first time — hearing his anger and contempt after all the time that had passed — the old feelings had slid comfortably into place like a sword into a perfectly fitted scabbard.

Now, however, he had witnessed a deep and sincere pain. Beyond Llan's simple lust and his irresistible need to prove himself better than anyone else — feelings which had led him to betray even the man who had bested him to become war-leader and had then taken him as his trusted friend and confidant — beyond all that lay a true hunger for Gwynhyafar's love and respect. Gowen had no doubt that Gwynhyafar had chosen correctly. He too had witnessed the ghostly figure and had even been charged by her with his own responsibility. Still, it was painful and confusing to see in the eyes of the man he had considered to be shallow, spiteful and vain, an emotion of such depth and sincerity that it glared from his eyes like an angry contradiction.

"Poor Llan," murmured Gwynhyafar, and Gowen could only nod in agreement.

"And I fear for you, friend," she said, turning a worried face to him. "He will not believe that ours is an innocent relationship. He already believes that we have betrayed him as he and I betrayed Artor. He will hate you even more, if that is possible. And he will carry out his threat. He will see you dead."

Gowen smiled sadly.

"In a way, lady... friend, I am already in the Land of the Dead. If I leave, it will only be to go to Tir na Óg."

Gwyhyafar frowned in confusion at the Gaelic term for the Land of the Young, but did not interrupt as he continued.

"I have lived a rich and wonderful life in my few years. It was a life that should have ended on a battlefield in Eire. Instead, I am here, returned to the place where I was born and grew to the age of understanding. There is some purpose in this, and when it is fulfilled, I begin to realize, I will not be returning to my life and to the one whom you saw in my eyes — my own love. I will be gone from both here and there forever."

He paused and sighed.

"I could resent the arbitrary ordering of my life, if I had not had the wonderful compensations of love and friendship that it has given me. It gives and it takes in equal measure. I could resent it, if I did not see in you and Artor and in my brother and Cei and Bedwyr and Peredur and Aran-Cet and even Llan the same playing out of immutable rules. It is as on a gwyddbwyll board, where only certain moves are possible, and the only choice is to play well or to play badly."

He put his hand lightly on her elbow.

"Do not waste your emotion on what cannot be changed. Do what you must. Be the example your people need you to be. It is a time of great danger, and you are one of the bulwarks against disaster."

As Gwynhyafar wept soundlessly, standing outside in the semi-dark, Gowen's friends and brother, who had followed him out of Artor's house, went to her one by one to offer her the hand of friendship. She still made no sound, but her tears became a torrent which she made no effort to control.

Thereafter any one of Cei's small company was prepared to hazard his life for her.

It was, of course, only a matter of time until Llan made a move against Gowen. He had now been warned by everyone close to him, by Gwynhyafar too, and yet again by Llan himself. He knew that they were right, but he knew just as surely the truth of what he had said to both her and the others. He was living on borrowed time, and he knew that it would not expire before he had fulfilled his destiny.

Nonetheless, he and each of those who cared about him paid particular attention to Llan and everything he did or said when he was in their company. Of course, no one knew what he did when he was not in Artor's great house, before the eyes of all. His patrol came and went on its rotation, as did Cei's. Llan himself no longer approached Gwynhyafar, although he could be seen from time to time casting a hungry glance in her direction and a murderous one toward Gowen.

Routine had set in again, until one early morning after the late-night return of Cei's patrol. Gowen woke to a softly insistent voice. (Even those who were not in his inner circle had heard that it was dangerous to prod him awake.)

He did not recognize the young warrior, although he seemed vaguely familiar.

"... Artor's lady..."

Gowen sat bolt upright.

"Gwynhyafar! What has happened to her?"

But the slim figure had already made its way through the sleeping warriors and was standing now just outside the entrance. Gowen followed quickly and demanded, with a peremptory motion of his hand, to hear more.

"She was taken just moments ago by three big men who left the compound with her."

"Show me the way they went!"

The young warrior led him quietly from the entrance of the warrior's house to the gate, where the sentry was propped up against the frame of the gate — bleeding from a wound at the back of his head, but still breathing.

Down the ramp they went, and across the clearing to a narrow path into the woods.

"I saw them come this way. The lady was able to shout your name before one of them knocked me down."

"Go back and rouse Artor and the other warriors. I will blaze a clear trail."

The young man nodded and turned toward the fortress as Gowen struck into the woods. Just before he turned out of sight, Gowen was able to glance back and see the young warrior staring after him, hardly two steps from where he had been. Impatiently, he waved him on and pressed further into the woods, following a trail left by men who apparently gave no thought to possible pursuit.

It was a long and hard trek, cross-country through the woods, and it was near midday when he began to sense them ahead of him and quickened his pace. It seemed odd, if they had left just before the young warrior woke him, that it had taken him this long to overtake three men on foot with a captive — even big men. And though he listened carefully, he heard no one approaching from behind him. That too was odd, for between him and his quarry, a very visible trail had been made for Artor and his men to follow at speed.

As he considered these odd facts, he stepped into a clearing, where a striking, raven-haired woman, with skin as white as the clouds on a fine day and black eyes as flat and expressionless as those of a raven, sat on a log and stirred a large cauldron over a blazing fire. He thought fleetingly of the story of Taliesin, until the woman reached into the cauldron with her long-handled ladle and brought up a piece of stewed meat.

"Accept my offering, Little One," she said, with a conspiratorial grin, and he recognized that the meat was from a dog. Cathbad's words came to him:

"Your first *geis* is that you must not refuse a proper offer of hospitality or sustenance made to you. Your second *geis* is that you must not taste the flesh of your namesake, the dog. Until you have fulfilled these *geasa*, you will not be killed."

This was that fated moment, for he had either to break the first geis or the second.

He smiled benignly at the woman and said: "I will choose to refuse your hospitality. Why should I accept it now, when I have rejected it before? Ever since you visited me as a horned heifer and a snake in the water and a wolf, I have known you would come back. What are you in this place?"

She smiled as at an old friend.

"I am who I am, but some of the more effete in this place like to call me Morgana la Fay."

She paused.

"You and I could have created such prodigies of war and slaughter... But the truth is, you were not meant to live beyond your own time, and even I could not have changed that."

Her tone now was almost shy.

"I asked to be the one to give you the final warning. I have never had a better helper," she smiled wryly as Gowen winced, "or a better opponent. Hail and farewell, O CúChulainn!"

This unexpected recognition from the Queen of Slaughter herself sent a flush of blood to his face and a warmth to his breast that dissolved the cold lump that had lodged there since the confrontation with the Ghostly Lady.

"Hail and farewell, O Battle Crow!" said Gowen, and pressed on into the woods again.

It was with a strange sense of peace that he continued tracking, allowing the stages of his life to play across the eye of his mind: Gwri, Cei and his friends, Roigh falling on him, Cathbad saying the great thing about him, the taking of a name, the earning of weapons and the tutelage under Scáthach, the winning of Emher thanks to Cúroi, the Championship, Mebd and the great Cattle Raid, Lugh, the return to a home that he no longer knew, Gwri and Lynedd and the final test, and now... whatever would come.

As he thought this last thought, he stepped into another clearing and saw, on the opposite side of it, Gwynhyafar, held by the arms by a huge figure on each side of her. Squinting against the sun, Gowen felt a spurt of recognition as he studied the two huge men. The size, the odd deformities of facial features and body parts — they were Fomhoire! Here, in Gwynedd! Fleetingly he recalled the tale of the great Bran and his conversation with the king of Eire who was courting Bran's sister: how the Gaelic king had expelled a family of monstrously strong and marvellously ugly people from Eire and lost track of them; how they had found a welcome in Dyfed and settled among the Cymry. These, then, were relatives of Foragall's allies in Leinster. They both stared at him with undisguised hatred.

"Free her and you will have the battle you want," he said.

At that moment the scene before him exploded into whirling bits of colour — slashes of reddest red and blackest black. He found himself stretched out on his stomach, hands flung forward, as a huge foot stepped into the small of his back and pressed unbearably. Peering through his pain, he saw that Gwynhyafar had been released and was standing indecisive and riven by doubt.

"Flee now, lady! Or I will have come for nothing!" And as she staggered across the clearing and, throwing an agonized glance at him, disappeared into the trees, he added sotto voce, "It was never you they wanted."

"Welcome, Killer of Foragall," rumbled the Fomhoire who was standing over him, and ground his foot more deeply into Gowen's back. This new pain was the impetus he had needed. The red film slid over his view; his skin burned like flame. He exploded upward, throwing the Fomhoire backward as if shot from a sling. As he landed on both feet, pulling his sword in preparation for his first swing, the other two Fomhoire stepped forward almost as one, and slashed at him with their long swords. Swiftly, he parried one blow, but felt the second cut into his left side.

It was not so far past noon that his strength had begun to wane, but that would come soon, and the wound to his side was leaking both blood and strength. Somehow, he had to despatch them quickly or he would succumb.

Only the heat of his battle rage kept him upright and moving. But he was moving backward, looking for any advantage, and now pressed by all three Fomhoire. In desperation, he crouched under a powerful swing by the man on the left and stretched forward in a thrusting stroke that drove into his middle opponent as Gwydion's thrust had driven into Pryderi so long ago. Hardly having made his thrust, he was rolling swiftly to one side, barely avoiding the powerful downward stroke of the man on the right.

He slowed his roll and flipped upright, but awkwardly, staggering, the wound in his side throbbing ever more fiercely. As the stricken Fomhoire curled up on the ground in a death agony, his two comrades closed on

Gowen, and he gave ground again, now holding onto control of his body by sheer will.

For the first time, he experienced hopelessness.

"Can this," he thought in his desperate confusion, "truly be the purpose of my return here? Just the destruction of three Fomhoire? Even if I can accomplish it?"

As he parried the first, mighty looping blow from the right, the man on his left turned suddenly sideways, as if in reaction to a challenge. Gowen gave ground again, feeling in his side the agonizing effects of blocking the last stroke. And then he saw from the side of his eye the bulky form of Aran-Cet confronting the other Fomhoire.

"Where... are... the... others," he gasped between sword strokes.

In rhythm with his own strokes, the big Gaul replied, "I know nothing... of otherrrs... I saw you leave with... your young gompanion... When you went... into the woods, he... went away and I... tried to follow you... I met the lady..on the way... I am not so fast, so I am... a little late... I am sorry."

Gowen smiled through his pain.

"Any debt you... ever owed me is... paid in full, friend."

Aran-Cet gave a roar of satisfaction and pressed his attack.

With only the one Fomhoire to face, Gowen had a chance. He kept giving ground until, summoning the last of his rage-strength, he leapt straight up and sliced across the Fomhoire's neck as he had the neck of the big Sassenach. As the head flew off at an angle to bump on the ground, the body pitched forward.

He looked to see if Aran-Cet required any help, but the big Gaul was just finishing his opponent with a mighty, two-handed blow, slashing into his unprotected neck at the shoulder and continuing downward so that it seemed he would split the man in half. He pulled his sword loose from the sagging body, straightened and grinned at Gowen, who began to smile back at him.

Then, suddenly, the big man pitched forward, to lie full-length, breathing still, but unconscious from a sharp blow to the back of his head.

Behind him stood a fourth Fomhoire, still holding the heavy club he had used to level Aran-Cet. To his right, smiling in satisfaction and holding his sword, stood Llan.

"Welcome to the end of your life, Gau-wain."

Gowen's stomach clutched in fear for his friend. Llan intercepted his glance at the prone figure.

"Worry not, Little One." With relish, he used the name the big Gaul had warned against when Gowen first returned. "He will be my witness that you were attacked by Fomhoire who abducted Guinevere. I will simply have to supply another dead body to make the tale ring true..." he pivoted left, bringing his sword-point around to to strike deep into the mid-section of his companion. The Fomhoire folded slowly forward and fell, already dead as Llan slid his sword swiftly out of the collapsing body. "... And that, as you can see, is already arranged. This poor fellow will be the one who struck your friend from behind and was then defeated by me in a fierce fight."

Smiling broadly, he moved toward Gowen, making patterns in the air before him with the tip of his sword. Retreating, Gowen knew that this was his last battle, but could not yet see its significance. Llan attacked strongly, but leisurely, using his greater reach to stay well away from a possible counter stroke. Gowen simply grew weaker as the life oozed from his side.

At last, he stumbled and fell backward. He lay on his back, sword at his side, still in the weakened grip of his right hand. As Llan stood triumphantly astride him, Gowen thought of Aoife and the lesson of deception and believed he could see how this might indeed be the fateful ending he had imagined.

"Any last word, pest?" Llan smirked down at him.

"Yes," Gowen whispered, and beckoned with his left hand for Llan to lean closer. Sure now that his enemy was finally dying, and anxious to hear his last words, Llan stepped forward and leaned over.

Gowen whispered, "Loyalty."

The triumph in Llan's features twisted into rage. His lip curled and he tensed himself to straighten and give the — unnecessary — killing blow.

At that moment, Gowen called on the last of his life-force to lift his sword one last time, straight upward, between Llan's legs, turning the keen cutting edge in a scalloping motion as he reached the apex of his stroke. The hilt fell from his numb fingers and the flat of the blade fell on his shin, yielding a pure, almost musical note. Llan sank to his knees, clutching the empty space between his legs, as blood seeped between his fingers. He stared at Gowen, less in hatred than in utter disbelief.

"Loyalty," Gowen whispered again, "will not be a problem, now."

His head lolled over to one side. He could see her now clearly — Emher, reaching out her hand to him, smiling. He smiled back.

Farewell Gowen! Farewell CúChulainn! Farewell Gawain!

Farewell Gwri! Farewell Curoi! Farewell Khuurkhi!

Farewell!

Farewell!